TE
BY DR

&

# THE ACCIDENTAL
ROMEO

BY
CAROL MARINELLI

MILLS
BOON

# BAYSIDE HOSPITAL HEARTBREAKERS!

*From no-strings flings to always and for ever*

Welcome to Bayside! The home of sun, sea, surf…and the hottest docs in town! In the heart of the Emergency Room the dreamy docs of Bayside Hospital work hard, saving lives, and flirt hard, winning hearts. But don't get too romantically involved, ladies! These passionate, enigmatic docs are strictly no-strings-attached…until they meet two very special nurses… Are these the only women who can see the men behind the heartbreakers and heal those closely guarded hearts?

**TEMPTED BY DR MORALES**

**and**

**THE ACCIDENTAL ROMEO**

**Both titles available now**

**by Carol Marinelli**

# TEMPTED
# BY DR MORALES

BY
## CAROL MARINELLI

Published in Great Britain 2014
by Mills & Boon, an imprint of Harlequin (UK) Limited,
Eton House, 18-24 Paradise Road, Richmond, Surrey, TW9 1SR

© 2014 Carol Marinelli

ISBN: 978 0 263 90745 2

Harlequir
renewabl
sustainab                                                                rm
to the leg

Printed ar
by Black

**Dear Reader**

As I wrote Juan and Cate's story it was never my intention to do two linked books. I adored Juan, and loved following his journey, but while speaking about my plot with my writing friend Fiona McArthur she said, 'I think you love Harry too.'

Is it possible to love two heroes at once?

Please don't think less of me, but my answer is YES!

They have both known tragedy, but in very different ways, and they both make me laugh. The funniest thing for me, while writing this, was that I discovered beauty really is in the eye of the beholder. Neither of my heroines remotely fancied the other's hero.

Their creator did, though! :)

I hope you enjoy their stories.

Happy reading!

*Carol* xxx

**Carol Marinelli** recently filled in a form where she was asked for her job title and was thrilled, after all these years, to be able to put down her answer as 'writer'. Then it asked what Carol did for relaxation. After chewing her pen for a moment Carol put down the truth—'writing'. The third question asked—'What are your hobbies?' Well, not wanting to look obsessed or, worse still, boring, she crossed the fingers on her free hand and answered 'swimming and tennis'. But, given that the chlorine in the pool does terrible things to her highlights, and the closest she's got to a tennis racket in the last couple of years is watching the Australian Open, I'm sure you can guess the real answer!

# CHAPTER ONE

'SORRY, JUAN, I didn't mean to wake you.' Cate Nicholls stopped twisting a long brown curl around her finger and cringed at the sound of Juan's deep, heavily accented—but clearly sleepy—voice when he answered the phone.

'It is no problem. Is that you, Cate?'

'Yes.' She blushed a little that Juan had recognised her voice. He had only done a few locum shifts at the Melbourne Bayside Hospital emergency department, but the tension between them sizzled. Cate had tried everyone she could think of before finally accepting Harry's suggestion and phoning Juan to see if he could come in. A fully qualified anaesthetist from Argentina, he was travelling around the world for a year or two and was as sexy-as-sin as a man could possibly be and still remain popular. 'I'm really sorry to have disturbed you. Were you working last night?'

'No.'

'Oh!' Cate glanced up at the clock—it was two p.m., why on earth would he still be in bed? Then Cate heard the sound of a female voice and cringed again as Juan told whoever the woman was that he took three sugars in his coffee. Then his silken voice returned to Cate.

'So, what can I do for you?'

'Sheldon called in sick and we haven't been able to get anyone else in to cover him.'

'Does Harry know that you're calling me?'

Cate laughed—Harry, one of the senior emergency department consultants, went into sulking mode whenever Juan was around; he was still annoyed that Juan had knocked back his offer of a three-month contract to work in the department. 'It was Harry who suggested that I call you.'

'So, what time do you want me to come in?'

'As soon as you can get here.' Cate looked out at the busy emergency department. 'It's really starting to fill up…' She paused for a moment as Harry said something. 'Could you hold on, please, Juan?' Cate called out to Harry, 'What did you say?'

'Tell Juan that even though we really need him to get here as soon as possible, he can stop for a haircut on the way if he feels so inclined!'

Juan's shaggy long black hair, unshaven appearance and relaxed dress sense drove Harry crazy and Cate was smiling as she got back to her conversation with Juan. 'I assume that you heard that?'

'I did,' Juan answered. 'Tell Harry that he loves me really.' Cate listened as Juan yawned and stretched and she tried not to think about him in bed, naked, at two in the afternoon. 'Okay,' he said. 'I'll just have a quick shower and I'll be there as soon as I can.'

'Thanks, Juan.' Cate hung up the phone and wrote his name on the board. Harry glanced over and gave a quick shake of his head.

'If ever there was a man inappropriately named, it's Dr Morales,' Harry said, and Cate had to laugh. Juan had quite a reputation, and even just writing his name down would have a few staff scurrying off to check their make-up and hair.

Cate refused to.

Washing her hands before heading back out to the patients, she saw her reflection in the mirror. Yes, her shoulder-length hair could do with being re-tied and her serious hazel eyes might look better with a slick of mascara, but she simply refused to make that effort for Juan.

She wasn't about to play with fire.

With three older brothers who had all been wild, to say the least, not a lot shocked the rather sensible Cate, but Juan managed to at times—either with his daredevil sports or with the endless women he briefly bedded. He raised more than a few eyebrows when he happily regaled his colleagues with tales of his trip around Australia, but what shocked Cate most was the internal fight she was having to put up to not simply give in to that sensual smile and dive headfirst into his bed.

They had hit the ground flirting but then Cate had backed off—soon realising that Juan and his rather reprobate ways were far more than she could handle.

Cate had returned from two weeks' annual leave, newly single after breaking up with her boyfriend of more than two years, and her stomach had turned over at the very sight of Juan. She'd never had such a violent reaction to anyone and, foolishly, she had told herself she was just testing out her flirting wings on the sexy locum, just indulging in a little play flirt the first time they had met.

Cate had never really thought he'd ask her to join him for a drink that night, though his eyes had said bed. She still burnt at the memory of their first meeting—

the rush that had come as she'd met his grey eyes, the desire to say yes, to hell with it all, for once to give in and choose to be reckless. Instead, she had refused his offer politely and, in the few times she'd seen him since then, Cate had played things down—denied the attraction that sizzled between them and tried her best to keep things strictly about work.

'Juan is a very good doctor, though,' Cate reminded Harry, because even if Juan was a bit of a rake, there was no disputing that fact.

'Yes, but his talent's wasted,' Harry said, but then sighed. 'Maybe I'm just envious.'

'I've never met a more talented emergency doctor than you,' Cate said, and she meant it. Harry was a fantastic emergency doctor as well as a highly renowned hand surgeon, only it wasn't Juan's medical talent that Harry was referring to.

'I meant maybe I'm envious of Juan's freedom, his take-it-or-leave-it attitude. He actually doesn't give a damn what anyone thinks. It would be lovely just to work one or two shifts a week and spend the rest of the time kicking back!' Harry gave a wry smile. 'But, then, Juan doesn't have four-year-old twins to worry about. Make that, Juan doesn't have anything to worry about.'

'Are things not getting any better?' Cate asked. She liked Harry a lot and had been devastated for him when his wife had been brought in last year after a car crash. Jill had died two weeks later in ICU, leaving Harry a single father to his young twins, Charlotte and Adam.

'The nanny just handed in her notice,' Harry said. 'Another one!'

Cate gave a sympathetic groan but Harry just rolled

his eyes and headed back out to deal with the patients. 'It will sort itself out,' Harry said.

'Ooh!' Kelly smiled when she saw Juan's name up on the board. 'That just brightened up my afternoon! With a bit of luck Juan will come out for drinks with us tonight after work.' Kelly winked.

'I'm sure that he will,' Cate said. 'I can't make it, though.'

'Come on, Cate,' Kelly pushed. 'You said that you would. It's Friday night, you can't sit around moping about Paul…'

'I'm not moping about Paul. When I said that I'd come out, I didn't realise that I was working in the morning,' Cate lied.

'But you said that you'd drive,' Kelly reminded her. 'It's still a week till payday.'

Yes, Cate thought, she had said she'd drive but that had been before she had known Juan would be working into the evening—he wasn't exactly known for turning down a night out.

Juan worked to live rather than lived to work—that had been his explanation when he had irked Harry by turning down his job offer. Juan had told Harry that he would prefer to work casual shifts at various Melbourne hospitals rather than be tied to one place. And, given he only worked one or two shifts a week, it had been thanks but, no, thanks from Juan. Cate had been surprised that Harry had even offered him the role.

He was, though, an amazing doctor.

He was amazing, Cate conceded to herself as she went to help Kelly make up some fresh gurneys and do a quick tidy of the cubicles.

Juan was also the last complication she needed.

Still, she put his impending arrival out of her mind, just glad to have the doctor shortage under control for now.

'Where's Christine?' Cate asked as she stripped a gurney and gave it a wipe down before making it up with fresh linen.

'Guess,' Kelly answered. 'She's hiding in her office. If you do get the job, please don't let that ever be you!'

Cate was soon to be interviewed for the role of nurse unit manager and it was fairly certain that the position would be hers. Lillian, the director of acute nursing, had practically told her so. Cate was already more hands on with the patients than most of the associate nurse unit managers, and if she did get the role she had no intention of hiding herself away in the office or going over the stock orders to try and save a bean. It had also been heavily hinted that, after Christine's haphazard brand of leadership, the powers that be wanted a lot more order in Emergency—and it had been none-too-subtly pointed out that the nurses were not there to babysit Harry's twins.

If she did get the job, Cate knew there was going to be a lot to deal with.

'Is this cubicle ready?' Abby, who was doing triage, popped her head in. 'I've got a gentleman that needs to be seen.'

'Bring him in,' Cate said. 'Kelly, if you could carry on sorting out any empty cubicles, that would be great.'

Kelly nodded and headed off and Cate took the handover as they helped the painfully thin gentleman move from the wheelchair to the gurney. His wife watched anxiously.

'This is Reece Anderson,' Abby introduced. 'He's

thirty-four years old and has recently completed a course of chemotherapy for a melanoma on his left thigh. Reece has had increasing nausea since this morning as well as abdominal pain.'

'He didn't tell me he was in pain till lunchtime.' There was an edge to his wife's voice. 'I thought the vomiting was the after effects of the chemo.'

'Okay, Reece.' Cate introduced herself. 'I'm going to help you to get into a gown and take some observations and then we shall get you seen just as soon as we can.' Reece was clearly very uncomfortable as well as dehydrated, and there was also considerable tension between him and his wife.

'The heat has made this last round of treatment unbearable,' his wife said. 'We don't have air-conditioning.' She looked more tense than the patient. 'I'm Amanda, by the way.'

'Hi, Amanda. Yes, I'm sure the heat isn't helping,' Cate said as she looked at Reece's dry lips and felt his skin turgor. 'We'll get a drip started soon.'

Melbourne was in the grip of a prolonged heat wave and more patients than usual were presenting as dehydrated. Cate had been moaning about the heat and lack of sleep herself, but to imagine being unwell and going through chemotherapy made her rethink her grumbles.

'Why don't you go home?' Reece suggested to his wife as, between retches, Cate helped him undress. 'I could be here for ages.'

'I've told you, I'm not going home. I don't want to leave you till I know what's happening.' Amanda's response was terse.

'You have to pick up the kids from school.'

'I'm going to ring Stella and let her know what's going on. She can get them…'

'Just go home, will you?' Reece snapped.

Cate looked over at Amanda and saw that she was close to tears.

'Just leave,' Reece said.

'Oh, I might just do that!' Amanda's voice held a challenge and Cate guessed this wasn't the first time they'd had this row. 'I'm going to ring Stella and ask her to pick them up.'

Amanda walked out of the cubicle and Reece rested back on the pillows as Cate took his baseline observations. 'I can't believe I'm back in hospital. Amanda should be sorting out the children, not me.'

Cate didn't comment; instead, she headed out and had a brief word with Harry, who was working with Kelly on a critical patient who had just arrived. He said he would get there just as soon as he could but, given how long the wait might be, Harry asked if Cate could take some bloods and start an IV.

Reece was pretty uncommunicative throughout but, as she went to leave, finally he asked a question. 'Do you think it's the cancer spreading?'

'I think it's far too early to be speculating about anything,' Cate said. 'We'll get these bloods off and a doctor will be in just as soon as possible.'

While she had sympathy for Reece and could guess how scared he must be, Cate's heart went out to Amanda when she found her crying by the vending machine.

'Come in here,' Cate offered, opening up an interview room to give Amanda some privacy. The interview rooms were beyond dreary, painted brown and with hard seats and a plastic table, but at least they were private. 'I know you must be very worried but it's far too early to know what's going on.'

'I can deal with whatever's going on health-wise,' Amanda said. 'We've been dealing with it for months now. It's Reece that I can't handle—his moods and constantly telling me to leave him alone.'

'It must be terribly hard,' Cate offered, wishing she could say more.

'It's nearly impossible.' Amanda shook her head with hopelessness. 'I'm starting to think that maybe he really doesn't want me around.'

'I doubt that,' Cate replied.

'So do I.' Amanda took a drink of coffee and slowly started to calm down—all she had needed was a short reprieve. 'You know, if that really is what he wants, then tough! I'm not going to walk away,' Amanda said, draining her drink and screwing up the cup as she threw it into the bin. 'Like it or not, I'm not going anywhere.' Amanda wiped her eyes and blew her nose then walked back to be with her husband.

Cate was wondering if she should try and find the intern to see Reece, though she did want someone more senior; then she considered calling in a favour from one of the surgical team and asking them to come down without an emergency doctor's referral, but then she saw Juan walk in.

He really was the most striking man Cate had ever seen. His tall, muscular frame was enhanced by the black Cuban-heeled boots that he wore. Today he was wearing black jeans with a heavily buckled belt and a grey and black shirt that was crumpled. His black hair was long enough that it could easily be tied back, but instead it fell onto his broad shoulders and, fresh from the shower, his hair left a slight damp patch on his shirt.

Cate's first thought on seeing him wasn't relief that finally there was an extra pair of hands and she could get Reece seen quickly.

Instead, as always, he begged the question—how on earth did she manage to say no to that? He was sex on long legs certainly, but more than that he made her smile, made her laugh. Juan just changed the whole dynamics of the place.

'You made good time!' Cate said, as he came over and she caught the heady whiff of Juan fresh from the shower.

'I got a lift.'

Ah, yes, Cate reminded herself, he'd had company when she'd called. Juan didn't have a car, he wasn't in any one place long enough for that, so instead he used public transport or, more often than not, he ran to work and treated everyone to the delicious sight of him breathless and sweaty before he headed for the staff shower.

'Where would you like me to start?' he asked. Juan was always ready to jump straight into work.

'Cubicle four,' Cate said, giving him a brief background on the way. She saw Reece's and Amanda's eyes widen just a fraction as a very foreign, rather unconventional-looking doctor entered the cubicle, yet Juan was so good with patients that within a moment he had Reece at ease.

Juan put one long, booted foot on the lower frame of the gurney and leant in and chatted with Reece about his medical history and symptoms before standing up straight.

'Can I borrow your stethoscope?' he asked Cate.

'There's one on the wall,' Cate said. There usually wasn't but the rather meticulous Cate had prepared the cubicle herself.

'I can't hear very well with them,' Juan said. 'I prefer yours.'

'I know! You took it home with you last time you *borrowed* it.'

'I brought it back,' he pointed out, but he took down one of the cheap hospital-issue ones and started listening to Reece's chest.

He cursed in Spanish and even Reece gave a small smile. 'They are useless. I should have brought mine but you said it was so busy that I was rushing to get here…' He winked at his patient and then Juan's full lips twitched into a small smile of triumph as Cate handed over her stethoscope.

'That's better,' Juan said.

Reece was soon back to feeling miserable as Juan examined him. He reduced Amanda to tears again when she tried to answer a question for him. 'I can speak for myself.'

'Okay,' Juan said, 'I am going lay you down and examine your stomach.' He turned and smiled at Amanda. 'Could you excuse us, please?'

Juan carefully examined his patient's abdomen as Reece tried to hide his grimaces.

'Reece…' Juan looked down. 'How long have you been sitting on this?'

'Since this morning.'

'Reece?' The doubt was obvious in Juan's voice.

'Last night...' Juan raised his eyebrows but said nothing, simply waited until Reece changed his story again. 'I woke up in pain the night before.'

'Is that one true?' Juan checked, and Reece nodded. 'Okay, I have to do a rectal examination.' As Cate helped Reece roll to his side, he was weary and close to crying. 'I'm sorry, Reece,' Juan said. 'I know it must be awful. It won't take long.'

He was so good with the patients. He never told them not to feel embarrassed, or that he'd done it a thousand times before; he just quickly examined him and as Reece was rolled onto his back again, Juan thanked him for his co-operation.

'Good man,' he said, and Reece nodded.

'What do you think is going on?' Reece asked, and this was where Juan was different from most doctors. This was where he was clearly senior because he gave Reece his tentative diagnosis.

'Your history makes things more complicated, of course...' Juan said. 'But I think you have appendicitis. I am going to ring the surgeons and get you seen as a priority.'

'Can I have something for the pain?'

'They don't like to give analgesia without first seeing the patient for themselves so they can get a clear picture.' Juan repeated what Cate had heard many times before, but again he showed just how experienced and confident he was as he continued speaking. 'Still, I will try bribing them by ordering a quick ultrasound while we wait for the bloods to come back. Hopefully I can give you something for the pain.'

It was still incredibly busy out in the department. Juan rang the surgeons and had a long discussion, then as he wrote up some analgesia he rang and arranged an ultrasound.

'Give Reece this for the pain and vomiting,' Juan said. 'I'll ring the lab and get the bloods pushed through. If we can get him round now for an ultrasound, the surgeons should be here by the time he comes back.'

'Sure.' Cate sorted out the drugs and then rang Christine and told her that she was taking a patient for an ultrasound and would she please come out of her office and work on the floor.

'That will go down well,' Kelly commented, picking up the constantly ringing phone.

'Do you know what?' Cate answered. 'I really don't care.'

Kelly held out the phone for Juan. 'A call for you.' He went to take it. 'Martina,' Kelly added.

Both women shared a look as he said a few terse words in Spanish and then promptly hung up. 'I spoke with Christine.' Juan looked at Cate. 'Did she not pass it on?'

'Pass what on?'

'I have had to speak to the nursing managers at the other hospitals where I work. Could you ask the nursing and reception staff not to put through certain personal calls for me?'

'Certain?' Cate checked.

'From Martina.'

'But if it's your mum or the girl you met last night…' Cate tried to keep the edge from her voice, but she felt like a secretary running his little black book when Juan was on call—women were ringing all the time '...then we're to put them through?'

'Okay, for *all* personal calls, just ask the staff to say they are not sure if Juan is working and that you'll take a message and leave it for him. I am just asking if the staff can be a bit more discreet.'

'The staff are discreet, Juan, but there's a difference between being discreet and rude. When it's clearly a personal call...' She took a breath. 'Fine, I'll speak to everyone.'

Juan got back to his notes and did not look up. It would simply open up a can of worms if he explained things.

He didn't want to explain things.

That was the reason he was travelling after all, no need for explanations, no past, no rules—just fun. Except Cate didn't want fun. She'd made that clear, even if not quite from the start.

He was going to do this shift and then go home.

Juan had just over two weeks to go in the country.

Had Cate said yes when he'd first asked her out they could have had an amazing few months.

Instead, she had made it very clear she wasn't interested in a brief fling with him.

She was interested, though.

Juan could feel it, he could smell it, he could almost taste it, but Cate refused to give in to it.

He wasn't going to try again.

Cate was a serious thing, a curious thing, and she was quietly driving him insane.

'Are you coming out for drinks tonight, Juan?' Kelly asked.

'Not tonight,' Juan said, and he heard Cate's small exhalation of relief.

Oh, well, Juan thought as he carried on writing up his notes.

She could relax soon.

He'd be gone.

# CHAPTER TWO

'HOW ARE THINGS?' Juan came in to speak with Reece soon after he came back from ultrasound. The surgeons had examined him there and had ordered antibiotics and changed his IV regime, and Reece was now being prepared rapidly for Theatre.

'You tell me,' Reece said. 'They said that appendicitis was serious in someone with my immune system.'

'That's why they're starting you on all these antibiotics. We need to get you up to Theatre before it perforates,' Juan said.

'I shouldn't have left it,' Reece said. 'I thought it was cancer.'

'Of course you did,' Juan said, 'but it is an appendix flare-up nevertheless. I had a pregnant woman just last week…' He didn't continue, there was a lot to be done.

Cate was trying to sort out the antibiotics that the surgeons wanted. It had been incredibly tense during his ultrasound, Reece telling Amanda over and over that she should just go home. Cate had, on her way back from Ultrasound, suggested that Amanda wait in the interview room, just to have a break from the snipes from her husband.

'Cate, can I see Reece's IV regime?' Juan asked,

and then spoke to the patient. 'Though you need to be operated on, I want you to have a bolus of fluids before you go up.'

He was so direct he overrode the surgeons' IV regime with a stroke of his pen.

Juan saw Cate's rapid blink—not many people would have changed Jeff Henderson's plan. 'I just spoke to him and discussed some changes,' Juan said. 'Reece needs to be better hydrated before he's operated on.'

'I bet that went down well,' Cate said, repeating Kelly's sentiment from a little while ago.

'Jeff was fine.' Juan shrugged. 'And, like you, I really don't care if I offend at times. This is better for the patient.'

He handed over the chart and then spoke to Reece. 'I'm going to put another IV in you so that we can push fluids in and then I shall speak with your wife.'

'Can you tell her that there's no point hanging around?'

'She's not going to want to go home while you're in Theatre,' Cate pointed out as she added the medication to the flask.

'I just don't want her here,' Reece snapped. 'I don't want to be a burden.'

'Then stop being one,' Cate said, and Juan's head jerked up from the IV he was putting in. He'd heard a lot of straight talking—emergency nurses were very good at it—but hearing what Cate had to say to Reece made him falter momentarily.

'The illness and the treatment you are on must be awful, for *both* of you,' Cate continued to Reece, 'but I can think of nothing worse than loving someone who is sick and being repeatedly told that they don't want you there, that you'd be better off without them.'

'I think she'd be happier—' Reece attempted, but Cate didn't let him finish.

'I'm quite sure Amanda would be happier if you graciously accepted her love and affection and her need to take care of you, to help you *both* get through this.'

Juan headed over to the sharps box. He could feel his pulse pounding in his temples, feel the roar of blood in his ears, and, for reasons of his own, he wished he hadn't heard that, yet he felt compelled to respond.

'She's right.' Juan's voice was husky and he cleared his throat before continuing. 'Cate is right, Reece. If your wife didn't want to be here for you then she'd have gone long ago.'

'You don't know that.'

'Cate…' Juan turned '…could you go and speak with Amanda and let her know what is happening and then bring her in?'

'Sure,' Cate answered. 'Reece, are you okay with me letting her know that you have appendicitis?'

Reece nodded. Clearly Cate's words had had an impact on him because he let out a sigh and lay back on his pillows, but as she walked out of the cubicle he met suddenly serious grey eyes. Only then did Reece realise that there was more to come.

'Right,' Juan said to his patient. 'While we've got a moment, I'll tell you *exactly* what I do know.'

By the time Cate returned from taking Reece to Theatre, the critically injured patient had been moved as well and the place was settling down. All the staff worked hard to clear the backlog and at six Juan looked up at the clock and spoke to Harry.

'Why don't you go home?'

She saw Harry hesitate. There were other doctors on but no one particularly senior.

Except the locum just happened to be Juan.

'Go and have dinner with your children,' Juan said. 'I'm sure we'll cope.'

Juan would more than cope.

Everyone knew it.

'You're sure?' Harry checked. 'Dr Vermont won't get here till ten.'

'Of course,' Juan said. 'Anyway, the nightclubs don't really get going till midnight.'

Harry gave a wry smile and headed for home, and Cate did her best to avoid the six feet three of testosterone who sat and worked his way through a huge bunch of grapes between seeing patients.

Relieved that Juan wouldn't be joining them on their night out, Cate had relented and agreed to drive her friends, but before she headed off to get ready she did have a question for Juan. He was sitting writing up his notes before handing over to Dr Vermont.

'What did you say to Reece?'

'Reece?'

'The appendicitis.'

'I'm not with you,' Juan said, still writing his notes.

'He was a whole lot nicer to Amanda when we came back in. He even thanked her for being there for him when I took him up to Theatre.'

'He must have listened to what you said to him.' Juan shrugged and Cate walked off with a slight frown. Yes, she had been direct while talking to Reece but *something* had happened while she'd been speaking with Amanda. She was sure of it, because they had returned to a very different man—and Cate was positive Juan had had something to do with it.

She just had no idea what.

The night staff came on duty and Cate handed over the patients, then headed to the changing rooms, where there was a fight for the mirror.

'I thought Christine was coming?' Kelly said. 'She said she was a little while ago.'

'No.' Abby laughed. 'When she found out Juan wasn't coming, Christine changed her mind, of course. He's made it obvious that he's no longer interested—you'd think that she'd have taken the hint by now.'

Cate changed quickly, moaning that her strapless bra dug in and gave her four breasts before pulling on a black halterneck she had bought the previous weekend.

'Is that new?' Kelly asked as Cate pulled on a pale lilac skirt.

'Yep.' Cate smiled. 'And so are these!' She held up the most gorgeous pair of wedges—they were nothing like her usual choice, and had been an absolute impulse buy.

Her first.

Cate did up the straps around her ankles and blinked back sudden tears. She was still in that wobbly post-break-up stage, still trying to work out what had gone wrong, what *was* wrong.

She'd been happy with Paul, just not happy enough. She had loved him in so many ways, but she still hadn't been able to give Paul the answer he wanted. The answer everyone wanted! Her parents had been equally shocked when the rather predictable Cate had made a rather unpredictable choice.

Why had she ended it?

'Because...' had been her paltry response.

Even Cate didn't really know why.

Juan tried not to notice when the late staff all emerged from the changing rooms, changed and scented, like a noisy flock of butterflies floating down the corridor—but there was only one who drew the eye.

She had make-up on, not much just enough to accentuate her wary eyes, and her mouth should not be allowed out, unescorted by him, when it shimmered with gloss. A lilac skirt showed off her tanned legs and he did his best not to notice, as they walked past the nurses' station, her back, which was revealed in a halterneck.

'I'm not staying long,' he heard Cate warning her friends as they said goodbye and headed out. 'I've got to be back here in ten hours.'

'Are you sure you won't change your mind, Juan?' Kelly called over her shoulder.

And he should leave well alone. Cate wasn't, Juan guessed, up to what he had in mind.

Except he couldn't get her out of his head!

Her words to Reece had lowered his defences, and the scent of her as she walked past, the sight of her bare skin...it was surely worth one more shot?

Juan wanted their time.

'I might see you there,' Juan called out to the departing group, and watched her bare shoulders stiffen, watched as she very deliberately didn't turn round.

As she, still, denied him.

# CHAPTER THREE

THE BAR WAS hot and crowded but it was equally hot outside; there was just no escaping the heat.

There was no escaping Juan.

She was terribly aware of him when, about an hour after they'd got there, he arrived.

He came over and bought everyone drinks, but Cate told him that she was happy with her soda water.

'When are you working with us again, Juan?' Abby shouted above the noise.

'I don't think I am,' Juan said. 'I have some shifts already booked in the city.'

'So this is your leaving do!' Kelly said.

'It might be…'

Cate stood there, watching her friends get louder, flirtier and more morose as they realised they might never see him again. By midnight, the night had turned into Juan Morales's unofficial send-off. So much so that there was now going to be an impromptu party back at his home.

Impromptu might just as well be his middle name, Cate thought as everyone asked her to come along.

'I'm working tomorrow!' Cate said it three times, not that anyone listened.

'It will be fun,' Abby insisted. 'Everyone's going back.'

Half the bar, it would seem, was lined up outside to take taxis to Juan's as, sober, fed up, tired and with her strapless bra digging into her, Cate headed out to her car.

'Thank you for this,' Juan said as he lowered himself into the passenger seat, far too tall for her rather small car. 'I really should get there first to let people in.'

'It's no problem.' Cate gave a slightly forced smile and then tried to turn it into a friendlier one as a couple of her colleagues and friends climbed into the back seat.

'You don't mind giving us a lift, do you, Cate?' Kelly checked, though not until she'd put her seat belt on.

'Of course not,' Cate said, and put the air conditioner on. The blast of cold air was especially welcome a moment later when Juan said, 'Cate, if you want to have a drink, you are very welcome to stay the night.'

Stay!

At Juan Morales's apartment for the night!

Cate turned and gave him the most incredulous smile she could muster, before starting the engine. 'Don't they have taxis in Argentina, Juan?'

He gave her a shameless smile back and then answered with his deep, heavily accented voice, which had Cate's stomach flip over on itself. 'I'm just letting you know that the offer is there.'

The offer had been there for a while now.

'I'm working at seven tomorrow morning.'

'You're staying for a drink, though,' Juan checked, but Cate answered him with a question of her own.

'Can you give me directions?' she said as she pulled out of the car park.

'Left ahead and then you go down…' He even managed to give a sexual connotation to the simplest directions, Cate thought, or was it that she was just incredibly aware of him sitting next to her?

Cate glanced over and caught a glimpse of his strong profile. His grey eyes were framed by dark lashes, his nose was straight and he had full lips that smiled easily. There was an exotic streak that seemed to run through every inch of him.

'Have you had your interview?' Juan asked.

'Not yet,' Cate said, surprised that he'd remembered. 'There are some external applications as well that they're going through.'

'So you would be the unit manager if you get it?'

'The nurse unit manager,' Cate corrected as she sat waiting for the traffic lights to change.

'Wouldn't you miss working with the patients?'

'I'd still be working with the patients,' came Cate's rather tart response, not that Juan seemed to notice the nerve he had just jarred, or, if he had, he chose to pursue it.

'Christine doesn't.'

She turned and met eyes that were more than happy to meet and hold hers. 'I'm not Christine,' Cate said, because rumour had it he'd been sleeping with Christine when he'd first arrived and Cate could well believe it. When Cate had come back from annual leave, she'd found Christine in floods of tears in the changing room and it hadn't been hard to work out why.

'No,' Juan said slowly and with a tinge of regret that made her throat tighten at the implication. His next loaded sentence seemed to insist she acknowledge the denied desire that simmered between them. 'You're not Christine.'

'The lights have changed,' Kelly called from the back.

As the car moved off Juan fiddled with her sound system and Cate cringed in embarrassment as a rather tragic break-up song came on.

'You should be listening to happier music,' Juan commented. 'All that will do is make you feel more miserable.'

'I'm not miserable at all.'

'Have you spoken to Paul since the break-up?' Abby chimed in from the back seat.

'Of course I have,' Cate said. 'It's all civil.'

'Which means that it was long overdue,' Juan commented, and Cate pursed her lips. It was the problem with being the so-called designated driver—you had to listen as things were discussed that generally wouldn't be.

'It doesn't have to be all smashing plates and tears,' Cate said, but didn't elaborate. Trust Juan to hit the nail on the head, though. Paul had been upset and uncomprehending at first, yet she had been calm and matter-of-fact once her decision to end it had been made.

Oh, she'd waited for the tears, for torrents of emotion to invade, for all the drama that seemed a necessary part of a relationship break-up to arrive—but they hadn't. She'd sat in her garden, sipping wine with her neighbour, Bridgette, with more a sense of relief than regret.

Juan was right, the break-up had been overdue.

'How much longer are you in Australia?' Kelly asked, and Juan turned a bit in his seat to answer and to chat with the girls in the back.

'Just over two weeks.'

'You should stay longer,' Kelly said.

'I can't,' Juan said, 'my visa expires the day after I leave.'

'Would you, though, if you could?' Kelly persisted.

'I think it's maybe time to move on.'

'Where now?' Cate asked, and Juan turned back to face the front.

'Turn right along the beach road and my place is about halfway.'

As she turned, the car jolted and Cate frowned. The car was not responding as it usually did, she could feel the groan of the engine.

'There's something wrong with the car,' Cate said, having appalling visions of breaking down a few metres from Juan's and, yes, ending up staying the night. The complication of a fling with Juan was something Cate did not need and frantically she looked at the dashboard. 'It's in manual…' Cate frowned but Juan had already worked it out—their hands met at the gearstick and Cate pulled hers away.

'My fault,' Juan said, 'my legs are too long.' He slotted it back into drive. 'My knees must have knocked the gearstick.'

God, he was potent. Cate's fingers were still tingling from the brief touch as she pulled up at his apartment. 'You are coming in?' Juan checked as she sat with the engine idling and there was a moment when she wanted to be the taxi martyr and drive off—but rather more than that, yes, she wanted a further glimpse of his world.

'Sure.'

Juan let them all in and it wasn't quite what Cate had

been expecting—it was a furnished rental apartment but a rather luxurious one with stunning beach views and a huge decking area outside. It was everything the well-heeled traveller needed for a few weeks of fun, Cate thought. Yet, despite the expensive furnishings and appliances, there was an emptiness and sparseness to it—a blandness even, broken only by his belongings.

Temporary.

Like Juan.

'This is the type of music you should be listening to,' Juan said, slotting his phone into some speakers. The room filled with music that under different circumstances Cate might want to dance to. Taxis were starting to arrive and, as more hospital personnel filled his home, Juan opened the French doors so that people could party inside or out, and then went to sort out drinks.

'What do you want, Cate?'

He made no secret that his interest was in her.

'I'll get something in a moment,' Cate said, and asked if she could use the bathroom.

'Straight down the hall,' Juan said. 'And to your left.'

She followed his directions but straight down the hall was his bedroom—the door was open, the bed rumpled and unmade, and for a wild, reckless moment she wanted to give in to his undeniable charm, could almost envision them tumbling on the bed, a knot of arms and legs.

Cate pushed open the bathroom door and let out a breath.

This wasn't like her at all.

She hadn't ever really envisioned herself that way with anyone, not even Paul. Bloody Juan had her head

going in directions it wasn't used to. A part of her
wanted to stop being sensible, ordered Cate and just
give in to the feelings he ignited—to be a little wild and
reckless for once. She knew that she was sending him
mixed messages, that at times she found herself flirting with him in a way she never had with anybody else.

Cate washed her hands and had to dry them on her
top because, of course, he didn't have hand towels, just
a wet beach towel hanging over the shower.

Whoops, there went her mind again, imagining that
huge body naked on the other side of the glass shower
door.

'Go home, Cate,' she said to herself. She was about
to do just that, but when she got back to the lounge Juan
handed her a large glass filled with ice and some dan-
gerous-looking cocktail.

'I'm driving,' Cate reminded him.

'I know, so I take care to make you something nice—
it is right to take care of the designated driver.'

It was fruity, refreshing and delicious, yet she didn't
want to be singled out for the Juan special treatment,
didn't want to be the latest caught in his spotlight, but
she knew that she was.

Cate danced a little, chatted with her friends, finished her drink and, having stayed a suitable length of
time, when she saw that he was safely speaking with
others, she said goodnight to Kelly.

'Stay for a bit longer,' Kelly pushed.

'I'm going to go.' Cate shook her head and slipped
quietly away and headed out to her car.

He really had chosen a lovely spot to live—there were
views of the bay to the front and behind was hillside. It
all looked so peaceful, it was hard to imagine that across

Victoria bush fires were raging, Cate thought, dragging in a breath of the warm, sultry night as she went into her bag for her keys.

'Cate.'

She jumped a little when she heard Juan call her name. Had she not lingered that second she would have been safely in her car; instead, she had no choice but to turn to him.

'Where I come from...' he walked slowly towards her, his boots crunching on the gravel '...you thank your host and say goodbye...'

'I didn't know you were such a stickler for convention.'

'I'm not,' Juan admitted, still walking towards her as she backed herself against the car. 'Just when it suits me.'

'Thank you for a lovely night.'

'And in my country,' Juan continued, 'the host would try to persuade you to stay for one more drink, would be offended that you were leaving so soon...' It was all very casual, except his hand had moved to her cheek and was moving a lock of her hair behind her ear.

'I'm good at offending people,' Cate said. 'There really is no need to take it personally.'

'Don't go.' He smiled. 'I only asked everyone back to get you here.'

She laughed.

She doubted it.

Actually, no, she didn't, she believed it. Anything was possible with Juan.

'I might not be called in to work again,' he said. 'So this could be it.'

'It could be.'

'I'd have liked to get to know you some more.'

She gave him a half-smile, but it wavered. Cate wanted to get to know him some more too, but for what? He made no secret that in a couple of weeks he would be gone. Juan seemed completely at ease with a brief fling, whereas it just wasn't in her nature.

Except, yes, she wanted more of Juan.

'Stay.'

'Juan…' Cate just couldn't do it and she tried to make a joke. 'I've got three brothers and they've all warned me about guys like you.'

'What?' He frowned.

'Come on, Juan.' She loathed how indecent he was. 'Won't whoever you were in bed with this afternoon mind?'

'What?' he asked again as the frown remained, but then it turned into a wicked smile. 'That was my cleaning lady,' he said. 'I fell asleep on the couch, watching daytime soaps.' He looked down at her, realised fully then that he hadn't had sex since he'd dumped Christine, since a certain Cate Nicholls had stepped into his life—how with one turn of his head he'd been very turned on. 'I love daytime soaps in Australia,' he said. 'They are filthy.'

Cate let out a small laugh.

She wasn't sure she believed him about the cleaning lady, but did it matter?

She wasn't his mother.

She wasn't anything and, yes, very soon he'd be gone.

She turned to go, only half-heartedly because he had moved in to kiss her, and not on the cheek.

One kiss couldn't hurt, Cate told herself.

It was time to have kissed someone else by now, Cate decided as his mouth met hers. Except she'd never known a kiss like it.

It was everything a kiss should be.

It was very slow and measured, his lips light on hers at first, nudging hers into slow movement. His hands crept around her waist and his tongue slipped in and slid around hers, slowly at first, letting her acclimatise herself to the taste of him, and she did, so easily. He tasted of raspberry and vodka and something else too, which Cate couldn't quite place.

He took things slowly, but not for long. Just as she started to relax, just as she thought she could manage a kiss goodbye with Juan, he breathed into her, shed a low moan into her, pressed into her, pushed in his tongue more deeply, and Cate found her missing ingredient—it was a dash of sin that he tasted of, because no kiss had turned her on so much. The press of his erection made her push her mound into him, the feel of his hot hand on her back had her skin turn to fire.

It wasn't just her first kiss after Paul, it was the first kiss she'd ever had that could propel her straight to the bedroom. She was kissing him back and with passion; it was still a slow kiss but their tongues danced with suggestion. His hand moved to her breast and how she wished she wasn't wearing a bra that was too tight and digging in, but a moment later she wasn't—as easily as that, Juan had undone it. Cate let out a small sigh of relief as her breast fell into his palm and then a moan of bliss as his hand cupped her and stroked.

'I want you...' He was at her neck and trailing his mouth down, she was stone-cold sober, yet almost topless and drunk on lust. He kissed back up to her mouth and she could feel the trail of wetness he had left on her chest—and how she wanted him. Her hands moved to his head and she felt the thick, long, jet-black hair that he refused to cut, felt the wedge of muscle of a man it would be so easy to be immoral with, understood exactly why women lost their heads to him, for she was losing hers.

She moved her hand down to his shoulder, her fingers sliding to his neck, but Juan's hands halted hers and moved them onto his chest. It jolted her, just a little, for in that moment not a fraction of their bodies had seemed out of bounds. Cate had been utterly lost but she returned to common sense and he felt it, their eyes opening together, and she saw the regret in his as she pulled her mouth back.

'We could be so good together...' His forehead was resting on hers and she was struggling to get her breath.

Yes, they could be so good together but he would be so bad for her.

Cate wasn't looking for forever but neither was she looking for one night, or one week.

She simply couldn't do the casual thing, never had and never could. Could not walk into work tomorrow with everyone knowing she had succumbed to Juan's undeniable charm.

How she wanted to, though.

How she wanted to give in to the urges that were pulsing through her as much as the music coming from his home, how she wanted to just say, yes, I can handle this. Except, stupid her, her body came attached to a heart that was already a bit bruised and did not need to be shattered by him.

Oh, it would hurt to have him and then not. That much Cate knew.

'Get over him, Cate!' Juan said.

She was so over Paul, not that he knew it. Cate did not dare reveal the truth, so she made a wry joke.

'By getting under you?'

'No,' Juan said. 'I want you on top. I want to watch you come.'

He was bad.

He was dangerous.

He was everything she wanted and yet everything she didn't.

'Thanks for a lovely evening.'

'Would you like to go out tomorrow?' Juan offered.

'No, thanks.'

'Cate…'

So she took a breath and told him, 'I'm not what you're looking for.'

'You don't know what I'm looking for.'

'I don't know what I'm looking for either,' Cate admitted, 'but it's not…' she tried to think of the right word and she didn't know how best to say it '…you.'

'Ouch.'

Cate smiled and climbed into her car and caught the lingering fragrance of Juan from when he had been in her vehicle, the expensive note that overrode others.

She knew that she hadn't hurt him.

Ouch would be sitting in the staffroom in a couple of weeks' time, hearing who he'd slept with next, or, if they did last the little time he had left in Australia, ouch would be waving him off at the airport. Ouch would be having had him and then trying to move on.

Cate had just ended one serious relationship—a

rebound with the name Juan attached to it was heading way too far in the other direction.

She reversed out and waved to him, and, yes, she regretted it plenty. She could see them alone in his bedroom. Many times she had envisaged him kicking those boots to the floor and letting herself be a notch on his temporary bed; many times she had wanted to let loose and be as superficial and as laid back about things as Juan.

So clearly she could see it now, could still taste him on her mouth as she drove off, her bra around her waist, her cheeks burning, her hands willing her to turn round and return to him.

Instead, Cate chose safety.

# CHAPTER FOUR

JUAN WOUND UP the party and did not invite anybody else to stay the night.

As the last taxi pulled off, he didn't even look at the clock or tidy up, he just undressed and headed to bed and tried to get Cate Nicholls out of his head.

She was way too serious for him.

Usually, he didn't want to hear about promotions and brothers and parts of the woman's history but with Cate somehow he did.

He thought about her hand on his neck, her fingers about to meet the thick scar and, no, he didn't want her knowing, would far prefer Cate thinking that he was shallow than to open up and confide in her...

That wasn't what this trip was about, he told himself as he lay there. Caught between awake and asleep, Juan was unsure if the kiss with Cate had been a dream, unsure even if his time in Australia was a mere figment of his imagination. He even wondered if Cate's words to Reece would disappear the second he awoke and he would find out it was all just another dream—because he was back there again, back in his head, trapped in his mind with a body that refused to obey even the simplest command.

In Juan's dreams he ran, his feet pounding the warm pavement as he dragged in the humid air.

In dreams, he threaded his beloved motorbike through lush Argentinian hills and made love to every single woman who had ever flirted with him—and there were many, perhaps Cate was one?

In his dreams, Juan jumped off bridges and felt the sting of icy-cold water as he plunged in.

In his dreams, he skied down mountains and did all the things he had never had time to do—Juan's focus had always been Martina, family and work.

He could hear the nurses, doing the two a.m. rounds, approaching the four-bedded ward, and Juan tried to haul himself out of the memory, tried to get back to kissing Cate, except he couldn't dictate his dreams and he couldn't erase his memories, and as the REM stage deepened a very natural reflex occurred.

'Hey, Juan.'

'I apologise.' Juan didn't need to look at the mirrors placed over his bed to know the sheet was tenting and that he was erect; instead, he stared at the ceiling as Graciela tried to catch his eye. 'Juan, it's natural,' Graciela said. They spoke in Spanish, Graciela, as always, practical—she was nearing retirement and had worked on the spinal unit for years. Graciela was more than used to young men finding themselves paralysed, used to the strange sight of a beautiful, fit body that might never move independently again and the humiliation a new spinal-cord injury patient faced regularly.

Yes, Graciela was kind and practical, it just didn't help now as she and Manuel rolled him onto his side. Juan was burning with shame in a bed in the Buenos Aires hospital he worked at.

Had once worked at.

Juan didn't want that part of his life over. Yes, he played upbeat for Martina and his family, insisted if there was a little improvement he could lecture and teach; but tonight the future, one where he could function independently, let alone hold another's life in his hands, seemed an impossibly long way off.

'Juan…' Manuel tried to engage with Juan. 'We still don't know the extent of your injury. You have spinal swelling and until…'

Juan closed his eyes. He didn't want hope tonight, he felt guilty that compared to his roommates there was a thin hope that his paralysis was not permanent; he just wanted to close his eyes and go back to his dreams but he knew he would not get back to sleep, knew that this would be another long night.

'You need a haircut,' Graciela commented as she washed his face. 'Do you want me to arrange one for you?'

'No.' Juan made a weak joke. He had been on his way to get his thick black hair trimmed when the accident had happened—it grew fast and he had it trimmed every couple of weeks. Always he had prided himself on looking immaculate, dressing in exquisitely cut suits and rich silk ties. Tonight those days seemed forever gone. 'I'm not risking that again.'

'How's Martina?' Graciela tried to engage Juan as they started the hourly exercise regime, moving his limbs and feet and hands. Martina had been here until eleven and Juan had pretended to be asleep the last two times the nursing staff had come around. It was important to know what was happening in the patients' lives as they adjusted to their injuries. 'Is she still worrying about moving the wedding date?'

There was a long stretch of silence before Juan finally answered, 'We broke up.'

'I'm sorry, Juan.' Graciela looked over at Manuel, who took over the conversation.

'What happened?' Manuel asked. He wasn't being nosey—the mental health of their patients was a priority, and he chatted as he moved Juan's index finger and thumb together and apart, over and over—as they did every hour—and then moved to rotating his wrist. Both simple exercises might mean in the future Juan could hold a cup, or do up a button, or hold a pen.

'We just…' Juan did not want to discuss it, still could not take it in, could not comprehend how every aspect of his life had now changed. 'It was mutual.'

'Okay.' Graciela checked his obs and shared another look with Manuel. 'I'll see you a bit later, Juan. Hopefully you'll be asleep next time I come around and I won't disturb you.'

Asleep or not, the exercises went on through the night.

Graciela moved on to the next bed, leaving Manuel to hopefully get Juan to open up a bit. Since his admission Juan had remained upbeat, insisted he was dealing with it, refusing to open up to anyone, and Graciela was worried about him, especially with the news of the break-up. Relationships often ended here; patients pushed loved ones away, or sometimes it was the other way around and the able-bodied partner simply could not cope with a world that had rapidly altered.

'Hey, Eduard.' She smiled down at the young man,

who gave her a small grimace back and moved his eyes towards Juan's bed. 'Is he okay?'

'He'll get there.'

For the first time Juan didn't think he would.

There was one thing more humiliating than a massive erection in full view of the nurses. It was starting to cry and not being able to excuse yourself, not being able to go to another room and close a door, to thump a wall, not even being able to wipe your own snot and tears.

'Let it out, Juan,' Manuel said as he covered Juan with a sheet and saw his patient's face screw up and tears fill Juan's grey eyes.

'I…' He didn't want to let it out, he had held it all in and he wanted to keep doing so. There was young Eduard in the next bed. He'd only been here for three days and Juan didn't want to scare him—Juan had been trying to cheer him up today.

He just couldn't hold it in any more.

The sob that came out was primal, from a place he had never been.

'Good man,' Manuel said.

Juan lay there sobbing as Manuel wiped his eyes and blew his nose. He was in hell and humiliated and scared and everything he'd tried not to be.

'Good man,' Manuel said, over and over.

He'd been a good man, Juan thought. He'd done everything right, everything had been in place—an amazing career, a loving fiancée. He *had* been a good man.

'No more…' Juan said, incoherent almost as he sobbed.

But there was more and tonight he let it out.

Graciela stood there and wiped Eduard's tears as

they glimpsed for the first time Juan's desolation and rage, and she swallowed a couple of tears of her own.

All Juan's roommates cried quietly along with him. Two had been there before, giving in to the grief and the fear in the still of the night, and Eduard soon would. There was no privacy in their worlds right now and all the men had heard the painful exchange between Juan and Martina.

All were with Juan as finally he gave in and wept.

No one was with him, though, when, eighteen months later, Juan woke up in a foreign country, feeling the desolation all over again.

## CHAPTER FIVE

'How has your week been?'

Cate stopped for a brief chat with her neighbour as both women headed for work. Bridgette and her husband James were both in the police. It was nice being neighbours with fellow shift workers and, over the summer, Bridgette and Cate had spent several afternoons lying in one or the other's garden and putting the world to rights.

'It's been good.' Cate smiled as she lied. It had been a long week spent trying not to think about Juan and trying not to worry about work. 'Have you had your interview?' Bridgette asked.

'Not yet, but I'm stepping in as Acting Manager on Monday.'

'So you're off the weekend?'

'No, I'm working it, but if I do get the job I'll have every weekend off.'

'No more shift work!' Bridgette exclaimed, and Cate gave a smile and a nod, then they chatted a bit about the unrelenting weather but soon enough Bridgette asked how Cate was doing since the break-up and if she'd met anyone else.

'Not really.'

'What does that mean?' Bridgette asked. She was far too perceptive sometimes!

'There is someone I like,' Cate admitted. 'Or rather there was. He's from overseas and he's heading off to New Zealand soon so, really, there's no point.'

'No point in what?'

'Starting anything.'

'What are you talking about?' Bridgette gave her a very queer look. 'He sounds perfect for having a bit of fun with after Paul! You're not looking for forever, are you?'

'No, but…'

'Let you hair down and live a little while you're single.' Bridgette held up her hand and flashed her wedding ring. 'While you still can…' She winked. 'I'll come around over the weekend and we'll have a proper chat.'

'Do,' Cate said. 'I'd like that.'

Cate drove to work and tried to ignore the small bubble of disquiet that kept making itself known.

It had been the same towards the end of her relationship with Paul—everything had been going well, they'd got on, she'd cared about him; but when Paul had suggested moving in, they had been together for two years after all, Cate hadn't wanted that. When he'd suggested that they look for somewhere together, Cate had really had to sit and examine her feelings.

Cate turned on the radio instead—she didn't want to examine them now.

The staff car park was busy and Cate had to park well away from Emergency, which usually wouldn't matter but the temperature had barely dropped overnight and Cate couldn't wait to be in the air-conditioned hospital. The sky was a curious pink, even though the weather warned of no change or storms. Then, a week to the day after they'd shared that sizzling kiss, Cate saw him.

Only a madman would go running in this heat, Cate thought. An incredibly fit madman, though.

Juan was at the entrance to the hospital when she got there, trying to catch his breath before heading inside. He was bent over, his hands on his thighs, as he dragged in the sultry air. He was dressed in grey shorts and a top and they were drenched, as could be expected, given the considerable distance to the hospital from his apartment and that he'd run with a backpack on.

'Don't you listen to the warnings on the news?' Cate's voice was dry, deliberately refusing to reveal any awkwardness about their kiss last week. 'During a heat wave you're supposed to avoid exertion.'

'That is for the young and elderly,' he said, somewhat breathlessly bringing himself to stand upright, which was a bit disappointing for Cate as she'd been enjoying the opportunity of shamelessly looking at his legs. Long and muscular, pale-limbed with black hair and with a weight around one ankle. Briefly she wondered why, but only briefly—because as he looked down and spoke to her there was another image now to add to the Juan file she had stored away in her head. Juan smiled and added, 'And I am neither young nor elderly.'

'I think it was a given that no one would be crazy enough to go running in weather like this,' Cate said, trying not to blush, because now he was standing upright he looked amazing—he wasn't just unshaven, he practically had a beard. Harry wasn't going to be pleased, though Cate didn't mind in the least. He looked like a huge sexy god, Cate thought, and then corrected herself, because that was probably a wrong thing to think. He looked like a huge sexy…man.

It would just have to do.

'If a bit of heat and humidity stopped us, then no one in Argentina would ever run,' Juan said as they started walking into the hospital.

'So you're working here today?'

'They caved again.' Juan grinned. 'I got a call late last night to ask if I could come in for the morning shift.'

'You've been coming here for nearly three months now,' Cate pointed out. 'If you'd just signed the contract in the first place—'

'I've liked working all over Melbourne,' Juan interrupted, still slightly breathless. 'I've met loads of great people. It has been good not being confined.'

'Confined?' Cate frowned. 'It's not a prison.'

'Restricted,' Juan said. 'I don't know the word I am looking for in English,' he admitted.

'Doesn't it drive you crazy, though?' Cate asked. 'Never knowing where you'll be from day to day.'

'I love it,' Juan answered. 'It's the best thing I could have done.'

Cate could think of nothing worse and she told him so. 'I worked for an agency when I was a student. I loathed not knowing where I'd end up, where they'd send me, who I'd be working with…' She gave a small shrug. 'Maybe I'm boring like that.'

'You're never boring.' He turned and gave her a smile, just enough of a smile to let her know that he was thinking about the other night. 'Are you going to Christine's leaving do?'

Cate nodded. 'Are you?'

'She invited me.'

He headed into the changing rooms and Cate went to the staff kitchen and filled a glass with ice from the machine and then poured a cup of black tea with sugar over it and took her drink into the staffroom, where it was lovely and cool.

'Morning…' Cate smiled at two familiar faces—Charlotte and Adam were sitting dressed in their pyjamas and watching television. 'Have you two had breakfast?'

'No, we haven't eaten anything.' Charlotte was the louder of the two. 'Daddy said he'd get us something from the canteen before he took us to childcare.'

'Do you want me to get you something now?' Cate offered, and when they both nodded Cate went back to the kitchen and made them some cereal and juice.

'Christine's not doing the jump any more,' Kelly said as Cate came back in and served up breakfast for the twins, 'so there's a space if you've changed your mind.'

'Not a chance,' Cate said. Some of the staff had come up with the idea of a skydive to raise some much-needed funds to refurbish the interview rooms—but even if the funds were needed, even if it was for a good cause, Cate could think of nothing worse than jumping out of a plane, let alone paying for it. She much preferred to keep her feet on solid ground.

In came Juan, with that potent post-shower scent that had Cate's toes curling in her shoes. He was wearing scrubs, yet he still had on his signature boots and he was simply like no other.

'We've got hospital razors, Juan,' Kelly teased. 'I can get you a couple if you can't afford them.'

'Ah, but then you'd have to suture me after,' Juan said. 'They are lethal.' He looked at the twins, who had paused in their breakfasts and were staring up at this very large, very commanding man. 'Hello,' he said and then made Adam laugh. 'Are you the new consultants that are starting?'

'No,' Cate said, 'the interviews only started this week. These are Harry's twins, Charlotte and Adam.'

'Daddy got called in,' Charlotte said. 'For a sick boy.'

'Well, that's no good,' Juan said, and then looked at Cate's glass. 'Did you make me one?'

'No.' For a moment she thought he was going to take a sip of her drink.

For a moment he thought about it!

'Hey, Juan.' Kelly wasn't going to miss an opportunity for a little extra Juan time. 'A space has opened up on the charity dive next Sunday. You like all that sort of stuff.'

'I do.' He went and read the notice. 'I'll still be here. I fly out on the Tuesday…'

'We'll all go out afterwards,' Kelly said. 'It could be your leaving do.'

'Another one,' Cate said, and he turned at the slightly tart note to her voice but just smiled.

'Are you doing the jump?' Juan asked her.

'Absolutely not.'

'You should.'

'Why?' Cate challenged, but Juan gave no answer and went to get a pen from his pocket but, as usual, he didn't have one and he asked Cate if he could borrow hers.

'No,' Cate said. 'You already owe me three.'

'Just to put my name down on the list. I'll give it straight back.'

She ended up relenting and handed him her pen.

'Where are you going to next, Juan?' Sheldon asked.

'New Zealand! The south island first.'

'How long will you stay?'

'I'm not sure—I'll see how it goes, but I've heard that the skiing is spectacular, so I might stay there for the winter.'

'Then home to Argentina?' Sheldon asked as Juan wrote down his name to do the skydiving jump.

'I'm not sure...' Juan said. 'I was thinking of Asia.'

How could he have no idea where he was going? Cate wondered. He was hardly a teenager. He must be in his mid-thirties and just drifting through life, if you could call jumping off bridges and rafting down ravines and biking through the hills drifting. Cate just could not wrap her head around Juan's way of living.

'Come on, guys.' Cate glanced at the clock and stood. 'We'd better get round there.'

'You're not the boss yet,' Kelly teased.

No, she wasn't the boss yet, Cate thought. She said goodbye to Charlotte and Adam and turned on some cartoons instead of the news, telling them that someone would be around to check on them soon—but she wondered how she could tell Harry that he couldn't bring in the twins or, rather, if he did that the nurses wouldn't be watching out for them.

As they walked through the obs ward on their way, Cate was just about to ask the nurse who was working there to keep an eye out for Harry's children. But, seeing that the supervisor was there checking the bed status, Cate decided otherwise.

'Last day in the madhouse!' She smiled at Christine, who had just arrived at work.

Her smile wasn't returned.

'Thank God!' Christine rolled her eyes. 'If you can watch the floor, Cate, I'm going to go make sure all the ordering is up to date. Given all the fire warnings in place, I think it might be a good idea to order some extra burn packs and IV solutions…'

'I already have,' Cate said, and saw Christine's jaw tense.

'Of course you would have,' Christine said, and flounced off.

Cate knew she had annoyed Christine but, then, everything seemed to annoy Christine lately. Cate didn't particularly want to go to the leaving do tonight, especially now she knew that Juan would be there, but it would look rude and petty not to go. Handover was about to start and as she went to make her way over to the huddle Cate searched in her pocket for her pen, but of course, yet again, Juan had failed to give it back.

'Here…' He walked past and grinned as he saw Cate going through her pockets and he gave her back her pen, or what was left of it.

'You've chewed it!' Cate moaned.

'So did you,' Juan said, and opened his mouth and curled his tongue just a fraction. 'I had to taste you.'

He could be so filthy.

'Juan!' Harry came over to where they were standing, Cate's cheeks still on fire. 'I didn't know that you were on this morning.'

'Neither did I till late last night.'

'Well, it's really good to see you. Renée called me in a couple of hours ago—I've got a five-year-old named Jason that I'm really concerned about and am thinking of transferring. It would be great if you could come in and take a look.'

'Sure!' Juan said, and walked with Harry over to Resus as Cate went over to the group.

'Wow! I think Harry just gave Juan a compliment. He said that he was pleased that he was here. That's a bit of a turnaround.'

'I'm actually very glad to see Juan here this morning,' Renée, the night nurse, said. 'The child Harry is concerned about has got Goldenhar syndrome. Have you heard of it?'

Cate shook her head. There were many, many different syndromes, some relatively common, some rare, as was the case with this admission.

'It mainly presents as facial abnormalities. In Jason's case he's got a very underdeveloped left ear and he was born with a cleft palate and other problems. I've looked it up on the computer if you want to read about it. The main problem today is that he has presented with severe asthma, for which he's had several ICU admissions. Usually he's seen at the children's hospital and, understandably, the parents tend to stay close but, given the heat, they thought a couple of days near the beach might be nice.'

'It should have been nice,' Cate said. 'Poor things.'

'Yes, Jason has a very tricky airway and is really difficult to intubate—he's had to have a tracheostomy in the past. I think that was why Harry was so pleased to see Juan. The on-call anaesthetist has already been down to check on him a couple of times.'

'How come Harry is here?' Cate checked. 'I thought that Dr Vermont was on call last night.'

'He was,' Renée said. 'He was here till one o'clock but then he was unwell and had to go home. Jason came in just before five. I tried to get the paediatricians down but they're busy with a sick baby and so really I had no choice but to call Harry in.' Renée grimaced. 'I didn't realise that he'd have to wake up the twins.'

'Well, it sounds like Jason needed someone senior on hand,' Cate said. 'So, what else could you do?'

'Do you want to go in and take over?' Renée suggested. 'From Monday you'll be spending a lot of time in the office.'

'No, I shan't be.' Cate didn't elaborate, it wouldn't be fair on Christine, but Cate had no desire to disappear for hours into the office, as Christine all too often did. Still, Cate knew that she wouldn't be able to get as involved with individual patients—like it or not, the more senior she had become, the more hands off her role had been, so it was nice to take the opportunity to look after Jason.

Cate took the handover from Mary, the night nurse, as Juan examined the young patient.

'The parents are incredibly tense.' Mary pulled Cate aside. 'I don't blame them a bit, it must be awful to be away from all the specialists they need, but I think they're really making Jason more upset. Harry was talking about transferring him to the children's hospital and getting them to send out their emergency transfer team, but Lisa, the mum, got really distressed. Apparently Jason is petrified of flying, especially given that he's had more than his fair share of emergency transfers.'

They went through the drugs Jason had been given so far, before a grateful Mary headed for home.

Juan had been speaking with the parents, and had only just started to examine Jason. The little boy was exhausted but, despite that, his eyes were still anxious.

'So, you're a regular on the ICU at the children's hospital, are you?' Juan asked, after listening to his chest, and Jason nodded. 'I was working there last week and I'll probably be there again soon. Do you know Paddy?'

'We know Paddy,' Jason's mum said.

'Ken...do you know Ken?' the little boy said. He could still talk but only just.

'Do you mean Kent?' Juan checked. 'The ICU nurse?' Jason nodded. 'He's good fun. I might just have to give Paddy a call and let him know that you're here.'

Cate knew Juan was just putting the boy at ease, letting Jason know that he knew the staff there, while letting the parents know he worked there too.

He must be as popular there as he is here, Cate thought, strangely jealous of the other worlds of Juan.

'I just want a look in your mouth, Jason. Can you open it, please?' Juan removed the mask that was delivering medication and shone a light in. He looked carefully and then replaced the nebuliser, which was nearly finished.

'Okay, Jason,' Juan said. 'Just rest now and let the medicine start to work.' Juan looked over at Harry. 'Continuous nebulisers now...' Juan said, which moved Jason from severe to critical; but Juan seemed calm and Cate was a little surprised how Harry was stepping back and letting Juan take over the case. She knew Juan was good and a trained anaesthetist, but as it turned out Cate didn't know just how good he really was.

'He does need to be transferred, Lisa.' Juan spoke now to the mother. 'But I'm happy to keep a close eye on him here at this stage. I think we can wait for the rush hour to pass and then we will go by road ambulance...'

'What if something happens in the meantime?' Lisa was clearly petrified of being stuck in the outer suburbs without all the specialist doctors. But it was then that Cate realised exactly why Harry had been so pleased to see Juan this morning, and why he was so readily stepping back. 'What if something happens in the ambulance?' Lisa said, her eyes filling with nervous tears.

'I have worked with a lot of children who have similar problems to Jason,' Juan said, and went on to explain that he had spent a year as an anaesthetist in America, working at a major craniofacial hospital, and was very used to performing the most difficult of intubations on children.

'You've seen children with Jason's problems before?' Lisa asked.

'I have.' Juan smiled at Jason but Lisa still wasn't quite convinced.

'Jason had to be put on a ventilator the last time he had an asthma attack,' she said. 'They couldn't wean him off and in the end they couldn't keep the tube in his throat for any longer and so he had to have a tracheostomy…'

'Let's just focus on today,' Juan said, and started checking all the equipment. Harry had already brought over the difficult intubation box and Juan commenced pulling up drugs and taping the vials to the syringes, as relaxed as if he were making a coffee rather than preparing for a difficult intubation, and chatting away to Jason as he did so.

In a child with severe asthma everything was assessed clinically, there were no blood gases taken as it would simply upset Jason further. The fact that he was petrified of flying was an important issue because it was important not to distress Jason, but if he became much worse, there would be no choice.

'What's the protocol for IV aminophylline here?' Juan asked, after having another listen to Jason's chest.

'We don't give it here,' Cate said, because it was a drug that required constant monitoring. 'It's only given on ICU.'

'This has just become ICU,' Juan said. 'I'm not leaving him.'

Cate looked over at Harry.

'Fine.' Harry nodded and rolled his eyes. 'In Juan we trust.' Which actually made Lisa laugh.

'How long are you on till?' Lisa asked Juan.

'All day,' Juan said. 'Don't worry, when Jason is transferred I will go with him.' He didn't need to ask Harry's permission. Yes, it left them a doctor down, which would have to be sorted, but that was simply how it must be and no one argued. You could feel some of the tension leave not just Jason's parents but Jason himself. Clearly black boots and long black hair and an unshaven doctor didn't worry Jason a bit.

'Well,' Harry said, 'I'll leave you in Juan's capable hands and I'll come back in soon and see how Jason is doing.' He looked at Cate. 'I'm just going to get the twins some breakfast and then take them over to child-care.'

'I've already given them breakfast,' Cate said, and Harry gave a grateful nod. 'They're just watching cartoons in the staffroom.'

'Thanks so much for coming in, Doctor.' Jason's father stood and shook Harry's hand. 'It meant a lot.'

'Not a problem,' Harry said.

It was, though, a huge problem, and Juan commented on it after they had set up the aminophylline infusion and were waiting for the paramedics to transfer Jason.

Juan had double-checked that he had everything and Cate had done the same until, happy they were well equipped, they moved to have a quick coffee at the nurses' station, watching Jason from a slight distance. They had no idea when they might get another chance to take a quick break because they would both go on the transfer with Jason and then rush back to work at Bayside—unless there were any emergencies on the journey.

'Harry got here at five a.m. to see Jason,' Juan commented.

'I know.'

'Did he bring the twins in with him then?'

Cate gave a small worried nod.

'And does he do that sort of thing a lot?'

'Harry's wife died last year,' Cate said, by way of explanation.

'I know that,' Juan said. 'I asked if he did this sort of thing a lot.'

'He hasn't for a while.' Cate sighed because it was clearly starting all over again and on Monday she'd be the one dealing with it.

'He needs to get a nanny or someone he can count on.'

'He had a nanny,' Cate said. 'She just left.' She glanced at Juan, but he didn't return her look as he was watching Jason. But she did see him smile when she revealed a little more. 'They tend to fall in love with him.' She watched as Juan's smile spread further as he responded.

'Then he needs to stop sleeping with them.'

'Stop it!' Cate blushed, but trust Juan to get to the heart of it. Harry was a widower and a very good-looking, well-heeled one at that. There were plenty of women only too happy to bring over a casserole as Harry had once said with a wink and a tired roll of his eyes—he'd thought they were just being nice at first. No doubt he was having the same trouble with his babysitters. The thing was, it wasn't the Harry she knew. 'He adored Jill.'

'Of course he did,' Juan said. 'Sex and love are two very different things. I hear he was wild in his student days.'

'Please!' Cate said. She didn't even want to think about Harry and his sex life, but then she confided in Juan a little of what was troubling her. 'I've been told that once I'm Nurse Unit Manger I'm to address him bringing the twins in. Christine just ignores it, and Lillian says it's been going on for too long.'

'It needs to be addressed,' Juan said, and he glanced over just long enough to see the flare of worry in her eyes. That much he could do for her. 'I will speak with him about it.'

'And say what?'

'Bro talk,' Juan teased. 'You are not allowed to know.'

'But you barely know him.'

'Even better,' Juan said. 'Aside from everything, it's not fair on the little ones to be dragged in here all time.'

Had she thought about it, she would have expected him to take Harry's side, to say that it was no problem. Juan really was the most curious mix—the last thing she had expected was for him to actually be prepared to address the issue with the boss.

She'd love to be a fly on *that* wall!

# CHAPTER SIX

JUAN DRAINED HIS mug and as they headed back, the paramedics arrived.

'So we're not competent enough for you, Juan?' Louise, half of the team that would be transferring Jason, teased as she walked into Resus with the stretcher.

'Jason has a very special airway, don't you, Jason?' Juan said.

Jason had, in fact, picked up considerably but he was on strong drugs that meant he needed very careful monitoring. All joking aside, it was good to have Matthew and Louise as the paramedics—they were an excellent team and Juan went through all the history and the equipment with them and told Louise the medications Jason was on.

'I want to get there quickly,' Juan said, 'with as little upset to him as possible.'

'Do you want one of his parents to come?' Louise checked, but Juan shook his head.

'I've already told them no. We're going to play chase.'

'Sorry?' Louise frowned but Juan just smiled.

There really wasn't room for either of Jason's parents to come in the ambulance, especially as there was the potential for an emergency on the way. Even with the anti-emetic he had been given, Juan was worried that Jason might vomit and that could prove urgent in itself with his poor breathing and difficult airway.

Fortunately, though, Jason was so taken with Juan and so delighted to have escaped the helicopter that he didn't protest in the least and neither did his parents. They headed off as soon as the paramedics arrived in the hope of beating the ambulance to the hospital. There was a good chance they might, as Juan took his time making sure everything was ready for the transfer, and ensured that Jason was as stable as he could be.

'Come on, then,' Juan said a good twenty minutes after Louise and Matthew had arrived. 'We've given your parents a good start, shall we see if we can catch them up? We might have to put the sirens on if we're going to have a chance.'

He winked to Louise, who smiled because she understood the game.

It was so much better with him than without, Cate thought as they sped with sirens and lights blazing to the city, trying to *beat* Jason's parents! The stars really had aligned for Jason today and they pulled up at the children's hospital without incident. Just knowing that Juan could deal with whatever presented had made a difficult transfer so much more straightforward. Juan was more than highly skilled—clearly his career had, at one time, been his major focus and yet here he was drifting around the world.

Cate wanted to know why.

She wanted to know more.

But soon he'd be gone.

'We got here first!' Juan said as the ambulance doors

opened and there was no sign of his parents. An exhausted Jason even managed a quick high five.

Jason was a direct admission to ICU and a very pretty nurse looked up and turned purple before smiling when she saw Juan walking in. From the general reaction to his entrance, Cate knew he was just as popular here as he was at Bayside.

'Juan!' A huge bear of a man came over and shook Juan's hand. 'I thought you were in New Zealand by now.'

'Soon! How are you, Paddy?' Juan said, and proceeded to hand over the young patient as, just a little behind them, Jason's parents arrived.

'You beat us!' Lisa kissed her son. She was looking a lot more relaxed in more familiar surroundings with staff that she was more used to. 'How was the journey?'

'It went really well.' Cate smiled. 'Juan will come and speak with you soon, he's just handing everything over.'

'He's good, isn't he?' Lisa said to Cate, glancing over to where Juan was chatting with Paddy.

'Very good,' Cate said, as Juan made his way over to them.

'Okay, the journey was without incident,' Juan said to Lisa. 'I've spoken with Paddy about all that has been done for Jason and you are safely in the right place.'

'Thank you so much.'

'No problem,' Juan said. 'I am just glad he is here without any more drama for you.'

'Well, we won't be going far again,' Lisa said, but Juan shook his head.

'Did you have a good week?'

Lisa nodded.

'Would he have got the asthma anyway?'

Lisa was nearly in tears as she nodded again.

'So he is here, where he would have been anyway, but also he has had a week at the beach, and that is a *good* thing.'

He gave Lisa a cuddle, just a brief one, told her what an amazing mother she was, and Cate felt a sting of tears at the back of her eyes as Juan peeled another strip off her heart and nailed it to the Juan wall in her mind.

Don't go!

She stood there and looked at him, hating that very soon there would be no more Juan. She didn't even try to fathom her strong feelings towards a man she didn't really know, because everyone was crazy about him, everyone wanted more Juan in their life.

He shook Jason's father's hand and, oh, what the hell, Juan gave him a hug too and then went to say farewell to Jason. Cate was more confused than she had ever been, because she didn't want, ten days from now, to have Juan gone from her life and to have done not a single thing about it.

Then he spoiled it by going missing as they were about to head back to Bayside.

'I'll go and find him,' Cate offered.

She soon did!

Talking to Nurse Purple Face and making her laugh.

'You're quiet,' Juan said as they rode back in the back of the ambulance with Louise.

'I'm just tired,' Cate lied, not sure if she was jealous or just cross with herself. Or was it regret that she simply couldn't push aside her usual rules, wave her knickers over her head and give in to him?

'Well, that was worth the trip for me,' Juan said, 'I

have my shifts for next week all sorted I am working Friday through to Saturday on ICU there.'

Cate glanced up.

He only did one or two shifts a week, she knew that, preferably one long one, and he'd just been given that.

Today really could be the last time she saw him.

Apart from tonight.

# CHAPTER SEVEN

CATE WAS SO distracted she didn't even hear Matthew talking on the radio until he called out to Cate and Juan. 'We've got an eighty-six-year-old in an independent living facility, she's waiting to be admitted for a chest infection but she's developed chest pain. Are you guys okay with us accepting?'

'Sure,' Juan said. 'So long as you go fast.'

On went the lights and sirens and Cate felt a flurry in her stomach as the ambulance sped off.

'You love this part, don't you?' Louise smiled.

'I do.'

'Are you still thinking about joining us?'

Cate shook her head. 'It's not for me. Sometimes I do still think about it, though.'

'You've thought of being a paramedic?' Juan's eyes widened in surprise.

'Cate came on a ride along with us,' Louise told him. 'About six months ago, wasn't it, Cate? I said to try a Saturday night in the city before she made up her mind.'

Cate could feel Juan's eyes on her.

'You didn't like it?' he asked.

'I loved it,' Cate said. 'It was an amazing experience but...' She gave a small shake of her head. 'It made me appreciate even more all the back-up that we have in Emergency, and I decided that it just wasn't for me.'

They were pulling into the independent living facility—the gate had been opened for them and a staff member directed them to the small unit where the patient was. Matthew and Louise took all the necessary equipment and then the four of them walked into a small house that was crammed full of furniture—huge old bookshelves and old-fashioned sofas—that looked a little out of place in the more modern surroundings.

'Her name's Elsie Delaney,' the on-call nurse explained. 'We had the doctor in to see Elsie last night for her cough and she was started on antibiotics for a chest infection. When I went to check on her this morning, she didn't look well and finally admitted she had chest pain. She's very independent and didn't want me to call you, of course.'

'Hi, Elsie!' Matthew walked in first and greeted the patient.

'What are all of you doing here?' came an irritated voice as the room started to fill up.

'You're getting the works today, Elsie,' Louise said. 'We had a doctor and nurse already with us, so that's why there are so many of us.'

The bedroom was as full of furniture as the rest of the house and, with Juan walking in front of Cate and his shoulders taking up most of the doorframe, it took a moment before Cate glimpsed Elsie.

She was tiny, sitting up in bed, her straggly white hair held back with a large, jewelled hair clip. She had a pink shawl around her shoulders and was wearing an elaborate necklace, and on her gnarled fingers were several rings.

She looked absolutely gorgeous, but she was wary and disgruntled and complained as Louise and Matthew did obs and attached her to a monitor while Juan slipped in an IV.

'I'm feeling much better,' she kept protesting.

Really, they weren't needed at all. Cate and Juan were completely supernumerary as Louise and Matthew had it all under control. They soon had a heart tracing and were giving Elsie some medication for pain and, despite having said she had little pain, as it took effect she lay back on the pillow. Elsie finally agreed that, yes, they could take her to hospital.

'Are there any family for us to inform?'

'She has a daughter, Maria, who lives nearby,' the nurse said, and spoke then to Elsie, 'I'll ring Maria and let her know what's happening.'

'She'll be very disappointed that I'm only sick and not dead,' Elsie said. 'It's the truth!' Elsie turned to Cate and winked, and Cate found herself smothering a smile. 'Does Maria even have to know that I'm going to hospital?' Elsie asked.

'Of course she does, Elsie!' the nurse answered. 'And you're wrong, Maria will be ever so worried.'

Elsie gave a huff to indicate that she doubted it. 'I'm not going out on a stretcher,' Elsie said.

'Fine.' Louise smiled. 'I'll go and get the chair.'

'Do you want to leave your jewellery here?' Cate suggested, knowing that one of the first things that would happen when they got to Emergency was that they would take it all off and lock it up in the safe. But Elsie wasn't going anywhere without her finery.

'And I want my photo album too…' She pointed to a shelf and Juan went over to fetch it.

'You might only be there a few hours,' the nurse pointed out.

'Then I'll have something to look at while I'm waiting,' Elsie retorted.

'Where's this, Elsie?' Juan asked, pointing to a picture in a frame where a younger Elsie was smiling into the camera against a stunning backdrop of houses and a glimpse of the ocean behind her.

'Menton,' Elsie said. The medication wasn't stopping her from talking! 'They call it the pearl of France. Have you been?'

'To France, yes,' Juan said. 'To Menton, no, but I want to now!' They chatted about it even as she was loaded into the ambulance and transferred from the chair to the stretcher. She was in a seated position for comfort and she and Juan chatted all the way to Bayside.

'I was there for six months,' Elsie said. 'Then I went back, oh, ten years ago now and it's still just as lovely.' She looked at Juan. 'Are you Spanish?'

'I'm from Argentina.'

'Well, I'll try not to hold it against you,' she said, and Juan laughed. Elsie peered at him for a while, slowly looking at his hair and then down to his boots before looking at Cate.

'He's a good-looking one, isn't he?' Elsie said.

'You just caught him at a good time,' Cate answered back.

'That's what I'm here for,' Juan responded, and Cate felt her cheeks burn a little, because a good time was *all* that he was here for—and she would do very well to remember that fact.

'So you don't live in Australia?' Elsie asked him.

'No,' Juan said. 'I am here for a working holiday.'

Elsie frowned for a while before speaking. 'You're a bit old for all that, aren't you?' And for the second time since meeting Elsie, Cate found herself suppressing a smile. Elsie was funny and wise and old enough to say what she liked and not care what others thought.

'Never too old, Elsie,' Juan said. 'Surely you know that?'

For the first time since their arrival it was Elsie smiling—at Juan. 'You're a charmer, aren't you?'

'Am I charming you, Elsie?' Juan smiled back.

Of course he was.

Christine didn't seem too impressed when they arrived back at the department. 'Finally, the wanderers return!' And she wasn't too pleased to have been forced out of her office during Cate's absence. 'I'm going to go and do some work now,' Christine said. 'There are incident forms to fill in. I don't want to leave them for you.'

'Sure,' Cate said, as Christine handed over the drug keys to her.

'She's a sour one!' Elsie muttered, as she was moved over onto a gurney.

Cate made no comment. 'I'm just going to go find you a gown,' she said to Elsie when she realised that there wasn't one. Now, that was one thing that *was* going to change when she was in charge. Cate really hated it when the cubicles were not properly tidied and stocked.

'Can't I just wear my nightdress?' Elsie grumbled, but Cate explained that she would need to take off her bra and necklace as the doctor would probably order a chest X-ray.

First, though, Cate did a routine set of obs and then headed off in search of the elusive gown. The linen trolley was void of them—the staff from the wards were always coming down and pinching linen from the emergency trolley and so Cate often hid a few pieces as soon as they were delivered. She went to her secret stash in the storeroom, where she kept a few gowns hidden behind the burn packs.

The phone was ringing as she made her way back and, with the ward clerk not around, Cate took the call—it was Maria, Elsie's daughter.

'She only just arrived in the department,' Cate explained. 'The doctor should be in with her soon.'

'She's talking?' Maria checked.

'Oh, yes!' Cate smiled, because Elsie hadn't stopped talking since she had laid eyes on her. 'Should I tell her that you're coming in?'

'No, no,' Maria said. 'I'll call back later this afternoon to see what's happening. It doesn't sound as if it is anything too serious. I don't know why they called an ambulance.'

'She developed chest pain,' Cate said. 'I'm quite sure it was more severe than even Elsie was letting on, though she's very comfortable now.'

'Still, I think an ambulance is taking things a bit far. We don't want any heroics.'

Cate blinked for a moment at the matter-of-fact way Maria addressed a rather sensitive issue. 'Is that something that has already been discussed?' Cate asked carefully. 'Does your mother have a DNR order?'

'No, but at her age surely we should just let nature take its course?'

Cate continued the difficult conversation, explaining that Elsie was lucid and comfortable and that it was something Elsie could discuss with the doctor if she saw fit. 'Is there any message that you'd like me to pass on to your mother?' Cate asked.

'Just tell her that I'll call back later,' Maria said, and then rang off.

Cate let out a breath, and when the phone rang again, on instinct she answered it, though she soon wished that she hadn't.

'Can I please speak with Dr Morales?'

'I'll see if he's available,' Cate said. 'May I ask who's calling?' As soon as the words were out she regretted them; she had made it clear that Juan was here but her mind had been so full of Elsie and her daughter that she had forgotten Juan's little lecture from last week.

'Tell him it is Martina.'

She found Juan in with Elsie, taking bloods.

'Sorry I took so long, Elsie,' Cate said. 'Your daughter just called...'

Elsie rolled her eyes and dismissed the information with a flick of her hand. 'You can ring her when I'm dead,' Elsie huffed. 'That will cheer her up.'

'She's going to call back later,' Cate said, making a mental note to speak to whichever doctor Elsie was referred to, so that Elsie's wishes could be discussed properly. 'Juan, you've got a call too—Martina is on the phone for you, I'm very sorry, I forgot and I—'

He interrupted her excuses. 'Tell her that I am with a patient,' Juan answered, labelling the vials of blood he had taken.

'Just to have her call back in ten minutes?' Cate checked, because Martina called fairly frequently. 'Why doesn't she ring your mobile?'

'Because I've blocked her.' He muttered something

under his breath in Spanish but then winked at Elsie. 'Excuse me, I need to take a phone call.'

'Be nice when you do,' Elsie warned, and Juan smiled and gave a small shake of his head.

'It gets you into more trouble sometimes.'

It did.

Juan had tried being nice, had tried being firm, had been downright rude a couple of times and the calls had stopped for a while. But as the date of what would have been their first wedding anniversary approached, Martina was more determined than ever to change history.

'Juan, I was hoping to speak to you.'

'I'm at work.'

'Then call me from home.'

'Martina—'

'You won't let me properly explain,' Martina interrupted. 'And I'm hearing from everyone the ridiculous things you are doing—that you are going to do a season of skiing. Why would you take such risks?'

'I'm not your concern, Martina. You made that very clear.'

'I would have come round. Juan, please, we need to speak.'

'Stop calling me at work,' Juan said, and hung up and sat for a moment, thinking of the man he had once been, compared with the man he was now.

Martina didn't know him at all.

She couldn't.

Not even *he* knew yet who the new Juan was.

'Poor Martina,' Elsie had said as Juan had left the cubicle to take the call and Cate had laughed. She loved old people, they knew about a thousand times more than the whole of the staff put together. It had taken

Elsie about two seconds to work out what a heartbreaker Juan was.

'I had one like that once,' Elsie said, nodding to the curtains Juan had just walked through, as Cate helped her undress and get into a gown.

'What, a six-foot-three Argentinian?' Cate quipped.

'No, a five-foot-eight Frenchman!' Cate wanted to put Elsie in her handbag and take her home. 'I was in my fifties and I'd been widowed for two years.'

'That's young to be a widow.'

'Don't waste any sympathy, I had a terrible marriage,' Elsie said. 'You can call me the merry widow if you must, but I was just sick of feeling like I was in my daughter's way and being told what to do. I took myself off to France—I'd always wanted to go and I was so glad I did. We had one week together and I had the best time of my whole life!' She pointed to a large silver bezel-set amethyst ring on her finger. 'No regrets from me,' Elsie said. 'We had completely different lives, it would never have worked long term but we kept in touch a little bit. He sent me a card now and then, and when he died ten years ago I went back and visited his grave and thanked him.'

She opened the album and showed Cate a picture of the love of her life, a love that had lasted just a few days.

'Have you ever been adored?' Elsie asked, and Cate frowned as she met Elsie's pale blue eyes.

'I don't think so,' Cate admitted, as the reason for her break-up was delivered to her, as the word she had needed was revealed.

'I highly recommend it,' Elsie said. 'Have you ever adored anyone?'

And Cate faltered. 'Adored?'

'It's a rare kind of love,' Elsie said, 'and I got to taste it.'

'Was it worth it, though, Elsie?' Cate asked. 'Lugging a broken heart around for the rest of your life.'

'My heart wasn't broken.' Elsie smiled. 'It soars every time I think of him.'

Cate's heart wasn't soaring, though, as Juan pulled her aside a while later and warned 'for the third time' that she had to have a word with the nursing staff and receptionist and remind them about privacy on the phone. They were not to reveal any of the staff rosters.

It was the closest she had come to seeing him angry or, rather, very disgruntled.

And so too was Cate, as she had a word with the staff as per Juan's instructions!

There she was, mopping up the chaos of his love life. It was a relief not to have slept with him.

Then she saw him laughing with Elsie, chatting with her as she was waiting to be moved to the ward, just standing by her gurney and putting a smile on the old lady's face. She was in a white hospital gown now, all the rings and jewellery off, but she had her pink shawl around her shoulders and was smiling as she showed him pictures.

No, it was no relief not to have slept with him.

It was simply self-preservation.

# CHAPTER EIGHT

'CATE?'

Cate heard her name being called over her side gate as she hung out her uniform. She was in a rush, she'd just come out of the shower and, yet again, she was driving, so she really didn't have much time. But that never stopped Bridgette, who would chat happily as Cate got ready.

'Come over, Bridgette, but I can't chat for long.'

'Going out?'

Cate nodded. 'Yes, and I have no idea what to wear.'

They headed into the kitchen and Cate put on the kettle and did her usual thing with tea and ice—it was the only way to get through the long hot summer. Then they headed upstairs to decide what Cate should wear. 'I need a new wardrobe,' Cate sighed.

'So do I.'

'No, I really need one,' Cate said. 'Everything I've got I wore when I was going out with Paul. I've got my black dress, my going-out-for-dinner dress, the dress I wore when I met his family...' It was hard to explain.

'What about this?' Bridgette pointed out Cate's lilac skirt.

'It's the one new thing I have but I wore it last week.'

'Are you missing him?'

'No,' Cate said. 'And then I feel guilty that I don't.'

'So who's this other guy?'

Cate was about to shake her head but there was no chance of Bridgette meeting Juan and it would be so nice to get her advice—even if she had no intention of taking it! Bridgette was a lot more open-minded than Cate and always made her laugh.

'There's a casual doctor at work,' Cate said. 'He's from Argentina and is travelling for a year or two…'

'Nothing wrong with a younger man.'

'He's not younger, though,' Cate said, because, yes, most doctors were in their twenties when they travelled the world. 'He's in his mid-thirties, I think. It sounds like he had a really good job and then just took off…'

'He's a bit young to be having a mid-life crisis.'

'He's not in crisis!' Cate laughed. 'He's having a ball. He's stunning, everyone fancies him, he makes no bones that he's moving on soon and that he's not interested in anything serious, not that it stops anyone.' She paused for a moment. 'He works all over Melbourne and from what I saw today he's having just as much fun at the other hospitals as he is at Bayside, but…' Cate took a breath '…we get on, he likes me…'

'And you clearly like him.'

Cate nodded. 'He leaves the country soon so it's not going anywhere except bed…' She looked at Bridgette. 'And that's just not me.'

'Who knows where it could lead?'

'No.' Cate shook her head. 'That's the one thing I

can't let myself think. The whole point is, it *will* go no-where and I don't know if I can get my head around that.'

'You take things so seriously.'

'I know I do,' Cate said. 'I don't want to, but I do. I want to be carefree, I want to just let loose and have fun and live a little…'

'Then do.'

To Bridgette it was that simple.

Maybe, Cate thought, it could be.

She thought of Elsie and her one wild fling, thought of Juan, who was, quite simply, beautiful, and she felt as if she was standing on the edge of a diving board and peering down.

She wanted to have done it, wanted to be climbing out of the water, high from the thrill. It was just throw-ing herself over the edge that Cate was struggling to come to terms with.

'I've got a dress you can have,' Bridgette said. 'It's too big for me but it would look great on you. It's still got the tags on. Go and get ready and I'll fetch it.'

They borrowed and swapped things all the time. Bridgette was always buying and selling things on the internet. Cate did her make-up until Bridgette returned.

'Oh!' She stared at the dress. 'White?'

'First after Paul.' Bridgette winked. 'You need sexy undies.'

Cate opened her top drawer and let out a sigh. Juan was right, her relationship with Paul had gone on too long—two years in and they'd long since passed the sexy underwear stage.

'You are joking?' Bridgette said, as Cate pulled out

some rather plain white panties. 'You'd be better off not wearing any!'

Well, that wasn't going to happen—so she had to wear the sensible ones.

Cate never usually wore white, but when she put it on she found it suited her. The dress tied under the bust and scooped a little too low and certainly, when she looked in the mirror, the word virginal didn't spring to mind.

'It's too much! Or, rather, it's way too little,' she said, pulling the dress down over her bottom.

'Go for it,' Bridgette said. 'Take a taxi.'

'I'd rather drive,' Cate said. 'Anyway, I'm working tomorrow.'

She put on her new wedges and there was a flurry of nerves in her stomach as she looked in the mirror, and then there was the most terribly unfamiliar feeling as she filled her bag not just with lipstick and breath mints but with a few condoms too.

It was so not her.

Just so against her nature.

Cate picked up Kelly and Abby and kept having to force herself to keep up with the conversation, her mind was so full of Juan.

There was a flurry of hellos as they entered the garden to the restaurant where Christine's leaving do was being held.

They had chosen outside, not just because of the balmy heat but because thirty Emergency workers tended to be loud at the best of the times.

Cate slipped into a seat beside Louise and, although she did best not to look over, the second she arrived she searched for him. She saw that Juan was already there. He was, of course, in the middle of the long table, sitting beside Christine and enthralling his adoring audience.

Maybe, Cate thought, all this indecision was for nothing, because he'd barely looked in her direction.

Maybe she'd said no one too many times.

'He could have his pick, couldn't he?' Louise said.

'Almost,' Cate sighed, they both knew who she was talking about.

'It's a shame he's leaving.'

'I just don't get the drifting-around-the-world thing,' Cate said. 'He wouldn't even commit to a three-month contract. I could understand it if he was in his twenties.'

'I don't need three months with him...' Louise nudged, and Cate pushed out a smile.

It was actually a very nice night—at first. The restaurant was set high on Olivers Hill and looked over Port Phillip Bay. The view was stunning and the drink was flowing a bit too freely because Christine's laughter was getting louder and louder, the stories at the table more outrageous. Cate laughed and joined in but her heart really wasn't in it. She just wanted to go home, not to be sitting waiting for a sliver of Juan's attention, not to be like Christine and hanging onto his every word.

And, yes, it hurt that he hadn't so much as spoken to her once.

It was still, at eleven p.m., unbearably warm and Cate blew up her fringe as she let out a long breath. 'Another sleepless night, tossing and turning...'

'Well, if you insist.' Juan's voice from behind her made Cate jump but she managed to answer in her usual dry fashion when she turned round. 'In your dreams, Juan!'

He lowered his head and gave her a brief kiss on the cheek, just as a few other colleagues had, but because it was Juan he took the tease one step further. 'Often.'

'You don't know when to stop, do you?' Cate really tried not to take his flirting seriously, for pity the woman who believed that any words that slipped from those velvet lips hadn't been used many times before.

'I brought you a drink...' Juan put a glass of champagne on the table.

'It's very nice of you, but I'm driving.'

'You can have one.'

'I don't want to have one.'

'I'll have it.' Louise smiled.

'Help yourself.'

He moved into an empty seat beside her—a few of the gathering had gone to dance and once she'd finished her drink Louise drifted off to join them.

'Are you looking forward to Monday?' Juan asked.

'I don't know that much will change,' Cate attempted.

'Of course it will.'

'It might only be temporary,' Cate pointed out. 'I might not get the job.'

'You know you will.' He saw the swallow in her throat. 'Is it what you want?'

'Of course it is.'

'Why?'

'Why wouldn't I?' She gave a small shake of her head. She wasn't about to discuss her career with a man who had turned his back on his.

'Have you thought about doing the sky jump?'

'The places are all taken.'

'You can have mine.' Juan grinned. 'I'd happily pay

to watch you jump out of a plane. I think it would be very freeing for you.'

'I don't need freeing.' Her eyes narrowed as she looked at him. 'I don't need a shot of adrenaline from jumping out of a plane to prove that I'm alive...' It annoyed her that he smiled. 'I don't.'

'I'm not arguing.' Still he smiled. 'I wish you good luck with your interview. If I come back in a couple of years, I expect you'll be carrying a clipboard and be the new director of nursing.'

'And what will you be doing in a couple of years?' Cate asked, because even though he was smiling she felt there was a challenge in his tone. 'Still roaming the globe, still doing casual shifts and not knowing where you're going to be each day?'

'I don't know,' he admitted. 'I try not to think that far ahead, but I am thinking ahead now—after you've dropped everyone off, come back to mine.'

'Pardon?'

'I would like to have some time to speak with you.'

'We're speaking now.'

'Okay, I would like to talk to you some more.' He would. Juan was more than aware that this might be the last time they were together and he cared enough about Cate to prolong the conversation. She clearly didn't want his career advice, so he switched track to something a little more palatable. 'I would like to be a bit more hot in my pursuit but I don't think you would appreciate it. You are senior, you don't need the Dr Juan walk of shame, so I'm inviting you to come over afterwards...'

'Why would I come back to yours?'

'Because, as I said when I brought your drink, I think about you often and think it is the same for you.

I believe if you want something you should at least try, and so I am.'

'I don't think—'

'Don't think, then.'

She couldn't really believe he could be so upfront about it.

'Juan…'

'I can't talk too long. Christine is being a pain and I don't want to upset her at her leaving do. We can talk some more back at mine.'

Cate excused herself and nipped out to the toilets. She wished for a guilty moment that she hadn't when she saw Christine in there in tears. Cate really didn't know what to say.

'It's hard, leaving,' Cate attempted, 'but you'll still keep in touch…'

'Do you really think I'm crying about that place?' Christine looked at her. 'I couldn't be happier to be getting away from it. It's Juan.'

'Oh.'

'I made a bit of a fool of myself,' Christine said. 'I asked if he wanted to come back after…' She cringed. 'I was very politely rebuffed. I told myself before I came out not to drink and Juan.' Cate gave a thin smile at Christine's pale joke—she knew exactly what she meant.

'Our livers will be thanking him,' Cate said, because she wasn't just being a martyr, driving everyone around—since she'd met Juan she'd been clutching water, terrified that a thimble of wine and all restraint would be gone.

'I should have known better.' Christine started the

repair job on her face. 'I knew it wasn't going anywhere, but it was so great being with him…'

Cate really didn't want to hear this; she didn't want to hear from Christine how good he was in bed. She was just about to excuse herself, skip to the loo, do anything to avoid that conversation. She had no idea what was coming next.

'It was all going great until you came back from leave.'

'What?'

'Oh, come on, Cate…'

'There's nothing going on between us.'

'I'm not blind.'

Cate just stood there; she knew this could get nasty and she certainly didn't have to explain one kiss to bloody Christine.

'What's going on between the two of you, then?' came Christine's slightly drunken demand.

'I don't know about you, Christine, but I left school years ago,' Cate said, and walked out.

She went to get her bag but she'd promised Kelly a lift.

Kelly could pay for a taxi for once, Cate decided. But there was no need to rush off. The drama was over—Juan had already gone.

Once the bill had been paid, even Kelly didn't want to head off to a club; so Cate drove her home and then dropped off Abby, which took her unbearably close to Juan's.

She couldn't just walk up the garden path for sex.

'Hi, Juan.' She could just picture it. 'I'm here.'

Cate was nothing like that, she did nothing like that. She had fewer regrets than Frank Sinatra.

Yet Cate didn't want to be sitting on a gurney in fifty years' time, speaking about this stunning six-foot-three Argentinian who had offered no strings, who had offered nothing but a night, maybe a couple of days...

'What did you do?' She could just see the young nurse asking her half a century from now.

'I went home.'

'Oh.'

'Nothing could have come of it,' Old Cate would rationalize. 'There was no point if it was going nowhere.'

Elsie would be disappointed

Bridgette too.

Even the imaginary nurse of the future would be disappointed in her tonight, Cate thought as she refused to give in to temptation.

She arrived home—there was a present on her doorstep and Cate opened the note with it as she stepped inside.

*Hope you don't get this till morning and you can take this beauty out for a whirl tonight.*
*B xxx*

Lilac velvet panties, still fresh in their pack, and they'd cost an absolute fortune, Cate knew, because Bridgette had been trying to sell them to her!

Wasted, she thought, crunching them into a ball in her fist and trying not to cry.

Lying in bed alone at two a.m., Cate was disappointed in herself too...at her wasted chance.

## CHAPTER NINE

IN HIS NIGHTMARES he relived it.

Juan had waited for Cate until one and then given in and gone to bed, but he left the lights on outside and in the hall, just in case she changed her mind. He dozed off, trying to keep one ear open for her car, trying to fathom what it was about Cate that held his attention so, when he found himself back in his hospital bed.

'I felt that!' Juan said.

Manuel was washing his arm and Juan felt something, a vague sting, but at least he felt it.

His breathing came faster, scared to hope.

It was two a.m., the nurses were doing their rounds the night after his meltdown.

His roommates had all been wonderful.

'Love you, Juan,' André had called to him that morning as Juan had woken up. He was so ashamed for what he had put his roommates through, not knowing it was part of the process, not knowing two of them had done it too.

'Love you, Juan,' José had called, and Juan had closed his eyes.

'Does it make me gay if I say I love you?' young Eduard had called out, and Juan had smiled at the ceiling.

'No,' Juan finally answered. 'I love you guys, too,' he said. 'Thank you.'

It had been a day of conversation, a day of comradeship in the room as they'd stared up at the ceiling and joked and laughed. With the nurses' help they had even video-called each other that afternoon, finally face to face with each other. Eduard had told them about his amazing girlfriend, Felicia, who was currently flying back from a student exchange in France and would be coming in to see him tomorrow.

Juan had woken at two a.m., as he always did when the nurses approached.

'Not like this!' Juan's eyes snapped open as he heard Eduard shout. 'I don't want Felicia seeing me...'

Poor man.

Juan closed his eyes in agony as he heard Eduard screaming to Graciela, who was by his side. Poor man. Juan wept as Manuel wiped his tears and Eduard's deranged, grief-filled rant continued.

Oh, Eduard!

Juan wanted to go over and hold him. He wanted to fix him, to heal him, but all he could do was lie in respectful silence, grimacing over and over in agony as Eduard let out his fears in a room, in a ward, that understood.

Poor man.

Good man.

He looked up at Manuel, saw that his eyes were filling up too, but he gave a small smile of comfort to Juan.

'It's okay,' he said quietly. 'He will be okay.'

Juan's eyes snapped open and his heart was pounding as he came out of the memory. He moved his hands and it was luxury, checked that his legs still moved and then his hand moved to the heaven of an erection he could feel, even if was unsated, and he cried in the darkness, feeling the hell of that night again.

He sat up and gulped water and then reached for his laptop. He blew his nose as he made the call on his computer and waited for the comfort of a familiar face.

'Juan!' Eduard smiled as he came into focus.

'Does it make me gay if I call you in the middle of the night to tell you I love you?' Juan asked.

'Bad night?' Eduard asked, and Juan nodded as he wiped the tears from his face. Their friendship was worth more than gold, silver and platinum combined. It was Juan's most treasured possession. André struggled with Juan, jealous at his recovery, but they were trying to work through it. José was doing well and had movement in his arms and they kept in regular touch. But it was Eduard and Juan who were closest. The bond they had made back then was unbreakable and Juan smiled to see Eduard's cheeky grin. 'Bad luck for you if you are gay,' Eduard said. 'Felicia and I are getting married.'

'Eduard…' Juan was smiling and crying and then just smiling. Eduard was quadriplegic, with some small movement in his left hand and wrist. How he treasured that movement, how grateful he was for the exercises the nurses had performed over and over so that meant, with special equipment, he could type, could raise a beaker and drink from it. 'She is so beautiful,' Juan said. 'She is amazing…'

'I know.' Eduard was serious. 'Juan, will you be my best man?'

'We don't have best men in Argentina,' Juan teased lightly, but then he was serious. 'Except, for all that has happened, we do. I would be so proud to be your best man.'

'I don't want you to come home if you are not ready. I understand why you had to get away…'

'You tell me the date and I will be there. Nothing would keep me from being there to share in your day.'

'We are sorting the date out. Juan?' Eduard's tone changed to being tentative. 'There is something I wish to discuss with you. We're so grateful, but you don't have to keep paying for my pills.'

'Are the pills working?' Juan asked, and grinned as Eduard gave a shy smile back. This was no crude conversation, there was nothing they did not discuss, and Juan, loaded with survivor guilt, refused to leave anything out of bounds.

'Yes,' Eduard said. 'We have sex and it is getting better. She enjoys it, I think, and I love her pleasure.'

'Then that money is there,' Juan said. He knew the tablets were expensive and the young couple could not afford many, knew what must sometimes be on Eduard's mind, so he said, 'If I kill myself doing all this crazy stuff I have left money for you in my will. You will be pleasing your beautiful Felicia all your life, my friend.'

'Thank you.'

'No need,' Juan said, and he meant it.

'I tried what you said with my mouth,' Eduard said, 'and she was not faking!'

'I'll teach you more tricks another time,' Juan said. No, it was no crude conversation—younger, far less experienced, Eduard had cried and cried to Juan about losing his ability to make love to Felicia, had doubted that he might ever please her again. But even as Juan smiled, it faltered. His tears were coming again, and he felt guilty because he was the one walking and yet he was the one crying. 'Sorry, Eduard, you don't need this today…'

'Hey!' Eduard said. 'It's me.'

'I know.' Juan looked at his friend and nodded, because they had agreed it went both ways. For it to work, Eduard had to be there for him too. How different Juan was from how he had once been—how much his priorities had changed since that day.

'I was going to call you on Sunday,' Eduard said. 'I know it will be a difficult day.'

It would have been Juan's first wedding anniversary.

'It's not just the wedding anniversary,' Juan admitted. 'I like someone, Eduard. For the first time in what feels like for ever there is someone that I cannot get out of my mind and yet I cannot get her into bed.'

'You can.'

'I leave a week on Tuesday.'

'You have to leave?'

'Yes,' Juan said. 'My visa expires and anyway I don't want to get too involved.' He trusted so few now, had sworn never to let go of his heart—to just love them and leave them. 'She reminds me a bit of your Felicia, she is loyal, she is so serious…' He smiled as he spoke. 'She is so sensible and cautious but I am sure she is wild too…'

'You've got it bad,' Eduard said. 'Have you told her about the accident?'

'No.'

'Will you?'

Juan shook his head. 'No, I don't want her sympathy.' He shared it with no one apart from the people who already knew. 'I don't want to even try to explain what happened, what it was like.' Juan thought for a long moment and Eduard patiently sat through his silence. 'I don't want to get involved or anything. Really, I just want it to be a week on Tuesday and to be gone…I think.' Juan honestly didn't know how he felt. 'Perhaps it is just that she has said no. Perhaps that is the reason I can't forget her. If I could sleep with her, maybe I'd get her out of my mind.'

'Have you cooked for her?' Eduard said, and Juan grinned. 'Has she had the full Juan treatment?'

'No.'

'Go!' Eduard said. 'Sort it now.'

Juan laughed.

They chatted a little while longer then said goodbye and Juan found himself naked in the kitchen at three a.m. He lit the gas under the frying pan then he went and put a towel around his hips to save the precious bits from any oil splashes.

Hopefully he'd be needing them tomorrow night!

# CHAPTER TEN

CATE WOKE TO the heat of summer and the scald of her own thoughts about Juan, insisting she should be proud of herself.

*Imagine how much worse you'd be feeling if you'd slept with him,* Cate tried to tell herself as she took her uniform off the line and quickly ironed it. *Imagine how much worse you would be feeling if you'd gone and got involved with him,* Cate told herself as she drove to work.

She had almost convinced herself she was proud for resisting, but it actually felt horrible, walking into the department and knowing she wouldn't see Juan.

That she probably wasn't ever going to see him again.

These last few weeks, when she should have been missing Paul, when she should have been trying to get over a two-year relationship, when she should have been sorting out what she wanted from her career, instead her thoughts and emotions had all been taken up with Juan.

Funny that a heart could be so raw and bruised by a man she barely knew when it was not damaged by the man she had spent two years with.

It surely just showed how right she had been to end things with Paul.

Cate looked at the roster, devoid of Juan's name, and thought of the sky jump next Sunday.

Her last chance to see him.

A farewell shag before he flew? Oh, God, she was actually thinking about it, Cate realised. *That* was how much she regretted saying no last night!

'How was Christine's leaving do?' Harry yawned. He had been working all night and was now about to go off duty until Monday.

'Good,' Cate said. 'Who looked after the twins last night?'

'Mum.' Harry sighed.

'Are you having any luck with getting a new nanny?'

'I've got a couple of people to see next week,' Harry said. 'But most of the people on the agency books want to live in the city, not a good hour away from it, and I've got the consultant interviews too.'

'Any luck?'

'Nope.' Harry shook his head. 'Same problem I'm having with the nannies—all the good ones want the bright lights of the city. Honestly, Cate, I need to sort something out as soon as I can. I can't keep just dropping everything and coming in because we don't have enough staff...' Harry shook his head. 'At least I don't have to think about it for a couple of days now. The department is Dr Vermont's problem this weekend. I'm going to spend some quality time with the twins.'

'You have a good one,' Cate said.

It was, thankfully, a busy morning, so there wasn't much time to dwell on Juan and the night that had never happened, but it was there in the back of her mind, just waiting for her thoughts to turn to it, and Cate was determined they would not.

She was heading off to lunch, having decided to spend the hour sorting out what would be her office come Monday. She did not want to sit in the staffroom and join in the post mortem about last night. There always was one after a department do. As the late staff trickled in, more and more would be revealed—who'd got off with who, who had said what, and people were already talking about Christine and the fool she'd made of herself last night.

Cate simply didn't want to hear it. She was just about to hand the keys to Kelly when she saw a well-dressed woman, looking a little lost, and Cate asked if she could help her.

'I've been told to come here to get my mother's valuables,' she said. 'I don't know who to ask for.'

'I can help you with that,' Cate said. 'Do you have the receipt?'

'Yes, it's in my bag.' She started to open it.

'It's okay,' Cate said, 'you can give it to me when you need to sign.'

Cate walked with her towards Reception, where the valuables safe was located. 'What ward is your mum on?' Cate asked, really just making polite conversation.

'She was on the emergency medical unit, but she passed away last night…'

'Oh.' Cate turned in surprise. She was used to upset relatives coming down to collect their loved one's valuables but this lady didn't seem upset in the least. Cate had assumed she was just collecting a relative's things to take home. 'I'm sorry to hear that,' Cate offered.

'It's a blessing really,' the lady said as she handed her the receipt and Cate looked down and saw Elsie's scrawling signature on the piece of paper. 'She just sat in her bed or her chair all the time, staring at photos. She couldn't really get out—it's no life!'

Cate didn't really understand the blessing. It might have been considered a blessing if Elsie had suffered a serious stroke or had been struggling with dementia, or had been in chronic pain. But, no, as she filled out the paperwork and Maria chatted on, it became apparent that Elsie had passed peacefully in her sleep—the nurse had gone to check on her at two a.m. and had found Elsie deceased.

Yes, perhaps it was a blessing to slip away like that, but as Cate handed over the envelope that contained the necklace and rings, tears were stinging at the back of her eyes. She wondered if the daughter had just sat down and spoken to her mother—if she had found out all the wonderful things her mother had done, all the stories Elsie had still been able to tell—would it have seemed such a blessing then?

Cate headed to the office and surprised herself when she started to cry, and it wasn't just over Juan, and that he was gone, her tears really were for Elsie. Death was commonplace here and so, of course, there were tears at times, although not usually for an elderly lady who had died of natural causes. Elsie had been so lovely and Cate had been so glad to know her even for a little while. She blew her nose into a tissue and when the phone rang in her new office, Cate picked it up with a sniff and gave her name.

'Are you crying because you regret not coming back to mine last night?' She heard his deep voice and smiled into the phone.

'Of course I am.' Cate attempted sarcasm, although she was speaking a bit of the truth.

'Or are you crying because you miss me?'

'It's just not the same here without you, Juan,' Cate teased, and then told him the real reason for her tears. 'Actually, I just found out that Elsie died in the night. I know she was old and everything…'

'She was a complete delight,' Juan said. 'She had a wild side to her, you know…'

'I heard about it!' Cate smiled. 'So, what can I do for you?'

'Well, this morning I went on a culinary trip of the Mornington Peninsula. We caught our own fish and then when we got back we cleaned and prepared them and were taught how to cook them…'

'That's very tame for you.'

'I can be tamed at times…' He said it in a way that had Cate blushing. 'So, I have some beautiful fish steaks that tonight I'm going to prepare with a *chimichurri* sauce, which I will serve with cucumber salad. I don't have a deep fat fryer so I cannot do *papas fritas*…'

'Sorry.' Cate frowned, not just because she didn't understand some of the words, more that she did not understand why he was reeling off a menu.

'French fries,' Juan translated.

'Haven't you heard of frozen chips?'

'I don't believe in them.' Juan tutted and Cate found herself both frowning and smiling at his strange response.

'So,' Juan said. 'Do we get to say goodbye, just the two of us? Will you join me tonight for dinner?'

Cate thought of Bridgette and the nurse of the future. She thought of Elsie and her Frenchman and then thought of a life with too many regrets, and even though she had been teasing him before, yes, Cate would miss Juan when he had gone.

It might as well be for a reason.

'Fish and salad sounds lovely.'

'Good.'

'What time do you want me to get there?'

'Whatever time suits you,' Juan said. 'I'll see you when I'm looking at you.'

Cate put down the phone. She couldn't wait until he was looking at her!

'No regrets, Elsie,' Cate said to the room.


She didn't feel quite so brave at six p.m.

What to wear when you knew it would be coming off?

Yes, she could eat her fish, have a lovely conversation and then go home—he wasn't going to be tying her to the bed, or maybe he was?

Strange that Cate shivered just at the thought, when she had never thought of such things before. But what she had meant was that Juan wasn't going to be forcing her.

She was consenting to be bad.

For the first time in her life.

Cate put on the lilac skirt and it would have to be the black halterneck again, though she loathed the strapless bra that squashed into her breasts and made her look like she had four. Then she remembered, with a thrill low in her belly, how easily he had removed it and the exploration of his hands during their one kiss.

Cate left it off.

Hardly daring, as she didn't have the biggest bust, but for sensible Cate it felt reckless.

And it felt even more reckless when she took off her skirt and shaved in a place she rarely did, her fingers lingering on her mound as she thought of Juan and what was to come.

'Me,' Cate said with a shocked giggle, and then dried herself and put the lilac velvet panties on.

She stopped for some wine on the way to Juan's, asking for help to choose one that went well with fish. She took the suggestion of a nice refreshing white but, as she approached his house, Cate worried about bringing wine—if she did, would he assume she was staying?

Was she staying?

Of course!

Cate had no idea what she was doing, even if Juan might think it easy for her. The thought of getting through the meal, knowing there was this big sexy slab of Argentinian for dessert, made her glow like the bush fires that were still raging.

When she got to the bottom of the hill, she was just about to turn the car round and go home, but the thought that he might see her doing that forced her to push on. She was determined not to appear nervous, absolutely determined to enjoy her one wild night, and, taking a deep breath as she approached his home, Cate parked and climbed out.

Juan opened the door before she knocked, took the wine and grinned, and she was relieved when he didn't welcome her with a kiss, for she was almost petrified of touching him.

'Did you go to the store on the corner of Beach Road?' Juan asked.

'Yes, why?'

'He suggested this one to me, too. I am still not up on

Australian wine.' Juan led her through. He was wearing black jeans and a silver-grey shirt and there was his bottle already open. He was chopping up cucumbers, it would seem, and sexy music was on.

'We put this one in the fridge...' Juan said, and took it. He went to get a glass, but first he seemed to remember what he had forgotten to do at the door. He gave her a brief kiss on the cheek, a sort of European greeting kiss, which was very nice and very friendly and very tame...

She glanced down to see that he was barefoot. Cate had never found feet sexy, but his were: he had very long toes, which made her aware that her own toes were curling. His eyes were looking not at her but at her oiled and scented body and at two thick nipples that were poking out like two mini-erections. There was a throb between her legs and, for safety's sake, she should have worn a bra, Cate thought.

'You're shorter without your high heels on.' Cate said and, as she spoke, even Cate didn't recognize her own voice—it was thick and loaded with lust—and it was then she found out how nice the wine she'd bought was, because she got a taste, and not from the glass.

He wedged her to the kitchen bench and she was kissing him back. Frantic, hungry, pre-dinner kisses. She wondered what on earth she'd been worrying about, wondered why on earth she hadn't spent the last few weeks being slammed up against his kitchen bench or taken on the floor.

'Sorry,' he breathed, prising his face from hers. 'That's why I didn't kiss you at the door...'

'It's okay.' Cate understood, she understood completely.

'I'll get you a drink,' he said, 'and then...'

Oh, what was the point? She was hauling him back now, because they *had* to have sex, they absolutely had to. Cate had never *had* to have sex before—it had never been an absolute command. Juan was kissing her again, lifting her up onto the kitchen bench and undoing the tie on her top.

'God, I've been wanting you for weeks,' Juan said.

She was naked from the waist up on the kitchen bench; she'd never been devoured like this before.

Not once.

Not once had she known the bliss of absolute unbridled lust. His tongue was at her nipples, licking, nibbling, sucking. He uttered breathless words that he would get to them later, that now, just now... 'I have to be inside you.'

Cate's hands were just as busy as she almost ripped off his shirt, because she wanted to, *had* to, see the bits of him she hadn't seen before. She wanted to prove to herself, as if she needed to, just how delicious he was. Cate pulled his shirt down over his shoulders but it was difficult to get the last bit over his arms as he was face down and buried in her breasts, but the second his hands were free Juan was lifting up her skirt. It was as if she'd known him for ever, as if it was completely normal to be heading for the zipper she was sliding down. Her only regret as she ran her hands over his delicious length was that, when she'd got ready for tonight, she had even bothered with panties.

Time really was of the essence but it didn't deter Juan; his fingers parted her and he was stroking her, his mouth a hot, wet demand on the senses in her neck.

'I want to see you,' Cate said, as she just about

pushed him off. She looked down at the sight of him huge and erect in her hands and moaned with want.

'We have to go to the bedroom,' Juan breathed. He went to lift her but she resisted, frantically patting the bench for her bag. Yes, she was taking a chance tonight, but not a chance like that—and the groan of relief from him as she pulled out some condoms was her delicious reward for being sensible.

'Good girl…' Juan said, grabbing the foil.

He had it on in an instant, and she should be ashamed of herself, Cate thought, except she wasn't.

She didn't even get to take off her panties. He merely pushed them aside and, huge and precise, he was inside.

'Oh…' He said something in Spanish, something that sounded crude, that matched their mood. He switched to English. 'I want to see you too,' Juan said. 'I *have* to see you.'

He took the knife he had been chopping the cucumbers with. She was trying not to come, trying to stay still as he cut off her knickers, and she felt the twitch of him inside her as he tried to hold back too, his eyes devouring her, freshly shaved and just for him.

They watched for a moment, just for two decadent thrusts, before her legs were tight around him and there was no need to look any more.

No, need for 'Is that nice?' she thought as he bucked inside her. No, 'Like that?' or 'Is that better?'

There was absolutely no need for Juan to question her enjoyment or pleasure, for Cate was sobbing it to the room. Her nails were digging in his back as he came deep inside her, as nearly three months of foreplay exploded inside Cate and she pulsed around him in turn.

'Dirty girl,' he said, as she swore for the first time.

'Beautiful girl,' he said, as he shot inside her again, as her deep pulses milked him dry. Then as she tried to get her breath back while resting her head on his shoulder, as she looked down at the chaos of their clothes, they started laughing.

Juan still inside her.

'I needed that bad.' Juan kissed her, kissed her and chased away the embarrassment that was starting to come.

'So did I.'

'Now,' he said, sliding out, remarkably practical as Cate sat there feeling dizzy, 'you sit over there on a stool and I can get you that drink, and then I can concentrate properly on making dinner.'

'Did you just say what I thought you said?'

Had they just had sex?

'Yes,' Juan said. 'You are a bad distraction in my kitchen.'

# CHAPTER ELEVEN

JUAN KEPT A very neat kitchen. All evidence was removed—he even tied up her halterneck for her—and then he parked Cate on a bar stool and threw her expensive knickers in the bin. He handed a glass of wine to her.

'Better?' Juan said.

'Better.'

She couldn't believe it. Five minutes in his house and she'd had the best orgasm she had ever had. She felt a little stunned, a little breathless but enjoying the view. She was sipping her wine as if it was normal to watch him cook and see the scratches on his back that had come from her.

'Can I help?' Cate offered, because wasn't that what you were supposed to say?

'Relax,' was Juan's response.

It was bizarre that, for the first time around him, she could relax properly.

Juan picked up the knife that had sliced her panties and with a smile that was returned he carried on chopping the salad.

He could chop too.

Fast, tiny, thin slices.

'You've done that before.'

'I helped in the family business,' Juan said. 'After school and during medical school. My family have a...' he hesitated for a moment, perhaps choosing the right word '...café.' He moved and took the fish steaks out of the fridge and she heard the sizzle as they were added to the pan.

'They smell fantastic,' Cate said. 'What was the marinade?'

*'Chimichurri,'* Juan said. 'It is Argentinian. There are many variations but this is my mother's recipe that I make for you tonight.'

It was soon ready and they took the food outside to the table that had been laid. There was even a candle and, as she took the seat looking out to the ocean, Cate blinked a little when he put a plate in front of her. It looked amazing.

'You can cook too!'

'You haven't tasted it yet.'

'Ah, but it's all in the presentation.'

'No.' Juan smiled as he sat opposite her. 'It is no good to look beautiful and taste of nothing, or, worse, when you do bite into it, to find out it is off.'

'Well, it's a treat to have someone cook for me,' Cate said. 'It's beans on toast more often than not at mine.'

Cate loaded her fork. Of course she was going to say it was lovely, of course she would be polite, she meant what she had said, it was nice to be cooked for, but, more than that, it could taste like cardboard and the night would still be divine.

'Oh!' She forgot her manners completely, spoke with her mouth still full as she took her first taste. 'It's amazing.'

It was. The fish was mild and so fresh it might just

as well have jumped out of the ocean and landed on her plate, yet the marinade… Cate was not particularly into food unless it was called ice cream, but there was a riot happening on her tongue.

'It is very fresh…' Juan took a bite '…and my mother's *chimichurri* is the best.'

'I think I'm having another orgasm,' Cate said.

'Oh, you will later,' Juan said. 'And you won't think, you'll know.'

But there was only so much you could say about fish and, with sex out of the way, conversation turned a touch awkward at first. They knew little about each other, and it was supposed to be that way, Cate told herself, but she couldn't help asking about his homeland when he spoke briefly about it.

'Do you miss it?'

'No,' Juan admitted. 'I speak to my family a lot and to my friends, of course.'

'What made you decide to travel?'

'The woman who rings…' There was a tight swallow in Cate's throat as she found out a little about the man. 'Martina. We were engaged but it didn't work out. I think when any relationship ends you start to question things,' Juan said. 'Don't you?'

'I guess.' Cate took a swallow of her wine.

'Did you?' Juan pushed, when normally he didn't. Normally he didn't want to know more, but with Cate he did.

'A bit.' Cate gave a slightly nervous lick of her lips and put down her knife and fork. 'That really was delicious.' She tried to change the subject, but Juan pushed on.

'Really, my parents were never pushy with my education. They thought I would join them in the family business but I wanted to do medicine, so I spent a lot of time studying as well as working part time for them. I never really took some time to do other things I wanted.' He gave a small shrug. 'Now seemed like a good idea. I think it is good to step back. It is very easy to get caught up in the rat race…'

Cate shook her head. 'I don't see it as a rat race. I have no desire to step off.'

'None?'

Cate took a deep breath, felt the bubble of disquiet she regularly quashed rise to the surface. 'I'm not sure that I'm happy at work.' She looked at his grey unblinking eyes. 'I'm not unhappy, but sometimes…' Her voice trailed off and Juan filled the silence.

'Is that why you considered being a paramedic?'

Cate nodded. 'But it's not for me.'

'What is for you?'

'I'm working that out,' Cate admitted. 'Don't you miss anaesthesia?'

'No,' Juan admitted. 'I expected that I would and I admit I enjoyed looking after Jason the other day, but I don't miss it as much as I thought I might. I had a lot of ego,' Juan said, then halted, not wanting to go there. 'I like Emergency, that was where I started, then I did anaesthesia and was invited to a senior role. I enjoyed it, but being back in Emergency I realise how I enjoy that too.'

'And your fiancée?'

'Ex.'

'Who still calls regularly.'

Juan grinned. 'She misses me, can you blame her?'

'Did it end suddenly?' Cate knew she was teetering

outside the strange rules of a non-relationship—it was just that she wanted to know more about him.

'Yes.'

'Were you…?' Cate's voice trailed off.

'I can't answer a question if you don't ask it.'

'Were you cheating?'

'No,' Juan said. 'I took our engagement seriously. It was ended by mutual agreement—now it would seem that she has some regrets.'

Cate looked at him, looked at that full mouth, slightly taut now, saw a flicker of pain in his eyes. He wasn't over her, Cate knew it.

And Martina wasn't over him, Cate could guarantee that. Imagine having that heart and losing it?

'All I've learnt is that nothing lasts for ever,' Juan said. 'So enjoy what you have now, live in the moment…'

'Well, that's where we're different,' Cate said, hoping that he'd leave things there, but Juan did not. His hand reached across the table and took her tense one.

'Why so cautious?'

She looked up, looked at him, and he saw the tiny creases form beside her eyes.

'We're just talking,' Juan said lightly, but he wanted to know more.

'Having three brothers makes you so…' She attempted to sound dismissive but it was an impossible task. 'All my brothers were quite wild, but my middle brother decided to steal a car with his girlfriend when he was eighteen,' Cate said. 'I was nine. He nearly killed his girlfriend—I just remember the chaos, the hospital, the court cases, what it did to Mum and Dad… "Thank God for Cate," Mum and Dad always said. I never caused them a moment's worry, I guess it became who I thought I was…' She looked back up. 'Now I'm trying to find out who I am. So, yes…' She gave a tight smile. 'I guess the end of a relationship makes you examine things.'

She was trying not to examine things a little later as they headed to his bedroom and she saw that huge white bed. She was trying to live in the now—except she knew she would remember and miss him for ever.

He undressed her and she was more nervous than when she'd arrived at his door as he took off his boots, as he kicked them to the floor, because a night in his arms was simply not enough.

He pulled her to the bed.

'You're shaking?'

'I…' She didn't know what to say. In Juan's world the bedroom wasn't the place to tell him you had the terrifying feeling that you loved him. 'The air-conditioning,' Cate said, and she lay there as he went to turn it down, lay in his bed and replayed his words, told herself she could just enjoy what they had now.

As he climbed into bed and started to kiss her, at first her response was tentative. It was too late to be chaste, Cate told herself, and, yes, there was the heaven of his touch.

She felt the skin of his back beneath her fingers, felt the strength of his arms pulling her closer, and she was a mire of contrary feelings, because she wanted this and yet she was scared to give in. His tongue was as necessary as water to her mouth, his scent embedded in her head for ever and his touch almost more than her heart could handle. Her hands moved over his shoulder, to his neck and then her fingers paused, felt the ridge at the back of his neck. Then Juan's hands were there, moving hers away.

Again.

Her eyes opened to him and they stared for a moment, still kissing, but a part of him was out of bounds and he felt her withdraw, knew that tonight was about to end, and he didn't want it to, so Juan moved to save it.

Cate felt the shift in him. It was more than physical— he dragged her back to him, not with passion but with self; he just brought her back to him with his mouth.

He kissed down her neck and to her breasts and Juan lost himself for a moment, just lingered. He wanted her hot beneath him, he wanted them both sated, or he usually did, but tonight he let himself pause. He tasted her skin and licked and caressed with his mouth and then moved down.

She could feel the scratch of his unshaven jaw, such a contrast to the warm wetness of his mouth.

'I'll be sitting on ice tomorrow.'

It was her last feeble attempt at a joke, because she felt like crying from the bliss. His mouth, his touch, was slow but not measured. There was no blueprint— he followed her gasps and breaths, guided by them. It was more than sex. Her hands went to his head to halt him, scared to hand herself over, and then she felt his tongue's soft probe and heard the moans from him— and she gave in to being adored.

Juan hadn't done this in a long time; he hadn't been so enchanted ever. He buried his tongue in warm folds and she gave in to his intimate caress. Cate wanted him to stop, because she could feel herself building, in a way she never had. She wanted the trip of orgasm, a textbook pleasing, not the new feeling of delayed urgency he stoked.

'Stay still.' He wasn't subtle, he held her legs wider open and she looked down at him. Every stroke of his tongue was dictated by her response and when she sobbed he went in more firmly; when she arched, his mouth held her down. He tasted her, he ravished her.

He adored her.

Why, she was almost begging as his mouth took her more fervently. Why did he have to take all of her? Why did he have to show her how good things could be? She was coming and fighting it; she was loving it and scared of it, scared of loving him.

Juan held her in his mouth and he just about came himself as he felt her throb and finally still.

'Cate.' He said her name as he slid up her body. He did not allow her time to calm; he had taken her rapidly once and she sobbed now as he took her slowly. It was torture to be locked with him, to be consumed by him, to gather speed together with each building thrust.

Cate arched into him, her orgasm a race down her spine and along her thighs. The powerful thrusts of him had her dizzy, the feel of his final swell that beckoned his end was like a tattoo being etched in her mind. And then he collapsed on top of her; incoherent thoughts were voiced. It was a moment she would never forget.

'We could have had three months!' Breathless, Juan berated the time lost to them.

Breathless, Cate thanked God she had waited, because she couldn't have given him months of this with the end looming.

She was beyond confused; his bed was no place to

examine her true feelings, because she was only here for one night, except both knew they had just gone too far.

They both lay, pretending to be asleep, until finally they were—but it was an uneasy sleep, a difficult sleep. Cate didn't want to get too close to the man who lay beside her and Juan, with a mind that raced through the dark hours, chose not to hold onto her throughout the night.

Juan woke at two.

He always did.

He moved his legs, just a little, he moved his hands and then remembered Cate's hands on his neck and the look they had shared. He wondered if she might guess.

Asleep, she rolled into him and after a moment he put his arm around her; the luxury of that she could not know. He allowed himself the bliss of contact as he faced tomorrow—the anniversary of the wedding that hadn't happened was the day he had dreaded the most.

He dreaded another day now, one week on Tuesday when he left Australia. It was already drawing eerily close.

# CHAPTER TWELVE

*'HOLA, MAMÁ!'*

Cate lay in bed, awaiting the promised coffee, but since Juan had got up his phone had rung three times and she had listened to him chatting away in the kitchen in Spanish, sounding incredibly upbeat.

Cate felt anything but.

Last night had been amazing, possibly the best night she had ever had, except she had got too close, had given away too much. Not just with words; last night had been way more intimate than she had intended.

Perhaps more intimate than Juan had intended too, for he didn't quite meet her eyes when he walked into the bedroom and waited while she sat up in bed and then handed her a mug. 'Sorry that the coffee took so long.'

'Is it your birthday?'

'No,' Juan answered. 'Why?'

'All the calls?'

'Just family.'

He wasn't so upbeat now; if anything, things between them were back to being a touch awkward.

'What time are you working?' Juan asked.

'Twelve,' Cate said, glancing at the clock. 'What about you?'

'I have the rest of the week off till Friday. I have to move out of here on Tuesday.'

'Where will you go?'

'I am staying with a couple of nurses I met, travelling, who work at the Children's Hospital.'

Nurse Purple Face, Cate thought. This was big-girl's-pants time: it was time to hide the truth and lie; it was time to smile and pretend it had been good while it lasted.

Good didn't even come close.

Cate gulped down her coffee and then climbed out of bed. 'Well, I'm going to head home.' She started to pull on her clothes.

'Have a shower,' Juan offered. 'I'll find a towel...'

'I'll get one at home.' She didn't want a beach towel or a Juan towel wrestled from a backpack. She wanted a cupboard with towels in it and a home that wasn't about to be abandoned without a backward glance a couple of days from now.

Even if the views were to die for.

Even if it had been fun.

'I'll see you.' He gave her a kiss and she returned it briefly, because it was very hard to not ask when, not to know if this was the last time.

'Cate...' He walked her to her car. 'I'll call you.'

'Sure.'

His phone was ringing again and she gave a cheery wave and drove off, her hands so tight around the steering-wheel that she turned the wipers on instead of the indicators as she turned into her street. She ignored the horn and the abuse from a driver behind.

She waved to Bridgette as she climbed out of her car.

'What time do you call this?' Bridgette joked, and

Cate gave another wave and bright smile but it died the moment the door closed.

*Pull yourself together, Cate,* she told herself.

She'd done it.

Slept with him.

Succumbed to him.

Now she just had to work out how to put together the pieces of her heart...

'Are you even listening?' Kelly asked as they sat in the staffroom, waiting for their shift to commence.

'Sorry?' Cate said. 'I was miles away.'

'It must be hell for those firefighters,' Kelly said, pointing to the news. 'Imagine having to wear all that gear in this heat and be near the fires.'

Cate couldn't imagine it. The fires were inching closer. It took up half the news at night and everyone was just holding their breath for a change to cooler weather to arrive, but there was still no sign of it.

They headed around to work and, though it would be tempting to hide in the office she still hadn't got around to sorting out, there were, of course, a whole heap of problems to be dealt with.

'I'm not happy to send him home, Cate,' Sheldon said.

There was a child, Timothy, who Sheldon had referred to the paediatricians. They had discharged the boy but Sheldon wasn't happy and wanted a second opinion.

Cate agreed with him, except Dr Vermont had called in sick.

Again.

Which meant there was no senior doctor to call in.

'What about Harry?' Sheldon said, but Cate shook her head.

'Harry needs this weekend,' Cate said. 'Unless there's a serious emergency, we should try not to call him. I've let him know that Dr Vermont is sick but...'

'What about Juan?' Sheldon suggested. 'He's senior.'

She could *not* face calling him, so instead she asked Frances on Reception to ring and ask if he could come in.

'He's not available today.' Frances came off the phone and then smiled as Jane, a new ward clerk, came over. 'I've got a job for you,' Frances said. 'Start from here and work your way down and see if you can get any of these doctors to cover from now until ten p.m. I've already tried the names that are ticked.'

Cate stood there as Timothy's screams filled the department and his anxious mum came racing out.

'Do you really think he should be going home?' she demanded.

'We're just waiting for someone to come and take another look at Timothy,' Cate said. 'Kelly, can you go and run another set of observations on him...' Cate let out a breath then turned to Sheldon. 'I'll ring Harry.'

Harry sighed into the phone when Cate called him and they briefly discussed Dr Vermont. 'He's never taken a day off until recently for as long as I've known him,' Harry said. 'Did he say what was wrong?'

'No,' Cate admitted. 'And I didn't really feel that it was my place to ask. I just said I hoped he got well soon and I would arrange cover.' She gave a wry laugh. 'Which is proving easier said than done on a Sunday afternoon. Sheldon is concerned about a two-year-old who's really not right. They've diagnosed an irritable hip and the paediatricians have discharged him…'

'Do you want me to come and have a look at him?'

'I want you to finally have a weekend off, without being called in.'

'Well, that's not going to happen for a while.' Harry let out another long sigh. 'Have you tried Juan?'

It was a compliment indeed that Harry was thinking of asking Juan to cover for the rest of the weekend because, despite his impressive qualifications, Juan only covered as a locum resident.

'We tried,' Cate said. 'He can't.'

'Okay, I'll be there in ten minutes but I'll have to bring in the children.'

'That's fine,' Cate said. 'I've got Tanya sitting in the obs ward, watching one elderly patient, I'm sure she won't mind.'

Juan ended the call with Frances.

He had thought for a moment about accepting the shift at Bayside but he knew that he might not be the best company today.

Martina would be ringing him soon, pleading with him to give them another go. She would say that she had just panicked, that in time, of course, she would have come around to his injuries.

Juan turned off his phone, not trusting Martina not to use a different number just so that he wouldn't recognise it and pick up.

He would go for a drive, Juan decided. For the most part, while in Australia, he had enjoyed not driving, but now and then he hired a car. It was just so that he could explore, but today he wanted to do something different.

Juan hired a motorbike—it was his main mode of transport back home.

Or once had been.

Juan felt the machine between his legs and guided it up the hills, felt the warm breeze whipping his face and arms, and he relished it.

The view was amazing; to the left was the bay, and ahead he could see the smoke plumes far in the distance where bush fires were still raging, swallowing hectares of land but thankfully no homes.

He had enjoyed travelling around Australia—it was an amazing and diverse country and it had been everything he needed. It had been the last few weeks that had made him feel unsettled, wondering if it was time to think of returning home.

He swallowed down a mouthful of sparkling water, thought about New Zealand and Asia, and was suddenly weary at the thought of new adventure. He just couldn't get excited at the prospect of starting over again, and finally he knew he had to acknowledge the day.

His family had been ringing all morning, trying to see how he was coping, whether or not he was feeling okay.

Juan really didn't know how he was feeling.

He sat there, staring into the distance, trying to picture how his life might have been had the accident not happened. He and Martina would have been married for a year now—perhaps there would have been a baby on the way by now.

Juan asked himself if he would have been happy.

Yes.

Then he asked himself if he was happy now.

There was no neat answer.

Juan dragged his hands through his hair and his fingers moved to the back of his neck. For a moment he felt the thick scar and recalled pulling Cate's hand away from it.

He hated anyone knowing.

Not just about the accident but about what had happened afterwards.

Still, eighteen months on, he could not quite get his head around the moment when everything had fallen apart—and it hadn't been the moment of impact.

Juan closed his eyes, remembered when he had looked up into the eyes of the woman he was due, in six months' time, to marry. He had realised then that it was not a limitless love.

Juan didn't want to dwell on it, he hated the pensiveness that swirled like a murky haze, that billowed in his gut like the plumes of smoke in the distance.

He should be enjoying himself, Juan told himself, heading back to his bike. He should be getting on with life, living as he had promised to on those dark, lonely nights when his future had been so uncertain. He should not be thinking about some imagined past that had never happened, a marriage that hadn't taken place. He should be embracing the future, living for this very minute, not dwelling on a wedding that had been cancelled and a future that had never existed.

He was happy being free, Juan told himself, and he intended to remain that way. He climbed back on his bike and started the engine, ready to move on with his life—as he had said to Cate last night, nothing lasted for ever. It was about enjoying what you had now—and Juan was determined to do that.

He *was* happy.

Juan rode the bike up the hill, along the curved roads, hugging the bends and telling himself he loved the freedom, loved the thought of a world that was waiting for him to explore it.

A small animal burst out of the bushes and his mind told him not to swerve, but instinct won.

The bike skidded and he tried to right it but failed. But he was skilled on a motorcycle and he was not going fast, so he controlled the landing. He felt the bitumen burn along his shoulder as he and the bike skidded into the bush, regretting that he had ridden without leathers.

Great.

He lay there a moment, getting his breath back, winded, a bit sore. His ego was a touch bruised, especially when Juan heard a voice and the sound of someone running towards him.

'Stay still!' He heard the urgent command. 'It's very important that you stay still.'

'I'm fine,' Juan called back, and moved to sit up, to get the bike off that was pinning him down.

'You *have* to stay still.' A man was looking down at him. 'I'm a first-aider.'

Brilliant.

'My wife's calling an ambulance.'

Better still!

'I'm fine, really,' Juan said through gritted teeth. 'If you could just help me move the bike.'

'Just lie still.'

'I know what I'm saying—I'm an anaesthetist,' Juan said. 'I work in Emergency…'

'They say that doctors make the worst patients.' Still he smiled down. 'I'm Ken.'

Trust his luck to get an over-eager Boy Scout come

across him. Juan lay there as Ken's wife came over, telling them that the ambulance was on the way.

'Hold his head, darling,' Ken said. 'I'll lift the bike.'

'What about the helmet?' She looked down at Juan. 'I'm Olive, by the way.'

'Don't try and remove it,' Ken warned. 'Leave that for the paramedics.'

His day could not get any better, Juan thought, lying there. Of course he could shrug them off, get up and stand, but they were just trying to help. He *should* be grateful, Juan told himself. Technically they were doing everything right, except, apart from a grazed shoulder, there was not a thing wrong with him.

He *was* grateful.

Juan looked up at Olive and remembered the last time he'd had an accident. He had been lying on his side, begging bystanders not to touch him, not to roll him, not to move him.

It's *not* like last time.

Over and over he told that to himself and held onto the scream that was building.

He'd explain things to the paramedics, Juan decided, closing his eyes and hearing the faint wail of a siren far in the distance. He tried to calm himself, but there was an unease building as he thought of the paramedics' response when he told them about his previous injuries. An appalling thought occurred when he tried to work out his location and the nearest hospital.

He did not want Cate to know.

Juan did not want his past impinging on the little time they'd had, yet he could hear the paramedics making their way over to him and knew that it was about to.

'Juan!' Louise smiled down at him, shone a torch in his eyes as she spoke to him. 'What happened to you?'

He told her. 'It was a simple accident. I have only grazed my shoulder. I'm not going to hospital.'

'Let's just take a look at you, Juan.' Louise was calm. 'Were you knocked out?'

'No.'

'How did you land?'

'On my shoulder.'

Her hands were feeling around his neck. 'Do you have any pain in your neck?'

'None.' He felt her fingers still on the scar and then gently explore it.

'Is there any past history that we need to know about, Juan?'

He stared up at the sky at the tops of the trees and he absolutely did not want to reveal anything, except only a fool would lie now.

'I had a spinal injury.'

'Okay.' Louise waited for more information.

'Eighteen months ago.'

He just stared up at the trees as the routine accident suddenly turned serious. 'I'm fine, Louise.' He went to sit up but hands were holding his head.

'Just stay still, Juan.'

'My neck is stable, better than before…'

'What injury did you have?'

'I had an incomplete fracture to C5 and C6.'

He lay there as they carefully removed the helmet and he was placed in a hard collar, and the spinal board was brought from the ambulance.

'I don't want to go to Bayside,' Juan said as they lifted him in.

'I'm sorry, Juan. We need to take you to the nearest Emergency.'

'Nothing is wrong.'

'We have to take all precautions. You know that.' Louise cared only for the health of her patients and pulled out the words that were needed. 'I'm following protocol.'

He couldn't argue with that.

The best that he could hope for was that Cate might be on her break, that he could somehow slip in and out of the department unnoticed by her. She might even be holed up in her office.

Except she wasn't Christine.

She wasn't like anyone.

Cate was like no one he had ever met.

Juan stared up at the ceiling of another ambulance and said it over and over again to himself.

It's not like last time.

# CHAPTER THIRTEEN

CATE REGRETTED THAT she'd had to ask Harry, she truly did, but she had never been more grateful about how approachable Harry was than when he came in to examine young Timothy.

The boy was, in fairness to the paediatricians, markedly more distressed by the time Harry arrived. Harry took some bloods, called the lab and asked for the tests to be put through urgently. Then he called the orthopaedic surgeons as it began to look more and more as though the child might have septic arthritis, which was a surgical emergency and needed to be dealt with as quickly as possible.

'They're going to take him up for aspiration of the hip under sedation,' Harry explained to Cate a short while later, 'and they're getting started immediately on antibiotics.' He was just writing up his admission notes when Lillian, the director of nursing, came and asked Cate if she could have a word.

'Over here.'

Lillian gestured to a place away from the nurses' station and as they walked up to the drug fridge and out of Harry's earshot, Cate took a deep breath, because she knew what was coming next. 'Why,' Lillian asked, 'is the student nurse sitting in the observation ward, drawing pictures with Harry's children?'

'Because Dr Vermont, who was supposed to be the on-call consultant this weekend, has rung in sick. Sheldon was worried about a patient the paediatricians have discharged and luckily for us Harry came in. As it turns out, it would seem that the child has septic arthritis.'

'Then why,' Lillian persisted, 'is a student nurse, who should be getting clinical experience, acting as a childminder, instead of being out on the floor?'

'Because she was already rostered on the observation ward…' Cate was saved from having to explain herself further when she looked up and saw that Louise was signalling her to come over so that she could have a word.

'Excuse me,' Cate said. 'I'm needed.'

'We'll discuss this later.' Lillian said. 'This really can't continue.'

Cate knew it wasn't over yet, but for now she was happy to escape a lecture and walked over to Louise.

'What you got for us?' Cate asked.

'A very reluctant patient,' Louise said.

'So, what's new?'

'It's Juan,' Louise said, and Cate felt the colour drain from her face. 'He didn't want to come here but I've stuck to protocol and brought him to the closest Emergency. He seems okay…' Louise frowned at Cate's pale lips. 'He came off a motorcycle. He's got a few cuts and a nasty abrasion to his shoulder, but he's had a previous spinal injury.' Cate stood for a moment as she heard that it wasn't whiplash they were talking about, that, in fact, Juan had broken his neck and had been paralysed for a period. She could almost hear her brain clicking as things fell into place.

'Incomplete C5 and C6…' Louise said, and Cate remembered her hands being removed from his neck.

'There's a slight weakness in his left leg,' Louise continued, 'but he insists that since the accident there always has been.'

Cate recalled noticing the weight on his leg as he'd run and thought she might be sick. She really knew nothing about him, yet he had insisted on finding out about her.

'We've taken all precautions,' Louise continued. 'I said I'd come in and try to do this as discreetly as possible.'

'Okay.' Cate nodded. 'Bring him in.'

If she had thought it might be hard facing Juan after last night, it was going to be close to impossible now.

'It had to be you.' Juan gave a tight smile as she came over. He was staring up at the ceiling and only glanced at her briefly. There were a few scratches on his face and his shirt was torn and she could see that his teeth were gritted and that he was struggling.

'Well, they came and got the most senior nurse on.' Cate tried for practical, tried to hold onto a strange anger that was building inside her. She was about to add that if he'd asked to be dealt with by someone he hadn't slept with then he'd be lying on that stretcher for quite a while.

She tried to hold onto the shout that was building.

'I don't need to be here,' Juan said.

'Then you shan't be for long,' came her pale-lipped response.

They slid him over on a board and Cate held onto

the top of his head and then covered him with a sheet to undress him, but as she went to unbutton his shirt he asked that she not.

'I'll just do some obs, then.' Cate said, knowing how embarrassed she'd be if the roles were reversed. Not that she'd have been riding a motorbike through the hills with a previously broken neck.

Neither would she have been white-water rafting.

Or considering hitting the ski season in New Zealand or, next Sunday, diving out of a plane.

Her hands were actually shaking as she did his routine obs and then a set of neurological.

Juan answered her questions. Yes, he knew where he was and what day it was.

As if he could ever forget.

Yes, he could squeeze both of her hands tightly.

'Just get the doctor in to see me,' Juan said as she lifted the sheet to see two black boots.

'Lift your leg against my hand.' He did with the right.

'And the left.'

There was perhaps a slight weakness. Cate wasn't sure she would even have noticed had Louise not pointed it out.

'That leg has some residual weakness from my previous accident,' Juan said.

'I'll just take your boots off.'

'Please, don't.'

'It's fine.' Harry swept in and picked up on the tension. 'Juan, how are you?'

'I've been worse,' came Juan's wry response.

'So I hear.'

'I thought Dr Vermont was on this weekend,' Juan said to Harry.

'So did I, but I'm afraid you're just going to have to make do with me.' Harry was brisk and efficient as he started his examination. 'Okay, Juan, you know the drill.'

He went through today's accident with him, which Juan could remember clearly. 'A small animal came out of the bushes, I swerved…'

'And your past medical history?'

'Can we just…?' Juan closed his eyes in impatience. Cate thought he was about to ask for the collar to come off, or to say that it was all unnecessary again; instead she raised her eyes slightly at what he said next. 'Can you leave, please, Cate?'

Two spots of colour burnt on her cheeks as Harry turned round and smiled. 'We'll manage, Cate.'

Had it been a door and not a curtain, Cate might have slammed it as she walked out. She simply didn't know why—she was not upset, she was angry.

Harry went round with him for the CT and Cate tried not to let his dismissal of her sting.

She tried her best to not give a sarcastic response when Harry came to speak with her some time later. 'All the tests look good and Juan's neck's fine. I've had the orthopods take a look at the images. He's got a lot of titanium in there! He needs a dressing to his shoulder—'

'I'll get someone to do it.'

'Cate…' Harry sighed. They had worked together for a long time and he knew her well, though he hadn't guessed until now that there was anything going on between them—Juan was for too depraved for Cate, or so Harry had thought! 'Juan didn't ask you to leave because he didn't want you looking after him.' He shook his head and tried to explain. 'He's a proud guy,

Cate. He's been through a lot…' Harry let out a breath through his teeth. 'I told Juan that you'd be in to do his shoulder and he's fine with that. I want him in the obs ward for a few hours, he's a little bit tender over his left kidney but it all looks fine. I want his urine tested and to be sure he's okay before I discharge him, because there's no one at home. Hourly obs, and I'll come in this evening again to see him.'

'Thanks Harry.' Cate attempted to snap back to normal. 'I really am sorry to rot up your weekend.'

'It's not a problem,' Harry said. 'It just makes me more determined that we hire the right staff. This place is running on empty…'

Harry headed off with the twins and Cate buzzed Tanya to tell her that they would have a new admission in the observation ward soon; then she prepared a trolley to sort out Juan's shoulder. She could feel tears pricking at the back of her eyes as she set up but she swallowed them down before making her way in.

Someone, perhaps Harry, had helped him into a gown and his clothes and boots lay in a heap beneath the trolley next to his crash helmet. His cervical collar had been taken off.

'Harry wants your shoulder cleaned and dressed and I need to look at the scratches on your face. Would you like someone else to come in and do that?' Cate checked.

'Why would I want someone else?' Juan asked, although Cate could tell he was just as tense with the situation as she was.

'I just thought you might.'

'Just do what you have to.'

Cate sorted out his face first, cleaning a few superficial abrasions and cuts and closing them up with couple of paper strips. They didn't speak much; Juan was more than used to staring up at a hospital ceiling in silence.

'I need you to roll on your side,' Cate said when she had finished sorting out his face.

'For what?'

'So that I can pick the road out of your shoulder.'

The gown was far too small for him and hadn't been tied up at the back. The abrasion was large and it would take a while to clean it up. Cate moved his hair out of the way and could clearly see the thick scar that ran the length of his neck and the clips scars either side—the reason why he had always halted her hands.

'This might sting a bit,' Cate said as she squirted a generous amount of local anaesthetic onto Juan's shoulder. She knew it must sting but he didn't wince. While she waited for it to take effect, Cate took a moment to get some more equipment for her trolley so that she wouldn't need to keep going in and out—they both wanted this over and done with.

Silence dragged on as Cate cleaned his shoulder. Thankfully he was on his side, facing away from her. It was already hard enough without looking at each other—it was going to take a long time to do it properly, and Cate would have loved to take the opportunity to hide in an office.

She knew the severity of his previous injury and she could not believe that someone who'd been given another chance at life could take it so lightly.

It was Juan who broke the silence. 'Cate, could I just explain—?'

'The same as you, Juan,' Cate said through tight lips, 'I really don't want to talk about it.'

'Cate, the reason I didn't mention it is that I don't want to be reminded every five minutes about it. I don't like talking about it.'

'That's fine.'

'Am I supposed to have given you a full medical history before I asked you to dinner?'

Cate was saved from answering when Kelly came in behind the curtain. 'We've got someone on the phone enquiring after you, Juan.'

'We've been through this,' Juan said. 'Just say that you're not sure if I'm on duty and take a message.'

'The call actually got put through to Reception.' Kelly grimaced, not that Juan could see it. 'Jane's new, she's the receptionist on duty and she didn't realise that you worked here. She thought it was your girlfriend enquiring as to how you were after the accident. It's Martina…'

'What did she say to her?' There was an ominous note to Juan's voice.

'That you were in X-Ray and she told her to call back in half an hour or so. She has just—'

The expletive that came from Juan's lips was in Spanish and possibly merited.

'She's a bit upset,' Kelly elaborated. 'I've tried to reassure her but she isn't listening to me, so I brought the phone down. I thought if you perhaps could speak to her, she would realise that you really are okay.' Kelly handed him the phone and, still on his side, Juan took it.

'I'll leave you to speak to her in private,' Cate said, as it was already more than awkward. 'I'll come and finish doing your shoulder afterwards.'

Cate turned to go but as she reached the curtain Juan

called out to her. 'Cate, would you mind speaking with her, please.'

'Juan…' She could not stand to speak Martina, given she had been in Juan's bed last night—except that wasn't relevant here. Juan was a patient.

'She is my ex-fiancée,' Juan said. 'Someone I specifically asked your staff not to give any information to.' And then he lost the warning note from his voice. 'Cate, I really don't need this today, of all days.'

'Sure.' Cate took the phone, doing her best to simply treat him as a patient. 'What would you like me to say to her?'

'Just say as little as possible. Tell her that it was a minor accident and that I'm fine.'

Cate took the phone and introduced herself.

'I would like to speak with Juan Morales.'

'I'm afraid that's not possible. Can I help you with anything?'

'I want to know what is happening. I'm in Argentina. Have you any idea how stressful this is to not be able to speak with him?'

'Juan had a small accident this afternoon. He's got some abrasions, which are being dressed at the moment. Apart from that, he's fine and will be going home later today.'

'How did it happen?'

'I'm sorry,' Cate answered. 'I can't give out that sort of information without Juan's permission.'

'He does this!' She could hear Martina's mounting exasperation. 'He wants to pretend he has not had an accident. He's going to kill himself one of these days; he just pushes everyone who loves him away. I don't know what he is trying to prove. Today would have been our first wedding anniversary and instead he's lying in hospital…'

'Give me the phone.' She didn't know if Juan had heard what Martina had said but she handed him the phone and Juan spoke in short, terse sentences, before ringing off.

The silence was deafening as Cate resumed cleaning his shoulder.

'She seems to think that because we were once engaged—'

'Juan.' Cate was struggling to keep her voice even, could scarcely believe the information she had just heard, understood now why his family had all been ringing him. 'You don't owe me any explanation. I don't blame Martina for being concerned. If I cared about you, I'd be concerned too.'

'Ouch,' Juan said as her tweezers picked out a particularly deeply imbedded stone, and Cate even managed a wry smile—she had no idea if he was referring to her words or the sudden pain in his shoulder.

She had no idea about Juan at all.

But wasn't that the whole point of a one-night stand or a brief fling? It was why she simply wasn't any good at them.

She carried on pulling out some of the deepest stones. He tensed a few times but said nothing and Cate got on with her work, trying not to look at the scratches on his back.

The ones that were courtesy of her.

Kelly noticed them, though.

She came in to get the phone and to ask Cate to cast her eyes over an IV flask—a simple procedure, but because the solution contained potassium it needed to be checked by two nurses. Cate nodded that all was fine.

'Your poor back, Juan,' Kelly said, eyeing the scratches and giving Cate a wink as she walked out.

'It shouldn't be too much longer,' Cate said. 'And then we'll get you round to the observation ward.'

'I don't need to be observed.'

'Harry thinks you do. If you choose not to follow in-structions I'll get the necessary paperwork…'

'I'm not stupid enough to discharge myself.' He turned, just a little but enough to nearly send the sterile paper sheet flying. 'Cate, I didn't tell you because I don't need your sympathy.'

'Oh, believe me, there's no sympathy coming from behind you, Juan.'

'You're upset.'

'No. I'm not upset.'

'I can hear your voice shaking.'

'I am so not upset, Juan.' She shook her head. This wasn't the place but, what the hell, she told him her truth. 'I'm angry.'

'Angry?' This time he turned enough to knock off the sheet completely and looked into her eyes and, yes, she was angry all right. 'Angry, about what?

'It doesn't matter. I'm going to get Kelly to come in and finish off your shoulder.'

'Why?'

'Because you're a patient and it doesn't look good for a nurse to be shouting.'

'Don't worry about that—I'm fine with the conver-sation.'

'Well, I've got work to do.'

'I don't understand what you're angry about.'

'Your carelessness,' Cate answered. 'Your lack of limits…'

'You know what, Cate?' Juan was surly and in no mood to sweeten things. It had been one hell of a day after all. 'I don't think you're actually angry at me. I think you're more cross at your own…' He couldn't think of the word he wanted so hers would have to do. 'Limits.'

'I'm going to get Kelly.'

'Fine,' Juan said. 'Go and count your stock.'

It was lucky for Juan she had already put the twee-zers down!

She asked Kelly to come in and take over and then walked to what would soon be her office. She took a long, calming breath and tried to remember what she'd been doing before she'd been called away for the prob-lems with Dr Vermont.

Stock orders.

Cate drew in a less than cleansing breath.

And there were outstanding complaints and incident reports to be dealt with too. Despite promising to com-plete them, Christine had left them unfinished.

Damn you, Juan, Cate thought.

At least she knew where she was going; at least she knew what was happening from week to week—at least she wasn't ricocheting around the world with a handful of titanium in her neck.

She *was* hiding in her office, though.

But at seven p.m., when Tanya hadn't had her break, Cate had to go in and relieve her. Thankfully, Juan was asleep.

'His observations are all stable,' Tanya said. 'Harry

just stopped by and is happy for him to be discharged in an hour or so. Or, if Juan prefers, he can stay overnight.'

'I'm sure he won't want to.'

Tanya also told her about the elderly lady. 'She's waiting for a bed on the geriatric unit and one might be coming up soon. I've just done observations and they're all fine. She's very deaf and she refuses to wear her hearing aid but she knows exactly where she is and what is happening.'

'Thanks.' Cate smiled. 'Go and have a break and I'll keep an eye on them both.'

Cate was glad that Juan was asleep as she took a seat and saw that his obs had only just been done. Determinedly, she didn't read his notes. She didn't want to know about his past and she really wasn't in the mood for conversation. The director of nursing was, though.

'Where's Harry?' Lillian asked as she walked through the observation ward.

'He's at home.'

'He's still on call, though?'

'Yes.'

'Cate, something has to be done,' Lillian said. 'What if he gets called in tonight?'

'I believe he's making arrangements, although the consultants' childcare plans are not a nursing concern.' Cate did her best to terminate the conversation but Lillian was having none of it.

'It becomes a nursing concern when it's the nurses who end up watching the said consultant's children. Cate, you're the acting nurse unit manager.'

'As of tomorrow.'

Juan's eyes snapped open as he heard Cate's tart response. He hadn't been asleep for a moment, but since his time on the spinal unit he was exceptionally good at pretending that he was.

'Well, as of tomorrow, Cate, it will be up to you to ensure it doesn't happen.'

'That what doesn't happen, Lillian? That we don't ask Harry to come in when we're without a consultant or concerned about a patient? Is that what you want?' Cate looked her boss in the eye. 'I happen to be very grateful that the nursing staff have a consultant who, despite personal problems, is prepared to come in at short notice when he's not even rostered on. I'm very grateful to have a consultant who will accept a worried phone call from a member of the nursing staff and get in his car and come straight in.'

'It can't continue.'

'I'm sure Harry is more than aware that the situation is far from ideal.'

Juan lay there and listened as the director of nursing pointed out some health and safety issues. He listened as the nurse who had admitted she liked working in Emergency because of the back-up she received from her colleagues backed up a member of her own team one hundred per cent.

'What if one of the nurses can't get a babysitter?' Lillian challenged. 'We can't run a crèche in the staff-room!'

'I'll cross that bridge when I come to it.'

'Not good enough, Cate.'

'No, it's not,' Cate responded. 'And it's a poor comparison. If a nurse can't come in I can ring the hospital bank to have them cover a shift or I can ask for a nurse to be sent from the wards. We have ten nurses on duty at any one time, but there aren't very many emergency consultants to call on at short notice.'

He heard the director of nursing walk off and he heard a few choice words being muttered under Cate's breath and he couldn't help but smile, but it faded as Cate took a phone call and then came over.

'Are you awake?'

Juan turned over and looked at her. 'I am now.'

'How are you feeling?'

He gave a wry laugh.

'I just took a phone call from a Ken Davidson,' Cate told him. 'Apparently he helped you today. He said he waited until your bike was picked up.'

'Did you get his number?' Juan asked, relieved that the call hadn't been from Martina. 'I need to thank him.'

'I did,' Cate said. 'He's also got your wallet.'

'Thanks.' Juan said. 'And I'm sorry for what I said before about you getting back to your stock. You do a great job—I guess I was just spreading the misery.'

Cate gave a small nod of acceptance. 'Harry's happy for you to go when you're ready or you can stay the night.'

'I'll go home, thanks.'

'Do you want a lift when I finish?'

'Do you always offer patients a lift home?' Juan asked.

'I would offer any colleague a lift home in the circumstances.'

'Then that'd be great.'

It was either that or ask to borrow fifty dollars for a taxi.

For Juan, it was Indignity City today.

Juan borrowed a pair of scrubs and she watched him try not to wince as he bent down to pull on his boots.

He carried a bag containing his clothes and crash helmet and they walked, pretty much in silence, to her car.

It wasn't how it was supposed to have been, Juan thought. He loathed all his secrets being out, but now they were and, as he had expected, she was acting differently with him.

'Watch the speed bumps,' Juan said as she drove him home slowly. 'I might jolt my neck and suddenly have no feeling from the chest down.'

'You don't need to be sarcastic.'

'You're driving as if you have a Ming vase rolling around on the back seat,' he pointed out.

'I'm a careful driver,' Cate said, about to add, *unlike some of us*, but Juan turned and saw Cate press her lips firmly closed.

'I should have just run it over,' Juan said. 'I should have killed the baby koala bear.'

'It wasn't a koala,' Cate said, and she almost smiled. *Almost*. But Juan knew she thought he shouldn't have been out motorcycling in the first place.

'So, I am supposed to walk slowly, not run, not climb, not surf or ski…' He looked over at her. 'Athletes go back and compete after the injury I sustained. I am not doing anything my doctor does not know about. I walk everywhere, I run most days. I take my health seriously.'

'I get it.' Cate gripped the wheel.

'I don't think you do.'

'I get it, okay?' There were tears in her eyes as she realised he was right, and yet her fear had been real. 'I just got a fright when I heard how seriously injured you had been.'

He looked at her tense profile.

'Fair enough,' Juan conceded. 'Do you know how my

accident happened?' Cate said nothing. 'I was going to get a haircut...' He gave a wry laugh as Cate drove on. 'It was embarrassing really on the spinal unit. There were guys who had been diving, playing sport, car accidents—I had been walking to get a haircut. A car driven by an elderly woman mounted the kerb and really only clipped me, but the way I fell...' He let out a long, exasperated sigh. 'It was bad luck, chance, whatever you want to call it.'

'So now you take risks?'

'Yes, because I never did before and look where it got me, lying on my back paralysed from the neck down. Now I live, now I do as I please...'

'It's all just a game to you, isn't it?'

'It's no game,' Juan said. 'I have ridden a bike for years, it is how I get around back home. I'm not on some daredevil mission. I'm living my life, that's all.'

'Well, your fiancée is beside herself.'

'Ex.'

'Because you're too bloody proud and have too much to prove.'

'You don't know me.' His grey eyes flashed back; it was the closest Juan had come to a row in a very long time. It was the closest he had come to anyone in a long time and that was what he had been trying to avoid, Juan reminded himself as they pulled up at his apartment and he climbed out.

'I know that today would have been your first wedding anniversary,' Cate called to his departing back, and watched as he turned slowly.

'It would have been, except Martina decided she didn't want to marry a man in a wheelchair.'

Cate sat there, her knuckles white as she clutched

the wheel. Of all the things he might have told her, that was the last she had been expecting.

'Juan!'

She went to step out of the car.

'Please, don't.' Juan put his hand up. 'Thank you for the lift.'

'Juan,' Cate said. 'I didn't know.'

'Because I didn't want you to know.'

'I don't want to just leave you—'

'Why?' His eyes flashed. 'I want to be on my own. I don't want a heart to heart, I don't want to sit and talk, I don't want company.'

Cate bit her lip as he threw out his final line.

'I never wanted you to know. I never wanted any more than what we had.'

She watched his departing back and, yes, she should leave it there, except she couldn't. If Juan didn't want kid gloves because of his injury, or because of the phantom anniversary, then he wouldn't get them from her, she decided as she opened the car window.

'Why didn't you just leave it at sex, then?' She watched his back stiffen but he didn't turn round. 'It was supposed to be sex and dinner, Juan, but, oh, no, you had to delve deeper. You had to take it that step further and ask about me and my past and future. So much for living in the now!'

She didn't wait for his response. She knew she wasn't going to get one; instead, she drove off as Juan let himself into his home.

His temporary home.

What had they had? Cate asked herself.

A whirlwind romance?

Holiday fling?

A rebound after Paul?

Not one of them fitted.

They didn't fit for Juan either. He turned on his phone and saw the many missed calls. He looked around the empty apartment and told himself it was time to move on. The day he had dreaded was almost over, yet, instead of dwelling on the woman he should have married a year ago today, it was Cate who consumed his thoughts.

She was right—it had been more.

# CHAPTER FOURTEEN

CATE HAD MORE than enough to keep her occupied.

Or she should have had.

Yet, despite working as Acting Nurse Unit Manager, despite telling herself over and over that Juan was not her concern, she could not stop thinking about him.

Through the week she attended meeting upon meeting, caught up with the backlog Christine had left and sorted out her new office. She was determined to make a stand and, even though there were so many other things that she should be doing, she put in mandatory appearances on the floor, though sometimes she wished that she hadn't. It felt different without Juan—even the knowledge that he might possibly be called into work, that she might see him again, had meant more than Cate had, until now, understood.

That was why she didn't do one-night stands, Cate told herself as she walked back from yet another meeting.

Then she felt her heart squeeze when she glimpsed him entering the department.

He had to save the best until last.

He was wearing black jeans and his boots but the silver buckle on his belt was larger than usual and the white, low-necked T-shirt he was wearing was too tight and showed his magnificent physique along with a generous flash of chest hair as well as his nipples. He hadn't shaved since she'd last seen him. He looked like a bandit, or an outlawed cowboy, Cate thought, waiting until he went into the department and then walking along behind him, almost willing him not to turn round.

'Juan!' Of course he was pounced on and Cate walked on quickly, rather hoping he had not seen her—his final words to her were still ringing in her ears and she wasn't quite sure she could pull off a farewell without tears invading.

Cate headed to her office and as she closed the door she let out a sigh. She'd left it neat but already her inbox was full again and there was a list of messages to attend to. Gritting her teeth, she went to take off her jacket but was interrupted by a knock on the door—she knew it was him.

'Nice jacket,' Juan said.

Cate loathed it.

She was to wear it to meetings, she'd been told, and it was an authoritative touch, apparently, if she was called on to attend to upset patients or relatives.

'How's it going?'

'I'll tell you when I find out.' Cate gave a terse smile. 'So far all I seem to do is sit in meetings.'

'Is that where you've just been?'

Cate nodded. 'I've just been to the nurse unit managers' meeting and after lunch it's the acute nurse unit managers' meeting!' She rolled her eyes. 'I didn't know that you were working.'

'I'm not,' Juan said. 'I had to come in and sort out the health insurance forms from my accident. It was easier to do it in person.'

There was a knock at the door, which was already half-open, and Harry popped his head in. 'Cate, I was just wondering if you could...' Harry's voice trailed off. 'Juan, I didn't know that you were on.'

'I'm not,' Juan said. 'I wanted to come in and say goodbye and I also wanted to apologise if I was a bit difficult on Sunday. I do appreciate all the care that was taken.'

'We do tend to panic a little bit when it comes to spinal injuries.'

'With reason,' Juan said. 'I was very lucky to recover so well—I know that is often not the case. I was also hoping to have a word with you before I go.'

'Of course,' Harry said. 'But you'll have to make it quick, I've got an interview in fifteen minutes.' He looked at Cate. 'I'm interviewing right through till six. If I run over, is there any chance that you could pick up the twins and watch them for five minutes?'

'I finish at five, Harry,' Cate said, and Juan watched her cheeks glow red as she attempted to say no to Harry and then gave in. 'Though I doubt I'll get away on time...' Cate gave a small flustered nod. 'Sure, don't worry about it. I'll collect the twins if you're running behind.'

Harry gave a grateful smile and, as he left, Juan told him that he would be there in a moment.

'So, this is the new assertive Cate?' Juan smiled.

'I can be assertive when it's required.'

'I know that,' Juan said, recalling how Cate had stood up to the director of nursing on Harry's behalf.

'I could make a stand today and tell him that I won't pick up the twins,' Cate said, 'but the fact is this place needs new consultants more than it needs me to get away on time, and if watching Harry's children for fifteen minutes facilitates that…'

'I lied,' Juan interrupted Cate, to tell her the real reason that he was there. 'It would have been just as easy to deal with the health insurance forms online.' He looked into her serious eyes and loathed having hurt her. 'I hated how we ended things the other day,' Juan admitted. 'It was supposed to be fun, it was supposed to be…' He didn't know how best to explain it. 'It wasn't supposed to end like that.'

She gave a watery smile. 'I know Sunday was a difficult day for you.'

'That was the reason I chose to take myself far away,' Juan explained. 'The last place I thought I'd be was in Emergency, being looked after by you. I overreacted.'

'I can understand why.' Cate gave a smile. 'How's the house-sharing?'

Juan rolled his eyes. 'Awful,' he admitted. 'I think I am maybe too old to share, they are getting on my nerves.' He didn't tell her Nurse Purple Face was sulking from his lack of advances, or how he had stayed in for two nights in a row for the first time since his arrival in Australia. Neither did he tell her just how much he wanted to see her again, so they could end things better.

'Are you going to watch the skydive on Sunday?' Juan asked.

Cate shook her head and then shrugged. 'I don't know,' she admitted. 'Kelly wanted me to go along for moral support but…' She was blinking back threatening tears, could not stand the thought of saying goodbye to him in a crowd, on another wild night out. It was perhaps better here, in her office, alone with him.

'Do you want to keep in touch?' Juan offered. 'I tried to look you up on the internet...'

'I changed my privacy settings,' Cate admitted. She could not stand the thought of keeping in touch with him, of watching his life from a distance. She could not imagine keeping up the pretence of being mere friends who'd had a thing going once, however briefly. 'I think we should just leave it as it is. It was fun.'

There was nothing fun about how she was feeling but she tried to keep things light.

'I brought you a present,' Juan said.

'Bought.' Cate smiled.

'No, brought,' Juan said, and went into his bag. It was perhaps the strangest present she had ever received and one only he could give. 'I made it for you before I left the apartment. I was cleaning out the fridge...' It was a huge jar of *chimichurri* and Cate had this vision of her dividing it up into freezer bags, sustaining the memory of Juan with one tiny taste each Sunday.

'Thank you.'

'I have to go. I need to speak to Harry. I never did get around to it.'

'You're not going to discuss the children?'

'Of course I am,' Juan said. 'I told you that I would.'

'But you can't...'

'I have dealt with colleagues,' he said. 'In another life, I was quite a demanding boss.'

'I can't imagine it.'

'I know,' Juan said. 'So...' He gave her a smile and pulled her into his arms, a sort of big-brother hug that lasted about a third of a second because she just melted against him. His touch was so fierce that she was at risk of breaking down and breaking the rules and admitting the heartbreak he was going to cause her.

'Please, don't say, "This could be it,"' Cate said.

'I won't,' Juan said, 'because it is.'

'You could come for dinner…' She could not stand to say goodbye like this, didn't want it to be a quick hi and bye in her office. They may not have counted for much but surely they counted for more than that. 'No big deal…' She pulled back, forced a smile. 'My neighbours will probably be there, it would just be nice to say goodbye properly.'

'It would,' Juan said, and his smile was slightly wicked. 'You know, though, that it will end in bed?'

'I would hope so if I have to cook.'

A two-night stand was surely better than one?

She gave him her address, signed over her heart to the certainty of more misery for the sake of tonight, but it would be worth it one day, Cate hoped. And, despite saying it was no big deal now, Cate, who never planned her meals, had to suddenly plan dinner!

'Bridgette?' Cate winced a bit as she called in a favour from her neighbour and friend, because it involved shopping and lighting a barbeque and putting dinner on. Oh, and could she also get wine and beer…?

'Anything else?' She could tell Bridgette was smiling.

'I can't ask.'

'You want me to make your bed, don't you?'

'And maybe a little tidy?' Cate cringed.

'So long as I get to meet the man I'm cooking and cleaning for!'

Cate hung up the phone, smiling. It was nice to have friends you could lean on, nice to have people who you had enough history with that you could call on at times like this—she wondered how Juan managed without them. She wondered how he functioned in a world without that team, people who stepped in for the big and the little without question. She headed out of her office and passed Harry's office, where a couple of people sat waiting outside to be interviewed. As she did so, she silently thanked Juan for the forced introspection.

Cate knew what she wanted now—to be a part of a team, to be a part of the back-up, not to be finding solutions to a problem that she didn't think was one.

Cate walked up to Admin and knocked on Lillian's office.

'Cate!' Lillian looked up. 'I was just about to email you. We've sorted out the interview times.'

'Actually, that's what I wanted to discuss.' Cate took a deep breath. 'I'm withdrawing my application.'

'Cate?'

'I'll stay on till you find someone suitable, of course. I'm going to have a think, but I might resign as Associate. I want to get back to nursing.'

'You're a good manager, Cate.'

'Maybe,' Cate said, 'but I think I'm a better nurse.' She shook her head. 'It's just not for me.'

# CHAPTER FIFTEEN

PERHAPS THE BIKE accident combined with the anniversary had unsettled him more than he'd realised, Juan thought as he stepped off the train that evening and walked in the direction of Cate's house. Saying goodbye had always been easy until now—it had always been about having fun, living life and then moving on.

And he would move on, Juan told himself. So too would Cate, he thought with a wry smile as he knocked at her front door and there was no answer.

She wasn't even home.

Juan had never been stood up and wondered if maybe she had just changed her mind or, more logically, she had been caught up at work, minding Harry's kids—then he heard the sound of laughter coming from the back of the house.

'Cate?' Juan peered over the gate. She was sitting at an outdoor table, dressed in shorts and that black halterneck and looking completely relaxed, smiling and laughing with a friend as she turned to him.

'Juan?' Cate gave a wide smile. 'Were you knocking? I should have said—if I'm outside, just come through the gate.' Cate walked over and unlatched it. 'Sorry, I never thought. Everyone knows…'

Everyone who was in her life, Juan thought, handing her a bottle of wine and taking in the gorgeous fragrance of meat cooking on the barbeque.

'This is Bridgette, my neighbour,' Cate introduced them. 'She came over to borrow an egg!'

'An hour ago,' Bridgette said, unashamedly looking Juan up and down.

Juan smiled and saw the nuts and the bottle of champagne on the table and, no, Cate hadn't been nervously awaiting his arrival—her world would carry on just fine without him.

'I'll leave you to it.' Bridgette went to stand.

'Don't go on my account,' Juan said.

Bridgette didn't need to be asked twice; she sat down again as Cate went to offer Juan a drink and then realised she needed a glass.

'I can get it,' Juan said, and held up his bottle of wine. 'Shall I put this in the fridge?'

'Please.'

As he walked through to the kitchen, Bridgette's eyes widened and her mouth gaped as she looked at Cate. 'Oh, my word!' she mouthed.

'Told you.'

'I've never considered a foursome till now.' Bridgette winked, making Cate laugh out loud.

Juan could hear the laughter coming from the garden. It was the strangest feeling, stepping into Cate's home—it was just that, a home. To the right were two sofas piled high with cushions and in the centre a coffee table brimmed with magazines. There were bookshelves, which was something he hadn't seen in a while, and he would have loved to browse but he saved that for the fridge! Smiling, he opened it and saw the contents were those of a busy single woman who didn't have much time to cook.

Yes, it was a home but more than that it was *her* home.

It was almost as if Juan recognised it.

It was a lovely evening. James, Bridgette's husband, came home from work and must have heard the laughter and known about the gate too, because he came straight from the car to Cate's garden.

Juan wanted time alone with Cate, yet he wanted this as well. For, somehow, this way he knew her more.

It was nice to pause, to enjoy the end of summer.

'There's a cool change coming tonight.' Bridgette fanned herself as Cate went over and lifted the lid on the barbeque and checked dinner.

'Your skydive might be rained off.' Cate smiled at Juan.

'No, it is forecast to be fine again for the weekend,' Juan said. 'Are you sure you won't change your mind?'

'Cate, skydiving?' Bridgette laughed. 'James had to come and change the light bulb on her staircase a few weeks ago!' Bridgette drained her drink and went to stand. 'Now we really do have to go.'

'Stay,' Cate offered, as Juan took up the knife and started to carve. Her offer was more out of habit than politeness. 'There's plenty.'

'I'll leave you two…'

'It's not a romantic dinner for two.' Cate grinned, trying to keep up the pretence for just a little while longer, trying to keep things casual for just one more night.

'James has to ring his mum,' Bridgette said as James frowned. 'It's her birthday.'

'Oh, God, so it is!' James suddenly stood.

'Take some lamb if you want, save you cooking,' Cate offered.

Juan had sliced the lamb in a way Cate would never have—thin slivers instead of her usual rather messy effort, and it looked somehow elegant. Bridgette licked her lips.

'Yes, please.'

She gave them some jacket potatoes too and a plate with the mango salad Bridgette had prepared.

'It's normally Bridgette and James feeding me,' Cate explained as she loaded the plates.

'Yes, you're not exactly known for your cooking skills.' Bridgette said. And then there was the most terribly awkward bit. 'It was lovely meeting you, Juan. Next time…' And Bridgette hesitated. 'Well, it was lovely meeting you.'

'Same here,' Juan said, and gave her a kiss then shook James's hand.

'They seem really nice,' Juan said when it was just the two of them.

'They are.' Cate nodded. 'Bridgette knows when I need tissues and when I need champagne bubbles!' She met his eyes. 'I just withdrew my application for the nurse unit manager's job.'

Juan gave a wry smile. For a moment there, he had thought the tissues or bubbles had been about him. 'How come?' he asked.

'I don't want to talk about it.'

'Why?'

'Because…' She blew a breath upwards that made a strand of hair lift on her forehead. 'Because I just spent nearly an hour going over it with Bridgette and…'

'She'll still be here next week?' Juan finished for her.

Cate nodded.

'You know...' Juan smiled. 'I've got addicted to day-time soaps while I've been here. If I miss a couple of episodes I can soon catch up. I love watching it when I wake up from a night shift. I can't believe I'm not going to find out what happened to the baby...'

Cate laughed.

'And I can't believe I'm not going to know what happens with you.'

It was the closest either of them had come to admitting how hard this was.

'Well, you're not going to find me with a clipboard as the director of nursing in a couple of years,' Cate said. 'I've just shot my career in the foot.'

'If it changes anything, I did speak to Harry,' Juan said. 'Things should improve there.'

'It's not just Harry. I haven't been as happy as I should be at work for quite some time now. That's why I was thinking about being a paramedic. I've been trying to sort out what I wanted, what was wrong, and when I actually sat down and really thought about it I realised I've only been unsettled since I started climbing the ranks. I know what I love, being a nurse in Emergency, and so that's what I'm going to do.'

'Good for you.'

'I might regret that choice when I get my pay cheque,' Cate sighed. 'And I might regret it again when the new manager starts. I think they're going to be pretty rigorous about who they choose.' She gave a shrug. 'Not my problem any more.'

It was such a bitter-sweet night.

Never had she laughed so much as he tried to teach her to tango and never had he relished more the sensual movement, the feel of a woman in his arms, the touch of another person and the ability to simply move.

To climb the stairs and see for the first time her bedroom. To have fingers that moved and could untie the knot of her halterneck—he took not a second of it for granted.

'I am going to leave you money by the bed.' Juan smiled as he undressed her. 'Not for the sex but for a new top...'

He made her laugh. 'It's my Juan top, the rest are...' Paul's name did not belong in this room any more, the only name that would be uttered here was Juan's.

She felt his mouth on her shoulder.

'You are over him?' Juan checked, and then made slow love to her.

Yes, she was over Paul, so much more than he knew.

Now she just had to get over Juan.

'The reason I didn't just leave it at sex...' Juan spoke to the darkness as they both tried to sleep later, answering the bitter questions she had hurled that night '...is because I care about you and what happens. If things were—'

'Please, don't,' Cate interrupted. 'I don't want to hear that if things were different we might have made it. I don't want to think how it might have been if we'd had more time, because...' It was as simple as that—his visa ran out next week. 'We don't.'

# CHAPTER SIXTEEN

JUAN WOKE AT TWO.

He was on his back, Cate curled up in a ball by his side. He could hear the rumble of thunder in the distance and, as always, he moved his hands and then his feet...

Just to check.

He wondered if it would disturb Cate if he went downstairs and made a drink, perhaps put on the television. He didn't even have a book with him to read.

'What was it like?'

Her question filled the darkness; he was glad she did not turn. The psychologist on the spinal unit had asked on many occasions and the nurses had been amazing, but he'd answered them all correctly and just kept it all in.

By day.

Martina certainly hadn't wanted to know and his parents and family he had not wanted to burden.

Cate didn't see it like that.

'You really want to know?' he said to the darkness.

'I do.'

'Stay there,' he said, and Cate screwed her eyes closed and did not turn to him.

'It was very busy,' Juan said. 'For the first few days

there are tests and Theatre and endless examinations and equipment and you keep waiting for things to change. Everyone is waiting for news, for updates and progress and it really has not sunk in. I had my fracture stabilised and it was wait and see. I had severe spinal swelling so they were unsure of the extent of the damage. I tried to stay positive for Martina and my family but I wasn't feeling positive at all,' Juan explained. 'I knew, almost as soon as I hit the pavement, that I had broken my neck.' He closed his eyes for a moment before carrying on. 'I did not believe that anything the surgeon could do would help.'

'You thought that was it.'

'Completely,' Juan said. 'All the tests, the tentative diagnosis, my family trying to keep positive, I went along with it for them, but in my heart I was sure it was permanent.'

'Were you scared?'

'You are too busy to be scared,' Juan said. 'The day is full. You start at six with obs and a drink, then breakfast, then wash, then doctors' rounds, then physio, visitors, more physio, exercises every hour...' He listed the day. 'Then at about ten you are settled and perhaps watch a movie. I used to sleep with the television on, but someone would turn it off and I used to wake...' He hesitated. 'You really want to hear this?'

'Yes.'

He told her about the nights.

Finally, he told somebody about the nights. How it felt to be trapped in only your head, how every missed opportunity, every wasted moment taunted, how the simplest things mattered in a way that they never had before.

'Every hour the nurses come around, day and night, and you have passive exercise. They move your limbs, your ankles, your hands. One of the nurses was trying to chat to Martina, trying to show her how she could move my fingers and wrists.' He lifted his index finger and thumb and, unseen by Cate, started pulling them together and then apart. '"That might mean he can hold a cup," the nurse told Martina, "or do up a shirt." And then she showed Martina how to turn my wrist in the hope I could one day have a drink by myself, and I saw her face…'

'Was she overwhelmed?'

'She couldn't do it,' Juan said. 'I saw her expression and when the nurse had gone she broke down.'

Then he told Cate about the night only three others knew about.

Because they had lain there in silence as they'd heard it.

'"I can't do this, Juan…" Martina couldn't even look me in the eye to tell me; instead she sat down by the bed.

'"It will be okay," I said.

'"When?"

'I just lay there. I'd have loved to know that answer too.

'"It's not what I envisaged, Juan. When you asked me to marry you, when I said yes, this was not how I planned things to be."' He'd hated how she'd attempted a joke. '"You always said that I would be a terrible nurse."

'"I don't want you to be my nurse."'

Cate listened as he told her some more of Martina's words, how worried she was about what others might think about her leaving him while he faced a future in a wheelchair.

'I told her that I would always say it was by mutual agreement and I would have stuck to that, except she calls me now. Martina has a different recollection of our conversation. She says she was in shock, that she just needed some time to adjust...'

Cate swallowed, wondered if it was pride holding him back from returning to Martina, but Juan shook his head when she asked him.

'I know, had I not got better, that I would never have seen Martina again.'

He told her how slowly, so slowly, sensations had started to come back. How it had hurt when they did, first his arms and then later his wrists. Then his thighs and slowly his calves and feet. 'I did the rehab, I dragged myself to physio, I learnt to walk, and then she started to visit. Martina had decided that maybe we could work through it, that maybe I did need her help after all. I needed her long before that,' Juan said. 'I certainly don't need her now. I flew to Australia. We were going to come here for our honeymoon but I came by myself. I was very thin and weak when I got here, but I spent months building my body up.'

Cate knew she had been right.

She had known so little about him.

'Martina wants it to go back to the way it was.'

'It can't?'

'No,' Juan said, 'because something like that is life-altering. You don't go back to how you were. When something that big happens, you find out who you really are...'

'And you are?'

'I'm still finding out,' Juan said. 'But I'm not the person I once was.'

She understood that.

Cate lay in the silence, listening to his breathing, and, even though it was nowhere near as severe as what had happened to him, Cate felt she had been through something life-changing. Juan had changed her. She couldn't go back to how she had been.

'I'm a different person now,' Juan said.

So too was she.

So different.

Cate woke to a sound that was unfamiliar—rain was beating against the window, heavy rain that was so needed. She thought of the firefighters and how thankful they would be for the reprieve, and the homeowners who had lived under the shadow of imminent danger for weeks now.

The threat had passed.

Just as Juan would soon move on.

All the attempts to safeguard her heart had been in vain and in a little while she would be doing what she most dreaded and saying goodbye to him.

She turned and looked over to the sight of Juan sleeping and smiled because she'd never thought she'd find the spill of long black hair on her pillow sexy, or that her toes might curl at what was now more than a few days' growth—he officially had a beard!

And she'd never thought she'd be so bold as to move over and start to kiss his flat nipples.

More than that she'd never felt so *inclined*, or had wanted another so much.

He felt her lips on his chest and he lay there; he

felt her mouth over his nipples and her tongue and he closed his eyes.

Juan loved sex, preferably quick. Hot, passionate sex was how things had had to be, not lying there with a mouth exploring, working its way down his stomach. He felt her hands move along his thighs, sensations returning, flooding his body, the slow burn of making love and being made love to.

He felt her hand grip his shaft, felt lips start to explore him, and for a second he wanted to stop her for, as it had in the hospital, sometimes feelings hurt as they returned.

Her mouth was hot and intimate and he moaned in pleasure and gave in to her.

Cate felt his hands in her hair, the gentle guidance of his palm. So many things had changed since Juan had come into her life—she could explore without shame and taste without guilt, just let herself live in the moment, for this moment at least.

He tasted of both him and of her, and she heard his ragged moan as she kissed him deeper, taking him further, and Juan gave in then.

The shout was primal and it came from somewhere he had never been.

She felt the jerk and the rush at the back of her throat and she was coming just from feeling him, from tasting him.

From adoring him.

# CHAPTER SEVENTEEN

'STAY THERE,' JUAN said as the alarm blared like a siren. 'I'll bring us coffee.'

It was stupid to lie there and listen to him in her kitchen for the first time and to think she could miss something that had only happened once.

She was very close to crying and absolutely determined not to.

He brought her coffee and they drank it in strained silence. Juan headed off to the shower and then came out and dressed. He sat on the bed and she watched him pulling on his boots for the first and last time.

He made every moment matter.

'It's good to hear the rain.'

'It is,' Cate said. 'I'll be told off now for ordering too many burn packs.'

'Better too many than not enough,' Juan said. 'I think you made the right choice about work.'

Cate nodded, she didn't trust herself to speak.

'I'd better go,' Juan said, when it was clear she was struggling. 'I start at eight...'

'Sure.'

'Thank you for last night, for all our times...'

'Go,' Cate said, 'or I'm going to fail...'

'Fail what?'

'Living in the moment, not getting too involved.'

'Will you be okay?'

'Of course, as long as I avoid any tall Argentinian doctors that happen to be passing through...'

'No regrets?'

'No.' Cate shook her head. 'I don't think so anyway. You?'

'Potentially,' Juan said. 'Will you be there on Sunday?'

'No...' Cate shook her head, she couldn't put herself through this again, but a part of her couldn't stand never to see him again. 'I don't know.'

He kissed her again but it didn't quite work out and he stood. 'I'm going to go.' She went to get up, to see him out.

'Stay there,' Juan said.

So she did.

Hearing the door close hurt a million times more than it ever had.

Cate did get up. She stood back from the window, watched him walk in the direction of the train station.

She knew then what she'd been scared of right from the very start—not the one night with him, not the casual aspect. It was this part she'd been dreading, and the next part and the next.

Juan did not look back.

He felt the rain on his face and he loved it, loved living, loved the freedom. It was time to move on, he told himself.

He took the train to the city and watched as a young woman in a wheelchair boarded and gave him a dark look as she caught him staring.

'Excuse me,' Juan said. He did not look away and

maybe their souls recognised each other because they got talking, so much so that Juan was going to be late for his final shift in Australia. He was sitting at a train station, having a coffee, when his new friend told him a truth.

'Maybe it's time to go home, Juan, and face things,' she suggested. 'Maybe it's time to stop running away.'

'I think it is.'

He was only ten minutes late for work and no one seemed to notice. He walked around the unit with Paddy taking the handover then told him he hoped that he had a good weekend.

'Jason!' Juan looked down at his very drowsy patient. 'Do you remember me?'

'Of course he does,' Lisa said. 'Jason, it's Juan, the doctor who brought you here.'

He saw Jason's eyes flicker open.

'You've had a rough time, haven't you, my friend?' Jason had gone downhill a few days after his admission and had been intubated two days ago. They were trying now to extubate him.

Juan looked over at Jason's mother and saw Lisa's eyes brimming with tears. 'We're hoping he finally gets the tube out today.'

'It will happen when it's ready,' Juan said. 'You will have heard the saying—difficult intubations mean difficult extubations. We expect this...'

Lisa nodded.

'We just want him home.'

There was that word again.

'He will be,' Juan assured her. 'It makes it no easier on you but this is, for Jason, normal.' Juan sat on the bed with his young friend. 'We're going to let the sedation wear off this morning and see how his breathing goes, and if he's keeping his saturations then we'll think about removing the tube later today.'

'Will you be here?'

'I'm on till tomorrow evening,' Juan said. 'We'll get through this.'

'Then you're off. To New Zealand, isn't it? Or so I've heard,' Lisa said.

'I'm not sure…' Juan looked up as Kent came over.

'You're popular this morning,' Kent said. 'I've just taken a couple of calls for you. I said I didn't know if you were working today but that I'd find out and pass the message on if you were.'

They were so much more efficient here than at Bay-side!

'Thanks,' Juan said to Kent, and then looked at the note. He grimaced when he read it and then put it in his pocket.

'So, you're not sure about New Zealand?' Lisa resumed the conversation.

'Nope,' Juan said. 'I think it might be time for home.'

He gave Jason's shoulder a squeeze and told him he'd be back to check in on him in a little while. He went out to the on-call room to make a couple of calls that he'd been putting off for way too long now.

'Martina.' He was kind, he was firm and there was no arguing with someone who had made up their mind. 'You need to stop calling me.'

They spoke for a little while and as Juan went to end the call she asked him a question.

'Can we at least be friends?'

Juan was about to say no, because he didn't need the

constant reminders, but perhaps that did not matter any more—maybe they could be.

'Some day perhaps,' Juan answered.

He rang off, but sat there for a very long time with the phone still in his hand. He understood fully why Cate couldn't stand to catch up with him on social media, how it would hurt to watch someone's life from a distance.

Martina didn't hurt any more.

He wasn't just letting go of a love that had once been, he was letting go too of the man that he'd once been. All the dreams and aspirations, even thoughts, that had existed were alien to Juan now.

The old Juan was gone and it almost hurt to finally let go, but there was a sense of relief when he did.

He *was* a different person.

A wiser person.

A happy person.

A good man.

The second phone call Juan had expected to be the tough one—but it turned out to be the most straightforward decision in his life.

He wanted to go home.

# CHAPTER EIGHTEEN

Soon she would have no regrets, Cate told herself.

In a few weeks from now, surely it wouldn't hurt so much?

Cate fervently wished that she could do the casual relationship thing, wished that she hadn't had to go and fall quite so hard. Walking to the shops on Saturday morning, Cate looked up at the rainbow that had come out, telling herself it meant something. She was determined to buy a delicious top with the money she'd found on the hall table after he'd gone.

No, it hadn't offended; instead, it had made her smile.

Cate wasn't smiling now.

Tears were precariously close and she could see Kelly coming out of the boutique. The last thing Cate wanted now was conversation and she turned to look into a shop window, hoping that Kelly wouldn't notice her.

It was an antique shop and Cate looked at the rings, her eyes catching sight of a bevelled silver one with an amethyst and she walked inside.

'Can I look at a ring in the window?' Cate pointed it out and the assistant chatted as she headed over to fetch it.

'It just went in the window this morning.' The assistant smiled as she handed it over and as Cate looked, there inside she saw the words she really needed to see, and she thanked Elsie and her lover for them.

*Je t'adore.*

Cate thanked the wonderful old woman who had given her that push to live a little more, as she wanted, rather than how she felt she should. She thanked too the man who had made her feel more adored than she ever had.

It wasn't an impulse buy, it was an essential buy, and as she handed over the money he had left, yes, it came from Juan.

'Cate!' Kelly saw her coming out of the antique store. 'What are you up to?'

'Shopping.' Cate was getting good at forcing that smile. 'Ready for your jump tomorrow?'

'I can't wait,' Kelly smiled. 'You should come.'

'I might come along and watch.' Cate wondered if it would just make things worse, but the chance of seeing him again, even the sight of him hurtling out of a plane, was surely better than not seeing him at all.

'I meant you should come and jump.'

'It's too late now, the bookings are all done.'

Kelly shook her head. 'There's a spot that's opened up. It's all paid for—it was too late for a refund.'

Cate twisted the ring on her finger and made the second most foolish choice of her life.

'I'll jump,' Cate said, terrified not just at the prospect of leaping out of a plane but at the thought of seeing Juan again and having to say goodbye—again. 'But I can't just take someone's place without paying. Who do I owe?'

'Juan.' Kelly said, and Cate simply stood as Juan

moved out of her life for ever, just as she had always known that he would one day. 'He said he'd been looking forward to it but had somewhere he needed to be. I think he's already gone.'

Cate made it home without crying and when there was a knock at the door she forced that smile and saw that it was Bridgette.

'Thanks so much for your help the other day,' Cate said.

'It was no big deal. I brought back your plates.' She handed them to Cate. 'The lamb was delicious.'

'Thanks to you.'

'So was Juan!'

'I know,' Cate said. 'He's gone to New Zealand...' She tried to sound upbeat. 'I knew all along he would, it was just...' She couldn't finish, couldn't pretend that it wasn't agony for even a second longer.

'Do you want...?' Bridgette stood there. By now Cate usually would have opened the door and invited her in. 'Do you want company?'

'No, thanks.' Cate shook her head.

'If you do?'

'I know,' Cate said, closing the door, her eyes so full of tears that as she walked into the kitchen she faltered and tripped and the plates crashed to the floor.

Yes, she could have broken her neck.

As easily as that.

She stared at the mess and then the tears fell.

It hadn't been a fling or a holiday romance, neither had it even been a rebound.

It was love and she'd lost it.

# CHAPTER NINETEEN

CATE FELT MORE than a pang of guilt for the lecture she'd delivered to Juan about being reckless to even consider the skydive. There was a disabled group jumping before the emergency team and Cate knew that she should have got her facts straight before accusing him of being careless.

But, then, she hadn't been thinking very straight at the time and, really—a motorbike?

Then she thought of Juan riding through the hills, the elation he must have felt, and still felt each day over and over again, as he chose to live his life the way he wanted to, and she smiled for him instead.

'You need to take that ring off,' the instructor told her, and Cate pulled it off and pocketed it, having visions of it knotting in the strings as she jumped into the sky.

'Are you okay?' Kelly asked through chattering teeth.

'I've never been more scared in my life,' Cate admitted. 'Tell me, why am I doing this again?'

'For a good cause?' Kelly offered as, instructions over, they walked towards the plane. Kelly wasn't looking quite so confident now.

'I'm sorry I pushed you into this, Cate,' Kelly said. 'I'm petrified.'

It came as little comfort to know she wasn't the only one as she sat with her fellow suicide and the plane rose into the sky.

Kelly went first. She left the plane screaming. Abby went second and one by one the rest followed.

Cate was last, which was so much worse in so many ways—there were no friends to bolster her, no one to watch her shame as she said, no, she couldn't do it.

'I can't,' she said, as she was strapped to her sky-diver. 'I've changed my mind.'

'All you have to remember is to lift your legs as we land.'

'I can't.'

'Cate…' The instructor was more than used to this, but when over and over Cate insisted that, no, this really wasn't what she wanted, he was about to relent and unstrap her.

'You'll regret it if you don't,' he warned her.

Cate had heard something like that somewhere before.

'I'll do it.'

The instructor took the small window but, even if he hadn't, now Cate's mind was made up there would be no changing it.

That much she knew about herself.

There was no feeling like it.

Even with her eyes closed, even pretending she wasn't really doing it, there was nothing, Cate quickly found out, like it in the world.

She screamed and screamed as she opened her eyes to a world that was amazing. The sky and the bay were dressed in vivid blues as far as the eye could see. Then she saw the white chop of the waves on the back beaches and the calm stillness of the bay, felt the pressure of the air, and Cate knew why she was doing this now.

*I'm doing this for me.*

She was doing it for the exhilaration of jumping out of a plane and feeling the pressure and the surprisingly strong cushion of thin air, for the fear and the fun and the uncertainty that all too often she had refused to embrace.

But finally she had.

Cate felt the chute jerk and the freefall break, and she thought about Juan, understood his need to embrace things, to experience and to fully sample the world. Floating above the tea trees, it happened then, just as Elsie had said it would—her heart soared for him.

'Juan!' Kelly turned. Still giddy from jumping, she smiled when she saw who it was. 'I didn't recognise you.'

'I figured it was time for a haircut,' Juan said. 'I wanted to come and watch the jumping but I am later getting here than I thought I would be.' His eyes scanned the gathering, hoping to get a glimpse of Cate; he had been to her home but she wasn't there and he had hoped she might have come along to give her colleagues moral support, but there was no sign of her.

'We're going out for dinner afterwards,' Kelly said.

Juan gave a noncommittal nod. 'How was your jump?' he asked her.

'It was the scariest moment of my life,' Kelly admitted. 'I feel terrible for pushing Cate into it, though

I don't think she'll jump. She was pea green the last time I saw her.'

'Cate's jumping?'

'There she is!' Kelly shouted, and Juan looked up, watched the two figures jumping out of a plane, and he grinned, for he'd known there was a wild side to her.

'Who'd have thought?' Kelly said as Cate's screams and laughter came into earshot.

Me, Juan said silently, because he'd seen a different side to her, the untapped spirit that lay inside and the quiet strength too. He could only smile that she wasn't crying or miserable, though his ego would have liked a slightly more subdued Cate after he had seemingly left.

No, he wouldn't, Juan decided as he watched her land, heard her laughing as she untangled herself and then, dusting down her legs, she walked to the group.

'That was amazing!' Cate shouted. 'I can't believe I'm saying this but I want to do it....' Then her voice halted as she looked at the group of colleagues and friends and saw that Juan was amongst them.

A different Juan because that long shock of black hair had been cut. She'd loved his hair, yet he looked incredible with it shorter too. And what was with the clean-shaven jaw?

'I thought you were in New Zealand!' She tried to hide her exhilaration; she didn't want her colleagues knowing what had gone on between them, but the unexpected sight of him was more breathtaking than jumping out of a plane.

'So did everyone.' Juan grinned.

'You've had a haircut!'

He nodded.

'How was it?'

Juan pulled her aside. She knew him, knew the big deal it must have been, and he told her the truth. 'Can you believe I broke into a sweat as I walked in?'

'Yes.'

'The girl must have been all of eighteen and could not have been more bored as she cut my hair. "What did you do to your neck?" she asked when she saw the scar.'

'What did you say?' Cate smiled at grey eyes she had thought she might never see again.

'That I went to get a haircut.' Juan grinned. 'She did not get the joke, of course. I think she thought my English was no good.'

'So how come you finally got it cut?'

'My gap year is over,' Juan said. 'It is time to get to work.' He saw her frown. 'Harry rang me at the children's hospital on Friday and said that he had found only one applicant suitable and that they really needed two. He said that he wanted me to work at Bayside. The applications have to be in Personnel by Monday and, given I was working till last night, this morning was our only chance for a formal interview.'

'For a three-month contract?'

'No.' They started walking towards the crowd, who were calling to them to get a move on. 'For a permanent role.'

Cate blinked, because seeing Juan every day was going to be hard. Yes, she knew they had something, should be pleased they didn't have a clock hanging over them now, but to get closer to him, to have to work alongside him…

'I might have to go to New Zealand while the applications are sorted. Harry is going to try and help to sort things with Immigration but we will have to see what happens.' Then he stopped walking and caught her hand and turned her to face him. 'Marry me?' He said it just like that, walking towards the shed where all their colleagues were. 'I was going to ask that we take things more seriously, that we see how things work out, but I already know what I want.'

'Marriage?' She looked at him. 'For a visa?'

'Cate.' He held her eyes. 'Ask yourself that question again. Why do you think I want this job, why do you think I want to be here?'

'Me?'

'You,' Juan said. 'We can live here or in Argentina, or...' He looked at her. 'I don't care. I just don't want to be apart from you. I take marriage seriously, and today I watched you jump out of that plane and, yes, like anyone, I had some concerns. If something terrible had happened, I would have been there. I knew it as truth as I watched you fall. I knew too that if something happened, you would be the first to say we have only been with each other a little while, it is not serious, that I don't have to hang around...'

She could feel tears stinging the back of her throat as he continued.

'I want the good and bad, in sickness and in health, and I want them with you.'

It wasn't a game.

The feelings she had been fighting, glimpsing, scorning herself for feeling had been real after all.

'Do I have to ask twice?' Juan said, and she shook her head.

'That's a yes,' Cate said, and it was hardly even a decision because it needed no thought when her heart knew the answer.

'I should warn you,' Juan said. 'I'm guaranteed to have a limp when I'm older.'

'I'll buy you a cane.' Cate smiled, and her heart swelled as she glimpsed the truth. They had a future, one where his black hair would go silver and he wasn't temporary but was there with her, for all of it. It was overwhelming, more overwhelming than jumping out of a plane, more exhilarating than freefalling.

'We're going shopping,' Juan said.

'Shopping?'

'For a ring.'

She caught his hand. 'I've already bought the ring, or rather you have.'

'What?' He half smiled and frowned as she took a silver ring out of her pocket and handed it to him. He turned it over and over in vague recognition.

'I used the money you left for me to get a top on this instead. It was Elsie's,' Cate explained. 'I found it in an antique shop in the village.'

He looked at the silver ring in his hand and read the inscription and then he looked at her, a woman who didn't want diamonds, who wanted only his love.

'*Je t'adore,*' Juan said, and took her right hand. 'We don't have separate engagement rings in Argentina, so this is your wedding band,' he told her. 'It is worn on the right hand till our wedding day,' he explained, slipping the ring on her finger, and it fitted perfectly. It was absolutely meant to be.

She could hear the screams and shouts from Kelly and Abby as Juan bent over and kissed her in full view of everyone. Readily, Cate kissed him back.

'They'll want us to go out and celebrate when we tell them,' Cate warned, as they started running over.

'No,' Juan said, and he thought about the friend he had made on the train, about the conversation that, since he had met Cate, had been running through his mind. He recalled the feeling of stepping into her house and hearing the sound of her laughter from the garden. 'We are going back to yours. It's time for me to stop running away.'

Juan took her hand in his. 'We're going home.'

## CHAPTER TWENTY

'I AM SO glad to be out of that place for four weeks.'

They were high above the clouds, on their way to Argentina to get married. Cate's family was coming out next week, but for now Cate and Juan were sitting sipping champagne. Cate felt guilty that Juan had got business-class tickets and it was nice to be grumbling about work but, in truth, to be happy at work, too. The new nurse unit manager had started and was making very sure that Cate knew who was boss. 'Marnie's awful.' Cate sighed. 'I don't think she understands that I resigned rather than that I was demoted and that I have absolutely no desire to do her job.'

'I like her,' Juan said.

'You like Marnie?'

'I do.' Juan shrugged. 'The place is running well. She's very strict and she takes no nonsense and Marnie's certainly stopped all the carry-on with Harry and his children.'

'Leave Harry alone,' Cate said.

'No. If something happened to you, would you want me dragging our baby in at four a.m.?'

'No,' Cate admitted. 'But we don't have a baby and—'

'We could,' Juan interrupted.

'Isn't it too soon?'

'Not for me,' Juan said. He'd seen the look in her eyes last night when Bridgette had told them she and James were expecting a baby.

Cate looked at him. Sometimes she had to pinch herself, sometimes she actually jumped when she walked into the house and he was still there.

'You were supposed to be a one-night stand,' Cate said. 'My wild fling. And now, here we are, talking about babies.'

'You don't do wild flings,' Juan said.

'I know.'

He sat as she contemplated the future. Cate was the least impulsive person he knew, but when she made her mind up, she made it up—he'd realised that.

'Next year,' Cate said. 'I want a year of just us and getting to know each other and being as happy as we are. Anyway,' Cate said, 'we need to save for it. I've just had my first full pay since I demoted myself.' She gave a small wince. 'And you've blown your savings flying my family out for the wedding and you've only just started back at work full time.'

'Whenever you're ready,' Juan said and he looked over. There was so much to learn, so much to know and so much that hadn't mattered to Cate that had mattered to so many others.

As they approached Buenos Aires some time later, Cate woke up and saw a pensive Juan looking out of the window, staring down at his home town. He only stopped when the flight attendant told him to close the shutter for landing.

'Nervous?' Cate asked.

'Not for myself,' Juan admitted. 'I never thought I

would be so ready to go back. I just wonder how they are going to react to me.' He gave her a smile. 'To the new Juan.'

They loved him.

All his family were there at the airport—as unconventional and as glamorous and as exotic as Juan. They welcomed Cate with open arms and it wasn't just blood family who were there to greet him on his return.

'This is Eduard,' Juan introduced them, and Cate hugged him as fiercely as Juan had. 'And this is Felicia…'

'We are so excited,' Felicia said. 'My English is crap.'

'I taught her,' Juan said.

'Of course you did.'

'We are so excited,' Ramona, his mother, told her as they drove towards their home. 'Pardon my crap English.'

Cate started to laugh. 'You have to tell them what they're saying,' she said to Juan.

'But I love it too much to spoil it,' Juan said.

They chatted about the plans for the wedding and the menu. Their English was littered with the swear words Juan had told them were the words Cate would want to hear.

'It sounds wonderful,' Cate said to the blue air, even though she had no idea what the dishes that were being talked about were.

'Wow!' Cate looked out of the window the whole ride from the airport and she had said it often. Buenos Aires was such a busy, vibrant city, a lot like the man it had produced, yet there was incredible elegance too.

'I was expecting fields and horses.'

'This is Recoleta,' Juan explained. 'We are nearly at

my parents'.' Cate swallowed as they drove down the very affluent streets. The houses were amazing, the streets lined with trees and golden streetlights. 'There is Medicina,' Juan explained, 'where I studied medicine…and over there is the best dance school. You have to learn the tango before the wedding.'

'Please!'

'You do. I have booked you for lessons, and over there…' her head turned to where he was pointing '…is where we will be having our celebration.'

He watched as Cate's jaw gaped. It was the most beautiful restaurant and she cringed when she thought of the cost, worried as her parents had offered to help pay for the wedding of their only daughter.

She doubted they were expecting something so grand.

'Don't worry.' Juan winked as he watched her lick dry lips. 'We're getting a good discount, given that it's the owners' son's wedding.'

'That's your parents' restaurant?' It was beyond amazing, a huge Parisian-style building, nothing like the corner café she'd been expecting.

'When you said you worked in the café after school…' She'd had visions of young Juan wrapping up kebabs and mopping floors.

'Oh, I meant restaurant,' Juan said, and she remembered then how carefully he had chosen that word.

'Liar!' Cate laughed.

'I was then.' Juan smiled. 'I told no one anything of my past. It is one of the best restaurants in Buenos Aires, perhaps the best. My parents are world-renowned chefs—they hoped I would follow in their footsteps and I thought about it for a while.'

'Oh.' Cate swallowed. 'So that fish that tasted more amazing than I could begin to describe, that marinade...'

'Is my mother's recipe,' Juan explained. 'I didn't go fishing that morning—but I knew I could seduce you with food...' He gave her a nudge. 'As it turned out, I didn't need it.'

'Stop!' Cate blushed at the memory of them in the kitchen.

'Juan is a beautiful cook,' Ramona sighed. 'A waste of your talent...'

They were all mad, all gorgeous and all about to become her family, and then Cate remembered. 'Oh, God! All those meals I've cooked you...'

'What meals?' Juan checked. 'You mean cheese on toast, egg on toast, beans on toast...?' How he teased. 'You do make a nice roast lamb, if a little dry.' He put his arm around her. 'I'm a good catch.'

He looked at her serious hazel eyes and he was certain.

More certain in love than he had ever been.

'And I am so glad that I caught you,' he said.

## EPILOGUE

IN CATE'S DREAMS she relived it.

'You look wonderful,' Juan said as he kissed her at the entrance to the church.

Cate had never seen Juan in a suit, and he looked exquisite. He had on a slate-grey tie that matched his eyes and she knew he would have been so grateful for the fingers able to knot it, so grateful for each button on his shirt that he was able to do up. The dawning smile on Juan's face when he saw her wedding dress made her blush. It was a very pale lilac, like the skirt she had worn when he'd first kissed her, and it had a halterneck top—together they smiled at the memories they had already created, in the knowledge there was so much more to come.

'We do this walk together,' Juan's rich voice told her as, with Juan's father and Cate's mother and Eduard behind them, hand in hand they walked down the aisle. And then they faced each other and offered their vows, and Cate needed no translation.

Every word was heartfelt in whatever language it was spoken.

Their future was together, come what may, Cate had

known as a very special ring was moved from her right hand to her left.

Caught between waking and sleeping on her first morning as Juan's wife, she remembered the reception, surrounded by family and new friends. Dancing a terrible tango and drinking *fernet* and cola, then coming back to the hotel.

Cate moaned in her sleep as she recalled their lovemaking, because if ever there was a bride more inappropriately named it was Mrs Morales!

'Cate?'

She heard her name being called but she didn't want to wake up, didn't want to move away from the bliss of being kissed by him. His tongue mingled with hers and she relished the scent of him, the feel of his hands roaming her body.

Juan checked her finger and the ring was there. He ran a hand along her legs and kissed her until they moved and wrapped tightly around him.

'Cate?'

She heard her name again and moaned as he slid inside her, wanted to be woken like this each and every morning. Her hands slipped up his shoulders and to his neck and he didn't halt her this time. Nothing was out of bounds now. Instead, she opened her eyes to him as together they lived the dream.

*  *  *  *  *

# THE ACCIDENTAL ROMEO

## BY
## CAROL MARINELLI

Published in Great Britain 2014
by Mills & Boon, an imprint of Harlequin (UK) Limited,
Eton House, 18-24 Paradise Road, Richmond, Surrey, TW9 1SR

© 2014 Carol Marinelli

ISBN: 978 0 263 90745 2

With love to Fiona McArthur
I love our chats
C xxx

# CHAPTER ONE

So IT HAD been too good to be true!

Marnie Johnson drove slowly down Beach Road with a sense of mounting unease. The modern apartments and townhouses she had inspected just a couple of weeks ago were slowly giving way to dilapidated renovators' delights with sprawling, overgrown gardens. These were the type of homes that would require a whole lot of TLC for anyone to live comfortably in them—and the one thing Marnie didn't have was time to give a new home a lot of attention.

Almost certain that she had the job of nurse unit manager at the Bayside Hospital on Melbourne's Mornington Peninsula, Marnie had spent the afternoon after her interview looking at suitable homes to rent and had fallen in love with this street in particular. Yes, it was expensive but it was still a lot cheaper than her smart city apartment. She had been taken in by the sun-drenched, sparkling apartments with views that looked out over the bay and the townhouses with their balconies perfectly angled—just right for relaxing after a busy day, and Marnie certainly intended to be busy.

When the job offer had been confirmed Marnie had found herself far more stretched for time than usual,

what with finishing up her old role and celebrating her
sea change with friends. Yes, it had been a gamble but,
after a lengthy conversation with Dave, the real estate agent who had shown her around, she had signed
a month's lease on a house unseen, having been told
that it was very similar to the ones she had inspected.

Similar!

The only similarity to the homes Marnie had been
shown was that they each had a front door. Not that
Marnie could see this particular one—it was ob-
scured by overgrown bushes and trees, and the grass,
as Marnie walked up the path, was waist high.

Never trust a real estate agent.

Marnie knew that but had been taken in when Dave
had told her that this home had just come on the market
and there were no photos yet. She had been so stretched
that, for once, the very organised Marnie had taken her
eye off the ball.

And look what happened when she did!

Pushing the door open, Marnie stepped inside and it
was easily as bad as she had been expecting.

Marnie pulled out her phone and when the real estate agent's receptionist answered she asked to be put
through to Dave. Marnie could hear the irritation coming through in her own voice—her usually lilting Irish
accent was now sounding a touch brusque and harsh
and she fought to check it.

'Dave is at an auction,' the receptionist that Marnie
had collected the keys from explained. 'I'm not expecting him to come back to the office today, though I can
call him and leave a message asking him to get in touch
with you.'

Marnie bit back a smart response—after all, none

of this was the young woman's fault. 'Yes, if you could ask him to call me as soon as possible, I'd appreciate it.'

There wasn't a hope that Dave would be calling back today, Marnie just knew it.

Tomorrow was Sunday and on Monday she started her new job and there simply wouldn't be time to arrange more inspections and shift her things again—she made sure that she led by example and she wasn't going to spend the first week in her new role trying to sort out somewhere else to live. She looked around at the grimy beige walls and told herself that once she had washed them down and cleaned the dusty windows, the place might not be so bad after all—though Marnie was sure she was fooling herself. As she wandered from room to room it grew increasingly hard to stay positive. The place didn't even have a bath—just a very mouldy-looking shower that would certainly need a good scrub before she used it. 'What is it with Australians and their showers?' Marnie asked herself out loud—she liked to have a bath in the evening to relax.

Letting out a sigh, she gave up dwelling on it—she'd been through far worse than this.

The removal truck would be arriving with her furniture at eight o'clock tomorrow, along with two of her brothers, Ronan and Brendan.

So she'd better get cleaning!

Marnie tied her thick black hair into a ponytail and headed out to her car to collect the bucket, bleach and vacuum cleaner that she had brought for the job, though she had expected it to be a far easier one. Still, if there was one thing Marnie excelled at it was organisation and cleaning. She'd have this place sorted in no time.

Men! Marnie thought as she lugged in the equipment. They took one look at her china-blue eyes and petite but curvy figure, saw her smiling face, heard her soft accent and thought that they had worked her out.

No one had ever worked her out!

Dave had no idea what he had let himself in for.

She took a call just as she was getting ready to start—it was Matthew, a friend that she went out with now and then.

'How's the new place?' Matthew asked.

'Grand!' Marnie lied. She certainly wasn't about to tell Matthew her mistake. He had thought she had gone a bit crazy when she had announced that she was leaving the city and moving out to the bayside suburb.

'You'll be back,' Matthew had warned. 'You'll soon be bored out of your mind.'

Marnie would like ten minutes to be bored, she thought as she chatted to him for a few moments and then ended the call.

It never entered her mind to ask him to come and help. Matthew was starting to get just a bit too familiar and Marnie didn't like that. She worked very hard at keeping all areas of her life separate. Family, work, social life—all were neatly separated, even her sex life. At thirty-one years old Marnie had long decided this was the way that worked best for her. She was an independent woman and certainly didn't want Matthew coming over to gloat about her real estate mistake and, worse, meet her brothers—that would render her relationship with Matthew far more than it was and Marnie had no intention of that happening.

Marnie opened every window throughout the house to let the sun stream in and then started her cleaning in the kitchen, gradually working her way outwards.

She stopped occasionally for a drink and to admire her own handiwork. She was like a mini-tornado once she got going. Rubber gloves on, Marnie washed down the walls and cleaned the windows. The curtains she took down and hung out in the sun and, before putting them back, she vacuumed and mopped the floors, all the while thinking about Monday and the challenges that lay ahead.

She was looking forward to running a department. She had been an associate in a large city hospital for a few years but, realising her senior had no plans to leave and loathing having to answer to anyone, when she had seen the job at Bayside advertised she had taken the plunge. As she worked on, Marnie thought back to her interview. The place needed a strong leader, she had been told—and Marnie was certainly that. Christine, her predecessor, had apparently spent more time in the office than taking care of the department. The off-duty was a joke—the shifts dependent, it would seem, on who had brought Christine the most coffee. For now the place was being run by Cate Nicholls, who had chosen not to take the role permanently as she was soon to be married.

The emergency department was woefully short of doctors, though that, Marnie had been told, was being addressed and there were two new consultants starting soon. Another problem that had been hinted at was that one of the consultants, Harry Worthington, who hadn't been present at Marnie's interviews, was using the nursing staff as a babysitter to his twins.

'Not any more!' had been Marnie's swift response, and she had seen Lillian, the director of nursing, not only give a brief smile but write something on the notes in front of her.

It was then Marnie had known she had the job.

Harry Worthington!

As Lillian had shown her around the department Marnie had learnt a little bit more about the staffing issues and had found out that Harry was a recent widow and single father to four-year-old twins.

Marnie hadn't let on that the name was a familiar one but she had smothered a little smile when she'd thought of the once wild Harry now a consultant and single father.

Who would ever have thought it?

Ready now to tackle the shower, Marnie took down the shower curtain and soaked it with a good measure of bleach then stripped off into her underwear. As she started to scrub the grimy walls she thought about her early student nurse days. She had done the first year of training at Melbourne Central before, for personal reasons, transferring to the Royal to complete her training—it had been at Melbourne Central that their paths had loosely crossed. Loosely because, apart from 'What's his blood pressure doing?' or 'Can you get me his file?' Harry had never so much as spoken directly to her when she had been there, though she had felt the ripple effect when he'd entered the ward or canteen and she had heard an awful lot about him!

As a junior doctor, his wild ways, combined with very good looks, had assured that Harry had never lacked female attention. The mere whisper that Harry would be at a party in the doctors' mess would guarantee that the number of attendees swelled. Marnie had been head over heels with Craig, her first boyfriend, at the time. Living away from home, away from her strict parents and the responsibility of taking care of her younger brothers, Marnie had been too busy embracing her first taste of freedom to give Harry Worthington more than a moment's thought. But, a fair bit older and a whole lot wiser, kneeling back on her heels, Marnie thought about him now.

She remembered that he was tall and very long-limbed. His hair was brown and had always been superbly cut because no matter what the hour, be it nine a.m. and just starting or eight p.m. and just heading for home, it had always fallen into perfect shape. He had surely invented designer stubble and there had often been sniggers in the staff canteen when a nurse had appeared with Harry rash! He had worked hard, partied harder and completely lived up to his decadent reputation—though everyone had loved Harry, from porter to consultant, domestic to senior nursing staff, patient to relative, he somehow had charmed them all!

Not her, though.

Now that she thought about it, now that she sat quietly, they'd had one brief conversation away from work.

'Come on, Marnie, stop moping around...' She could hear her flatmates urging her to go out and, even though she hadn't felt like a party, to keep them from nagging, Marnie had agreed. She had stood there clutching lemonade and watching the good times unfolding as, unbeknown to her flatmates, Marnie's world fell apart. In the end she had decided to just slip away.

'Leaving so soon?'

Harry had caught her as she'd headed for the door and had offered to get her a drink. Marnie had looked into very green eyes and watched them blink as, completely impervious to his charm, without explanation, she'd simply walked off.

Marnie wondered how the charming Harry would be faring these days! He'd be in his late thirties by now—surely all those years of excess would have caught up with him. Marnie stood and turned on the shower, aiming the water on the walls and laughing to herself at the thought of a ruddy-faced Harry, who surely by now had a paunch.

Oh, and a single father to twins.

There'd been no chance then of him charming her and there'd be even less now—she could truly think of nothing worse than a single father.

Marnie was decidedly free and single and liked her men to be the same.

Selfish, some might think, not that Marnie cared a jot what others thought.

As evening descended, perhaps the light was just being kind but the place looked far nicer than it had when she had arrived. Though Marnie would never admit the same to Dave when she spoke to him about it on Monday, she actually liked the main bedroom—it had high ceilings and a huge bay window, as well as a fireplace, which would surely be gorgeous for snuggling up in bed with a good book or a man in winter.

Not that she would be here in winter, Marnie reminded herself. She would see this lease out, given she had been foolish enough to sign, but she would be finding herself a new home and Dave certainly wouldn't be her agent of choice.

Marnie made her final trip to the car and pulled out

her yoga mat, which would serve as her mattress to-night, a duvet and pillow, and a box of personal effects.

Marnie set out her toiletries in the now sparkling bathroom and had a shower then headed to the main bedroom. There she put out her clothes for the morning and set up her bed for the night. Then she put her photos up on the mantelpiece.

First she put up the family favourite—Marnie and her parents with her five younger brothers, all together on the day Ronan had graduated.

Ronan, her youngest brother, was unashamedly Marnie's favourite. She had been nearly eleven when he was born and Marnie had had a lot to do with raising him—changing his nappies, getting up to him at night, feeding him before she went to school. It was funny to think of Ronan now at twenty-one—he was a gorgeous geek who loved computers and playing the piano, though not necessarily in that order.

Marnie placed the photo above the fire and took out another. There she was, a fourteen-year-old Marnie with her best friend Siobhan on the day the Johnsons had left Ireland to emigrate to Perth, Australia, and start a new life. Though the two young girls were smiling in the photo, Marnie could see the tears in both their eyes—for Marnie and Siobhan it had been a terribly difficult time. Marnie hadn't wanted to leave her home, her school, her dancing and her friends, especially Siobhan. Still, she had made the best of it and had started to make friends—only then her father's work had dictated that the family again up sticks and move from Perth to Melbourne.

'You'll soon make new friends,' her mother had again insisted.

Yes, Marnie had made new friends but none had come close to Siobhan.

Marnie chose wisely and so when she gave her heart it was for ever and she and Siobhan were still best friends nearly twenty years later. They shared daily emails and video-called often, as well as catching up every couple of years face to face. Marnie smiled as she put out the photo and was still smiling when she pulled out the last one—but maybe it had been a long day, because she felt the sting of tears at the back of her eyes. Marnie cried rarely and she hadn't expected to feel that way today. She was tired, she reasoned, as she gazed on the familiar and much-loved photograph of an eighteen-year-old Marnie holding Declan.

*Finally* holding Declan.

It was such a bitter-sweet time because until he had been two weeks old Marnie had never got to hold him, though her body had ached to, her breasts leaking as much as her eyes as she'd peered into the incubator and craved the feeling of holding her son in her arms. Until the day of the photo his tiny body had been smothered in tubes and equipment but, when it had been deemed that nothing more could be done for Declan, they had all been taken away. She and Craig had been given a comfortable room away from the hustle and bustle of the neonatal unit and had had a few precious hours alone with him.

Her parents Marnie had allowed in only briefly.

'There will be time for other babies.' No, her mother hadn't been insensitive enough to say it on that day. It had been said when Marnie had first told her she was pregnant—that there would be plenty of time for other babies later down the track had been a large portion of her mother's advice.

No, there would be no other babies.

Declan was her son and he forever had her heart.

Marnie ran her finger over the image and felt not the cold of the glass but the soft warmth of her baby's skin. She looked into his dark blue eyes that were so weary from fighting and, just as she did every night, Marnie said goodnight to him.

Setting the photo down, Marnie set her alarm for six and then settled down on her yoga mat to get ready for an uncomfortable night, sleeping on the floor.

Not that she minded.

Yes, Marnie had been through far worse.

# CHAPTER TWO

'I THINK YOU'VE already met Marnie…' Lillian, the director of nursing, said as she introduced Marnie to Dr Vermont.

'I have.' The elderly doctor shook her hand and Marnie smiled back at him warmly. 'We met at Marnie's first interview. I was thrilled to hear that you had accepted the position,' he added to Marnie. 'Hopefully you can bring some order to the place.'

'I have every intention to.' Marnie smiled again. She had, on sight, liked Dr Vermont. He was old school and liked things done a certain way and had had no qualms in telling her such, which was exactly how Marnie liked to work.

'Harry!' Lillian called, and Marnie turned to the sight of Harry Worthington, fast realising that instead of his wild youth catching up with him, he had left it behind, only to improve. Rather than the scrubs she remembered him wearing, that tall, muscular physique was now dressed in a well-cut charcoal-grey suit. He seemed taller, a touch broader, but there was far from a paunch; if anything, he was slimmer than the Harry of yesteryear. He wasn't quite perfection. It was no longer designer stubble that graced his jaw—Harry needed a good shave! He also needed to put on a tie. He had an unfinished look to him that ten minutes would soon take care of. Perhaps, though, the most surprising thing to see was that the once terribly sexy, laid-back Harry was now late and clearly rushing with a little boy and girl hanging off each hand as Lillian made the introductions.

'This is Marnie Johnson, the new nurse unit manager. You didn't manage to come in for her interviews.'

'No, I was on night duty for the first and on a day off for the other,' Harry explained, 'but Dr Vermont has said many good things about you.' He let go of his daughter and shook Marnie's hand, albeit briefly, because the little girl, as soon as she was let loose, started to wander off.

'Charlotte!' Harry warned, giving a brief eye-roll to Marnie before retrieving his daughter's hand. 'How many times do I have to tell you? You're to stay with me.'

'But I'm hungry.'

'That's because you didn't eat your cornflakes,' Harry said to his daughter as he returned to the group, and Marnie watched as Lillian's lips pursed in disapproval. Marnie couldn't see that there was an issue—clearly, Harry had just arrived for work and was taking his children to day care. It was hardly his fault that there was a group to meet him.

'You and Marnie might already have met.' Lillian pushed on with the conversation when really it would be far easier to make the introductions once Harry didn't have his children with him. 'Marnie, didn't you train at Melbourne Central?'

Harry frowned. He looked at Marnie's raven hair and china-blue eyes and couldn't quite believe they might

have worked alongside each other for three years and
that he didn't recognise her at all.

'No,' Marnie corrected Lillian. 'I only did my first
year of training at Melbourne Central. After that I transferred to the Royal.' She turned to Harry. 'I do remember you, though…' Marnie said, and suppressed a smile
at the slight flare of concern in his eyes—perhaps Harry
might be a little uncomfortable with people who could
remember him in his wilder days.

Perhaps, Marnie thought, noticing again, after all
these years, his stunning green eyes, it was time for
some fun. Dr Vermont was talking to Harry's son and
Lillian was briefly distracted by her pager going off and
Marnie simply could not resist a tease, even though they
had barely ever spoken. 'You remember me, though,
don't you?'

'Actually…' Harry let go of Charlotte's hand again
as he rather worriedly scratched at the back of his neck.
'Now I think back on it…'

'Surely you remember,' Marnie implored, enjoying
herself.

'Charlotte!' Harry called, but Marnie could hear the
relief in his voice at a brief chance of escape.

'I'm just about to take Marnie on a tour and introduce
her to everyone,' Lillian interrupted the fun. 'Marnie,
do you want to go and get your jacket before I show
you around?'

'I'm fine.' Marnie shook her head. 'We'll just get on.'

But Lillian had other ideas. 'We actually like the
managers to wear their jackets, especially for things
like formal introductions—it adds a nice authoritative
touch.'

'I don't need a jacket to be authoritative,' Marnie responded, and it was Harry who was suppressing a smile now as he watched her walk off.

Not many people spoke to Lillian like that.

Clearly Marnie was setting the tone.

'I think,' Dr Vermont said as Marnie clipped off with Lillian moving fast to catch up, 'that Marnie Johnson might be just what the doctor ordered—did you see Lillian's face when she said that she didn't need a jacket?'

'I did.' Harry grinned.

'So, do you remember her from Melbourne Central?'

'I don't.' Harry swallowed, paying great attention to Adam and failing to see the twinkle in Dr Vermont's eyes.

'She seems to remember you!'

'I'd better get these two over to day care,' Harry said, again glad of the excuse of the twins to escape. He walked behind Marnie and Lillian on his way to day care, trying and failing not to notice her very petite, trim figure in the navy dress. She had stopped to shake hands with Juan Morales, one of the new consultants who was just finishing up after a night shift. 'And Dr Cooper starts when?' Harry heard Marnie asking as he walked past.

'In four weeks' time, I believe,' Juan answered.

Harry didn't hang around to hear the rest of the conversation. Just wait until Lillian and Marnie found out that he had approved Juan's annual leave, commencing in one week's time! Yes, the place was almost running well with Juan finally on board, but it was all about to go to pot again some time soon.

Harry signed his name alongside Charlotte's and

Adam's in the day-care register and tried to focus on today instead of worrying about the weeks ahead.

Since Jill had died, he had learnt that it was the best he could do.

'Are you picking us up?' Adam asked.

'I'll do my best to be here at six,' Harry said. 'But if it looks as if I won't be able to get away on time, I will ring Evelyn and she'll pick you up.'

Harry could not stand Adam's nod, or that his son was trying not to cry. He knelt down to look Adam in the eye. 'We had a good weekend, didn't we?'

They'd had a brilliant weekend—the first in ages.

With Juan working, both Harry and Dr Vermont had finally had a full, undisturbed weekend without being rung for advice or called in urgently. Dr Vermont had taken his wife away to celebrate their upcoming wedding anniversary, which fell today. He himself had taken his children to the beach on the Saturday and had spent Sunday finally tackling the garden then watching movies in the evening.

Simple pleasures perhaps, but they hadn't shared a weekend so straightforward in ages.

'I just…' Adam started, but he didn't finish and Harry waited. He was worried about Adam's talking, or rather the lack of it. 'It doesn't matter,' Adam said.

Oh, but it did.

Harry looked at Adam's dark, serious eyes, so like his mum's. And, like Jill, Adam never complained about Harry's ridiculous work hours, which only served to make Harry feel worse. 'Hey,' Harry said. 'Tonight we're going to take those bruised bananas and make banana bread.' It was completely off the top of his head. 'So tomorrow you and Charlotte will have something nice waiting for breakfast that you can eat in the car if we're in a hurry.'

'Promise?' Adam checked.

'As much as I can promise,' Harry said, because the very nature of his job meant that nothing could be guaranteed. 'But if we don't get to make it tonight then the bananas will be even blacker tomorrow and the banana bread even sweeter.'

Finally, Adam smiled.

'I hate banana bread!' Charlotte, the louder of the two, had to have her say as Harry gave her a kiss goodbye.

'I know.' Harry smiled. 'But you do like eating the frosting.'

'Can I make the frosting?' Charlotte was more easily cheered, though, unlike Adam and Jill, she did protest loudly whenever Harry was late picking them up or was called into work.

'Yep,' Harry said, and then, because he had to, he qualified again. 'If I get home in time.'

'Try,' Charlotte said.

It was all he seemed to be doing these days.

He hugged them both and then, as good as gold, they headed off to join their little friends to start their very long day.

Something had to give.

Harry headed back towards the department and tried, for now, not to think about the unpalatable decision that he was coming to.

As well as being an emergency consultant, Harry was also a renowned hand surgeon. He was reluctantly considering moving into the private sphere and focusing on his second love—hands. Emergency and single fatherhood, he had fast found out, simply didn't mix.

Harry had decided that he was going to take some annual leave while he made his decision. Once Juan was back from his honeymoon and Dr Cooper had started work and the department was adequately staffed, he could take some proper time off and work out what to do.

He just needed to get through the next few weeks.

Harry headed straight for the changing rooms and took the ten minutes Marnie had noted that he needed. He quickly shaved, combed his hair and added a tie, then walked back into the department, and the first person he saw was Marnie.

'That's better!' Marnie commented, when others perhaps would not have.

'Better?'

'You've shaved, put on a tie...'

'I don't need a tie to be a consultant.' Harry made light reference to her jacket comment to Lillian but still he bristled. She should see how Juan dressed some days, stomping about in Cuban-heeled boots, and, until recently, Juan's black hair had been longer than shoulder length—imagine what she'd have had to say about that! Harry had always prided himself on his appearance and tried to look smart for work, and he really didn't need a lecture today.

Heading to her office, Marnie gave it a good wipe down with alcohol rubs and then, deciding it was too drab, she rang a local florist and asked for flowers to be delivered. Then she asked Cate Nicholls, who had been filling in after Christine had left, to bring her up to date with certain protocols and paperwork.

'Most multi-trauma goes straight to the city, though

it depends on transport availability, so we can get a sudden influx,' Cate explained, but Marnie had gone through most of this at her interviews. The paperwork took a while—there were all the patient complaints and staff incident reports to go through.

'They're mainly about waiting times,' Cate commented.

'And cleanliness,' Marnie observed, flicking through them. 'Is there a protocol for cubicle preparation for the patients?'

'Not one that's written as such,' Cate said.

There soon would be! Still, Marnie moved on to the budget lists and all the stuff that Cate had loathed but which Marnie just loved to tackle.

'I hope everything is up to date,' Cate said. 'If it's not...'

'I'll just ask you,' Marnie answered.

'I won't be around, though,' Cate reminded her. 'I'm going on annual leave next week.'

'Of course, you're getting married...are you going anywhere nice for your honeymoon?'

'We're getting married in Argentina,' Cate answered. 'Juan and I—'

'You're marrying Juan?'

'That's right.'

'The new doctor?' Marnie checked, and Cate nodded.

'How long are you going to be away for?'

'Three weeks.'

Cate was still smiling. Perhaps, as most would be, she was waiting for congratulations—she just didn't know Marnie, whose only interest at work was work.

'Are you saying that Juan's got three weeks off!' Marnie exclaimed. 'But he's only just started.'

By nine a.m. both Lillian and Cate had glimpsed what was to come.

By midday the rest of the staff were starting to.

'Are there four of her?' Kelly, one of the nurses, grumbled as she sat on a stool beside Harry.

'Sorry?' Harry looked up from the notes he was writing. 'Four of who?'

'Marnie.' Kelly sighed. 'It seems that everywhere I go, there she is.'

Harry grinned. Marnie certainly wasn't hiding in the office, as Christine had—she darted in and out and wherever you looked it seemed that she was there.

Harry *had* noticed and, as if to prove Kelly's point, Marnie soon appeared.

'Where are the nursing roster request forms kept?' Marnie asked Kelly.

'In here.' Kelly opened a drawer and pulled out a large diary, which Marnie took.

Then Marnie sat on a stool at a computer, quietly working her way through the rosters before disappearing.

'See!' Kelly said. 'She's everywhere...' She launched into another moan but her voice trailed off as Marnie returned with not just a new diary but instructions.

'From now on, all of the off-duty requests are to be written in the new diary, along with a reason for requesting that date,' Marnie said, as she pinned up a laminated note stating the same. 'If you would prefer to speak to me personally, rather than write your reasons down, that's fine.'

Satisfied the note was up straight, she turned and

Harry realised that, though the nursing rosters had
nothing at all to do with him, he was watching her.
He quickly looked away, telling himself he hadn't just
been admiring the rear view of the new nurse manager
and the way her dress had lifted just a fraction as she'd
pinned up the note.

Surely he'd remember if anything had ever happened
between them?

Surely?

'Do you have a moment?' Marnie asked.

'Sure.'

'Not here.'

Harry had guessed this would be coming—Cate had
warned him that Marnie had been less than impressed
about Juan taking time off. With a slight roll of his eyes
he headed to her office and took a seat, leaning back
in the chair and stretching out his legs, absolutely refusing to jump through hoops for Marnie, as everyone
else seemed to be.

'I was just looking through the doctors' roster and
it would seem that we are very short of senior medical staff.'

'We have been,' Harry said. 'But things are steadily
improving. We've got Juan now and there's another new
consultant—Dr Cooper—starting soon.'

'Which would be great but I've just found out that
Juan has been given three weeks' annual leave, starting well before Dr Cooper commences.'

'He's going home to Argentina—you can hardly go
there for a long weekend.'

'But that will leave us with just you and Dr Vermont
to cover the department.'

'I'm aware of that.' Harry was more than aware—

things had only just started improving and now the nightmare was going to begin all over again, not that he was going to reveal the logistical nightmare to Marnie. 'Juan's getting married,' Harry pointed out, assuming that there the discussion would end.

He just didn't know Marnie.

'Could he not have delayed his wedding till Dr Cooper had started?'

'It was a whirlwind romance,' Harry answered with a wry smile.

'Please!' She rolled her eyes. 'There's no such thing and, even if there was, surely true love could at least wait a month.'

'Apparently not!' Harry said. 'Look, Juan is an amazing doctor and believe me when I say such a highly skilled doctor is usually pretty hard to entice to come and work at Bayside Hospital. Once immigration and everything is sorted, Juan's going to be a huge asset to the place but he only agreed to take the role if I accommodated his annual leave request.'

'You *acquire* annual leave,' Marnie said. 'Juan hasn't acquired any, from what I can see.'

Harry tried a different tack. 'The guy broke his neck a while back, he was barely able to walk when he got to Australia. As well as getting married, he really wants to return home and let his family see how well he's doing.'

Oh, but Marnie was having none of it. 'So Juan breaking his neck means you have to bend over backwards and break yours to accommodate his love life?'

Harry was sure then that he hadn't slept with her!

He'd certainly remember—Harry had never met anyone like her in his life! 'You're not a romantic, I take it?' Harry's voice was dry.

'There's not a single romantic bone in my body,' Marnie said. 'But so long as you can assure me that the department will be adequately covered with senior medical staff then it's not my issue.'

'It will be covered.'

'Good.'

Harry stood up and turned to go, but how well they might have known each other was driving him crazy, so he decided to simply bite the bullet and ask, 'What year were you at Melbourne Central?'

'You really don't remember?' Marnie said. 'I was blonde then, if that helps.'

'Blonde?' Harry looked at her very thick black hair. 'That would have taken some peroxide.'

'It did,' Marnie said. 'You still don't remember me, do you?'

She loved his discomfort—loved the small swallow in his neck—and she watched as he drew in a breath while attempting to come up with a suitable answer. Then those green eyes met hers and a smile spread on Harry's lips, lips that had been just a little insolent and teasing in their day, Marnie recalled, and they were becoming that now.

'How could I ever forget you, Marnie?'

The little game Marnie had been playing had suddenly gone too far because it was Marnie, most unusually, who struggled to calm a blush, and she rapidly decided to put an end to it, while still keeping the upper hand. 'It's okay, Harry, I've been teasing you. You don't have to worry—I'm very possibly the only student nurse at Melbourne Central that you didn't sleep with.'

'Glad to hear it,' Harry said, still smiling back at her,

except the smile sort of wavered, because maybe that wasn't the right answer to give.

What was the right answer to a statement like that? Harry wondered as he walked off.

He couldn't make Marnie out. She was a strange mix. Forthright yet distant, funny yet stern but, even if he was smiling at the little game she'd played on him, Harry knew as he headed back to the patients that the holiday was over. Not that you could ever call this place a holiday, but there would be no asking Marnie if she could keep an eye out for the twins in the staffroom, even if it was right near her office. There would be no appealing to her feminine side and asking her to grab them from day care, or would she mind if one of the nurses in the obs ward kept an eye on them for an hour.

Harry just knew it.

# CHAPTER THREE

YES, MARNIE WAS everywhere.

As Harry sat having his lunch he found out, if he hadn't known already, just how forthright she was—the pint-sized Marnie didn't even try to mince her words when she answered a personal call.

Marnie didn't excuse herself from the staffroom to take the call—instead, she tucked the phone between her neck and chin and squirted salad dressing over her home-made salad. As she thanked Dave for returning her call, she stirred in the dressing.

Oh, her accent was as soft as butter as she spoke but you could almost feel it choking the rather unfortunate Dave's arteries.

'Absolutely, I signed the contract but let me ask you this, Dave—was one month's rent really worth it? I certainly shan't be staying on when my lease is up.' Harry listened as she made it very clear that she wouldn't be using him in the future and hopefully, if the hospital grapevine served her well, neither would anybody else from Bayside. 'So, to be clear,' Marnie concluded, 'you have my notice and I have photos of before and after so I'll be expecting to receive my deposit in full—the place was nothing but a filthy swamp before I set to work.'

'Ripped off?' Kelly asked, and Marnie nodded.

'It's my own fault for signing a lease on a place that I hadn't seen. He only showed me the first half of Beach Road…' She didn't elaborate and she didn't sit around for much longer—after finishing her salad, Marnie stood and left the staffroom.

'I can't make up my mind whether or not I like her,' Kelly grumbled.

'Well, I've made up my mind and I don't.' Abby, another of the nurses, sighed. 'I was given a ten-minute lesson on the correct way to wash my hands, as if I didn't already know. I think that she's got OCD!'

'She's got ADHD,' Kelly grumbled. 'She just never stops.'

'Ladies!' Dr Vermont said, and didn't even look up from his newspaper as he delivered a warning for the nurses to stop gossiping.

Though, a few hours later, he indulged in a little gossip of his own as he put on his jacket to head for home. 'What do you think of Marnie?' Dr Vermont asked Harry.

'I don't know what to think,' Harry admitted. 'She's not exactly here to make friends, is she? Marnie doesn't seem to care who she offends.'

'I like that about her,' Dr Vermont said. 'The trouble with Christine was that she was either your best friend or your worst enemy.' He thought about it for a long moment. 'I know that it's very early days but so far I'm impressed.'

Dr Vermont was more than a colleague to Harry. He was a friend and mentor and Harry admired him greatly. If Dr Vermont liked Marnie, that was high praise indeed and almost as good as a reference.

'Well, so far so good,' Harry conceded. 'But enough about this place—hadn't you better get going?'

'Sorry that I have to dash off.' Dr Vermont didn't elaborate. They both knew that it was his wedding anniversary today and Dr Vermont was kind enough to realise that milestones such as the one he and Marjorie had just reached might cause a twinge of pain for Harry.

'You go and enjoy yourself,' Harry smiled. 'Forty years is quite an achievement.'

'I know that it is,' Dr Vermont agreed. 'We've got all the family coming over tonight…' He paused as Harry took a beautifully wrapped bottle from his desk and handed it to him.

'Well, you'd better hide this from them, then.'

Dr Vermont thanked Harry and after he had gone to celebrate with his wife and family Harry sat for a long moment.

Jill had been dead now for more than a year and a half. Birthdays and two Christmases had passed. Two wedding anniversaries had been and gone as well—and still it hurt. Some days more, some days less, but the pain was always there. Not just for Jill and all that she was missing out on, but for himself and more pointedly for the twins. Harry twisted the ring on his finger—he still couldn't bring himself to take it off. It wasn't just the hurt, there was also guilt—perpetual, constant guilt about whether or not he was doing a good job with the children. Certainly they weren't being brought up as Jill would have wanted. She had wanted to stay home at least until the twins had started school.

Yes, he was doing his best—he was just all too aware that it wasn't quite enough.

Harry headed back out to the department, which

was, for once, quiet. The late staff were all trying to pretend to be busy as Marnie sat at the nurses' station and went through the policy manual, and of course she was making notes and had several questions for Harry.

'Sheldon just brought back a puncture wound of the hand for review in the hand clinic tomorrow.' Marnie had been surprised; it was a very small injury that could easily have been followed up by a GP. 'When I questioned him he said it was policy. Now I've checked and it says here that all hand injuries, regardless of how small, are to be brought back the next day for review in the hand clinic.'

'That's right.'

'All?'

'All.' Harry nodded. 'A lot of things get picked up in the hand clinic and for the most part the patients are in and out in less than a minute. It's worth it, though, because something that seemed minor at the time is often picked up. I've found it works better to just bring everyone with a hand injury, no matter how small, back the next day for review.'

'Fair enough.' Marnie turned the page and then glanced up at the clock. 'What time do you finish?'

'Now,' Harry said. 'Day care closes at six.'

'Dr Morales comes on at nine?' Marnie checked.

'That's right. Though you can call me for anything you're concerned about—all of the staff know that.'

'They do,' Marnie said. 'I'll see you tomorrow, then.'

'You shall.' Harry smiled. 'It's nice to meet you, Marnie, and I'm very glad that we never...' He halted. He wished he could take that back and wondered what had possessed him to even go there in the first place.

'New girl's tease.' Marnie smiled. 'I couldn't help myself.'

'I thought it was supposed to be the other way around, that we were supposed to be teasing you.'

'I make my own fun,' Marnie said.

She really was the oddest mix and, if there was any doubt as to that, she proved it when she continued talking. 'I should be offended really that you're so relieved nothing ever happened.' Marnie winked. ''Night, Harry.'

He turned to go but as he did so the alert phone rang and Miriam, one of the late staff, took the call. 'There's a multi-trauma coming in, they've just diverted and are bringing him here,' Miriam said. 'ETA ten minutes. Harry, would you like me to run over and grab the twins for you?'

'That would be great,' Harry said, taking off his jacket but pausing midway as Marnie's soft voice carried the length of the nurses' station and promptly halted everyone.

'Instead of running over to day care, Miriam, shouldn't you be setting up for the multi-trauma?'

Miriam hesitated and when Harry gave her a nod, instead of racing to get the twins, Miriam headed into Resus.

'You'd better get going,' Marnie said to Harry. 'You don't want to get caught up in this.'

No, he didn't want to get caught up but if it was serious he would call for the trauma team to come down and if it wasn't serious Sheldon could deal with it, except Marnie was already speaking into the phone.

'Could you fast-page the trauma team to come to

Emergency?' she said, but as she replaced the receiver Harry was waiting for her.

'They might not be needed.'

'Hopefully not,' Marnie said, 'but if they are then surely it's better for the patient to have them waiting here.'

Harry heard the overhead intercom crackle into life to summon the team.

''Night, Harry,' Marnie said again.

For Harry it was the strangest feeling to be leaving the department knowing full well there was an emergency on its way in.

He was always running towards an emergency; instead, this evening, he was walking away.

It just didn't feel right.

And however assured Marnie was, he couldn't help but wonder how she'd deal with a less-than-impressed trauma team if she'd called them at five to six for something minor, just when they were due to go home…

Harry paused as he reached day care, dropped one ball from the many he was juggling as he heard the sound of his colleagues' footsteps racing down the corridor to greet whatever was being brought in.

Harry let out a breath and walked into day care. No, he wasn't the first parent to get there but at least he wasn't the last.

'Daddy! We thought you'd have to help with the emergency!' Charlotte squealed, and flung herself at him. Her brown curls were bobbing and her green eyes, the same as her dad's, were smiling with excitement as she realised it was home time. *And* she remembered the promises made.

'Can I make the frosting?'

'You can.'

Even though the trauma team was arriving, the blasted intercom was summoning the team for the second time as Harry signed the twins out.

As he walked down the corridor, carrying Charlotte and holding Adam's hand, he felt Adam still as the stretcher was raced in. He looked down and saw Adam blinking. 'He'll be okay,' Harry assured him.

But the injured man on the stretcher didn't upset Adam, he'd seen way more than most children had already. No, he was bracing himself for his father to return them to day care, Harry realised, or to pop them around to the staffroom; instead, they headed to the car.

'Who's looking after him?' Adam checked, because normally his father was needed.

'He's going to be fine,' Harry said, wishing for the hundredth time his children didn't know or see so much, but the hospital day-care centre was his only choice if he was going to work here. 'There is a team of specialists waiting for him.'

Harry strapped the twins into their car seats and drove the short distance home as Charlotte filled him in on her day, talking non-stop till they were turning into their street.

'How about your day, Adam?' Harry asked, trying to encourage Adam to speak.

'We did paintings.' Adam looked at his father as if Harry must have briefly lost his mind. 'Charlotte just told you.'

'I know.' Harry smiled. They were just so different. Charlotte liked every gap in the conversation filled with her voice, whereas Adam was only too happy to sit back and listen.

Evelyn came out to help him with the twins as they pulled into the driveway, but as she ushered them in, knowing he wouldn't be able to relax till he knew things were okay at work, Harry told Evelyn he'd join them soon. He stood in the hallway, took out his phone and called Emergency. It was Marnie who answered.

'How's the multi-trauma?' Harry asked.

'All good,' Marnie replied. 'Well, not so good if you're the patient, but it's all under control. He's just heading round for an MRI.'

'I can come back if you need me,' Harry said. 'My babysitter's here.'

'There's really no point,' Marnie said. 'As I said, it's all under control. The team have been fantastic.'

'Shouldn't you be at home?' Harry asked, glancing at his watch. She'd been there since long before nine after all.

'Shouldn't you be?' Marnie asked, and Harry gave a thin smile as he heard the chatter coming from the kitchen.

Marnie had made a very good point.

Happy that the patient was being well looked after, Harry headed into the kitchen and to the delicious scent of dinner. 'Smells good,' Harry said.

'I'm trying something different.' Evelyn smiled at the twins. 'Tonight we're eating Russian!'

'Ooh!' Charlotte was delighted, Adam not so sure, and Harry was simply grinning because Evelyn was so Australian she thought beef stroganoff was exotic.

Having Evelyn look after the children had, absolutely, been the best idea Harry had had.

Actually, it had been Juan's idea that he get an older carer for the children.

Yep, *mea culpa*, Harry had slept with the last nanny and the one before that.

It was exhausting being a widower at times!

Seriously.

Harry didn't want a wife—he'd had Jill. Sex, though, that was another matter entirely. Why did women always have to complicate things by falling in love?

At least Evelyn didn't read a single thing into it when Harry suggested that instead of dashing off she join them for dinner.

'Are you sure?' Evelyn checked, but she was already pulling out a chair. 'How was work?'

'Good,' Harry said, because, given he was home on time, it must have been a good day. 'We've got a new nurse manager just started,' Harry said. 'She seems very efficient.'

'She's rude,' Charlotte said.

'Rude?' Harry looked at his daughter, who was spooning sour cream onto her dinner, and tried to recall them meeting her. 'How can you say Marnie's rude? You barely even met her.'

'She didn't say hello to us,' Charlotte said.

'It was her first day,' Harry commented. 'I'm sure she had other things to think of.' Though, as Harry wrestled the sour cream from Charlotte, he did dwell on it for just a second. Charlotte was right, well, not the rude part but usually people did comment on the twins, especially when they realised that they were twins. Charlotte, Harry decided, was just far too used to having people drop to their knees and tell her how cute she was.

Dinner was nice and Harry refused Evelyn's offer

to stay and do the dishes. 'I can stack a dishwasher!' Harry said, as he saw her to the door.

'If you need me tonight,' Evelyn offered, 'you just have to call.'

'I shan't tonight,' Harry said. 'Juan's on. Things might get a bit busy, though, once he's off on his honeymoon.'

'No problem.'

Evelyn really was fantastic, Harry thought as he saw her out. Evelyn was their next-door-but-one neighbour. She had lost her husband many years ago and desperately missed her daughter, who had moved with her husband and baby to China. Evelyn had actually cried when Harry had taken up Juan's suggestion to get someone older and Harry had asked if she could be there for the twins.

For cash!

Perfect.

Evelyn was saving up to go and visit her family in China and she got to spoil Charlotte and Adam in the interim.

The twins went to day care but on the odd day they were sick, Evelyn was there, and if Harry was on call, Evelyn slept in the nanny's room. She didn't even mind the odd time when Harry had to call her during the night.

It wasn't a complete solution but for now it was working.

Wow!

It was just after seven. Dinner was done and the dishwasher was on.

'Can we make the banana bread?' Adam asked.

'Yep.'

Oh, the bliss of the absence of parental guilt, Harry thought as Adam mashed bananas. In no time there was the lovely scent of banana bread filling the house as he got the twins bathed and ready for bed.

'The frosting!' Charlotte said. 'You promised that I could make the frosting.'

'I know, but the bread had to cool.' Harry looked up the recipe on the Internet and squeezed some orange juice, which Charlotte mashed into cream cheese. By nine p.m. the twins were in bed, there was a slice of banana bread wrapped for Adam's breakfast and a small bowl of frosting for Charlotte. And there was just a glimpse of order to the home for the first time in a very long time.

Harry lay back on the couch and yawned.

They'd made it through another day.

He thought of Marnie stopping Miriam from going to fetch the children, and the strangest thing was he was actually grateful for it. Harry didn't want people rushing to pick up his children and he loathed all the favours that he constantly had to ask.

It was Marnie who had done him a true favour today.

She'd given him an evening at home with the twins.

# CHAPTER FOUR

'Excuse me!'

Harry's tongue rolled in his cheek as he heard Marnie's beguilingly soft voice. She walked over to Sheldon, the resident, who was washing his hands at the surgical sink.

Poor Sheldon, he had no idea what was coming.

Harry did. Marnie had delivered Harry exactly the same lecture she was now giving Sheldon.

'You see these long taps, Sheldon?'

'Yes.'

'Well, it might surprise you to hear that they're not designed for helping doctors who happen to have big hands.'

Harry couldn't resist looking up. He could see Sheldon blushing and Marnie smiling as she delivered a very firm lecture but in the sweetest voice. 'And, neither were they designed for busy doctors so that they could just push them back quickly. The designers were far more thoughtful than that—do you know why the taps are so long, Sheldon?'

'Okay, Marnie, I get it,' Sheldon said through gritted teeth.

'But I don't think that you do. You see, they're designed

that way so that you can turn them on and off with your elbows. I'll show you…'

'I already know,' Sheldon said as Marnie demonstrated how to turn the taps on and off with her own elbows.

'You know that?' Marnie checked. 'I'm so sorry, Sheldon, I didn't think you did because when I saw you just washing your hands…'

Harry shook his head and got back to his notes as Marnie continued to give Sheldon a lesson on handwashing. She was obsessed with cleanliness and handwashing was at the top of her list, along with cleaning the curtains and light switches.

'What,' Marnie had demanded, 'is the point of cleaning your hands and then opening a filthy curtain with them?'

Oh, and she had a thing about sunlight.

'It's cheaper than bleach,' Marnie had said when she had called Maintenance down to prise open windows that had never, in all the time Harry had been there, been opened. 'Sunlight kills everything.'

In the two weeks that Marnie had been at Bayside she had turned the *Titanic*.

The place was glistening, the cupboards were well stocked, and breaks were being taken, though heaven help you if you left the kitchen without washing and putting away your coffee cup.

Love her or loathe her, there was no doubt that the place was well run under Marnie's command and, as a consultant in the busy emergency department, Harry should be feeling extremely pleased at that fact.

He was pleased.

It was just…

Marnie did not give an inch. No, Harry didn't want favours, but a bit of flexibility wouldn't go amiss either. With Juan now in Argentina and Dr Cooper's starting date still a few weeks away, for Dr Vermont and Harry the wheels were again starting to come off. They were relying heavily on locums—some were excellent, others not. But locums were exactly that, they didn't have the investment in the place that the regular staff had. Sheldon, for one, was becoming increasingly exasperated about who the latest boss was and at what point he should call the regular senior staff in.

'Marnie!' Harry heard the surprise in Sheldon's voice and looked up as Sheldon spoke on. 'Did anyone ever tell you that you could be a hand model?'

'I get told it all the time!' Marnie said.

'I'm serious.' Sheldon was turning her hands over and examining them. 'They're amazing.'

'I know they are,' Marnie said. 'Really, I should just take the plunge and get them insured and go off and make my fortune.'

'Harry,' Sheldon called, 'have you seen Marnie's hands?'

'Er, no,' Harry lied. He'd noticed them when Marnie had given him the little hand-washing lecture the other day and Sheldon was right—they were incredible. Her skin was unblemished and pale, with long, slender fingers that tapered into very neat, oval nails. They really were beautiful.

'Show Harry,' Sheldon said.

Marnie duly walked over and held out her hands. Emergency was a mad place at times, so this sort of thing wasn't in the least peculiar. Even Kelly came over to admire Marnie's hands.

'They're lovely,' Harry said.

'Harry's got a bit of a *thing* about hands,' Kelly teased, but even she was surprised when Marnie took it a stage further.

'Do they turn you on, Harry?' Marnie said. Harry couldn't help but smile back and Kelly gave a slightly shocked laugh. Marnie was a minx—sexy yet cold, flirtatious at times but only when it suited her mood. And... Harry liked her.

Yes, it was another reason Harry wasn't feeling best pleased. Liking Marnie was too inconvenient for words.

'I have an *interest* in hands,' Harry said, and Marnie smirked at his response, 'not a fetish.'

'You *really* should be a hand model,' Kelly said, peering at them and then at her own.

'And who would keep you lot in place?' Marnie asked. 'Though I do know what you mean. Sometimes I look down at them and find myself smiling.'

No one was smiling a little while later when the nursing off-duty was revealed. It was the first one Marnie had done and a group of nurses had fallen on the diary the moment that it had appeared.

Abby, who loathed night duty, found that she was about to do her first stint after two years of having managed to avoid it.

Harry, who should be moving on to the next patient, couldn't help but stretch out his patient notes just so that he could listen as Abby voiced her concerns to Marnie.

Of course, they fell on deaf ears.

'I hate nights too.' Marnie smiled. 'Which is one of the reasons that I went into management, though I'm doing a stint myself soon, just to see how the place runs at night. We can be miserable together.'

Harry didn't look up as Abby slunk off, only for Kelly to take her place. 'Er, Marnie…' Kelly started. 'I wrote in the request notes that I don't do early shifts at the weekends, yet you've put me down for an early shift on Saturday next week and again a fortnight later.'

'I saw that you had requested that, Kelly, but you didn't write down a reason. I really am trying my best to accommodate everyone. Why can't you do an early shift on a Saturday?'

'Well, the thing is…' Kelly attempted, and Harry listened to the discomfort in her voice as she tried to give a suitable reason. 'I like to go out on a Friday night.'

'Of course you do!' Marnie answered calmly. 'We all love to go out and get blethered on a Friday night— heaven knows, we need it after a week in this place— which is why we share around the pleasure of a lie-in on a Saturday. Everyone takes their turn.'

And with that she walked off.

'I want to loathe her,' Kelly said. 'I have every reason to loathe her and yet…'

Harry glanced up. There was Marnie, catching the poor maintenance man before he escaped as she had plenty more jobs for him.

'She's efficient,' Harry said.

'She's cold,' Kelly corrected. 'She's been here for a couple of weeks and, do you know, nobody knows one single thing about her.'

Kelly was right and it was unusual. Emergency was a place that thrived on gossip, yet Marnie just didn't partake. Yes, long before he'd noticed her beautiful hands he had noticed that there was no wedding or engagement ring. Not that that meant anything—after all, he still wore his. He'd also noticed a large bunch of flowers has been delivered on the day that she had arrived. But, as she had taken delivery and inhaled the fragrances of the bouquet, Marnie had offered no explanation as to the sender. She never spoke about last night or what her plans were for the weekend. All she really spoke about was work and yet, no matter how he tried to tell himself it didn't matter, Harry kept finding himself wanting to know a little bit more.

She was intriguing.

It was as if she looked at the world through a different end of the telescope from everyone else—a case in point was Juan. All the staff raved about Juan and how lucky Cate was, how wonderful the wedding would be and what a great catch he was.

Marnie screwed up her nose.

'He's a fine doctor, but he'd drive me bonkers to live with,' Marnie said. Everyone was trying really hard not to like her but sometimes she just lit up the department with her commentary. Just like the windows she insisted on opening, she made the drab suddenly brighter.

'But he's gorgeous,' Abby said.

'He's a bit too New Age for me and I'd get tired of him being, oh, so understanding.' Marnie seemed to think about it for a moment and then shook her head. 'Imagine trying to have a row with that…'

'So you like a good row?' Harry asked.

'Of course,' Marnie said. 'Can you imagine trying to row with Juan? "No, I don't want my shoulders massaged…"'

Yet as funny and as intriguing as she could be, Marnie was also, as Harry had guessed she would be, completely immutable in certain areas.

'Marnie…' Harry approached her after taking a call.

'Day care just rang and Adam's not feeling too well. There's still a bit of a backlog and I thought I might just pop him in the staffroom—'

'Harry,' Marnie interrupted, 'the staffroom really isn't the place for a child that is not feeling well.'

'I know that but it will only be for an hour. I'm just asking if the nurse in the obs ward could pop her head in now and then.'

'Sorry.' Marnie didn't look remotely sorry as she shook her head. 'She's got post-op patients to keep an eye on. If Adam is unwell, he needs to be at home.'

'You know...' Harry gritted his teeth and stopped the words from coming out as they reached the tip of his tongue.

'Feel free to say it,' Marnie invited.

Instead, he chose a different tack. 'Fine, if no one can keep an eye out then I'll ring my seventy-year-old babysitter and ask her to drive over...'

'Grand.'

Except, when he rang Evelyn, Harry received the worrying news that she had just been to the doctor. The rash that she hadn't told Harry about just happened to be shingles and she wouldn't be able to help out with the children for a few days at least.

'Don't worry about the kids, you just get well, Evelyn,' Harry said. He didn't want to worry Evelyn with the places his mind had suddenly gone to—namely the twins contracting chickenpox. They had been immunised, surely? But, then, Jill had seen to all that. As both a doctor and a parent Harry's mind was racing through several scenarios even as he put down the phone. 'She can't come,' a rather distracted Harry told Marnie.

'Then you'd better get Adam home.'

'You know, you really are inflexible at times,' Harry snapped.

'Oh, but I'm very flexible, Harry,' Marnie responded. 'In fact, if twenty critically ill patients came pouring through that door at this very moment you'd see just how flexible I can be. I know exactly where my staff are and what they are doing, and I can call them at any given time because they are *not* keeping an eye out for a sick child.'

She made a very good point; unfortunately, Harry was in no mood to see it. He was trying to do the best by the department and do his best by his children too. He was worried that an unwell Adam might be in the early stages of chickenpox, which meant, if he was, no doubt any day Charlotte would be too. Marnie just didn't seem to understand.

'You just don't get it,' Harry said, picking up his jacket. 'You're not a mum.'

# CHAPTER FIVE

IT HURT.

And it still hurt as Marnie drove home but she did her best to push it aside when there was a knock at the door a little while later and it was her youngest brother, Ronan.

He'd just started work and was frantically saving up to move out from home, but every now and then he came and stayed for a couple of days with Marnie.

'How's the new job?' Ronan asked.

'Frustrating,' Marnie said. 'It would be a great department if there were enough staff and people didn't keep using the place as a drop-in crèche...' She stopped herself from elaborating. 'Don't mind me,' Marnie said, but Harry's words were still smarting and, in no mood to make dinner, she suggested that they eat out. 'My treat,' Marnie said. 'On the condition that you have dinner waiting for me tomorrow when I get home.'

It was nice to get out. Marnie drove along the beach road and into the small town and they soon found a gorgeous pub and sat outside, overlooking the bay, in the late sunlight.

Ronan, who was permanently hungry, dived into a huge steak while Marnie had prawns and a mango salad and enjoyed just sitting back and relaxing in front of the view, as she had promised herself she would of an evening. She wouldn't trade places with anyone. Watching a family on the next table, the mother spooning puréed pumpkin into a hungry baby's mouth as the father tried to amuse an overtired toddler, Marnie was very glad to be able to simply linger over her meal with her brother. She listened as Ronan told her about his work, and then got to, perhaps, the real reason he had asked to visit.

'You know what Mum's like,' Ronan said. 'I'm just warning you that she was upset you didn't come and visit at the weekend, or the last.'

'She surely knows how busy I am with work,' Marnie said. 'And moving! She could've come and helped with the move, like you did—she knows she doesn't need a written invitation to come and see me.'

'I think that she's just upset that you've moved so far.'

'It's not as if I've gone back home to Ireland.' Marnie sighed. 'I'm an hour's drive away.'

'She thinks you're punishing her for us emigrating…' Ronan attempted to make light of it but it was a bit of a dark subject and Marnie had to push out a smile.

'I'll try and get over one evening, but…' Marnie shook her head; maybe she was avoiding her parents a bit at the moment but she just didn't want to discuss it with Ronan. Or rather she simply couldn't discuss it with anyone in her family. *That* time of the year was coming up. The time of year that no one in her family ever spoke about because no one in her family knew what to say.

Declan would soon have been thirteen.

She looked over to the little family at the next table— the toddler was eating ice cream now, the baby falling asleep on its mother's lap, and sometimes, just sometimes, she *would* like to trade places.

Marnie took a long sip of her iced water and couldn't come up with a suitable line as to why she had been avoiding her mother, so she settled for the usual instead. 'I'm just busy, Ronan.'

So too was Harry.

After an evening spent trying to find vaccination certificates, as well as asking his parents if they could have the twins for a couple of days, Harry was in no mood for a very groomed Marnie the next day. She was busily writing on the white board while telling Kelly, who was frantically fishing to find out more about the elusive new manager, that the prawns she had had last night at Peninsular Pub were the best she had tasted.

He doubted Marnie would have been eating alone.

Yes, his response was terse when Marnie had the gall to ask him how Adam was.

'He's at my parents',' Harry said. 'Along with Charlotte.'

'Is she sick as well?'

'Neither is sick. Well, Adam's got a bit of a temperature,' Harry said. 'But my babysitter has shingles and I can hardly send them to day care knowing that any minute now they could break out in spots.'

'Weren't they immunised?' She was so annoyingly practical; she might just as well have been asking if the puppies' shots were up to date.

'You'd have to ask my late wife,' Harry snapped. 'I can't find the records.'

Ooh, they bristled and they snapped their way through the day, though the animosity was put on hold when a worried-looking Kelly came over and had a word with Harry, just as Marnie was finishing checking and ordering the scheduled drugs.

'I've got a seventeen-year-old girl in who's pregnant and bleeding. Sheldon estimates her to be around twenty-four weeks. The thing is, her parents are with her and Emily keeps insisting that she doesn't want them to know that she's pregnant. They keep asking for updates and are getting really angry that I won't let them in to be with her and that the doctor hasn't been in to speak with them. I'm just not sure how to deal with patient confidentially and Sheldon's concerned...'

'I'll come now,' Harry said, but as he made to go so too did Marnie.

'I'll come with you,' Marnie said, then spoke with Kelly. 'I'm happy to deal with her and the family.'

'Please.' Kelly let out a sigh of a relief. 'I don't blame Emily a bit for not wanting to tell her parents. They're not exactly the most approachable pair.'

Emily was very young, very scared but very determined that this baby was wanted. Sheldon had already started an IV and an ultrasound machine was being wheeled in as Harry and Marnie took over. 'Reece was going to come over at the weekend and tell my parents with me,' Emily tearfully explained as Harry gently examined her abdomen. 'Do we have to tell them now?'

'Well, we don't have to tell them,' Marnie answered, 'though I think they might start to guess what the issue is when they see you strapped to a foetal monitor or they see the sign for Maternity when I take you up.' Harry saw the small smile on Emily's lips as Marnie softened things with wry humour. 'Do you not think they have an idea?'

'I'm not sure,' Emily admitted. 'Dad did say that I was putting on weight and I was about to say something but then Mum said it was because I was spending all my time sitting down, studying.' Emily started to cry. 'They're going to be so angry.'

'They're going to be concerned,' Harry said, squirting some jelly on Emily's abdomen.

Marnie bit down on her lip because, as good a doctor as Harry was, until you'd been there you simply didn't understand.

Harry hadn't been there.

Marnie had.

She took Emily's hands. 'We can tell your parents for you.'

'You don't understand…'

'I do,' Marnie said. 'Sometimes news like this is better coming from someone who's not so involved. Once they know about the baby and have calmed down, they can come in and speak with you.'

'They'll never calm down.'

'Let's just see,' Marnie said. 'For now you just worry about staying calm. The last thing we want is you stressing yourself and raising your blood pressure and things.'

'Why am I bleeding?'

'It looks as if your placenta is lying rather low,' Harry said, running the ultrasound probe over Emily's stomach, and Marnie watched Emily's face as she stared unblinking at the screen and saw her baby for the first time. 'The heartbeat is a good rate and strong,' Harry said, pointing to the screen.

'Can you tell if it's a boy or girl?'

'The one time I tried I got it wrong.' Harry smiled. 'I'm going to get the obstetricians down and they'll examine you but for now I'll let your family know what's going on, if that's okay with you?' Emily gave a wary nod and then Harry asked about Reece and got a bit of history before they left to tell her parents. Marnie gave Emily's hand a little squeeze before she left.

George and Lucia really were a rather formidable pair—the air was thick with tension as Marnie and Harry came in and sat down.

'It's ridiculous the length of time that we've been kept waiting,' George said by way of introduction.

'Well, we've been with your daughter,' Harry calmly responded. 'I just wanted to have a chat before you went in.'

'We'd like to see her,' Lucia said, instead of asking what was wrong with her daughter.

'I'd like to speak with you before you do.'

'I really just want to see her,' Lucia insisted. 'If you could just let us know what cubicle she's in.'

They knew, Marnie realised, they simply didn't want to hear it, and thankfully Harry wasted no time getting to the point.

'Emily is pregnant,' Harry said to the two rigid faces. 'We estimate that she's about twenty-four weeks, though when she sees the obstetrician she'll have a more detailed ultrasound to confirm dates.' They all sat in silence for a moment, Harry and Marnie waiting for questions as the parents awaited the doctor's solution. 'This must come as a bit of a shock,' Harry offered.

'She's in her final year at school,' George said, as if that might change things, then he turned to his wife. 'I told you that she shouldn't be seeing him. I knew this would happen.' His fists balled as he gritted his teeth.

'She's got school to think of,' George said, and then turned back to Harry. 'She can't have it.'

'Emily wants to have the baby,' Harry said, 'and, as I've said, she's about twenty-four weeks' gestation and bleeding quite heavily. She's terribly worried for her baby and frankly so am I...'

'Baby!' George simply would not accept it and Marnie was pleased this conversation was taking place well away from Emily. 'How is she supposed to take care of a baby? She's still at school herself and doing very well. She's completely messed up her life.' He started to stand and his wife went to grab his arm.

'George, please.'

'Please what?' George demanded as he started pacing. 'How the hell is she supposed to support it?'

'Sit down,' Harry said. 'The last thing Emily needs now is to be upset.'

'Well, she should have thought of that. Maybe she should think of that...' George started heading for the door but then, realising he didn't know what cubicle Emily was in, he turned to Marnie. 'You'll take me to my daughter now.'

'Emily's not allowed visitors at the moment,' Marnie responded. 'At the moment she needs calm.'

'Don't you tell me what my daughter needs.'

'I really think,' Marnie continued, 'that it might help if you go for a walk before you visit Emily, or go to the canteen, or even just sit here and get used to the idea for a little while.'

'What would you know?' George shouted, and Harry was about to step in, perhaps even get Security, because there was no way he wanted Emily being subjected to her father's anger. But Marnie didn't need his help.

'I know plenty,' Marnie said. 'I can remember every word my parents said when I was eighteen and I told them I was pregnant.' She looked at Lucia. 'My son died when he was two weeks old and, given what had been said, I wouldn't let my mother comfort me. I still can't. I can guarantee that your next conversation with your daughter will be replayed in her mind for the rest of her life.' It was Marnie who stood then. 'She's in cubicle seven but, again, I suggest that before you go in there you take some time and really *think* about the kind of parents you want to be during this difficult time for your daughter.'

Yes, she loathed bringing her private life to work but she'd loathe even more Emily's parents speaking in haste.

Marnie walked into the cubicle, glad that it appeared George wasn't following. Emily was being seen by the obstetrician but she looked over anxiously as Marnie stepped in.

'How are they?' she asked, and Marnie hoped it would soon be the other way around—with her parents asking how Emily and the baby were.

'They're just taking it all in,' she said. 'You just focus on yourself for now.'

Her parents must have been doing some thinking because it was a good half-hour later, when Emily was about to be wheeled up to Maternity, that they came in.

'You could have told me,' were her mother's first words.

'I tried,' Emily said, and now Marnie said nothing as she escorted them up to Maternity and saw Emily settled in. Steroids had been started to mature the baby's lungs in case it needed to be delivered, but for now the bleeding had slowed down and things seemed a whole lot calmer.

'Thanks, Marnie,' Emily said, once Marnie had handed over to the midwife taking over Emily's care and had popped in to say goodbye.

'I'll pop back and see you when I...' Her voice trailed off as a very pale and clearly terrified young man came into the ward.

'I told you not to come yet,' Emily said tearfully.

'I couldn't just stay at work.'

Marnie watched as, instead of anger, George somehow found it in himself to go over and shake Reece's hand, and as Marnie headed back down to the department she knew that of all the things that had moved her about today, Reece had moved her very much. A young man who, instead of letting Emily deal with it alone, had been brave enough to leave work and come and face the music.

She could still remember the feel of Craig trembling beside her as they'd told her parents. She hadn't wanted him there but had been so proud that he had insisted on it.

Was it any wonder they had broken up even before Declan had been born?

Yet he had still been there for the birth of his son.

She could see Harry chatting to a colleague and Marnie decided she would go to lunch.

She was a touch embarrassed that she'd told her tale in front of him, but then, he wasn't the first colleague that had heard the same. Part of her job, and the reason she loved it, was that you saw people at their most raw and could actually make a difference. It had just felt a little awkward and clearly Harry thought it an issue because a few moments after she'd sat down he knocked at her office door.

'How's she doing?'

'Better,' Marnie said. 'The bleeding has stopped and the parents are a lot calmer. Her young man just arrived and George actually shook his hand.'

That wasn't what Harry was there for.

'I'm sorry for what I said yesterday,' Harry said, and he sat down when Marnie really would have preferred a more fleeting visit.

'It's really not a problem—believe me I've heard that, or similar, many times before.'

'I didn't know,' Harry said, then shook his head. 'Not that that's an excuse. I'll be more careful when I say things like that in the future.'

'Good.' She gave a small smile; he really did look uncomfortable and that had never been her intention. 'Harry, I don't broadcast what happened to me to everyone but, on the other hand, I don't hide it either. I am a mother, I had a son. I felt today that it was appropriate that I tell those parents what had happened to me before they marched into Emily and made exactly the same mistake my parents made…'

'A lot of parents do.'

'Well, hopefully Emily's parents shan't now,' Marnie said. 'I certainly didn't tell them to make you feel uncomfortable.'

'They didn't take it well, then?' Harry asked. 'Your parents?'

'No.' Marnie hesitated. Normally she'd add something sharp here, like, 'Just because you know about it doesn't mean that I want to discuss it.' Except today, right now, she did. Maybe it was because Harry, given he had lost his wife, surely knew grief. Or maybe it was just with Declan's birthday coming up and Ronan hinting that her mother was upset, it had all been brought to the surface.

Then she looked up to his green eyes that were waiting patiently and realised that maybe it was just because it was Harry. 'They're very strict,' Marnie said. 'Or rather they were when we were younger. My mum went crazy when she found out. She said that it would kill my granny and my father…' She gave a tight smile. 'Though not till he'd killed the baby's father.' Marnie closed her eyes at the weary memory of that time. 'All the usual stuff.'

'Like?'

'I'm sure you can guess.' Marnie gave a tight shrug. 'She also made it very clear that she didn't think I should keep my baby. Anyway, a few months later when my son was on the neonatal unit, the person I wanted was my mum but at the same time I didn't want her. We can't discuss it, even now.'

'Have you tried?'

'Nope.' Marnie shook her head. 'And I won't be trying either.' She looked at Harry. 'It couldn't end nicely.' Marnie felt uncomfortable now; the only person she really discussed Declan with was her friend Siobhan and, feeling she'd said more than enough, Marnie changed the subject. 'I'm just very glad that Emily's father didn't march in and vent his spleen. She had a big abruption, and she could start bleeding again any time soon,' Marnie said. 'That baby's far from safe.' She wanted to stop talking about it, she wanted to just end the conversation, to dismiss Harry and get on with her day, except Marnie felt her nose redden and Harry saw a flash of tears in her eyes.

'Marnie...' Harry was struggling for words—he was used to death, both personally and professionally, and had it been anyone else he'd have stood, gone over, but it was Marnie, and he didn't. Not because he didn't want to, more because of how much he did.

'It's fine.' Marnie filled the silence. 'I'm fine. It was all just a bit too close to home.' She blew out a breath. 'It's his birthday coming up.'

'Look, do you want to...?' Harry's voice trailed off as there was a knock at the door.

'Matthew!' Harry noticed that she flushed a little as a rather well-dressed man entered. 'What are you doing here?' Marnie asked.

'I had a client nearby,' Matthew said. 'I thought I might see if you were free for lunch. Oh, and I wanted to tell you in person that I got the tickets.' He handed an envelope to Marnie. 'Opening night, don't ask me how I got them!'

'Oh!' Marnie's anger at having her workspace invaded was temporarily thwarted because, more than anything, she loved the ballet and the opening night had sold out the day the tickets had been released. 'Wow!'

'It might be better if you look after them,' Matthew said, not even bothering to introduce himself to Harry, who had already made up his mind that he didn't like him.

'I'll leave you to it,' Harry said, and walked out.

Harry wasn't sure if he was jealous of Marnie's freedom or just plain jealous—Harry had been very close to suggesting they leave the department and get lunch.

Stupid idea, Harry, he told himself. Those days were long gone—he kept things well away from work.

A moment or so later he looked up from a patient and saw them walking out of the department, Matthew sliding a hand around Marnie's waist.

He didn't like that and neither did Marnie—she wriggled out of Matthew's embrace and it was clear she was cross.

'Are you going to show me where you live?' Matthew asked as she got into his car and he started the engine.

'Sure,' Marnie said, her tongue firmly in her cheek. 'My brother Ronan is over for a couple of days. You can say hi if you like...'

'Maybe not, then.'

Sitting in a bayside café a little while later, Marnie told him that she was far from impressed.

'Why would you drop in on me at work?' Marnie asked.

'I told you—I was in the area and I wanted to give you the tickets for the ballet or I'd end up losing them. I'm going straight from here to the airport.'

Marnie refused to buy it. 'Until recently I lived a stone's throw from your office and I would never have dropped in on you!' She was angry, very angry—part of the loose arrangement they had was that there would be no popping in. She and Matthew went out now and then. They were social and, yes, they slept together, but they did not invade each other's lives and that was the way Marnie wanted it. 'Whatever possessed you?'

'Okay, okay,' Matthew said, deciding against suggesting that she call in sick this afternoon. 'I shan't stop by again.' He watched as Marnie's hand, which had just dipped her bread in oil, paused over the salt. 'I wouldn't want to disturb anything.'

'Excuse me?'

'You and your colleague looked very cosy.'

'We were talking about a patient!' Marnie so did not need this. 'He's got two children...' Marnie shook her head and then reached for her bag. 'I need to get back.'

They drove in silence. Marnie was still cross, not just that Matthew had dropped by at her work but cross with herself for all she had told Harry. Cross too that Matthew had interrupted them.

'The ballet will be great,' Matthew said, as he dropped her off. 'Get you back to civilisation.'

Far from being offended, she actually laughed. Maybe she did need a night of being spoilt, it might stop the constant thoughts about Declan's birthday.

And about Harry.

As she went to get a drink of water from the staff kitchen she was met by a very stony-faced Harry, who was rinsing his mug.

'Nice lunch?'

'Lovely, thanks.'

'Your boyfriend—?'

'Boyfriend?' Marnie rapidly interrupted. 'I'm thirty-one—I'm a bit old for boys.'

'Sorry.' Harry gave a wry grin. She was the most impossible person he had ever met, yet, for reasons of his own, which he didn't really want to examine, he ploughed on. 'Your partner, then?'

'Partner?' Marnie challenged him right there and then. She was sick of men and the different rules that applied to them, and Marnie told him so. Despite never gossiping herself, Marnie was very clued in and had heard all the rumours about Harry. 'Is that what you called your last nanny? Your partner, your girlfriend?' Harry let out a breath as Marnie continued, 'Or did you upgrade her title to your live-in lover?'

'I was just going to say he seemed nice.'

'Well, I'll let you know when I need your opinion.'

Marnie dived into work, refusing to go to her office because that would look like she was hiding. And why would she be hiding? There was nothing to feel embarrassed or awkward about—a friend had merely dropped in to take her to lunch.

It was just that Marnie didn't like her worlds colliding and, as the afternoon progressed, the tension seemed to increase. Near home time she glanced up and briefly caught sight of a very dark-looking Harry walking past, and she knew it wasn't just that Matthew had dropped by that was unsettling her.

It was Harry.

In a nice way, though.

There was a tiny flutter in her chest as she met his eyes and it was still fluttering as she looked away and tried to concentrate on what Kelly was calling out to her.

'Sorry?' She looked at Kelly.

'There's a guy on the phone for you,' Kelly repeated. 'He says it's personal.'

'I'll bet it is,' Harry muttered, but thankfully well out of earshot.

What the hell did Matthew want now? Marnie thought as she made her way over. Only it wasn't Matthew calling her at work and she saw Harry's jaw grit as she said another man's name.

'Ronan, what are you doing, phoning me at work?'

He wanted to take the receiver from her and replace it. He wanted to turn her round and tell her part of the reason for his dark mood.

He couldn't get her out of his mind.

# CHAPTER SIX

HARRY REACHED FOR his jacket. It was ten to five and he was in no mood for *another* dose of salt to be rubbed into a very raw wound, and anyway he had to get to his parents to pick up the twins and inspect them for chickenpox.

Fun!

'Are you heading off?' Dr Vermont said, and Harry nodded.

'You're not in tomorrow?' Dr Vermont checked.

'I can't leave them with my parents for too long,' Harry said, and Dr Vermont nodded. He knew Harry's father's health wasn't brilliant and the twins were hard work at the best of times. By the time Harry had signed off on some paperwork, Marnie had gathered her bag and was walking briskly through the department, jangling her car keys.

'You're in a rush, Marnie,' Dr Vermont commented, because Marnie never usually left till well past six. 'Is everything okay?'

'I'll be back,' Marnie said. 'My brother just called and he's cut himself—his finger. I'm just going home to fetch him and bring him in.'

'I'll stay around to see him,' Dr Vermont said, and

Marnie gave a grateful smile, though, in truth, it was a bit of a forced one because she desperately wanted Harry to offer to stay back. He was, as she was starting to find out, not just considered the best hand surgeon in the hospital but one of the top in the country.

Harry made no offer; instead, he joined her as she headed out.

She walked to the car park with him. Their footsteps were rapid and the atmosphere between them was tense but it was Harry who broke the strained silence. 'Do you think it's serious?'

'It's deep. I told him to make dinner and he couldn't find my tin-opener so he decided to use a knife…' She was waffling, stupidly feeling guilty for insisting that Ronan cook, but she was evading the real answer, not because she didn't want to tell Harry, more because she didn't want to think what it might mean to Ronan. 'He says it's bad.' Harry could hear the slight panic in her voice as she elaborated, 'I'm worried he might have cut a tendon.'

'You haven't even seen it yet.' Harry was practical.

'He plays the piano.' Marnie glanced at Harry. 'I mean—he plays it really well.' She closed her eyes for a second. If Ronan had indeed injured his tendon it was going to be a tough few months ahead for him, with no guarantee his hand would return to full dexterity.

'If he has injured his tendon, Dr Vermont will refer him to Stuart. He's on tonight and he's a great surgeon.'

She wanted Harry.

They were now at her car and, given how inflexible Marnie had been with his children, she was in absolutely no position to ask him a favour, except it was Ronan. For that reason, and that reason only, Marnie swallowed her pride and went to speak, but the words wouldn't come out. Harry watched as she ran one of those very beautiful hands through her dark hair as again she tried to swallow her pride.

For Ronan, Marnie told herself.

'If it needs doing, is there any chance of you repairing it tomorrow?' There were two spots of colour appearing on her pale cheeks. 'If Dr Vermont orders it to be elevated tonight, you could—'

'I'm not coming in tomorrow.'

'Oh, I thought you were on.'

'No.'

When Harry didn't elaborate, Marnie just nodded and got into her car. She loathed that she'd asked him but, more than that, she loathed that he'd said no.

When she got home, Marnie let herself in and Ronan called out to her. 'I'm in here.'

He was sitting on the floor of Marnie's bathroom with his hand wrapped in a towel and he was holding it up.

'You don't have a bath to sit on,' was the first thing he said, and Marnie managed a smile as, first things first, she washed her hands.

'It was the first thing I noticed about the place too.' Marnie knelt down beside him and gently pulled down his arm.

'Sorry about the towel.'

'Don't worry about it,' Marnie said.

'I made a mess in the kitchen.'

'Ronan, stop.' She unwrapped the towel and Marnie, who was very used to looking at injured fingers, surprised herself by feeling a bit sick when she examined

Ronan's cut. Marnie blew out a breath as she saw the white of Ronan's partially severed tendon as he attempted to move his finger.

'Don't try to do anything for now,' Marnie said. 'I'll put a dressing on it and we'll get you to the hospital.'

She went to the kitchen and it was a bit of a mess with Ronan's blood, as he'd said. She reached for a glass and took two long drinks of water then refilled the glass.

It was ridiculous really, Marnie thought. There wasn't a single thing at work that made her feel faint but as soon as it was family, it was a different matter entirely.

She stood, remembering the nurses insisting she wait outside as they stuck another needle in Declan...

Not now!

Marnie tipped the water down the sink, got out her first-aid box and headed back to Ronan. She sorted out the wound, wrapping the injured finger in a saline dressing and bandaging it, then applying a sling, before she got him into the car and headed to the hospital.

'It's bad, isn't it?' Ronan asked, as Marnie concentrated on driving.

'I think you've done your tendon,' she admitted.

'That can be fixed, though, can't it?'

'Of course it can.' She glanced over and smiled but said nothing more just yet. Ronan's tendon could certainly be fixed but it would take a lot of time and patience to get back the function that Ronan had had.

She wished that Harry was on tonight.

The department was quiet and Marnie took Ronan straight through and into a cubicle, where she told him to lie down.

'I don't need to lie down,' he said, then changed his

mind. He was tall and geeky and didn't try to hide it, and Marnie loved him for it. 'I do feel a bit sick.'

'I know,' Marnie said, because the phrase 'as white as a sheet' could have been coined just for Ronan—Marnie was quite sure that had he not lain down when he had he would have passed out.

'Can a have a glass of water?'

'Nothing.' Marnie shook her head. 'You can't have anything till a doctor's seen it. Just wait there and I'll go and get you registered and then…' Her voice trailed off as the curtain opened and Harry walked in.

'Harry!' Marnie couldn't quite believe that he was here—especially since she'd seen him drive off.

Harry couldn't quite believe it either. He'd got five minutes down the road, feeling as guilty as hell for saying no to Marnie's brother, when his phone had rung with the news from his mother that Adam was coming out in spots.

Harry had pulled over and sat with his head in his hands, listening to the sound of the traffic whizzing past.

Of course, if Adam had them, then Charlotte would get them soon.

Something had to give and at that moment it did.

Adam was fine when Harry rang back—he was the centre of attention for once when usually it was Charlotte.

'He's tired, though,' his mum explained. 'I was just going to put him to bed. Why don't you stay here tonight? It would be a shame to wake him.'

Harry hesitated. He had been about to say yes, but at the last moment he asked his aging parents for yet another favour.

For the last time.

Sure, he'd need them in the future, Harry didn't doubt that, but the madness had to stop and so he had ended it.

'Marnie.' He gave her a tight smile and then aimed a much nicer one at Ronan. 'So, I hear that you've cut your finger, cooking.' Harry helped Ronan out of the sling and when he saw the neat dressing he made a wry joke about Ronan's big sister having a fully equipped first-aid box.

'Yeah, well, she might have a well-equipped first-aid box but she doesn't have a tin-opener,' Ronan said, as Harry washed his hands and put on some gloves while Marnie removed the dressing.

'I do have tin-opener,' Marnie scolded. 'Just because Mum keeps hers in the second drawer, you didn't think to look in the third.'

Harry grinned to himself at the good-natured banter between brother and sister and then he came over and carefully examined the wound as well as testing for sensation in Adam's finger. 'You're a pianist, Marnie tells me?'

'I'm a computer programmer,' Ronan said.

'Well, you'd need your fingers working for that...' Harry opened a needle and checked Ronan's sensation more thoroughly as Marnie stood wondering if Harry was thinking he'd been brought in under false pretences.

'He's a very good pianist,' Marnie said. 'I didn't mean to make it sound like he was a maestro.'

'You didn't,' Harry said. He looked at Ronan. 'I'm sure you've realised that this injury is more than just a straightforward cut that can simply be stitched.'

'I pretty much knew straight away,' Ronan said. 'Will I still be able to play?' he asked, and Marnie found she was holding her breath as Harry dealt with the issue that she hadn't been able to talk about during the journey to the hospital. 'I mean, will I still be able to play at the level I was?'

'First I have to do my part,' Harry said, 'then the rest is going to be up to you.' Harry was honest. 'You'll be in a splint afterwards and looking at a lot of hand therapy. It's early days yet. For now we have to repair it and then see where we're at.'

'Harry's an amazing hand surgeon,' Marnie said. 'You couldn't be in better hands.'

'Excuse the pun,' Harry said, and Ronan gave a pale smile, then Harry went through more of what Ronan could expect. He was very calming—even as he discussed the extensive rehabilitation ahead. 'Right, we'll get you around to our minor theatre. The tendon's still partially intact so I'll be able to do it under a block, but first I need to go and get something to eat as it might take a while.'

'Can I have a drink?' Ronan asked.

'Sorry,' Harry said with a brief smile. 'That was cruel of me. No, you can't have anything in case you do end up needing a general anaesthetic.'

'You're doing him tonight?' Marnie checked.

'I told you I was!' There was a slight edge of irritation to Harry's voice when he addressed Marnie, which he quickly fought to check. 'I'm not available tomorrow and the sooner that it's repaired the better.'

'I can assist.'

Harry rolled his eyes. 'Have you looked in the mirror?' Marnie hadn't. 'Even your lips are white. I'll ask Kelly.'

Kelly came in and introduced herself to Ronan and

Marnie excused herself as Kelly said she was going to get him into a gown and prepared for Theatre.

'I'll be waiting in my office,' Marnie said, but of course it didn't end there because Kelly was asking about Ronan's next of kin. 'I should ring Mum and tell her.'

'Not tonight.' Ronan shook his head. 'Please, Marnie, can that wait till tomorrow?'

Marnie was only too pleased to agree.

She gave Ronan a brief cuddle and then headed to the kitchen for another glass of water, where she found Harry feeding bread into the toaster.

'Thank you for coming back to do this.'

'It's fine,' Harry said.

'What about the children?'

'Charlotte and Adam are staying the night at my parents'. I'm going to get them tomorrow.'

'I feel awful…'

'Well, don't. You were right not to want Adam hanging around the department—he has got chickenpox.'

'Oh, no,' Marnie said. 'I feel terrible that he doesn't have you tonight.'

The toast popped up and Harry started buttering it but he did turn and speak at the same time. 'Marnie, it's my job—it's what I do. It's what I've been *trying* to do since Jill died. I can't count the times I called Jill and said someone had come in and that I needed to be here…'

'It's appreciated.'

'Good. I am the best hand surgeon in this hospital. I'd want me for this.'

'I'd want you to,' Marnie said, and from nowhere, absolutely from nowhere, a blush spread over her cheeks and, given how pale she had been, there was no chance of hiding it. 'I meant—'

'It's fine.

The strangest thing was, as the colour soared up her cheeks, Harry, who never blushed, thought that he might be as well.

Or was it just terribly warm?

'The thing is—' Marnie started, but Harry interrupted.

'Right, now I would just like ten minutes' peace before I go and do surgery,' Harry said, and, taking his toasted sandwich, he stalked off to his office rather than the staffroom, but there was no peace to be had there either.

There was an inbox that was so full it spilled over the edges and he daren't check his emails because he'd need a week to get them clear.

Harry ate his sandwich then changed into scrubs and headed into the minor theatre where Ronan lay, chatting with Kelly, who was setting up for the operation.

'I was just telling Ronan that he's got his sister's hands.' Kelly smiled.

'I don't remember Marnie's being quite so hairy,' Harry said, as he put in the nerve block that would ensure Ronan couldn't feel anything during surgery. 'Your accent isn't as strong as Marnie's. Though I guess you were much younger when you came to Melbourne.'

'We came to Perth first,' Ronan told him, and it wasn't, Harry noted, just Ronan's hands that were similar to Marnie's—he could talk for Ireland too. 'But Dad got transferred to Melbourne a couple of years later. I don't really remember Perth. I think I remember more about Ireland, though I'm not sure if it's from going back or Mum talking about it. I've been back twice now, though Marnie goes back far more often. She misses it like crazy.'

Harry looked up. 'Didn't she want to emigrate?'

'No,' Roman said. 'Though she didn't want to leave Perth either. She always said the moment she turned eighteen and she had her own passport she'd be straight back to Ireland, but she got into nursing...' Ronan didn't continue.

He didn't have to.

Harry pretty much knew what had happened from there. As he waited for the block to take effect, he spent a moment thinking about Marnie.

Harry's heart seemed to constrict for a moment.

No wonder she was so tough, she'd had to learn how to be.

He checked each finger in turn, making sure that the anaesthetic had taken full effect before starting.

It was a very intricate operation, which required Harry to wear magnifying glasses and to focus extremely hard, but every now and then Kelly would take his glasses off and he would sit up straight for a moment and take a very brief break. Sometimes he found himself listening to Ronan and Kelly talking, mostly about music and computers, but now and then the conversation drifted to Marnie.

'I fight all the time with my sister,' Kelly was saying.

'It's not worth fighting with Marnie,' Ronan said. 'It's her way or the highway.'

Ten years older than Ronan, Marnie had, it would seem, been a second mum more than a sister to him.

Funny that he found out more about Marnie during a

sixty-minute operation than he had in all the time he'd worked alongside her.

'You're done,' Harry said, finishing off the splint. 'For tonight you'll stay in and we'll keep it elevated. You'll be given analgesics as it's going to be painful as sensation starts to return and I want to start you on antibiotics. The last thing we want is an infection.'

'Harry will come in and see you tomorrow,' Kelly said, 'and then you'll probably be discharged home.'

'Actually, I'm off tomorrow,' Harry said. 'It will be Dr Vermont and then there will be follow-ups in the hand clinic and a referral to the hand therapist.' He really couldn't tell Kelly and Ronan his news before he'd told Dr Vermont.

And Marnie too.

'Take care,' Harry settled for instead.

He had a drink before heading into Marnie's office, and when he got there she was sitting with her head in her hands, just as he had in the car earlier, as if bracing herself for the news that her brother had died!

'It's a tendon!' Harry said.

'I know.' Marnie looked up and there was a grimace on her face as she tried to force a smile. 'I just came off the phone to my mother—you wouldn't believe me if I told you how difficult that conversation was. She actually rang me and I caved and told her about Ronan's accident.'

'Oh.' Harry was surprised. He'd got the impression they barely spoke. 'I thought you didn't…' Harry halted. It was none of his business.

'We may not talk about certain things,' Marnie said, 'but, as difficult as they can be, I love my parents very much.' Marnie lifted her eyes to the ceiling. 'Ronan's accident is all my fault.'

'Of course it is,' Harry said calmly.

'If she woke up tomorrow and the sky was purple, she'd be on the phone, blaming me.'

'Well, if you'd just kept the tin-opener in the second drawer, all this could have been avoided.' Harry wagged his finger and somehow made her smile, and then she looked away because Harry was usually in a suit. She didn't think she'd seen so much of his skin before, at least, not this close up. His arms were very long but muscular too, and she could see just a smattering of chest hair when Marnie was rather more used to smooth. He looked tired yet there was a certain air of elation to him that Marnie didn't quite understand.

'I've managed to convince her to not visit till tomorrow, it would be after ten before she got here. How did the repair go?'

'Very well,' Harry said. 'Kelly will be bringing him round to the obs ward soon....' His voice trailed off as his pager went and Harry read the message, then asked if he could use her phone.

'Sure.'

'Hi, Mum,' Harry said. 'Yes, sorry about that, it took a bit longer than I thought. Put him on.' Marnie tried to look away as he chatted to Adam but her eyes kept drifting towards him.

To think she'd expected him to have a bit of a paunch by now—he had a very flat stomach and very muscular legs and, as he sat on the edge of her desk as he spoke, Marnie could see the hair on his arms.

He was, as if Marnie didn't already know, very, very beautiful.

Dangerous too.

Dangerous, because Marnie rarely opened up to anyone, yet with Harry she did too easily. Even the brief conversation about her phone call with her mother was far more than she would usually share and Marnie's foot tapped, with tension rather than impatience, as Harry spoke on.

She wanted to get away from him.

She wanted to go home, just so she could give herself a good talking to.

After speaking to Adam, he chatted at length to Charlotte, though he could see Marnie's foot tapping in mid-air out of the corner of his eye, but then she stood and went and stared out of the window as Harry laughed and talked on. 'What do you mean, it's not fair?' He spoke a little while longer and then said goodnight and put down the phone.

'Charlotte's jealous that Adam has got chickenpox,' Harry said to Marnie, who was still looking out of the window. He watched her shoulders move in a small laugh and then wretched guilt at keeping him from his children caught up and Marnie turned her head.

'Say it,' Marnie challenged, her blue eyes glittering.

'Say what?' Harry frowned.

'Go on,' Marnie insisted. 'Say whatever's on your mind.'

Harry gave a wry grin. 'Such as…'

'It's different when it's you or your family,' Marnie offered, turning to face him.

'That's not what's on my mind.'

'Hypocrite, then?' Marnie suggested.

'No…' He was walking towards her.

'Just say it.'

'You're quite sure?' Harry said, and it was at that moment exactly that she realised that Harry had something else on his mind, something very similar to what was on hers as she saw the burn of arousal in his eyes. 'You're quite sure that you want me to say what's on my mind?'

She looked at him properly then, saw the Harry she hadn't seen in a very long time. There was an energy to him that had been missing, an energy that she hadn't seen since a certain night in the doctors' mess when he'd asked why she was leaving so soon—only this time it was potent.

If he'd been on the other side of the desk, she might have had a chance to deny him. Might have been able to rein in common sense and come up with some witty retort that would end things before they were started.

Except he was standing in front of her. She could smell the lust, the want, the need, and it was intoxicating and, quite simply, Marnie couldn't resist. One small nod was all the affirmation needed for Harry to tell his truth.

'I want you.'

His mouth came down and crushed Marnie's. He was so tall he had to, not just stoop but almost lift her to exert the pressure that this kiss demanded.

Marnie was no stranger to lust but she'd never felt it as ferociously or as deliciously as this.

Every snap, every snarl, every flirt, every tease was now being paid back tenfold by the probe of his tongue and the roaming of his hands.

Or was it her hands? One was in his hair, messing it to the way she had first seen it, the other moving down over his arm, but only so she could force a space to get to his back and to the taut buttocks she had admired from behind on far too many occasions.

It was lust uninterrupted, Marnie for once out of control, and she liked it.

'I remember you now…' He was opening the buttons to her navy dress and not for a moment did she think of halting him. Whatever was wrong in the world, this was the antidote and for now, this moment, they celebrated their discovery. 'Harry…' She could feel his arousal pressed into her; one hand was lifting her dress and he moaned into her mouth as he felt her soft thigh. As he slipped his hand higher, it was Marnie who moaned.

'Not here…' Marnie pulled back but her words were contrary to her actions; she was kissing his face, her hands lifting his top just to get to his skin, just to bury her mouth in his salty chest and taste him. 'Not here…' Marnie moaned again, and Harry almost came as he looked down at her licking her lips. 'Harry.' She was wrestling for control. Hell, she was the nurse unit manager, her mother could have changed her mind and arrived any minute, Kelly could knock at the door…

'I don't get involved with anyone at work.'

'Not a problem.' Harry turned the lock on her door and then picked her up and lifted her over to the desk. 'I just resigned.'

# CHAPTER SEVEN

'YOU WHAT?'

He was back to her mouth but now Marnie understood his earlier elation.

'Harry? You can't.'

'I already have.' He looked down at her breasts, pale in their bra, and he wanted to bury his face in them, to simply forget, but he knew then that the moment was over and, still breathless, still hard, still wanting, he did the right thing and started to do the buttons up.

Yes, it had been about escape, Marnie realised, for a man who wasn't thinking particularly straight, and it was time for her to steer things towards reason.

'Harry…' She was struggling to get her breath back too. His groin was still leaning into hers, her body still tingling and aroused, and it would be so much easier to dive back to his mouth, but instead she offered no resistance as he straightened up. In fact, she shivered a little at the coolness when he was gone.

'I apologise.'

'For what?' Marnie attempted to laugh it off. 'I didn't notice me doing much resisting, but I don't think a quick shag on the office desk is going to solve things.'

He smiled at her directness. 'I don't think anything

is going to solve things,' he admitted. 'Might be nice to give it a try, though.'

Marnie retied her hair and brushed her dress down then unlocked the door. 'As if the person on the other side wouldn't know what was going on!'

Harry wanted to pull her down to his lap, perhaps take it more slowly this time, take her home even—after all, he had the house to himself. He didn't want to think about what he had done—the handing-in-the-notice part, not the Marnie part. He'd love to think more about that! No, it was handing in his notice. His ten-past-five phone call to Admin that he didn't want to examine, but Marnie refused to let it drop.

'You love your job, Harry.'

'I love it when I get to do it,' Harry said.

'So what are you going to do?'

'Go private,' Harry said. 'Hand surgery…'

'Will it be enough?' Marnie asked. 'Harry, you love this place…'

'I love my children more,' Harry said. 'There will still be accident and emergency departments needing a consultant in a few years' time—right now the children need some stability.'

'You can give them that,' Marnie said, horrified to think of the department without him. Harry and Dr Vermont were the lynchpins of the place. Yes, there were new doctors starting but they needed guidance.

'It's not up for discussion,' Harry said. 'The deed is done.'

'How long's your notice?'

'Two weeks,' Harry said, 'but I'm not working it. I'm taking parental leave to look after the children.'

'That's it?' Marnie said, understanding more and

more where the emotion of the night had come from. Harry really was leaving the place.

'That's it,' Harry said. 'There will probably be a leaving do in a couple of weeks, which I'll do my best to get to—' his voice was wry '—providing I can get a babysitter.'

'Harry—'

'Leave it.'

Sex would have been so much easier.

Harry hadn't cried since the night before he'd lost Jill. He hadn't been able to, there had been two bewildered twins to look after and Jill's shocked parents as well as his own—all his grieving had been done on the ICU ward before the machines had been turned off, yet, on this day, he was precariously close to breaking down.

He loved his job—an A and E consultant was all he had ever wanted to be and it was killing him to walk away.

Yet it was impossible to stay.

'Come home with me?' he said, looking at her very full mouth.

She could feel his eyes there, wanted again the weight of his kiss, but not like this…

'Harry, if I come home with you, it will be to talk some sense into you.'

'You can talk sense into me over dinner.'

She was tempted, so tempted, and that was the problem.

She wanted dinner with Harry, and bed, and she wanted to know so much more about him. She looked into eyes that were as come hither as they had been all those years ago, only now it would be so terribly easy to say yes.

Dinner with Harry would be lovely.

Bed even better.

There was just one little problem.

Make that two.

How could she best put it?

'I'm busy tonight, Harry,' Marnie said. 'What about Saturday?'

It hit Harry where she had intended to—right below the belt. Ardour faded as Marnie flexed the freedom muscle she guarded so fiercely. It would take a whole lot more than the occasional night off, babysitter permitting, to lure Marnie.

'Saturday might be a problem.'

Yes, she'd rather thought that it might.

'I'm going to go,' Harry said, but Marnie hadn't finished discussing her favourite subject.

Work.

'Harry, you're rushing into this decision—'

'I'm not rushing into anything,' Harry interrupted. 'If anything, this is long overdue. I'll come in and say goodbye to everyone when the time's right, but now I need to take care of my kids.'

He left her in the office, stunned from the news, from his kiss, from the sudden absence of Harry.

He wanted his last walk through *his* department alone.

''Night, Harry,' Kelly called.

''Night,' Harry called back. 'Thanks for your help with Ronan.'

He nodded to Helen, the locum who was covering for tonight, and, yes, the place was going to struggle, but it would soon move on. Juan would be back and Dr Cooper would start.

He'd just miss it so much.

Dr Vermont broke the news to the staff the next morning.

'We all know what a struggle it's been for Harry since Jill died. It's not an easy decision to make but for Harry it must have been the right one.'

Marnie felt terrible—she kept beating herself up, wondering if she'd just been a bit more flexible the outcome might have been different. And, on top of all that, over and over she kept remembering the steamy kiss they had shared. Yes, she fancied Harry, but the impact of him close up had shaken her more than she had thought it would. Still, she didn't have much time to dwell on it. As the staff spilled out of the staffroom, all talking about the news of Harry's sudden departure, Marnie walked straight into her parents.

'Mum!' Marnie gave her mother a smile and a kiss.

'What was he doing, using a knife to open a can?' Maureen accused.

'You can't blame Marnie for this.' Ronan laughed and tried to sit up with one hand attached to a pole as Dr Vermont came over to visit the patients in the obs ward.

'Mr Johnson,' Dr Vermont said, and Marnie smothered a smile as her father stepped forward, because Dr Vermont was speaking to Ronan. 'I hear everything went very well last night.' Marnie took down Ronan's hand from the pole and Dr Vermont checked the colour and sensation in the tip of Ronan's heavily splinted finger. He asked Ronan to try and move the finger and

Marnie watched with relief as the pink tip lifted just a little.

'You can feel this?' Dr Vermont checked as Ronan closed his eyes.

'Yes.'

Marnie let out a breath and then smiled as Ronan again said he could feel the touch of the needle as Dr Vermont checked the other side.

'It's doing everything it should,' Dr Vermont said. 'I'll see you in two days and then...' He hesitated as he looked at the address on the admission notes. 'Do you do want to be followed up here?' Dr Vermont checked. 'I see that you live quite a distance away.'

'Here would be great,' Ronan said. 'I can catch up with Marnie when I have an appointment.'

'It's the only way you'll get to see her,' Maureen Johnson muttered, and Marnie chose not to respond to her mother's barb and stayed silent as Dr Vermont spoke to Kelly. 'Could you schedule in some hand appointments for Mr Johnson?' he asked, and then turned to Ronan. 'If we book the next couple in, at least you'll know what you're doing.'

He gave a few more instructions and then moved on to the next bed.

'You can get dressed,' Marnie said to her brother a little while later when Kelly had come off the phone.

'I'll give him a hand,' Kelly said, as she pulled the curtains around the bed. 'I've made the appointments. We'll see you the day after tomorrow and then again on the twenty-third. Is that okay?'

Ronan looked up at his sister, but thankfully the curtain swished past and Marnie had a second to collect herself before she answered for him.

'The twenty-third's fine,' Marnie said, and deliberately didn't look at her mum as the one date they all dreaded was, for the first time in a very long time, mentioned.

Trust the Irish to not make a fuss when it mattered!

# CHAPTER EIGHT

'This too will pass,' Dr Vermont said. 'It's my favourite saying and one I've used often over the years working in this place.'

It was two in the morning and Marnie was on her first night shift at Bayside. It had been difficult logistically without Harry as they struggled to cover the department but, more than logistics, he was sorely missed by everyone, including Marnie.

Especially Marnie.

She was missing him on a whole different level, though—the flirting, the teasing, just the fun of having someone as shamelessly male as Harry around.

Not that she told that to Dr Vermont, of course. They were going through the doctors' roster for the next couple of weeks and trying to cover the gaps as they ate Marnie's chicken and mango salad that she had brought in from home.

'I've been through staff shortages, work to rule, the whole lot,' Dr Vermont continued. 'And, though it feels like it will never end, invariably it does. It will all get sorted, and I'll say it again—this is not your fault.'

Dr Vermont was lovely and extremely practical when Marnie had confessed what was on her mind.

'Even if you had let Charlotte, or was it Adam, lie on the sofa, this still would have happened.'

'I was trying to make things easier for him,' Marnie admitted. 'I know I looked like I was being mean when I told him to go home a couple of times but I was trying to show him that he wasn't completely indispensable...'

Dr Vermont laughed. 'Well, you did!'

'I know.' Marnie ran a worried hand over her forehead. 'I was trying to prove to him that we could call the trauma team or the medics, that it didn't have to all fall to him,' Marnie explained. 'I just wish that I'd handled things a little differently. I wish—'

'Marnie,' Dr Vermont interrupted, 'Harry has been struggling to find balance between work and home since Jill died. I honestly don't know how he's managed to do this job for so long without a partner. Marjorie, my wife, managed to have a career and raise our family, but we had a lot of support too. Harry's sister and parents all live a couple of hours away.'

Dr Vermont thought for a moment. 'I could not have done this job and raised a family without Marjorie. Even when the place is fully covered you can still expect to be called in. I can't tell you how many nights I've been on take and yet I've still rung Harry to come in to give an opinion, or there's been a multiple trauma and another pair of hands has been needed. Marjorie was more than used to it—long before coffee machines were around she made sure there was a flask of coffee by my bed so that I could have a drink as I drove in.' He smiled at the memory and so did Marnie. 'What I'm trying to explain...'

His voice trailed off and Marnie looked up from her salad, waiting for him to continue. 'Dr Vermont?'

Marnie stood. For a bizarre, still hopeful, second, she hoped that he might have fallen asleep in mid-sentence, but even as she called his name again, Marnie knew what was happening. As she dropped her salad and raced around her desk, he took a couple of laboured breaths and she watched as Dr Vermont's skin tinged to grey and he let out an ominous gurgle.

'Dr Vermont!' Marnie shouted, as she tried to locate a carotid pulse. Her mind was in twenty places—she held onto his shoulder as he toppled forward and Marnie knew she couldn't get to the phone or door without him falling to the floor.

'Can I have some help?' Marnie shouted, trying to break his fall and kick the chair away at the same time, but no one was answering. 'Can someone…?' She laid Dr Vermont on the floor and raced to open the door, shouting loudly for help as she grabbed the phone from her desk.

Summon help, the nursing part of her brain told her, yet she wanted to start compressions. Marnie put out a crash call, explaining to the startled switchboard operator that she had to be specific. 'Code red, Emergency Department, in the nurse unit manager's office.' She was shouting, Marnie realised, when usually she was calm. 'Make sure you say that.'

She started compressions as the intercom crackled into life. But, alerted by her shouting, Clive, the night porter, came running.

'Oh, no…' he moaned, but he knew, without Marnie telling him, exactly what to do.

'I'll get help.'

'Get the crash trolley as well,' Marnie called, as she carried on with the compressions.

There was nothing emergency staff dreaded more than family or friends being brought in, but to have a colleague suddenly collapse at work was truly awful.

The staff came running and in no time Marnie's office looked more like the resuscitation room. Eric, the on-call cardiologist, arrived first. His shocked expression as he saw Dr Vermont lying on the floor, his shirt open, his glasses off, was one Marnie would never forget.

Abby was trying not to cry as she charged the defibrillator and Marnie could see the resident's hand shaking as he delivered yet another shock.

'Nothing.'

'We need to get him to Resuscitation,' the cardiologist said. He was breathless from running but helped to lift Dr Vermont onto the trolley that Clive had brought in. They sped Dr Vermont through the department and the resuscitation continued en route—Marnie kneeling on the trolley to continue the compressions as Abby pushed oxygen in with an Ambu bag.

The night supervisor came, as she often did when an emergency page had been put out, but she too had run just a little harder when she had heard the strange alert.

'It's Dr Vermont,' Marnie said, stepping down as Eric took over the compressions, frantically trying to pump the medications through Dr Vermont's system in the hope the next shock would have some effect.

It didn't.

'We need to let his wife know,' the night supervisor said as the team grimly worked on.

Marnie's hands were shaking as she went through the contact sheets, dreading the thought of calling Mrs

Vermont in the middle of the night to tell her that her husband was critically ill.

'Get Harry to call her,' Eric shouted over. 'Has he been told what's going on?'

'Harry no longer works here,' Marnie said, and Eric shot her a wide-eyed look.

'I can guarantee Harry would want to be the one to tell her,' Eric said.

'Even if he's on leave, Harry needs to be informed,' the night supervisor said. 'Right now the emergency department doesn't have a consultant.'

Harry didn't deliberately not pick up the first time the phone rang. He was putting anti-itch cream on a miserable Adam, who had woken at one a.m. and couldn't get back to sleep.

'So much for a mild dose,' Harry said to his son. Apparently you could get a mild dose after a child had been immunised. Harry had found all the immunisation records and had spent half an hour looking at Jill's handwriting—she had recorded every milestone, every little detail of their little lives and, yes, bang on the suggested dates, Charlotte and Adam had received their immunisations.

Adam getting chickenpox was just another thing that had gone wrong on top of another thing that had gone wrong, Harry was thinking when the phone rang.

Would they not just let him leave? Harry sighed, letting it ring out, but then, worried it might be his parents, he tucked Adam in and went and checked the machine.

'Harry, it's Marnie, could you call me back at work please?' He could hear the strain in her voice. 'I'm sorry to call you but it is an emergency.'

What the hell was he supposed to do from here? Harry thought, picking up the phone when it rang again.

'Harry, it's Marnie.'

'Marnie, I've got a child who's sick—'

'Harry, please,' Marnie broke in. 'I have some very difficult news to tell you.' Harry heard she was struggling and the line went very quiet for a moment before he spoke.

'Go on.'

'Dr Vermont collapsed a short while ago,' Marnie said, and she heard his sharp intake of breath as she spoke on. 'He's in full cardiac arrest.'

'Oh, no.'

'We're doing everything we can but I have to tell you, Harry…' She glanced over, they were still going but more and more it was looking hopeless. 'It doesn't look good at all.'

'Is Marjorie there?'

'It's only just happened,' Marnie said. 'I was just away to inform her when Eric said that you'd want to know and perhaps be the one to tell her.'

Harry sat on the edge of his bed and he remembered the kindness the Vermonts had shown him; he remembered all they had done for him when Jill's accident had happened, and, yes, it was right that he be the one to tell Marjorie.

'I've got the twins…' He didn't want to wake them up and drag them out; he didn't want that for them but sometimes, no matter how inconvenient, certain things just had to be done. There was no choice—the doctor in charge of the department was critically ill, no doubt the staff were distraught and, given Dr Vermont had given more than thirty years of his life to the place, certainly his wife deserved to hear it from him. 'I'll ring her now and then I'll pick her up,' Harry said. 'Marnie, I'll have to bring the twins in.'

There was no argument this time.

And no little barbs either.

It was all too sad.

'Adam's infectious, probably Charlotte is too,' Harry said.

'So were half the patients that came through tonight,' Marnie said. 'The observation ward is empty, I'll make up two beds and close it off for further admissions.' Her voice was back to practical and it helped because Harry felt as though the whole pack of cards was falling again, just as he'd almost rebuilt it.

'Do you need Marjorie's number?' Marnie asked.

Of course, he already had it.

Harry rang off and he'd have loved to gather his thoughts for a moment but instead he dressed and then woke the twins and put them into their dressing gowns.

'I'm sorry, guys,' he said as he carried them down the stairs and out into the night, 'but Dr Vermont is very sick and we need to go and get Marjorie so that she can be with him.'

Only when they were strapped in and already nearly back to sleep did Harry stand in the driveway and call Marjorie.

He told her what was happening as best he could, and of course he knew Marjorie well, knew she would be dressing as they spoke and about to get into her car and fly through the night to be beside the man she had been married to for forty years.

'I'm on my way now, Marjorie,' Harry said. 'I'll be there in a few minutes.'

He was—Marjorie was out on the street and she was trying not to cry as she climbed in

'You shouldn't have brought the children out,' Marjorie told him. 'I could have got there myself.'

Except her knees were bobbing up and down as she tried to sit still, the adrenaline coursing through her as the enormity of what was happening started to take hold. 'Is he....?' She couldn't even say it. 'I'd rather know now.'

'They were working on him when I last spoke to the hospital,' Harry said.

Harry didn't know if it was a good sign or bad when he saw Abby and Marnie waiting for them in the ambulance area.

'There's half the hospital in with Dr Vermont,' Marnie said as Harry came around and briefly pulled her aside. 'Abby said that twins would know her.'

'How is he?'

'We're just waiting for Marjorie,' Marnie said, taking a sleepy Charlotte as Abby carried Adam, freeing Harry to help Marjorie into the department.

Harry knew from her voice and words that they were just keeping things going till Marjorie arrived.

'Hello.' Marnie felt the sleepy weight of Charlotte stir in her arms as she lowered her onto a bed. 'Daddy's just in with a patient; he said to make sure you had a comfy bed. I'm Marnie.'

'I know,' Charlotte said, and turned over and went back to sleep.

Adam was a bit tearful and asked where his dad was. 'I'm here, Adam.' Harry came in at that moment. 'You can go back to sleep.'

'How's Dr Vermont?'

'He's not well at all,' Harry said, 'but Marjorie's with him so that's good. You just turn over and go to sleep and I'll let you know more in the morning.'

Marnie felt a swallow in her throat at the disruption to their little lives. Saw how, with barely a murmur of protest, Adam did as he was told and rolled over.

'What's happening round there?' Marnie asked once they had moved away from the sleeping twins.

'Marjorie told them to stop.' Harry's voice wavered and Marnie watched as he struggled to keep it together. After all, less than half an hour ago he'd been putting cream on Adam's spots.

He went over to Abby, who was sitting at the desk, crying quietly, and put a hand on her shoulder, but he spoke to Marnie. 'I think you might want to put the ambulances on diversion—a lot of the staff are going to be really upset.'

'Sure.' Marnie nodded. 'I've arranged for a couple of nurses to come down from the wards to help out.'

'Good. Are you okay?' Harry asked.

'I'll be fine,' Marnie said, though she could feel tears stinging at the back of her nose, but, really, it wasn't her place to be upset. She'd only known Dr Vermont a short while and, more importantly than that, she was the manager. Like Harry, tonight really wasn't about her—it was about doing their best for Dr Vermont and his family and the colleagues who would miss him so much.

'Who found him?' Harry asked. 'Eric said that he collapsed in his office.'

'We were in my office,' Marnie corrected. 'We were having supper and talking…' She pressed her fingers into her eyes for a brief moment and then recovered. 'He just stopped talking in mid-sentence.'

'You might need to speak to Marjorie,' Harry said, as he headed back out there. 'She might want to hear what happened from you.'

Marnie nodded. 'Harry!' She called him back. 'I don't know his first name.'

'Gregory,' Harry said. 'Gregory Vermont.'

Marjorie was as lovely as Dr Vermont had been and, though devastated, she was very stoic too.

'He spoke very highly of you,' Marjorie said when she'd been in to see her husband and was sitting down in his office, which was filled not just with his many certificates but with photos of his family too. 'He said you were going to bring a bit of order to the place...' She swallowed. 'Harry said that you were with him when it happened?'

'We were in my office,' Marnie said. 'We were having our supper break and talking about...' She glanced at Harry, who filled in for her.

'The Harry problem?'

'The staff issues,' Marnie said. 'He was actually talking about you. How you'd managed to have a career but how he couldn't have been an emergency doctor without all your support.' There was a flash of tears in Marnie's eyes as she recalled the conversation, such a simple one at the time but it was so much more meaningful now. Marjorie gave a grateful smile as Marnie recalled Dr Vermont's final moments, gave her the comfort of knowing he had been speaking about his wife and a marriage that had so clearly worked.

'He was telling me how you used to keep a flask of coffee by the bedside. Then he just stopped speaking, Marjorie,' Marnie said. 'There was no pain, no discomfort, I promise you that. For a moment I honestly thought that he'd fallen asleep...'

She heard a sniff and looked over. It was Harry. He'd been holding Marjorie's hand but now it was more that she was holding his.

'He thought the world of you,' Marjorie said to Harry, and Marnie watched as Harry nodded.

She felt as if she was glimpsing something incredibly private as, just for a moment, Harry gave in to his grief and screwed up his face, trying and failing not to weep.

'When you came to do your residency, he said what a great emergency doctor you'd make,' Marjorie said, and Harry nodded again but pulled himself together, when perhaps he didn't have to. Dr Vermont and Marjorie were, Marnie was fast realising, so much more than a colleague and his wife to Harry. They clearly went back years.

Marjorie went to sit with her husband again and to speak with her family, who were starting to arrive.

It was a wretched night and looked no better by morning. Marnie had placed the department on bypass so that no ambulances were bringing patients in, though the walking wounded still trickled in. There were a couple of ward nurses helping out and one of the surgeons had come down to assist too. The nursing staff had known Dr Vermont for a lot longer than she had and needed each other more than they needed her, so Marnie took herself around to the observation ward and sat with the twins. She went through the doctors' rosters and tried to work out how the department could possibly work without even one senior doctor.

'Are you okay?' Harry came in a little later to check on the twins. He didn't want to wake them again and also wanted to be there to tell the day staff the sad news himself when they started to arrive.

'Of course.' Marnie nodded. 'You?'

'I just can't take it in,' Harry admitted, sitting down at the desk beside her and talking in a low voice so as not to disturb the twins. Harry picked up the doctors' roster. It was already a mess—a mass of red crossings-out and locums and gaps in the schedule, and that had been before Dr Vermont had so suddenly died.

'So much for leaving,' Harry said.

'What are you going to do?'

'I don't know,' Harry admitted. 'I've just about used up every last favour. I'll have to do something, though. I simply can't imagine this place without him. He and Marjorie were so good to me when Jill had her accident...' He hesitated, not sure if Marnie was interested in hearing his thoughts or if she was just being polite.

'Go on,' Marnie offered, but Harry looked over at the sleeping twins and shook his head. 'Not here.'

They moved to the small kitchenette where they could talk and still keep an eye on the children.

'Jill was on ICU for two weeks after the accident.' Harry paused for a moment, which he so rarely did—he simply didn't have the time or the reserves to examine the past, but the emotion of losing such a close friend and colleague forced a moment of reflection. 'Jill had massive head injuries.'

'How?'

'A car accident. The only saving grace was that she didn't have the twins with her at the time. I knew as soon as I saw her that things were never going to be the same again and so did Dr Vermont. Even if she had lived, her injuries were so severe that things would never have been the same,' Harry explained. 'Dr Vermont told me that the time Jill was on ICU was my time. I can't really explain it, but we both knew at some level how difficult things would be, whether she lived or died. Cathy, my sister, had the twins and brought them in now and then to see their mum.

'Dr Vermont took care of the department. Marjorie brought dinner in for me every night and clothes, and just did so many things for me that I didn't even notice. I was so focused on the time I had left with Jill. I think I did all my grieving in ICU. I have bad days of course, but, really, when she died it wasn't about Jill, or Jill and I any more, or me, it was about the twins and work and just surviving.' He looked at Marnie, suddenly aware that his words might be hurting her for reasons of her own. 'Was it the same for you?'

'No,' Marnie admitted. 'The whole time Declan was in ICU I was convincing myself that he'd live and making plans for taking him home. Right till the last day I thought that he'd make it.' Marnie shook her head—she just didn't want to go there.

As the day staff arrived and the news was broken there were tears on the floor and more tears in the staffroom. Marnie worked her way through the contact sheets, ringing the staff who were not on duty today, or not due in till later, to let them know what had happened.

It was a department in mourning but, of course, the patients continued to arrive.

'I've come to get the twins.' It was Harry's sister, Marnie could tell. Her face was strained and yet she gave Harry a hug when he came over.

'I'm sorry, Harry. I know he meant the world to you.'

'Thanks.'

'The thing is…'

Harry halted her.

'I know you can't keep doing this,' Harry said for her. 'If you can just help me out till the funeral.'

It was close to eleven by the time Marnie got home and she had to be back there at eight for her night shift.

Despite the warmth of the house, Marnie was shivering as she climbed into bed and recalled her last conversation with Dr Vermont.

This too will pass.

Yes, Marnie thought, her body tired but her mind just too busy for sleeping.

When?

# CHAPTER NINE

THERE WEREN'T JUST cracks appearing, there were gaping holes in the roster and a couple of nights Marnie was close to putting the department on bypass again. Harry's sister had taken the children for the rest of the week and he was covering the department as best he could but, of course, he couldn't work twenty-four hours a day. He told Admim that he would work till the funeral on Thursday but, after that, it was up to them to find a replacement.

Sheldon was looking boot-faced when he came on duty on the morning of the funeral to work alongside yet another locum and one he didn't particularly like.

'Harry's hardly going to miss the funeral,' Marnie pointed out. 'But cover's been arranged for the weekend. Helen Cummings is covering the night shifts and she's really good. I worked with her a lot at the Royal...'

'What about next week?' Sheldon said, but Marnie had no answer.

'Who's in charge this morning?' Lillian asked.

Marnie explained what had been arranged. 'Miriam's working till ten then going to the funeral. I'm going to have a couple of hours' sleep in the on-call room and then we're running a skeleton staff till two p.m. and the place will be on bypass.'

Marnie watched Lillian's lips disappear. Putting the department on bypass cost the hospital a lot in fines, but Marnie almost dared Lillian to question the decision on the day of Dr Vermont's funeral. It was going to be huge—several surgical lists had been rescheduled so that colleagues could pay their respects, a huge entourage would be leaving from the hospital, then there would be drinks and refreshments for those who wanted them after the official wake. Whoever had said no one was indispensable had never met Dr Vermont.

'We're all trying our best,' Marnie said. 'I called Dr Cooper but he can't start any sooner as he's working his notice till the last day. I think I might have to call Juan...'

'He's on his honeymoon.' Even the hard-nosed Lillian was reluctant to go that far, or perhaps she knew Juan too well. He was one of the rare few who had worked to get balance in his life and knew his priorities. Terminating his honeymoon wouldn't be an option. 'I doubt he's going to fly back from Argentina,' Lillian said, but Marnie just shrugged.

'Well, he is a consultant, perhaps he'd want to know that the place is collapsing.'

'Rather you than me,' Lillian said.

Marnie checked the local time in Argentina on the computer and, seeing it was early evening, decided to give it a try, but even the switchboard operator was reluctant to give her an outside line.

'Yes, it's a mobile I'm trying to call!' Marnie rolled her eyes at Miriam, who had just come on. 'Well, I don't know his landline number in Argentina, he could be anywhere. I just want to be put through to his mobile…' She was halted from continuing as the receiver was taken from her hand. Marnie turned to the delicious sight of Harry in a black suit and tie and, though it was expertly knotted, it was just a tiny bit off centre and his collar needed arranging, but thankfully she managed to resist, focusing instead on the gorgeous waft of cologne.

'Our mistake,' Harry said to the switchboard operator. He hung up the phone and then looked down at Marnie. 'You'd really do it, wouldn't you?'

'Watch me!' Marnie said, trying to get at the phone, but Harry blocked her.

'You cannot call a man on his honeymoon to fly back to work.' Harry hadn't done a lot of smiling this week and he was trying not to now as he looked down in disbelief at Marnie. 'We're trying to prevent the next consultant dropping dead from a heart attack, Marnie.'

'Well, I'd want to know.'

'Really?' Harry checked. 'Lying by the pool on your honeymoon, next to the man of your dreams, you'd really want a phone call telling you to get back here.'

'Ha,' Marnie said. 'I hate sunbathing and there'll be no ring on this finger…' She held up that perfect finger in an almost inappropriate gesture. 'Anyway, Harry, you've no right to be stopping me. Soon this place won't be your problem any more.'

'Well, for this morning it still is and you are not ringing Juan.'

'Fine,' Marnie said, and turned to Miriam. 'I'm going to the doctors' on-call room to have a sleep. Wake me when you want to start getting ready for the funeral.'

She looked back to Harry. 'Good luck today. Are you speaking?'

'I am.' Harry grimaced. 'I'm just going to go and get my car washed and then—'

'You should have washed it on your way home last night.'

'I was tired.'

'Bet you wish you'd done it last night this morning!'

'No,' Harry lied. 'Actually, I'm going round to my office now to read through the speech and then go and sort out the car...'

'Keep it short.'

'Sorry?' She was telling him how to speak at a funeral!

'Short's better,' Marnie said.

'This from a woman who never stops talking? So you're an expert in funerals now, are you?'

'Actually, now you mention it...' She gave him a smile but then it turned to a more sympathetic one. 'I hope it goes as well as it can.'

'Thanks.'

'Harry.' She looked up at him, those blue eyes blazing, her lips worrying. 'I'm sorry, I just can't stop myself. It is a funeral you're going to after all...' Two very cold but terribly beautiful hands were at his neck, fixing his collar and tie.

'I can dress myself.'

'I know,' Marnie said, 'but you were right, Kelly.' She briefly glanced at Kelly, whose cheeks turned to ruby as she found out first hand that Marnie knew exactly what was being said about her. 'I think I do have a touch of OCD and I just cannot let you go without fixing your collar, Harry.' Oh, it was perfect now, collar down, knot in the centre. 'After all, you're representing the department!'

It wasn't intimate in the least, Harry told himself, and that was confirmed two minutes later when he saw her in the corridor, dusting down Eric's shoulders with a lint brush she just happened to keep in her office.

No, it wasn't intimate, but why could he still feel her fingers on his neck?

Why, when he saw from his office Marnie disappearing into the on-call room, did he sit there, wondering if she'd undress for bed?

Oh, help, Harry thought as she came out shoeless in stockinged feet with her hair down and returned a moment later with a pair of scrubs in her hand to change from that navy dress into pyjamas.

No, the little finger gesture hadn't been inappropriate—what was inappropriate was his thoughts on the morning of Dr Vermont's funeral.

He got up and closed the door, so as not to think of her.

It didn't work.

She'd drive you crazy, Harry told himself.

And as for bed, Harry attempted to alleviate the ache in his groin with the thought of Marnie moaning that she'd just changed the sheets, or maybe putting little towels down in case he dared to so much as spill a drop.

'Filthy business!' He could almost hear her saying it and, yes, that thought almost worked, except he remembered only too well their kiss and two minutes later Harry gave up focusing on the speech and headed out to get the car washed.

Anything for the distraction.

Marnie, his mind had decided, would be deliciously filthy.

'Marnie!'

Marnie peeled her eyes open as she heard Miriam's voice at the door. 'Marnie.'

'I'm up,' Marnie called, and on autopilot headed to the sink and brushed her teeth. There was *nothing* worse than a two-hour sleep after a night shift.

Well, there was a whole lot worse, Marnie told herself as she washed her face, but the point she was making to herself was that getting up from a short sleep, when you really needed a long one, was one of the reasons she had always loathed nights.

Marnie stood shivering in scrubs and a cardigan in the kitchen, pouring herself a very strong coffee as Harry breezed in with a load of glasses that were on loan to the department. He did a double-take when he saw the usually very groomed Marnie a good inch shorter without her low heels and as pale as the milk she was pouring into her coffee.

'I know.' She rolled her eyes. 'It should be me they're burying today.'

She dealt with death and all the horrible stuff with a black, wry humour that would offend some, but never him. Somehow, on not quite Harry's worst day, but it was certainly there in the rankings, she made him smile.

It felt strange as everyone started to leave. The department was on bypass and quiet, but all morning it had been a hub of activity, a meeting centre. Abby's tears had already started as everyone filed out to get into the cars and Harry put his arm around Abby and then patted his pockets.

'Here,' Marnie said, handing him a box of tissues from the bench, and then they were gone.

The department was eerily quiet. The locum was calm and efficient with the few patients they had but there was an immense sadness that simply wouldn't abate. Every time Marnie looked at the clock or paused a moment she thought about that last conversation with Dr Vermont or wondered how Marjorie was faring.

Harry too.

For that morning, at least, the focus wasn't on rosters or filling in shifts, it was on the huge loss—the tremendous gap that a wonderful man had left.

Staff started to arrive early in the afternoon and the staffroom filled with hospital personnel—those who had been to the funeral and those who hadn't been able to get away for it.

'How was it?' Marnie asked Harry. He seemed beyond exhausted, but had that grim-faced look of just pushing through.

'Awful.' Harry wasn't stopping. 'I just came in to drop some supplies off. Marjorie asked me to take some of the food from the wake for everyone here. I told her it had all been catered but she wanted to contribute to it too. Can you help me get some stuff out of the car?'

'Sure.'

'Where are the twins today?' Marnie asked, as they walked out into the sunshine on what would normally feel a glorious day.

'At Cathy's till this evening.' There were mountains of food, tray after tray of sandwiches and boxes of drinks, and they ended up loading one of the gurneys and covering it with a sheet before pushing it through the department and round to the staffroom.

'So, this is your last day?' Marnie asked.

'It has to be,' Harry said, as they unloaded the food and set up. 'Cathy's had to take this week off work.' He didn't want to think about it now—for the most part, they had Friday and the weekend covered.

'You go home, Marnie.' Miriam, back from the funeral, her eyes red rimmed, took over unloading the boxes. 'You must be exhausted. I hope you're not driving.'

'No.' Marnie shook her head. 'I'm taking a taxi.'

'I'll drive you,' Harry said.

'Shouldn't you stay for a bit…?' Marnie started, and then stopped. After all, it was the story of Harry's life at the moment and the reason he had no option but to quit his job.

'They're talking about building an extension in his name,' Harry said. As they walked to his car, Marnie was shivering again. 'The Vermont Wing.'

'That would be nice.'

'Well, there won't be a Worthington Wing.'

'Just as well,' Marnie said as they climbed into his car. 'Try getting your lips around that after a night shift.'

Harry actually laughed. 'Beach Road?' he said, because he remembered everything she had ever told him.

'The dodgy end.' Marnie smiled.

'I can't believe he won't get to retire,' Harry said as they drove out of the hospital. His phone was bleeping away but he just ignored it. 'Though he'd have hated retirement—even Marjorie said as much—he loved that place.'

'You do too.'

Emotional blackmail wasn't going to work on Harry.

He never took his eyes off the road. 'I love my kids. I need to put them first. Charlotte's becoming more pre-cocious by the minute, Adam...' He liked it that she didn't push things, just waited as he voiced a potential problem that he hadn't discussed with anyone. 'I think he's got a speech delay.' His knuckles were white on the wheel. 'I've been thinking it for months and I haven't even had time to do a thing about it.'

'Looks like I'll be ringing Juan to come back from his honeymoon, then.'

'You really aren't romantic?'

'Not at all,' Marnie said. 'Men always have to com-plicate things.' She watched as Harry's tense mouth curved into a smile—his problem was the same, but with women, of course. 'They say they want an inde-pendent woman,' Marnie continued. 'They insist they do but then they get all misty-eyed and start to ask strange things like could I possibly iron a shirt? Or they think that just because you had sex last night it means you're going to be overtaken by this sudden urge to cook for them...'

Harry laughed, really laughed, for the first time since he'd taken the call about Dr Vermont. It wasn't the saf-est conversation to be having right now. He turned and glanced at her. There was a smile on her lips as she looked out of the window, a smile that told him she knew she was flirting. His phone bleeped again. Harry went to get it, but seeing cyclists up ahead knew bet-ter than to risk it, but he was worried that it might be work. 'Can you get it out my pocket?'

She most certainly could.

Harry was used to making strange requests such as that one, used to concentrating on stitching, or something similar, as someone found his phone and held it for him to speak into. He could feel her bony fingers against his chest as her hand slipped inside his jacket and Marnie could feel the heat from his skin through his shirt.

'Mind on the road, Harry,' Marnie said, and he smiled. The air was almost crackling between them. 'You've a text from Cathy.'

'Which means Charlotte,' Harry translated. 'At least it isn't work.'

'What you need,' Marnie said, 'is a wife.'

'I've got one,' Harry said, and in a gesture that certainly wasn't insolent—in fact, for Marnie it was the nicest thing he could have done—Harry held up his ring finger.

'I know,' Marnie said, because she did know. She had a son. It didn't go away because time had passed.

He pulled up at her house and opened up the message.

'So that's that, then,' Harry said as he read it.

'Sorry?'

'I wasn't going to say anything but I was hoping that I might be able to juggle things next week—the incubation period is just about up and there was this tiny window of possibility that the twins could go back to day care on Monday...' He gave a wry laugh as he read out the text. 'Charlotte has spots—don't worry, right now she's delighted.'

'Poor Atlas,' Marnie said as she watched the load he was carrying drop just a touch heavier on his shoulders. She looked at his profile and knew she'd miss him.

A lot.

'Do you need to get back?'

'I'll call her,' Harry said. 'And see how she is.' Except his phone battery was almost flat. 'Can I use yours?'

'Sure.' She went to go in her bag to get it but changed her mind. 'Use the landline.'

'Marnie…' Harry started, and then changed his mind. 'Sure, a coffee would be great.' It was a long drive to his sister's after all.

But Marnie was over playing games.

'Harry, you *know* we're going to sleep together. So we can make this all awkward and have a coffee that neither of us wants and then a quick fumble at the door…' She loved it when he smiled.

'Won't it complicate things?'

'There's nothing complicated about sex.' Marnie smiled. 'And we don't work together any more.'

'I think—'

But she halted him. 'You've done enough thinking for the day.'

She was possibly the perfect woman for Harry right now, he decided as he tasted her moist, full lips.

And there was nothing nicer than the warmth of his kiss when you were freezing, Marnie told herself as his arms slid around hers. And could there be anyone better than Harry to get your second wind with? Because suddenly Marnie wasn't remotely tired.

'Come on,' Marnie said. 'Let's get you to bed!'

But first he called Charlotte and congratulated her on her spots.

'I'll stop and get some more supplies before I come and get you,' Harry said. 'Yep. Don't worry, I won't get there till dinner.' Marnie was taking off her cardigan as Cathy must have come on the phone. 'She's worried I'm going to pick her up before she gets to eat your pizza.' He looked at Marnie as he talked on about how today had gone well. Well, as well as funeral could go. 'Thanks for this week,' Harry said. 'No, Cathy, I get it. I know you can't take another week off…' He hesitated. 'No.' Harry's response was firm. 'Mum and Dad are okay for the odd night, but it's not fair to ask for a week.'

They just stared for a very long moment and there was something lovely about no longer working together, something really nice about being two people who were quite comfortable keeping their sex lives separate from the rest of their lives.

They both knew the other's rules.

They'd both wanted the other on sight.

'Come here,' Harry said, and it took just two words. Marnie stepped into his space and Harry looked down, lingering a moment safe in the knowledge there was no need for holding back now.

'You drove me crazy this morning.'

'I know.'

'You always do.'

'I know.' Marnie smiled.

She felt his mouth on hers, felt her tongue slide in and, yes, it was nice not to think.

Marnie, though she would never admit it to herself let alone Harry, was taken slightly aback by her own reaction to his mouth. She'd missed it, had been thinking about their kiss far more than she perhaps ought, and now he was back, his mouth sinking into hers, its demand building. She opened her eyes and saw Harry's were closed and it was an incredible turn-on to see him simply indulge. So lovely to feel his hands stop fighting their need for contact and roam free, down her waist, then to her bottom, and despite his height they were an incredible fit, Marnie thought, so incredible that it would be terribly easy to forget about bed.

Harry lifted her top, slid it over her head and moaned as his hands felt the bare skin he had craved. His fingers unhooked her bra and his mouth was enough to make her sink to her knees with Harry joining her.

'Harry...' She pulled back and he opened his eyes, waited for the inevitable excuses and the reasons that this was a terrible idea, but he still didn't know Marnie.

'I need to have a shower,' Marnie said, and he laughed for the second time in a very short space of time and, no, he didn't mind the delay in proceedings, especially with what she said next. 'I'd like to be clean before we get dirty.'

Marnie headed into her bedroom and picked up the alarm. 'What time do you need to leave?' she asked.

'Six.'

'I'll set it for five, then.' She was almost clinical in her approach yet for Harry it was sexy. He liked independence; heaven knew, there were so many people dependent on him. He liked the rarity of Marnie and her utter ease, combined with the delicious trepidation that he felt as she headed for the shower.

He heard the taps turn on as he closed the curtains of her bay window and undressed. It was an adult reprieve that had been building and with someone who fascinated him more and more. Someone with whom he could be himself, or rather he could go back to the man he had once been.

Naked, he walked into the bathroom and pulled back the curtain, stood watching her washing her hair, and she opened her eyes and smiled.

'You didn't come empty-handed, I hope.'

'No.'

'Come in, then.'

He picked up the soap and put the little silver wrapper in the holder, and there was nothing to stop them now.

'I hate showers,' Marnie said, looking down as his large hands lathered the soap and then slid over her breasts. 'Or maybe I don't.' He was as slow and as deliciously thorough as she had thought he would be. Marnie watched as he soaped her breasts, her nipples stretching and puckering, and then she took the soap from him, lathered her hands and then dropped it.

It was Harry who paused, stared down as her hands stroked the length of him, over and over. He stood, staring as if in some delicious hypnotic trance that they'd be jolted out of any second. Marnie knew it too, she felt the swell and the lift of the balls she cupped in her hand and she was so turned on watching Harry that she wouldn't have cared if his hand hadn't halted her.

He was struggling to hold back, and he kissed her till he was back from the edge. The shiver that went through her had nothing to with exhaustion or cold as Harry lowered his head to her breast.

Her breasts had been on his mind for so long, that long glimpse of them nestled in her lacy bra had been dancing in his mind's eyes since the kiss in her office. The taste of her wet, warm flesh in his mouth was more than worth the wait.

Marnie watched his tongue taking its time, building her urgency, and before she even begged she watched as her nipple disappeared into to the soft vacuum of his mouth. She felt his hand slide up her thigh and she just about folded over, holding onto his head for support.

Maybe she did like showers after all, she thought as Harry tended to the other breast for a while, ensuring she was flushed and dizzy from his generous tastings before his mouth moved down.

'Harry…'

He ignored her, knelt down and parted her legs. He retrieved the soap and washed her intimately, teasing out her clitoris till it was as erect as he'd left her nipples and then burying his face in her sex as his fingers slid deep inside.

Marnie usually took for ever to come but not this afternoon. She was pressing Harry's head in, watching him feast, buckling her legs to him, then accidentally blasting them with cold water as she grabbed a tap for support as she gave in to his mouth.

Harry loved the icy blast to his shoulders as he felt her heat in his mouth; he loved hearing the very controlled Marnie losing it to his tongue then shivering in his arms.

'More hot I think…' Harry said.

It was steamy, it was lovely and Harry had but a few minutes' patience left in him. He stood and watched as she tore the wrapper and both looked down as she gave him a little stroke and a tease.

'Sometimes I look down and just smile,' Marnie said at the sight of her hands tenderly wrapping her present as she slid the condom down.

'We'll slip,' Marnie warned as he picked her up, and she slid down on his length and Harry did his best to hold her, hot and slippery in his hands; but there was just a little too much energy between them, the sex they wanted a touch too vigorous to assure safety. 'We're going to end up in Emergency,' Marnie warned as he tried to get back to her breasts and she wrapped her legs tighter around him.

'They might have to send the flying squad out to us,' Harry said, giving up on the pleasure of her wet breast. She put her arms around his neck and still they kissed, but it was terribly difficult in her tiny shower and Harry wanted to see more of her.

He turned the taps off and carried her to the bed, letting her back till her shoulders rested and Marnie looked up to the stunning sight of him, dripping wet and devouring her with his eyes.

Her ankles were wrapped around his hips and he had one hand under her buttocks, the other stroking her as he thrust into her, but she pushed his hand away and gave full invitation.

She'd thought Harry sexy but she knew now just how sexy he was. Felt the grip of his hands on her hips and the delicious sight of him for once concentrating on himself. It was bliss to be moved by him, to be taken. The slap of wet skin and the feel of Harry unleashed deep inside, so potent even the soles of Marnie's feet seemed to contract as she started to writhe beneath him, not that Harry let her go anywhere.

He held her hips so tight as he shot into her that Marnie fought to arch, the suppression forcing the channels of energy back to where Harry delivered his final thrusts deep inside her. It tipped Marnie into the deepest orgasm of her life—her thighs shaking, her bottom lifting, grateful for the hands that held her firm as she rode the deep waves that coursed through her.

And Harry watched her collapse.

He could hardly breathe, he could see the flush on her cheeks and breasts and the tension in her throat as she spasmed around him. He watched and felt as slowly it all dissipated, yet the sight was almost enough for him to go again.

Yet almost better than the sex for Harry was afterwards. He kept waiting for the comedown, and so did Marnie, but right now it was just a matter of sleeping.

For the first time in what felt like for ever the world was a worry-free zone.

# CHAPTER TEN

'PRESS SNOOZE,' MARNIE said.

'It's on your side.'

It was very hard, trying to reach the alarm with Harry spooned into her and his strong arm holding her tight.

Marnie pressed snooze and felt his erection nudging, pulled a little packet from the drawer and, really, she'd have loved not to bother. And Harry would have loved not to bother either.

They were too sensible for that.

It did break the moment, though, a moment that neither usually minded breaking, but Harry soon got back behind her. 'Where were we?' he asked, nuzzling the back of her neck. The alarm going off the second time didn't actually ruin things as she reached over and turned it off. It felt natural for Harry to pull her back to his warm body and slide himself in.

Marnie loved half waking to Harry. She loved this slow, lazy sex where she barely had to move, and she loved his breath in her ear.

'I remember you now,' Harry said. 'I offered to buy you a drink.'

'No,' Marnie corrected, as he rocked deep inside her. 'The drinks were free that night.'

'I offered to get you a drink…'

'No,' Marnie corrected again, but she couldn't really think straight. She was trying to turn her head to meet his mouth, trying to stop her own orgasm because she didn't want it over just yet, or maybe she did because conversation was forgotten now as both surrendered to the bliss and then lay there for a few moments afterwards. Harry stroked her stomach; Marnie felt him soften and gradually slip away.

She didn't want him to leave.

Harry didn't particularly want to go home either. On a wretched, black day he'd glimpsed peace and it would be so incredibly easy to just drop all balls completely and close his eyes and sleep.

But he never would.

'I'd better go soon.'

She turned to him and decided that, yes, he'd better because she was so comfortable, so warm, so *enjoying* being with him; it would be too easy to kiss him, or for them to both close their eyes and convince themselves they could wake up if they had just five minutes' more sleep.

'Go on.' She disentangled herself and for Harry it was incredibly hard to haul himself out of bed.

'When the twins are better…'

'Harry…' She shook her head, didn't really want to spell out to him that a single father of two wasn't quite the date she had in mind.

He picked up his shirt and held it up. 'You couldn't give this a quick iron, could you?'

'Don't even joke.'

As he did up his shirt, Harry caught sight of a blonde Marnie holding her son and, yes, he hadn't been lying, he did remember her now.

'I asked why you were leaving,' Harry said. 'You didn't answer.'

'Yes, well, you wouldn't have liked it if I had,' Marnie said. 'I'd just found out I was pregnant.'

'What went wrong?' He wondered if he'd asked too much. There were so many no-go areas with Marnie— it would seem from her previous response that dinner and a bottle of wine was a no-no, yet, Harry realised as she started to answer him, she was prepared now to talk a little about her son.

'Premature,' Marnie said. 'Poor little thing didn't stand a chance—I had a placenta the size of an AA battery...' It was a dark joke and Harry didn't smile; he just picked up the photo and looked at them both as Marnie spoke on. 'So not only was he premature, he was also small for dates. Then he got an HAI and was just too small to fight it.'

No wonder she was obsessive about hand-washing and curtains being changed, Harry thought—a hospital-acquired infection explained a lot of things but it was as if she'd read his thoughts.

'I was always a clean-freak.' Marnie smiled. 'Even before Declan got so ill but, yes, I go a bit overboard at work.'

'I don't blame you.'

'You'd better go,' Marnie said. It felt strange to watch him holding her picture. It felt strange to be discussing that time with anyone other than Siobhan, who, even on the other side of the world, still nursed her through the yearly hell of birthdays and anniversaries and all the things you really needed a cuddle for, but a computer screen or telephone call had to suffice.

Harry didn't want to go, not just because he wanted to climb back into bed and forget the world for a moment. It was more that there was so much to Marnie that he'd like to know, so much about today he was having trouble letting go of.

So many things that he didn't want to end, and so he tried again.

'Do you want to go out at the weekend?'

'I'd imagine you'd have trouble getting a babysitter for twins with chickenpox.'

'I guess...' He felt strange walking off, as if he'd been using her, when for Harry it had been anything but. 'Have you had chickenpox?'

'I have.'

'Maybe you could come over. I could cook.'

'Harry, don't spoil it.' She was incredibly direct.

She made no excuses, Harry noticed as he dressed, and he should be glad of it. Glad for a woman who knew what she wanted—and a single dad to twins wasn't high on her list.

She was just moving to the top of his.

Marnie was lying in bed, watching him as he did up his tie but then, as he came over and sat down to kiss her goodbye, she suddenly found a solution.

This too will pass.

She could almost hear Dr Vermont say the words.

'Thank God we don't work together...' Harry gave a rueful smile as she reached for his tie and, as Marnie so loved to do, straightened it.

'About that,' Marnie said.

'About what?'

'Do you have a bath?'

'Yes.'

'How about I move in for a week?'

Harry grinned. 'This from a woman who doesn't even want to come out with me for dinner.'

'I'm not talking about dating or romance,' Marnie said. 'I'm talking about me moving in and, between us, taking care of the children. Harry, you're in the eye of the storm at the moment but in a week's time you'll have your lady back to help with the children, Juan will be working… If by then you still want to take yourself off and become hand surgeon of the year…' She made a little joke and then stopped because actually she was completely serious. 'My moving in for a week would give you a pause.'

'Why would you do that?'

'Because, I don't want the department that I've just started running to fall apart.'

'I can't drag you from your home.'

'It's hardly a home,' Marnie said. 'I've only been here five minutes!'

She simply didn't get attached to anything, Harry realised, but it would be so very easy to get attached to her, and he wasn't just thinking about himself when he spoke.

'It would be too confusing for the children,' he said, because, for all his faults, he had managed to keeps his flings well away from them, and Marnie in his bed for a week… He shook his head but then realised that for Marnie this *was* strictly business.

She really could separate the two.

'I'm not going to be sleeping with you, Harry, especially if there's a chance we are going to continue working together. There'll be no confusion.' Marnie smiled. 'I only want you professionally, Harry. It will be a working arrangement.'

'I can't ask you to take time off work to look after my kids.'

'Who said anything about that? I have the weekend off already, a day off in lieu of nights on Monday, and I'll take a management day on Tuesday and sort out those bloody rosters once and for all from home.'

His mind was turning faster. It was maybe, possibly doable.

'I could do a couple of nights on the days you're working. If I can sit down with Helen and work out some shifts…'

'We can work it,' Marnie said. 'It's just one week. I need a doctor for my department, Harry. I have no intention of failing.'

He looked at Marnie, sitting on the bed, the tiniest yet strongest woman he had ever met, and the most determined too. 'I doubt you could.'

# CHAPTER ELEVEN

'I FEEL LIKE Mary Poppins,' Marnie said as Harry opened his front door.

'Oh, you're no Mary Poppins.' Harry grinned, taking her case. He was looking more rumpled than usual and that clean-shaven look of yesterday was fading. 'Come in. Charlotte's just starting to realise that chickenpox isn't so much fun after all.'

No, Marnie was no Mary Poppins. Mary was a good girl who didn't notice things like Harry's bum as she followed him through to the lounge, but, then, she'd never seen Harry in just a T-shirt and jeans and barefoot too. Oh, she'd seen him in a suit, in scrubs and stark naked, but there was something very attractive about him in a T-shirt because it showed off his very flat stomach and in jeans his legs just looked longer.

No, she was no Mary Poppins, but Marnie was still a good girl because she didn't give that bottom a pinch as they walked and she kept her thoughts well to herself too—butter wouldn't have melted in her mouth as she gave his children a smile.

'This is Marnie,' Harry introduced her. 'You both met her at the hospital.'

Adam looked up and smiled and said hello, but Charlotte's eyes narrowed. 'A nurse isn't a nanny.'

'I'm not a nanny,' Marnie said. 'I'm here to help look after you so that Daddy can work.'

'Have you looked after children before?'

'Charlotte,' Harry warned.

'It's fine,' Marnie said. 'I don't mind being interviewed—I'd want to know who was looking after me too.' She turned to Charlotte. 'I've looked after plenty of children and I have lots of nieces and nephews and many younger brothers, so I've have a bit more of a head start than most.'

Harry showed her around—it was a lovely old home, though the stairs creaked terribly as Harry lifted her case upstairs.

'It's a beautiful home.'

'It's needs a demolition ball,' Harry said. 'It looks nice but everything needs fixing, apart from this…'

He opened a door and Marnie almost whimpered at the sight of a beautiful bathroom—it was completely white except for a few dots of dark tiles on the floor. 'It's the one thing that has been renovated,' Harry said. 'I think they gave up after that. I can't wait to see the back of it.'

Marnie was surprised. Surely this home would be filled with memories and the last thing he would want was to let it go, but he must have read her confusion.

'Oh, no…' Harry shook his head. 'We'd just sold our house and were looking for somewhere when Jill died… It was hell—the buyers had sold too and there was no getting out of it. I didn't want the upheaval for the children.'

'Poor things.' It just poured out of her mouth. 'I hated

moving, more than anything, I hated leaving Ireland and then when we had to leave Perth...' Marnie stopped. She didn't really like talking about herself but she was just trying to say that she understood how hard it must have been for the children to move so close to losing their mum.

'It wasn't exactly great timing,' Harry said when Marnie went quiet, 'but there was no real choice, so I rented this. Your friend Dave put me onto it.'

'Ah, Dave!' Marnie gave a bitter smile.

'It was supposed to be for six months...' He turned round and there was Charlotte, standing at the top of the stairs watching them.

'I'm itchy,' she said.

'I'll just show Marnie her room and then I'll come and put some cream on.'

They walked down the hall and he opened a door and put Marnie's case inside. 'I hope this is okay.'

'It's lovely.' It was, a large room with an iron bed dressed in white linen and lovely wooden furnishings that mismatched perfectly.

Charlotte, who had followed them, stood in the doorway and watched as Harry showed Marnie how the dodgy windows worked. 'Do you want to come in and help me put some things away?' Marnie offered.

'We're not allowed in the nanny's room,' Charlotte said, and huffed off.

'Fair enough,' Marnie said.

'She's normally much more friendly.'

'She's normally not covered in spots,' Marnie pointed out, as Harry, a touch awkward now, headed for the door. 'Do you want to go through our diaries?' Marnie suggested. 'Get it out of the way?'

'Sure.'

'I'll just unpack and I'll be down.'

Marnie unpacked her case—it only took a moment. She put her clothes in the wardrobe and hung her dressing gown up on the door and sorted out her toiletries. She put Declan's photo in the drawer of the bedside table. She didn't want questions if the children came peeking, but she couldn't bear to leave him at home, then she headed downstairs.

It was a working arrangement.

They sat at a large table and drank tea as they tried to sort out the upcoming week. 'I phoned Helen and I've got the shifts she can do, as well as Lazlo, he's on now and I'm going in tomorrow.'

'Who's Lazlo?'

'He used to work there and said that he can come in for a couple of shifts…'

Marnie looked at the schedule and saw Harry pencilled in for a shift on Friday night.

'I'm out that night,' Marnie said, and didn't elaborate, but Harry's jaw did tighten just a fraction as he recalled that she was going to the ballet.

With Matthew.

'Not a problem.' Harry cleared his throat before continuing. 'Okay, if I can get Helen to cover that night I can, if it's okay with you, be on call for the rest of the weekend and then Juan's back.'

It *was* a working arrangement.

She made that very clear.

When Harry opened a bottle of wine once the kids had gone to bed, Marnie politely declined.

'I'm going to have that bath.'

'Sure.'

She was a strange person, Harry thought—Marnie didn't even come down and say goodnight. But, ages later, when he headed for bed himself, he could hear her chatting away in her room and it took a moment for it to click that she was on the computer.

'You're living with him?' Siobhan checked, and Marnie was very glad for her headphones. 'You've slept with him and you've moved in but there's nothing going on?'

'You're making this more complicated than it is,' Marnie said.

'What does Matthew have to say about it?'

'I don't discuss things like that with Matthew,' Marnie said, but she did worry for a moment. 'Matthew and I...' She looked at Siobhan, who'd been married for nine years now and just loved hearing about friends with benefits and her best friend's rather glamorous life. 'I don't know,' Marnie admitted.

'What would Harry have to say about Matthew?'

'Nothing!' Marnie said. 'Because he's not going to find out.'

Except Harry had been there when Matthew had invited her to the ballet.

Marnie's conscience was pricking as she turned off the computer and tried to get to sleep.

She and Harry had been a one-off, an indulgence, safe in the knowledge they wouldn't be working together again.

*See what happens when you take your eye off the ball,* Marnie scolded herself.

It certainly wouldn't be happening again.

No, there was no hint of anything. The next morning she was up and dressed and even had lipstick on as Harry held up the kettle and asked if she wanted tea.

'Leave the tea bag in this time,' Marnie said.

'You're sure you don't mind doing this?' Harry checked. 'Charlotte's been up half the night crying. It's hardly a great day off for you.'

'Harry, I'm just relieved to know that the place is being looked after. It's been nothing but a headache trying to get the department covered.' She turned as Adam came down. 'Good morning.'

'Morning, Marnie.'

She was *lovely* to Adam. She chatted away and found out that he'd like cornflakes and juice and yet, Harry couldn't put his finger on it, she still held back. Then Charlotte appeared.

'Do you want babies?' Charlotte asked as Marnie sorted out her breakfast.

'Charlotte,' Harry scolded.

'It's fine.' Marnie smiled. 'No, Charlotte, I don't want babies.'

'Why?'

'Because…' Marnie filled a bowl with cornflakes as she spoke '…I like my work, I like my holidays, I like lots of things. And,' Marnie added, 'as I told you, I had lots of younger brothers. I've changed more nappies than most!'

'Don't scratch,' Harry warned, as Charlotte started to.

'I keep forgetting.'

'I'll paint your nails red later,' Marnie said. 'That will remind you.'

After Harry had gone, she did paint Charlotte's nails red and then she went about opening the windows and stripping the beds between putting on anti-itch cream at various times throughout the day.

'Do you like our house?' Charlotte asked as she showed her the cupboard at the top of the stairs where the fresh sheets were kept.

'I think it's lovely,' Marnie said, as she pulled out some sheets. 'Right! Which ones are yours, Adam?'

'The blue ones, silly,' said Charlotte. 'Mine are pink.'

Harry could not have done it without her.

The children could not have been better looked after and a wary Charlotte had quickly warmed to Marnie's chatter and rather offbeat humour. Despite refusing to iron a thing for Harry, Marnie hauled out the ironing board on the Tuesday evening and made a major dint in the piles of children's bedding and clothing.

'Do you ever stop?' Charlotte asked. She was helping Marnie to fold things as a distraction from scratching.

'Not till the work's done,' Marnie said.

Only Harry noticed that Charlotte's smile wavered.

# CHAPTER TWELVE

'YOU'VE DONE WELL during an extremely difficult time.'

She was sitting in a management meeting. Lillian had blinked a bit at the budget report, and there had been a couple of explosions. The maintenance hours had trebled and there had been fines for the department for twice being on bypass. That had been nothing to do with lack of beds or waiting times, though—in fact, waiting times were down as Marnie was very clued up about the wards hiding beds and had threatened a few times to go up and make a bed herself unless the patient was accepted soon.

Patient complaints were down too.

Marnie put out fires as they happened rather than letting them simmer and, overall, she was pretty pleased as she made her way back down to the department.

No one knew she was staying at Harry's. Certainly no one could know that the reason she hadn't arrived until ten past nine this Thursday was because of the patient Harry had been stuck with. There had been a couple of raised brows as she'd rushed in because she was so rarely late.

But, apart from that, things had ticked along.

Marnie was enjoying her time with the twins—she

liked children. She had been adored by her brothers as they'd grown up and was now a favourite aunty. Yes, she liked children, she just didn't want any of her own.

She'd had her baby and wasn't going to put herself through it ever again—she admired those that did.

Making her way back from the meeting, Marnie walked into the pre-natal ward and couldn't help peeking in.

'Hello!' She knocked on the open door and smiled as Emily looked up from the book she was writing in.

'Marnie!'

'Am I disturbing you?'

'Not at all.' Emily smiled. 'I'm on bed rest till the baby is born. I've never been more up to date with my homework.'

Marnie looked at the huge pile of books by her bed. 'You've got no excuse not to get a good grade,' Marnie said. 'How have your parents been?'

'They've been marvellous!' Emily said. 'I can't believe how good they've been, even though I do I think Dad's disappointed.'

'Maybe he's just worried,' Marnie offered.

'I guess,' Emily said, 'but we've spoken about what we're going to do and they're looking at doing up the granny flat so that Reece and I can live in that.'

'Wow.' Marnie smiled.

'Reece has got another job while I'm on bed rest…'

'You're going to get there,' Marnie said. 'It sounds like you're both using this time to put your heads down and get a future happening.'

'We will.' Emily nodded. 'I wanted to nurse before all this happened but now I'm thinking of teaching.'

'You'll get school holidays off!' Marnie smiled. 'And

that's something to think about because, by the time you're qualified, you'll almost have a school-aged child.' She looked at a very mature seventeen-year-old. 'What a great teacher you'd be,' Marnie said, 'having already earned your qualifications in the school of life.'

'Thanks, Marnie.'

'I shall come and see you again, if you like.'

'I'd love it.'

That night she told Harry about visiting Emily as they ate dinner before Harry went to work.

Charlotte and Adam had already eaten and were making a lot of noise upstairs as cabin fever started to seriously hit.

'I stopped in on Emily today. She's doing really well.' Marnie smiled. 'She's got her head down studying, hoping to be a teacher, and Reece is working an extra job.'

'They still have to be teenagers, though,' Harry said, mashing butter into his potato.

'She won't have time for being a teenager once the baby comes along. It's good that she's getting ahead.' Marnie stopped. Even she could hear that she sounded like her own mother and she tried to soften it. 'It's going to be hard for her but Emily will get there.'

'Did you work right through your pregnancy?'

'I went on bed rest when it was clear my placenta was failing,' Marnie said. 'But I'd have been straight back to my studies even if Declan...' She really didn't like talking about it. There was an uncomfortable silence and after a moment Harry filled it.

'What were your friends like?' Harry asked.

'Siobhan was great,' Marnie said. 'She's my best friend in Ireland, but can you believe she came all this way for the funeral? She'd saved up enough to go travelling for a year and she spent half of it getting here to help console me.'

'What about the girls you trained with?'

'Scathing.' Marnie pulled a face. 'Well, they weren't really friends, we'd all started just a few months back, and I think they thought I was mad to be going through with it.'

'And after you lost him?'

'It was awkward,' Marnie admitted. 'They were busy being teenagers and I guess I wasn't my sunniest. I took my nursing very seriously...'

Oh, he could just imagine that she had!

'That's why I transferred to the Royal. I just didn't want to be around anyone who knew what had happened so I gave myself a fresh start. Of course, I was always an old head on young shoulders even before...' She looked up at him. 'I did know what was involved having a baby—I was nearly eleven when mum had Ronan. I got up to him at night. It might have been an accident but I did know what I was taking on.'

Harry took the plates to the sink. He could see her sitting there, staring, and he thought about a teenage Marnie, let loose for the first time. Those first few months of freedom and, oh, what a price...

'Marnie. Why don't—?'

'I'm going to get the children ready for bed.' She just halted him. Marnie didn't want pensive conversations that changed nothing. 'You're off tomorrow?' Marnie checked their plans before she headed off.

'Yep, but I'm on all weekend.' He felt as guilty as hell, not that Marnie seemed to mind.

'That's fine. What time do you have to be in Saturday morning?'

'Eight.'

'I'll make sure I'm back early, then.'

'Early?'

'Saturday morning,' Marnie said. 'I told you I'm out Friday.'

'Of course…' Harry shook his head. 'I forgot.'

He hadn't forgotten, not for a moment, he'd just kind of hoped things might have changed.

But, then, why would they?

Marnie wasn't giving her heart away to anyone.

# CHAPTER THIRTEEN

'I've booked The Langham.'

Marnie was trying to get Charlotte to brush her teeth when Matthew called.

Marnie loved The Langham—it was a beautiful hotel on the river and possibly her favourite place on earth, but not even the prospect of The Langham could soothe a rather awkward conversation.

'Who's that?' Matthew asked, as a very demanding Charlotte called out for Marnie.

'I'm just watching a friend's children for a couple of days.' She didn't give him a moment to question it. 'I'll try to get there for six.'

'Who were you speaking to?' Charlotte asked, when Marnie hung up.

'A friend,' Marnie said. 'And you should be paying more attention to your teeth than my phone calls—you didn't do the back ones.'

'I hate brushing my teeth.'

'I'd noticed!' Marnie said. 'You'll end up like Adam.' Marnie smiled at Charlotte's brother. 'All your teeth will fall out. Show me...' she said, and Adam took his finger and wobbled a tooth that was barely hanging. Marnie felt a curl in her stomach as he pushed it too far.

'Stop now!' Marnie said, but Adam just laughed and wiggled it harder.

They were fun but exhausting and, as Marnie cleaned up the bathroom, she told herself there'd be fluffy towels and champagne waiting tomorrow.

It just didn't cheer her as much as it usually would.

Marnie was in bed early, knowing the chances of a full night's sleep were remote, and that was confirmed at two a.m.

'Daddy!' Marnie heard Charlotte's first cry and got up and headed to go to her, then turned and put a dressing gown on over her pyjamas.

'It's Marnie, Charlotte,' Marnie said, as she opened the door. 'Daddy's at work, remember—I'm looking after you tonight.'

'I itch.'

'I know,' Marnie said. 'It's that horrible chickenpox but they'll be gone soon. Shall I put on some lotion?'

Charlotte nodded.

'Would you like a drink?'

Charlotte nodded at that suggestion too.

'Why don't you go off to the loo,' Marnie said, 'and I'll be back with a drink and some nice cold cream?'

Marnie was very used to patients waking at two a.m. and more often than not it was the need to go to the toilet that had woken them. So she turned on the lights for Charlotte and then headed down the stairs, made her a drink and found the cream.

Charlotte was back in bed by the time Marnie got back up there and, despite the hour, Charlotte was her usual talkative self as Marnie dabbed on the cream.

'What's a code blue?'

'Why do you ask that?'

'Code red is for a fire and all the doors close,' Charlotte said, and Marnie's hand paused as she realised that the children must hear the overhead intercom alerts in the crèche. Well, of course they would, Marnie reasoned. If there was a fire or the crèche needed to be evacuated, then they needed to hear the alerts too, but it didn't sit right with Marnie that the twins heard them.

'So,' Charlotte pushed. 'What's a code blue?'

'It's when certain doctors are needed.'

'Like the trauma team?'

'Yes,' Marnie said. 'Right, you're done.' As Charlotte lay down Marnie tucked the sheet in around her and went to turn out the light. ''Night, Charlotte. You just call if you need anything.'

'Can you read me a story?'

'I'll tell you a story,' Marnie said, because the light was already off and Charlotte didn't need any more stimulation. Marnie sat on the edge of the bed and told her the same stories she had told Ronan when he had been little. About the fairies that lived at the bottom of the garden and all the good work that they did.

'In your garden?' Charlotte asked.

'In my garden back home in Ireland.'

'But what happens when you move?' Charlotte asked, and Marnie had been about to say they stayed to help the next lot of children who lived there but she could hear the anxiety in Charlotte's voice. She remembered that they'd already moved at a very difficult time and would perhaps soon be moving again.

'The fairies move with you,' Marnie explained, and in the darkness she could see Charlotte's eyes shining, waiting for her to go on. 'They fly along with the removal truck.'

'So the fairies from our old house are here?'

'Of course they are,' Marnie said. 'We'll take a little treat down for them at the weekend.'

Charlotte seemed to like that idea and it was she who said goodnight this time, but as Marnie went to go Charlotte halted her.

'Did your fairies move with you?'

'Of course,' Marnie said, but if she'd been making things up before, now she really was lying. All the lovely imaginings of her childhood were still there in Ireland, all the games and the fun and the innocence were still there in her old home and garden.

'Maybe not all of them, though.' Charlotte yawned. 'Fairies are very small and Australia is a long way to fly.'

She really did need to get out more, Marnie told herself as she climbed into bed, because all this talk of fairies and flying and her fairies being left behind had Marnie suddenly on the edge of crying.

It had been an emotional time, she told herself. The department was struggling not just with the doctor shortage but with the aching gap Dr Vermont himself had left behind.

But it wasn't just that.

She'd never expected she might get attached to Charlotte and Adam—Marnie's heart lived on ice—yet getting up to them at night, hearing their chatter, the things they said that made her laugh... Marnie could almost hear the drip of her heart thawing and it wasn't just that she didn't want it to, or that it terrified her, there was also an appalling sense of guilt because she was a mother of one and in a few days' time it would be Declan's birthday.

Not here!

Marnie lay in bed and refused to give in to tears—she was here to look after children. What if Charlotte called or Adam woke up?

She needed tomorrow, Marnie told herself as she lay there, trying to picture the ballet while frantically trying not to picture afterwards.

She wanted a night at The Langham with Harry.

Or just a night with Harry would do.

'Marnie!' She was almost asleep when she heard her name called.

'I'm coming,' Marnie said once she had ungritted her teeth, grateful for the three a.m. reminder of why she didn't want a single father!

She needed a night away to get back to herself and normality, instead of crying over fairies and made-up stories.

Harry let himself in the following morning a little earlier than usual. The place had been quiet and he'd slept most of the night in the on-call room.

He was greeted by the sight of Marnie's small case and a slightly flustered Marnie who, as usual, was fully dressed and had her hair tied back and make-up on.

'I was just taking that out to my car.'

She'd hoped to do so before Harry got home or the children were up. She'd hoped to completely avoid any discussion about tonight.

She was looking after his children, Marnie told herself as she took out the small case. Certainly she was entitled to a night off.

Harry was trying to tell himself the same. 'How were the twins?' he asked, as she came back in.

'I never heard a peep from Adam, and Charlotte just got up a couple times because she was itchy.' She hesitated a moment, it was none of her business after all. 'She was asking what a code blue was and things. Did you know they hear all the intercoms?'

'I know,' Harry said. 'They have to be on.'

'Even so…'

'Marnie, I'd love them to be somewhere local but I struggle to get across the corridor to pick them up as it is.'

'Of course.' She changed the subject. The child-care arrangements really had nothing to do with her after all. She just loathed the hospital being so much a part of their young worlds.

Except it wasn't her place to loathe it.

'You'll be tired, watching them all day,' Marnie said.

'I got a few hours' sleep last night,' Harry said. 'Anyway, I'm not working tonight.'

'No.'

'About tonight…' Harry turned to fill the kettle, trying to work out what to say. He'd hoped for a busy night so he wouldn't have had time to dwell on it. What had happened to the wild Harry of old, or even the not-so-wild Harry of late who would have loved a woman who didn't want to get serious…?

He loved this woman.

No.

He tore his head from that thought, told himself that he was just a bit infatuated, that was all. Intrigued perhaps. Or maybe it was just his ego because the one woman who didn't want him…

The one woman.

'I think the kettle's full,' Marnie said, as water gushed into the sink.

'Daddy!' Charlotte was delighted to see him. 'Morning, Marnie.'

'Morning, Charlotte.'

'Can we take the treat to the fairies today.'

'I'm off to work,' Marnie said.

'When you get home, then?'

'I'm away tonight,' Marnie said, but again didn't elaborate. 'I'd better get going.'

It wasn't even eight o'clock.

'See you, Marnie…' Charlotte was hanging by the door as Marnie put her jacket on, and Marnie gave Charlotte a lovely smile and a wave as she headed out the door, but it was clear to Harry that Charlotte wanted a kiss.

Yes, they all wanted more from Marnie.

She'd be gone on Monday, he told himself.

It would be a relief, because it was killing him to have her here yet not.

In bed at night.

But not his.

## CHAPTER FOURTEEN

THE DAY WENT far faster for Marnie than it did for Harry.

While he was trying not to pace at home and trying not give any leeway to the mounting disquiet that churned every time he thought of her out on her date tonight, Marnie never got a moment to think till she was flying through the door to her home just before five.

She'd left work early for once and, incredibly organised, her overnight bag was already packed. Even as she undressed, Marnie had flicked on her heated rollers and turned on the taps.

Okay, she conceded as she pulled on a shower cap and hopped under the water, showers were good for some things—at least she didn't have to wait for a bath to fill.

And showers were good for other things too, Marnie thought dreamily, recalling Harry, his hands soaping her body.

Marnie didn't really do feelings and as for loyalty, she wasn't deep enough into anyone to demand such a thing—but her moral compass was spinning in circles as, turned on for Harry, she turned off the taps and did her best to get ready...

For Matthew.

Her hair she piled into rollers.

Her make-up she had down pat and she was soon painted and sitting on the edge of the bed, pulling on gorgeous underwear and stockings and then arranging her cleavage into a very lacy bra. She took out her dress and laid it out on the bed—it was a gorgeous deep navy in the softest velvet and had cost a small fortune.

Yes, all the things she could afford because she didn't have children, and it wasn't just the financial benefits Marnie was taking into account as she quickly dressed—there was time to stop and get her nails done, time to linger in the make-up department, splurge on the ballet and a night at The Langham without having to worry about babysitters.

She wanted this life, Marnie insisted to herself. But her hands were shaking and she tipped on far too much perfume.

She'd been desperate to go when she'd heard the ballet was on—especially as it was Declan's birthday next week. She'd known she'd want a night staring in the dark and just seeing beauty, and then sex for sex's sake at a beautiful five-star hotel with her friend with benefits. Matthew didn't even know about Declan— he'd made a brief comment when he'd seen the silvery lines on her stomach and she'd mumbled something about being a fat teenager.

Marnie pulled out her rollers and sorted her hair, smiled at her reflection because she looked like some high-class tart standing fully made up in her underwear.

She'd be pushing it to get to the hotel, so she dressed quickly, doing up the zipper and then putting on her shoes before transferring all she'd need from her handbag into her evening bag.

'Tickets might help,' she told herself, and unzipped the flap in her bag, and then Marnie stilled.

'Oh, no!'

She'd put them in her computer bag. Marnie remembered now but it didn't stop her from tipping out her handbag in the futile hope that they'd suddenly appear—that she wouldn't have to stop by at Harry's to get them.

*It's tickets!* Marnie told herself.

She was simply making a big deal of it.

If she rang and warned Harry that she was on her way, then she might not even have to see him; she could just let herself in, fly up the stairs and fly out.

It really was no big deal, Marnie told herself as she dialled Harry's number.

'Harry!' Marnie cringed at her own voice, it came out too jolly and bright. 'I just need to stop by and grab something…'

'Something?' The last thing he needed was to see her on her way out. What if that bloody Matthew was driving her? No, he didn't like the idea of Matthew sitting in the car outside, but how could he put it delicately? 'I think it might be a bit confusing for the children.'

'Confusing?' Marnie checked—was this man serious? 'Did your previous nannies not go out?'

'Of course they did. I meant—'

'So the children won't be confused,' Marnie said, snapping off the phone.

It was the adults who were confused.

Harry was making dinner when he heard her key in the door and her breezy call, and he just called out hi and carried on chopping.

'Marnie…' Adam shouted. 'Look.'

Adam, who never asked for attention, was asking for it now. She could see him standing in the living room, holding his lips open like a horse.

'Adam's tooth came out,' Charlotte informed Marnie. 'He was eating popcorn.'

Marnie walked down the hallway and looked at Adam's gap and said all the right things as Harry stood in the open kitchen, chopping away. He felt like the most boring person in the world. He should be wearing a cardigan and slippers, Harry thought to himself. He was doing his best not to look up as Charlotte chatted.

'So the fairies will come tonight…' She stopped talking long enough to take in Marnie in her very lovely velvet dress and very, very high-heeled shoes. 'Marnie! You look…' Charlotte turned round to her dad. 'Doesn't she look beautiful, Daddy?'

Harry had no choice but to look.

In a very dark navy—or was it black?—velvet dress, she had stockings on and high heels and her hair was curly and worn down, her cleavage was gleaming white and her lips were painted red. Harry took a moment to find his voice.

'Very nice.'

'Where are you going?' Adam asked.

'Just out.'

'Where?' Adam persisted.

'Adam!' Harry warned, and then he let Marnie know he knew *exactly* what was going on. 'Marnie's going to the ballet, aren't you, Marnie?'

'I want to go to the ballet,' Charlotte said. 'I'm going to start ballet, aren't I? Soon, Daddy—you said, didn't you?'

He could barely get them home for dinner on time,

Harry thought—try adding in dance lessons too. Only it wasn't Charlotte's excitement and chatter that had him chopping and chopping, it wasn't that Marnie was going out and he was at home, and it wasn't her freedom. It was none of those things.

It was jealousy.

It was possessiveness that was filling his throat from the stomach up. A black jealousy that was as sickly and sweet and as potent as the perfume she had put on for *him*, Harry thought, shooting her a look that made Marnie turn and run.

As Marnie raced up the stairs to retrieve the tickets, Harry's possession seemed to chase her.

She stood in her bedroom, trying to get her breath for a moment—she didn't deserve that look!

She was looking after his kids, for God's sake, she wasn't his wife.

For Harry, the alarming thing was that it felt like it.

It felt, as he stood there pulverising the vegetables, as it might have felt if Jill had stood there dressed to the nines and wafting perfume. *I'm just going out to the ballet and for a shag afterwards, darling. Don't wait up!*

He was as angry and as defensive and as pissed off as he would have been had it been Jill clipping down the stairs. That meant something he didn't want it to mean, that it couldn't mean, because Marnie didn't want kids and family, she'd made that perfectly clear.

It was business to her.

It was supposed to be business to him—he was more than used to the nanny racing out the door on a Friday night, or their boyfriends dropping in.

He and Marnie had slept together *once*.

It was no big deal to him.

Usually.

'See you,' she called from the hall, and he heard the door open.

'See you,' he tried to call out, but the wrong words came out. 'Could I have a word before you go?' Harry said. He nearly added, 'Young lady.'

He felt like her father as he strode down the hall.

He felt *nothing* like her father as he caught her arm and turned her round. 'Call me old-fashioned,' Harry said, 'but I'll tell you this much…I don't like this, Marnie.'

'Harry, I'm only here to help with—'

'I don't care,' Harry interrupted. 'I don't care if it's too much too soon, I don't care if you don't want to hear it, but…' He tried to stop himself, she was thirty-one, he could hardly tell her she'd be better be back here at a reasonable time, that if she slept with him…

His eyes did the talking and so did hers. Marnie was not a woman who liked to be told.

'I don't know where we're going, but there are certain things that you can't come back from,' Harry said. 'And this is one of them.'

'Oh, but it's all right for you.'

'No,' Harry said. 'You have every right to be as angry and as pissed off as I am right now if I…'

Marnie wrenched her arm from his and clipped out to the car.

Bloody men!

Sleep with them once and the next thing you know you're ironing for them, watching their kids. He'd be asking what was for dinner next!

Harry let out a few harsh breaths as he stood in the hall after she'd gone.

'Daddy?' called Charlotte.

He ignored it.

'Daddy!'

He tried to ignore it a second time.

'Daddy, what have you done to the potatoes?'

Harry walked back into the kitchen, saw the mountain of minced potatoes he'd produced and gave a wry grin as he came up with a suitable answer. 'They cook faster if they're small.'

Even Charlotte didn't seem convinced.

'Marnie looked pretty, didn't she?' Charlotte simply didn't let up. 'Is she going out with her boyfriend?'

'Charlotte.' It was Adam who fired Charlotte a warning. Perhaps it took another guy to get it, Harry thought.

What the hell was wrong with him—issuing warnings like that?

A few weeks ago, Marnie would have been the perfect woman—no strings, no commitment. Marnie had been everything he'd wanted in a woman.

He just didn't want that any more.

Marnie wasn't faring so well either.

The traffic was hell as she approached the city—there was a match on at the MCG and Marnie could cheerfully have turned round and headed for home, except she had the tickets.

She was angry with Harry for making such a big deal of things, but it felt like a big deal—she didn't want to see Matthew.

She didn't even want to see Harry.

Right now, Marnie wanted a night at home to curl up alone and try and sort out her feelings.

'Where are you?' Matthew rang and she told him she

was running late and that rather than going to the hotel first she would meet him at the Arts Centre.

It was busy and there really wasn't much of a chance to talk. Marnie bought a programme and they ordered a drink and one for the interval, and then Matthew tried to make her smile. 'We could always skip the ballet and head straight to the hotel.'

And she took a breath and just said it. 'I think I might skip the hotel.'

'Marnie?'

'I need to be back by seven.' He just looked at her, nonplussed. 'I told you, I'm looking after a friend's children.'

'Who's the friend?'

'Just someone from work.'

'That was quick,' Matthew said, and Marnie sucked on her lemon. It was far sweeter than the conversation. She knew he was referring to how Marnie didn't exactly jump into friendships. 'I assume it's the doctor you were holed up in your office with.'

'Matthew, we agreed that we don't have to run every detail of our lives—'

'No, *you* decided that, you're the one who decides how much to give,' Matthew said, and Marnie could feel the people beside them briefly turn and then halt their conversations so they could listen to hers.

Matthew looked at her. 'The doctor wants a wife… Well, God help him, then,' Matthew said, 'and God help…' He halted then but Marnie knew what he'd been about to say and she challenged him.

'Meaning?'

'I never pictured you as a stepmother.'

'Oh, for the love of God.' Marnie rolled her eyes. 'I'm looking after his kids for a week.'

'Would you move in for a week to help look after mine?'

It wasn't really the time to point out that he didn't have any—even if the question was hypothetical, Marnie knew then the answer.

There'd be no Mary Poppins stopping at Matthew's door.

Even if she hadn't recognised it at the time, she had moved in because it was Harry.

When she said nothing, Matthew drained his drink. 'You're the coldest person I know, Marnie. The good doctor just hasn't worked it out yet.'

He left her standing there and Marnie wasn't about to follow.

She sipped on her drink as the bell went and people went through. She could just go home, Marnie realised, and have the evening alone she'd so desperately craved.

Shouldn't it hurt more? Marnie thought.

But it wasn't Matthew leaving that was hurting her now.

She wanted superficial. She wanted, for want of a word, relationships where it didn't feel as if you might die if the other person were to leave.

Yes, she wanted to go home, yet more than that she needed escape.

Marnie sat watching the ballet with an empty seat beside her, but not even the dancers held her mind for more than a moment. She wanted something she had never wanted before. It wasn't just Harry and giving things a go that scared her so—it was pink tights and

Charlotte and the serious eyes of Adam and his wobbly tooth that had made her stomach curl, and her stomach only curled for family. Marnie was petrified—if she did try to make things work with Harry, she had to love them.

What if it didn't work?

She wouldn't lose one, she'd lose three, and Marnie truly didn't know if she could stand to lose like that again.

It was a wretched night, a long, lonely drive home, and she was too upset to go to Harry's—she simply didn't want him to see her as confused and raw as this.

She'd feel better in the morning, Marnie assured herself as she let herself into her own home and set her alarm.

But she didn't.

'Hi.'

Harry couldn't even look at her as she let herself in at six a.m. 'I was just up with Charlotte, she should sleep for a couple more hours.' He was putting the medicine back in the cabinet and wearing only hipsters. He hadn't expected her back just yet, but more worrying than that was the effort needed to keep his voice normal, to somehow try and pretend that he hadn't said what he had last night.

Clearly, given the hour, it hadn't mattered a jot. She must have spent the night with him.

'I got a programme for Charlotte.'

'She'll love it.' Harry glanced up. There were the smudges of last night's make-up under her eyes and her hair was still curly, and his skin was alive and screaming for her, though his head denied that fact.

'About last night...' Marnie attempted. Usually she

could talk, usually she found it easy to say what was on her mind, but in this she was utterly confused.

'I don't want to talk about last night,' Harry said. He was doing everything he could not to think about it.

'Matthew said—'

'Oh, so you're going to stand there quoting him now!'

She didn't want to quote Matthew, she was trying to tell him how scared she was, to warn Harry that he might be making the most terrible mistake. Marnie truly didn't know if she was capable of love. 'He said...the doctor wants a wife, and if that's the case—'

'Believe me,' Harry swiftly broke in, 'if I was on the lookout for the perfect wife...' He stopped himself. Last night's anger hadn't been dimmed by sleep— Harry had barely had any. A night spent watching the clock, a night knowing she was out and with *him*, despite the fact that he'd told her they could never come back from that!

Yes, Harry was having trouble keeping this pleasant.

'Harry, please...' Marnie walked towards him. She had never wanted the feeling of somebody else's arms around her more. She had never wanted to halt a row more, and words were failing her this morning, so she attempted a more basic form of communication— one that had always worked till now. 'I don't want to argue.'

He could smell the remnants of last night's perfume as her hand moved to his chest. His mind put it more bluntly than he chose to voice, but as her mouth moved towards his, as much as he wanted that kiss, he really didn't know where she'd been.

'It's a bit much, Marnie.' He pushed her off. 'You

know, I never thought I'd say this, but I think I'm over meaningless sex.'

She went to kiss him but he moved his cheek and then he put his blunt thoughts into words

'I don't know where you've been.'

It was no surprise that she slapped him.

# CHAPTER FIFTEEN

MARNIE STRIPPED OFF and pulled on her pyjamas and lay there bristling with anger, wishing Harry would just go to work, but she could hear him downstairs on the phone and then the anger faded as realisation hit.

She hadn't told him.

In all her attempts to tell him how she was feeling, she hadn't told him the one thing that he'd needed to know.

She hadn't been with Matthew.

Marnie was half expecting it when she heard the creaking stairs and then heard him walking towards her room and a soft knock before he came in.

She wished he would just leave it, yet she was glad that he didn't.

'I'm sorry.'

He handed her a mug of tea.

And he'd left the bag in!

'You should be at work.'

'I rang Helen and said I'd be in late.'

'Why?'

'To apologise. I was jealous,' Harry admitted. 'It was jealousy speaking. Just pure and simple jealousy.'

'We'd had the tickets since before—'

'I know.'

'Nothing happened. Last night.'

'Marnie, you don't have to explain yourself to me—the thing is, you don't owe me anything. It's me who owes you. And the department,' Harry added. 'The lines got blurred. Well, they did for me and I loathe what I just said.'

'Matthew and I had words as soon as we got there,' Marnie said. 'I didn't even want to go but I had the tickets. He didn't even stay for the ballet...' Marnie gave him a small smile. 'Where's Juan when you need him?'

'Sorry?'

'Instead of rowing, I could have been having a shoulder massage,' Marnie said. 'He'd be far more understanding.'

'I'm not Juan,' Harry said, and he smiled at her.

'I'm glad.'

'Though I reckon even Juan's understanding might have been pushed to the limits last night.' He looked at Marnie all rumpled in bed and that was the trouble, he liked what he saw. As naturally as breathing, Marnie moved her legs as she took a drink of her tea and Harry sat down.

'I'm confused, Harry.' She was nothing but honest as she put her mug down. 'You're the last thing I want but also the only thing I want.'

'And I feel the same about you.' He gave a half-smile and she swallowed.

'I have to love your kids?'

'Marnie...' he looked at her '...no one is asking you to suddenly love anyone.' He didn't know how best to explain it. 'You're just so closed off...' He put his hand up to her cheek and his thumb smudged a bit of last night's eyeliner away. 'You've got me rearranging you now.' He was so gentle as he told her the bit that was hurting. 'You're wonderful with them, absolutely lovely...' Then he said it, because he could—they both managed to speak their truths. 'You're just as lovely as you'd be with any patient.' He watched the wetness of a single tear fall and slither beneath the pad of his thumb. 'I just wish you'd open up a bit.'

'I don't know how.'

'I know.'

'The deal was I just looked after them,' Marnie said. 'You were the one who didn't want them getting confused.'

'Yep,' Harry agreed, 'but that deal ends on Monday.' He watched her swallow. 'If you're ever here after that, you won't be sleeping in this room. You're not a fling, Marnie, that I'm going to hide from them.'

'I'll be your girlfriend?' Marnie tried to tease, waited for him to say, as she once had to him, that he was a bit old for that, but Harry wasn't joking now.

'Yes,' Harry said, and she saw his eyes drift briefly to his ring and he addressed it. 'We've both got things that we need to sort.'

And just when Harry thought she was considering the possibility of them being together, he felt her pull back, simply retract, and he *had* to reach her.

'We've slept together once, Harry.'

'Twice.'

'Well, technically twice...' Marnie started, but his mouth was on hers and he mumbled the word into hers.

'Twice.'

He kissed first her mouth and then her face. Marnie felt the scratch of his chin on her cheek and it was sublime. He moved to her neck and lifted her hair and nuzzled at the sensitive skin as he lifted her top.

'The children...' Marnie said, as he pulled her top over her head.

'They're asleep,' Harry said, 'and they'd never come in.'

'You've made sure of that!' Marnie said, trying to keep things light, but Harry refused to be drawn. He didn't want to joke; instead, interspersed with soft, deep kisses to her stomach, he was peeling her pyjamas down her hips and then sorting out the little clothing he wore. Then he joined her, face to face, both naked.

Not for the first time.

It just felt like it as he kissed her.

Slowly, deeply, he lingered, on her mouth, her neck, her breasts, as his hand crept lower, and she moaned as his fingers stroked her. She wanted him inside her, yet she was holding him as he stroked her, forgetting to kiss, forgetting everything except the bliss of his fingers and the feel of him in her hands.

'Please,' Marnie said, guiding him to her entrance and then remembering. 'We need—'

'Not yet.'

He stroked first with his fingers and then teased her with what she wanted. Harry's hand closed around hers, both stroking him till Marnie could only marvel at his control because she was coming, just from watching him and feeling the wet velvet strokes, but even as she came he was pressing her onto her back.

'Harry.' Marnie wanted her breath back, wanted to collect her thoughts, which seemed to be dancing in the air around the bed. She felt a flail of panic as she realised she was being made love to—and Marnie didn't do that. She wanted to halt him, to stop him, to remind him how casual they were, except right here, right now, they were not. Her legs parted to him and her eyes opened to him and he waited.

He waited till she could wait no more.

'I'm on the Pill.'

It was the second time in her life she'd got carried away, but this time it wasn't a mistake.

She heard the delicious moan of relief and want as Harry moved in but his eyes didn't close.

It wasn't the absence of a condom that rendered this unprotected sex—her heart was bare and stripped and the tears she had held back last night were there in her eyes, and there was anger too for somehow he exposed her.

'Crazy about you, Marnie.' He looked at her as he said it, and she pressed her lips tighter and swallowed back the words she wanted to say, for she *was* crazy about Harry.

It was sex, Marnie told herself—so why were her eyes closing and why was her mouth demanding his? Why was she now pinned beneath him, wrapped around him? She wanted to pierce the silent morning with a scream, but on the periphery she knew they were trying to be quiet. She could hear them building, could feel Harry's back sliding beneath her fingers, and then the moment of perfect acceleration as he drove her to the edge and joined her falling.

Marnie lay there afterwards, breathing in his scent, feeling his chin in her shoulder, and she should be jumping up as she had once, gripped with panic and guilt, but beauty laced with fear silenced her for a couple of moments.

'You're not being fair on Helen.'

'I know.' He rolled off her and smiled.

'Love me and leave me,' Marnie joked, but it was a very dangerous joke and, perhaps wisely, Harry didn't answer.

She'd be out the dodgy windows if he did.

Instead, he gave her a small kiss and climbed out of bed and, of course, there were the practicalities to discuss.

'I'll be back by eight on Monday.'

'Are they going to day care?'

'Not sure,' Harry said. 'I'll give Evelyn a call over the weekend and let you know.'

'You'll call the twins?'

'Of course,' Harry said. 'They call me all the time when I'm on take.'

She'd never worked a weekend with him.

It was a little awkward as he went to go.

'Harry?'

He turned.

'Did you remember to be a fairy last night?'

'Amazingly—yes,' Harry said. 'A very grumpy fairy.'

He wasn't grumpy now.

Marnie lay in the bath after Harry had gone to work and thought about his words earlier about the way she was with the twins.

He hadn't offended her—Harry had spoken the truth.

Yes, this last week she had looked after the twins and had a nice time with them, looked after their itches and given them their medicine. Harry was right, she gave as much of herself to them as she would to a patient.

It was all she ever gave to anyone.

How, though?

How do you open up when you don't know how?

Marnie got out of the bath and, wrapped in her dressing gown, she headed to the bedroom to dress and put on her make-up.

Her uniform, Marnie realised.

Every morning she presented herself as neatly as she would for work.

This morning, though, the very meticulous Marnie pulled back on the pyjamas Harry had so firmly discarded, combed her hair and, instead of blasting it with the hairdryer, tied it back damp.

The children were still asleep so Marnie made herself a large mug of tea and some toast and, instead of unloading the dishwasher, went and sat down and tried to relax, though it wasn't long till she heard footsteps.

'Oh!' Charlotte blinked in surprise at the sight of Marnie in pyjamas, drinking tea and looking through her ballet programme.

'I got this for you,' Marnie said.

'For me?'

'Come and have a look,' Marnie said, and Charlotte climbed onto the sofa beside her and Marnie showed her the programme and they oohed and ahhed at the costumes until Adam appeared. He showed Marnie the money the fairy had left him and then turned on the TV to watch some cartoons.

'I'd give anything to have been a ballerina,' Marnie said, getting back to the programme, looking at the gorgeous costumes she had barely taken in last night.

'You could change jobs,' Charlotte suggested.

Marnie laughed at Charlotte's simplicity. 'I think I've left it a bit late.'

'Were you good at ballet?' Charlotte asked.

'I've never done it,' Marnie said. 'I did Irish dancing.'

'What's that?'

'Irish dancing,' Marnie said, as Charlotte sat there nonplussed, and then Marnie did something she never did, or hadn't in what felt like for ever. 'I'll show you.'

The sound of Charlotte laughing and Adam joining in too made Marnie dance faster.

'Stop.' Charlotte was standing on the couch, both crying and laughing; Adam was curled up, laughing too.

'I haven't got to the really fast bit yet.'

It was *their* day.

They made a tiny miniature feast for the fairies and had their own picnic in the living room—Marnie opened the French doors and let the sun stream in as they sat on a blanket and pretended they were in a field.

Harry rang that evening to say goodnight but Marnie made sure she was busy upstairs, blushing a bit at the memory of the morning, still feeling a little as if she was playing house.

'Can we put more food out for the fairies tomorrow?' Charlotte said, but Marnie shook her head.

'They'll be too fat to fly if we keep feeding them. Now, you get some sleep.' She gave Charlotte a smile and headed out of her room and then into Adam's.

''Night, Marnie.'

'Would you like a story?' Marnie said because, unlike Charlotte, Adam never really asked for anything, and she smiled when he nodded.

It was a slightly different version of the one she had told Charlotte, and her nieces and nephews and brothers, but it was lovely to see Adam smiling and asking questions, though not as many as Charlotte had.

'Are we going back to day care on Monday?'

'I think so.' Marnie smiled but it faded after she had turned out the light and closed the door and realised this could well be her second-last night at the house.

Charlotte had the same question the next day after lunch. As she seemed a little bit tired and tearful, Marnie had suggested she have a little sleep, but it had been met by scorn.

'I don't need a sleep.' She looked at Marnie and made a quick amendment. 'Though I still don't feel well,' she added hurriedly. 'When do we go back to day care?'

'I'm not sure,' Marnie admitted. 'I think Daddy was going to call Evelyn over the weekend.'

'I'm going to ring him,' Charlotte said, but was upset a few minutes later when she came back into the lounge. 'Daddy can't come to the phone.'

'He's just busy,' Marnie said, because she'd just been watching the news. There had been an emergency in the city and now a pile-up more locally. 'He'll call you back as soon as he can.'

Even though there was nothing she could do to help, Marnie still called Emergency and spoke with Kelly.

'We're a bit snowed under,' Kelly said. 'But we're coping. Thankfully it happened just after the late staff came on, so there were plenty of us.'

Yes, there were plenty of nurses but as Harry examined a potential spinal injury, he wished there were a few more consultants.

An eighteen-year-old who had got his driving licence on Friday had taken a friend out and met up another newly licensed friend.

And his friend!

Harry had seen it and heard it and dealt with it more times than he should be able to remember.

Yet he remembered each one.

The trauma team had taken the first driver straight to Theatre and Harry was dealing with the passenger, who, though conscious, was displaying worrying signs. 'Squeeze my hands,' Harry said, and the patient did so. 'Okay, try and lift your left leg…'

'I can't.'

'Okay. Can you wiggle your toes for me?'

'Harry!' He could hear Kelly calling him from behind the curtain. 'Harry, now, please!'

He needed two of him.

'You paged the second on trauma?' Harry checked with Miriam, who nodded. 'Fast-page them again,' Harry said, and quickly gave Sheldon some instructions.

'Harry!' Kelly was calling him again as he stepped in. 'He's not responding…'

'Carl!' Harry pinched the young man's ear; he had been talking just a few minutes ago when Harry had been called for the spinal injury. When pinching his ear failed to elicit a response Harry tried a sternal rub. 'Carl!' Harry ran his pen over the young man's nail bed and watched as he extended to pain.

'Start some mannitol,' Harry said, prescribing an IV solution to reduce intracranial pressure. 'Let's him round for an MRI.'

'Are you going with him?' Kelly checked, and just as Harry was coming to an impossible decision, just as he heard the roar of the storm become louder, a deep accented voice brought calm.

'Can I help?'

'Juan!'

'I heard on the radio that there had been a big accident. I thought you and Dr Vermont might need a hand.'

There wasn't time for conversation, let alone to break the terrible news. 'I've got a query spinal in the next curtain who I'm very concerned about...'

'I've got it.'

For Harry there was almost a feeling of dizziness—it was such a relief to know that Juan was back, that there was another consultant to share the load, to know that he didn't have to think about the young man in the next bed—he was getting the best of care from Juan. Harry could focus now on Carl.

The afternoon passed in a blur of MRIs and transfers, but later, as Juan returned from Theatre, where his patient had been taken for halo traction, he caught Harry as he came off the phone.

'So, is he playing golf?'

'Sorry?'

'Dr Vermont.' Juan rolled his eyes because Dr Vermont did love his golf at weekends, or rather had.

'Juan...' There was no one critical now, it was time to tell him properly before he heard it in passing. He asked Juan if he could have a word in his office and once there Harry closed the door. 'Dr Vermont passed away.' He saw the shock on his colleague's face. Even though Juan was fairly new to the department, it was still a terrible shock. 'He was doing a night shift and suffered a massive myocardial infarction.'

'Who was on?'

'Sheldon,' Harry said. 'And Eric was the cardiologist. They did everything they could, of course.

He was having supper with Marnie in her office and just...' Harry shook his head and gave a weary shrug.

'Poor Marnie.'

'Yep,' Harry said. 'She got help, she did everything right, but there was nothing to be done.'

Juan was stunned. He asked about Marjorie. 'They were having their fortieth wedding anniversary.'

'They had it,' Harry said. 'It was after that.'

'So how have you managed?' Juan asked.

'Barely,' Harry said. 'Juan, there's something else I ought to tell you—I handed my notice in a few days before Dr Vermont died. The twins have both had chickenpox, something had to give. Oh....' he gave a wry laugh '...and my babysitter got shingles.'

'So you're leaving?'

'I don't know,' Harry admitted. 'Now that you're back, hopefully things will be better, but I need to put the children more to the front than the back of the queue. Speaking of which...' he grimaced when he saw the time '...I was supposed to call Charlotte.'

'Go home,' Juan said.

'You're not due back till tomorrow..'

'What did you just say about putting your priorities in order?' Juan checked. 'Go and spend the evening with your children.'

Harry smiled. It was so good to have Juan back. 'How was the wedding?'

'Amazing. I will tell you about it properly later. Right now I am going to call Cate and let her know I am here for the night.'

'Thanks.'

'Who's been helping with the children?' Juan asked.

'They've been here there and everywhere,' Harry

said, which was in part the truth. It had only been since Marnie had stepped in that things had been so stable, but certainly Marnie didn't want anyone knowing she had temporarily moved in.

Temporarily.

Marnie was starting to sort out her case, and was just putting Declan's photo in when there was a knock at the front door and she opened it to a lady who introduced herself as Evelyn. 'Harry rang me last night and told me the twins had been sick.'

'I'm Marnie,' she said. 'A colleague of Harry's. I've been watching the twins over the weekend while he's been working.' It was easier than saying she'd been here for a week.

'Evelyn!' Charlotte came charging down the stairs.

'Charlotte! I've missed you so much!' Evelyn was so effusive and loving and the children ran to her. 'I was so upset to hear you'd got chickenpox.' As she hugged the twins Evelyn looked over to Marnie. 'If I'd known I was infectious, I'd have stayed well away.'

'They're fine,' Marnie said.

'Poor Harry, how on earth did he manage?'

'It's been a bit of a juggle but he got there.'

'Well, I can help now.' Evelyn was clearly at home here. While she chatted to Charlotte, who was filling her in on every detail of her spots, Evelyn was filling the kettle.

Charlotte was so thrilled to see her that when Marnie's phone rang, Charlotte barely looked over as Marnie excused herself and headed upstairs. She was feeling horribly rattled and suddenly entirely replaceable.

'Hi, Mum.' Marnie did her best to sound cheerful, not that Maureen appreciated the effort.

'I know you're busy, Marnie, but it's been more than a month since you visited.'

'I know, Mum.'

'Well, on Thursday Ronan has his hand appointment. I was thinking, your father and I could bring him and then, when you've finished work, we could go out for dinner.'

Was she serious? Thursday was Declan's birthday.

'Ronan said you liked the prawns at the pub—'

'Mum.'

'And your dad loves a nice steak.'

'Mum!' Marnie picked up Declan's photo from the case—did her mother really think she wanted to be sitting eating prawns and talking about the bloody weather? 'I've got plans that day.'

'I know you do, Marnie, but, I think it would be nice if we could all be together.'

'I told you, I'm busy.'

She turned off the phone and stared at Declan.

Her son.

Did her mum really think they could get through the night of his birthday not talking about him?

Avoiding his memory and the terrible hurt.

Guilt filled Marnie as she looked at a photo that had been placed in a drawer while she'd played houses, looking after someone else's children, telling fairy tales that, yes, she'd once told Declan, even if he'd been far too young to understand them.

A part of her knew her guilt was misplaced, but this was her hardest time. She wanted it to be the week after next when she was over the hurdle of Declan's birthday.

But a fortnight from then it would be the anniversary of his death.

It never entered her head she could share her pain.

Oh, God, tears were filling her eyes but, as she was fast finding out, there was no such thing as suitable quiet time with a house of four-year-olds. She could hear Charlotte racing up the stairs, calling her name.

'Marnie!'

'I'll be there in a minute.'

'Daddy's home!'

Marnie headed downstairs to find Charlotte telling Harry about their weekend as Evelyn looked on happily.

'The fairies came and ate the food we left them...'

'Wow!' Harry said, but she could see it was all a bit forced. Still, he made plans for tomorrow with Evelyn and once she was gone and Charlotte was upstairs, Harry let out a sigh of relief.

'How was it?' Marnie asked.

'Grim,' Harry admitted. 'Juan's there now. I can't tell you how good it felt to hand the lot over to him.' He glanced at the television that was on in the background, the news regaling them with details of the accident. 'Who'd have teenagers?' Harry said, and looked over at Adam as Marnie busied herself wiping the bench down, terrified she might break down, because right now she'd give anything to have one. 'I've got it all to come,' Harry said.

'We'll be good.' Adam smiled.

'That's what they all say!'

'Can you read me a story?' Charlotte was walking in with a book. 'Mummy, can you—?'

'Marnie!' She snapped a little more than she'd intended. 'It's Marnie,' she said again, and Charlotte's cheeks went very pink and she turned and ran off.

'Adam,' Harry said, 'go and help Charlotte choose a story and I'll be in.' As Adam walked off he turned to her. 'It was a simple mistake,' Harry said. 'She's four.'

'I know,' Marnie said. 'I just…' She couldn't explain it properly, the little reference to teenagers, hearing Charlotte call her Mummy—it hurt and it hurt and it hurt and she wanted the hurt to stop. 'I'm not going to have her call me Mummy and get all confused.'

'Sure.'

'Harry, I think I ought to go,' Marnie said, and Harry stood silent. 'I've got so much to do at home…'

She was back to being the babysitter and there was nothing Harry could do.

'Stay for dinner?'

'I'd rather not. I'm ready for home.' She gave him a tight smile. 'I'll go and speak to the children.'

She was terribly nice to them.

Harry stood at the door as she said goodbye to Charlotte and told her she was sorry for snapping.

'Some things make me sad.'

'Like what?'

'Like—' Marnie was as honest as she could be with a four-year-old '—I don't have children.'

'You said you didn't want babies.'

'Well, most of the time I feel like that,' Marnie said. 'Just not all the time.'

Harry hadn't seen her with the children over the weekend. He watched as she was very kind and very honest with the twins…but, yes, she held back. 'I'm going to go back to my house now,' Marnie said. 'Dr Juan starts tomorrow, your spots are all gone…'

'Will we see you again?'

'Of course!' Marnie said. 'I'm sure you'll be dropping in to the department.'

It wasn't what they wanted, though.

They got their first and last kiss from Marnie.

Just a brief one.

She didn't want them, Harry realised.

Which meant she didn't want him.

'Thank you.' Harry helped her take her stuff out to the car.

'It's been great,' Marnie said, and then she sent their relationship straight back to where it had started. 'Not that we'll be telling anyone at work about it.'

'Of course.'

'If I had an umbrella I'd put it up!'

He couldn't even smile at her pale joke.

'Next week,' Harry said, 'once Juan's back, I'd like to take you out to dinner to properly say thank you.'

'There's no need for that.'

No, she could not have made it clearer.

'I really am grateful,' Harry said, remembering the reason Marnie had been there.

The only reason.

Work.

'We got through it,' he said.

'We did!' Marnie smiled. 'Two consultants and another soon starting! We'll be back on track in no time.'

## CHAPTER SIXTEEN

IT REALLY WAS business as usual.

At work at least.

The house had been as cold as a morgue after she'd gone.

It was strange, because there were always nannies and aunts and people coming and going, but without Marnie it felt like some sinkhole had opened up and plunged them back into darkness.

'I love Marnie…' Charlotte was crying.

'Charlotte!' He'd been about to tell her she was too dramatic, but she did love her, Harry realised, and Adam did too, because Harry could hear him crying in his bedroom. 'Marnie adores you.'

'Then why isn't she here?'

It was one question he couldn't answer.

He wanted to remind the twins she'd only been there for a few days, yet by the end of a week without Marnie—near midnight on the Sunday night—Harry had done what he'd thought he'd never be ready to do and taken his ring off.

He loved Jill so much but it felt wrong to be wearing it when he was mourning someone else.

All he knew now was that being in bed with Marnie

was amazing, but more than that, when she laughed, when she smiled, or when her honesty was so breathtaking your biscuit snapped in mid-dunk, Harry wanted more.

But Marnie didn't want intimacy.

Marnie didn't want them.

You had to admire her really.

Harry sat at work, late afternoon on the Wednesday, trying to write, trying not to turn to the sound of her voice.

'Did you forget how to use surgical taps when you were on your honeymoon?' Like a hawk swooping, she was off her stool and straight onto Juan. 'I'll remind you how to use them, Juan.'

'Marnie, I'm not about to see a patient…'

'It's about good habits,' Marnie said. 'Which means if you use the surgical sink then you're to use it as such and turn it off with your elbows.' She was demonstrating again and Juan was grinning.

'Show me again, Marnie,' Juan said.

Harry could stand it no longer and anyway he had somewhere he needed to be. In an attempt to cheer Charlotte he'd rung up about ballet lessons and she had her first one at five. 'Got to go,' Harry said.

'Before you do I need you to witness my signature.' Juan had an interview with Immigration the next day about getting permanent residence in Australia. 'For the immigration forms…'

'No problem,' Harry said. 'I need to get Charlotte changed here anyway. I'll just go and get them and, if you can have everything ready, I'll sign them on my way out.'

Marnie didn't hide in her office, neither did she

disappear, but she was glad she was with a patient as she heard Charlotte's excited chatter from behind a curtain a little later.

'I want to show Marnie.'

'She's busy,' Harry said. 'Come on.'

'But I want her to see—'

'We'll be late,' Harry said.

She waited just a moment before walking out, relieved that they'd gone, but then Harry dashed back.

'You've pocketed my pen,' Harry said to Juan, who was always borrowing things and forgetting to give them back. 'I was just—'

'Marnie!' Charlotte was running behind him. 'Look!'

She had on pink ballet tights and a pink headband and she looked so gorgeous and excited that Marnie wanted to drop to her knees. She wanted to tuck in her curls under the headband and to tie her cardigan properly, because Harry's attempt at a bow was already unravelling, but she just stood and smiled as Charlotte spoke. 'I've got my first ballet lesson.'

'Good toes, naughty toes,' Marnie said. 'Have a wonderful time.'

She said everything right, Harry thought, and she smiled as she did, but it was like watching the security screen shoot up at the bank, he thought as Marnie stepped forward then halted.

'Come on, Charlotte,' Harry said. 'You don't want to be late.'

Marnie stood watching as Harry took his children's hands and walked off, and he didn't look back—his priority was his children.

No matter the cost.

She felt Juan watching her and turned quickly, taking

out an alcohol wipe to clean down the bench. 'That'll be you before you know it,' Marnie said, trying to make conversation, embarrassed to have been caught watching Harry and the twins. 'Dashing off to take your little ones to their activities.'

'I hope so,' Juan said, and got back to his work. Marnie just stood there cleaning, hating how easy and honest his answer had been—that Juan could admit his hopes for the future, that he wasn't whipping out an alcohol wipe and cleaning something that didn't even need to be cleaned.

'Marnie—' Juan started, perhaps sensing her sudden distress.

'Don't!' Marnie snapped, and walked briskly to her office. She didn't want Juan waving his fairy dust on her and giving her one of his, oh, so meaningful talks.

Oh, she couldn't deal with this today.

Or tomorrow.

Especially tomorrow.

# CHAPTER SEVENTEEN

'HI, JUAN!' CHARLOTTE was still practising her dance moves when Juan arrived unexpectedly. She was sitting on the floor and doing good toes, naughty toes.

'Marnie said that's what we'd do!' she said to Harry, and Juan saw his colleague's jaw tense and knew that he was right.

'Sorry to drop in,' Juan said. 'I messed up the form.'

'It looked fine to me.'

'I had to do it again.'

Harry wasn't in the mood for conversation, though Juan was chatting about work—Helen was covering tonight and considering a permanent position. He witnessed Juan's signature again but tensed when he still hung around. 'I'd invite you for dinner but it's nuggets and tinned spaghetti...' As he served up dinner, Harry turned briefly to Juan. 'Don't you have a new wife to get home to? You're barely back from your honeymoon.'

'At least we had one. I hear Marnie was going to ring and try to haul me back.'

Her name was everywhere.

'Yes, well, it worked out without her having to.'

'She wouldn't have had much luck, anyway.' Juan shrugged. 'I turned off my phone.'

'Wouldn't that be nice?' Harry said, taking the children's dinner over and calling them to the table.

'How did you manage?' Juan, oh, so casually asked.

'Marnie looked after us,' Charlotte said, as Harry poured the twins drinks.

Harry's smile was wry as he ruffled Charlotte's hair.

'I'll see you out,' Harry said. He needed to be on his own with his children right now.

'Harry,' Juan said. Since his return he'd been worried about Harry. Juan had thought it was grief and from the look of his friend it was, yet it wasn't just Dr Vermont he was grieving for. 'If you want to talk—'

'I don't,' Harry broke in, though he'd love to open up to someone who had been out there a bit more recently, to discuss how the hell this friends-with-benefits thing worked, or just the hell of loving someone who didn't want love.

Yes, he loved her.

And because he loved her, he knew Marnie would loathe it to be discussed. She would hate Juan, and therefore Cate, knowing what had briefly gone on between them.

So he said nothing—he just wished Juan good luck with Immigration tomorrow.

'I should be back by midday.'

'No problem,' Harry said.

He was glad that everyone wasn't rushing to get to the department, that finally there was some calm to the place.

Just not to his heart.

'What time's hand clinic?' Kelly asked.

'Three,' Harry answered.

'I'm going to go and set up while it's quiet.'

Harry said nothing. He was past multi-tasking—just filling out a doctor's letter was taking all his concentration. Marnie was holed up in her office and Harry would love to do the same, except Juan wasn't back yet from Immigration.

'I'm here to see Marnie Johnson.' Harry glanced up as Kelly asked a man in a suit if she could help him.

Perhaps it was one of her brothers, Harry attempted, but he didn't have an Irish accent.

It had nothing to do with him, Harry told himself and carried on writing as Kelly buzzed Marnie and she came through to the department.

'Craig.' He heard Marnie's voice and deliberately didn't look up. 'I said to text when you were here and I'd meet you outside. Kelly, I'm going to be away from the department for my lunch break.'

Now, as she walked away, Harry did look up.

There was a wedding ring on Craig's finger. Harry could see it as he put his arm around Marnie's shoulders, but unlike with Matthew she didn't wriggle away.

Instead, Harry watched as her hand moved up to catch his.

Did she have to rub his face in it? Harry thought.

Was she so cold she could nip off to lunch with a married man and not care who knew?

Even him?

Yes.

It got worse as he took his lunch break.

'Guess who got picked up by a man and has now rung in with a sudden migraine?' Kelly smirked as she plonked herself down and opened her sandwich.

'Oh, but she'd have something to say if we did it,' Abby bristled.

But there was no Dr Vermont to say 'Ladies,' so Harry had to sit through it.

It was a relief to go back to work.

For ten minutes.

'Ronan.' Harry forced a smile as yet another reminder of Marnie came through. 'How are you?'

'Nervous,' Ronan admitted, as Harry carefully took the splint off and examined his finger for sensation.

'I couldn't be happier with it,' Harry said. 'It's going to take time to get back full range and function…'

'I know.'

'But for now everything looks better than I'd expected. Keep the splint on and I'll see you again in two weeks, but you can start now with the hand therapist.' He couldn't not mention her. 'Marnie is—'

'Oh, no, don't disturb her,' Ronan interrupted and shook his head and Harry frowned because it sounded as if Ronan was avoiding her.

'I was just about to say I'd let her know you were here, but she's actually off sick.'

'Okay.' Ronan stood and, although he was usually articulate and friendly, he didn't express concern or say that he knew; instead, he was suddenly awkward and Harry watched as Ronan shrugged and blushed and then shook Harry's hand.

Harry knew.

He knew then what day it was today—the day the Johnsons always avoided each other, the day that no one could discuss.

'Don't bring the next one in.' Harry halted Kelly and buzzed through to the main section. 'Is Juan back yet?'

'He's just getting something to eat before he starts,' Miriam answered, but Harry had other ideas.

He found him in the kitchen.

'Juan, can you take over hand clinic? I need to go.'

'Now?'

'Now.'

He just walked away from hand clinic, from Emergency, from all of it, without a backward glance and went to his car.

He drove to her street. If there was a car outside then he'd just keep going and come back later, but he guessed that there wouldn't be—Harry knew she would get through it and then want to be alone.

She didn't have to be.

That much he knew.

'Marnie…' He knocked and she didn't answer, so he knocked again. 'I'm not going till you open the door.'

'Make yourself comfortable on the doorstep,' came the smart answer.

'I know that it's Declan's birthday.'

There was no movement for a moment but then the door opened. Marnie looked as if she did have a migraine. Her already pale face was a chalky white and her eyes were glittering more with pain than tears.

'I don't talk about it.'

'But you can.'

He took her in his arms.

'I don't know how to,' she admitted, because it was easier to sob into a phone to Siobhan and then end the call when it got too hard.

'We'll work it out.'

'I've just been to the cemetery,' Marnie explained. 'I couldn't face coming back to work. Craig, that's his father, well, we don't go every year, sometimes he's away with work, but this year we went together. His wife's pregnant with their third…' She looked up at Harry. 'I am pleased for him and there's nothing like that between us, it's just…'

'Hard?'

'Not all the time,' Marnie admitted, 'but this birthday has been a bad one. He'd have been a teenager today.'

'I'm so sorry.' He still held her in his arms.

'I'd have a thirteen-year-old and be dealing with acne and rebellion and dirty bedrooms.' She leant on him. 'I want him to be thirteen.'

'I know.'

Harry did know. He knew about impossible wishes and guilt, because if his wish for Jill had come true, then he wouldn't be here with Marnie.

But he wanted to be here.

Especially now that she let him be.

She cried and she cried and he held her and then she cried for other things.

'I'm sorry I snapped at Charlotte.'

'Forget it.'

'I can't.'

'She loves you. Adam loves you.' He looked at her. 'I love you.'

'I'm so scared,' Marnie said. 'I'm so scared to fall in love and to love and—'

'You don't have a choice,' Harry said. 'In case you hadn't noticed, love doesn't let you choose. If it did, you'd be an amazing cook, a stay-at-home kind of woman…'

'You'd be bored.'

'I know.' Harry smiled. 'And you wouldn't have chosen a single father.'

'How do you know that?'

'You told me,' Harry said. 'Several times.'

'I didn't choose a single father,' Marnie said. 'I chose you and your children...' She thought of Adam so guarded and Charlotte so dazzling. 'They chose me.'

And on a day when she ached for her own son, there was room too for his, because a while later she found herself talking about another child who had wormed his way to her heart. 'Adam doesn't have a speech problem,' Marnie said, as she drank yet another mug of tea that Harry had made her. 'He's got the same problem that Ronan had—an older sister who says everything for him.'

'Perhaps.'

'No perhaps about it,' Marnie said, and just as she was almost smiling, Harry changed her world.

'Come home.'

'Not like this.' Marnie crumpled, terrified at the final hurdle. 'I can't go there all sad.' She used his trump card. 'It will confuse them.'

'Do you think they've never been sad?' Harry asked.

'Of course they have.'

'So let us take care of you today.'

Marnie didn't know how to have her heart taken care of, Harry realised. She was an expert in every department but that one.

He packed her overnight bag and led her to his car, and in no time they were back at Harry's.

'You can't tell them about Declan...'

'Come on.' Harry took her hand and led her up the

path and he saw their little worried faces as Marnie came in and it was clear that she had been crying.

'Hi.' Marnie stood there shy and awkward as Harry had a word to Evelyn, who made herself scarce.

'I'll be over in the morning,' Evelyn called.

'Thanks, Evelyn,' Harry said, and then led Marnie to the lounge.

'Okay.' He looked at the twins. 'You know how you feel sad about Mum sometimes?'

Charlotte nodded.

'How I feel sad sometimes?' Harry checked. 'Well, that's how Marnie feels today. I'm going to go and run her a bath and then make something to eat, so for now can you guys look after her?'

He left them to it.

'Sorry I was mean, Charlotte,' Marnie said.

'That's okay,' Charlotte said.

'You can call me whatever you want,' Marnie said. 'Well, so long as you remember Miss Manners.' She smiled and so too did Charlotte, but then Marnie stopped smiling and she wanted to turn and run because tears were threatening, but instead of running she sat down.

There was one good thing about grief, they knew what to do. Adam climbed on her knee and hugged her and she hugged him back and buried her face in his hair and just held him.

'Sorry,' Marnie said as she started to cry.

'Don't be sorry,' Charlotte said, and cuddled her too, and the twins were like little grown-ups and babies at the same time; they had been through so much and therefore could give so much.

Harry came in a little while later to find his three favourite people all cuddled in on the couch.

'Your bath's ready.' He took her hand and led her up the stairs and told the twins to wait there. Harry was so careful not to flaunt anything in front of the children but as natural as breathing he led Marnie up to the bathroom. There were bubbles and towels and not a hint of anything but love in the room as he helped her out of her clothes and into the warm bath and then left her.

'Is she okay?' Adam checked.

'She will be,' Harry said, and they headed to the kitchen to sort out something for Marnie to eat.

'Did her husband die?' Adam asked, as they loaded a tray.

'No,' Harry said.

'Her baby died,' Charlotte whispered. She was far too wise. 'I saw the photo…'

'Yes,' Harry said. 'Marnie's baby died a long time ago but it still hurts. Today would have been Declan's birthday.'

'We could make him a cake.'

'Charlotte!' Harry warned, and then almost dropped the kettle when he heard Marnie's voice and realised that she must have heard that little gem. 'She didn't mean—'

'It's fine.' Marnie smiled and gave a very worried-looking Charlotte a hug. 'It's a lovely thought but right now I'm so tired.'

'Go to bed,' Harry said. 'We'll bring this up.'

They headed upstairs together and Marnie went to turn left for her old bedroom, because surely it was too soon to do otherwise?

But it wasn't too soon. It was now.

'This way,' Harry said, and she stepped into her new bedroom. And was there any nicer way to be installed in your new bed than to have a very excited Charlotte pulling back the cover and Adam waiting with a tray? It was normal, it was natural, and it was the nicest way it could have happened.

'Okay,' Harry said, sending the twins away and pulling the curtains and putting on the bedside lamp. 'Have something to eat and a rest.' He looked at her glittering eyes and it was a relief to sit down on the bed and to take one beautiful hand in his and hold it as he perhaps said the entirely wrong thing.

'Why don't you ring your mum?' He held on tight to her hand as she pulled away. 'You need your mum.'

And her mum needed her too.

'My battery's flat.'

'There's a phone by the bed.'

An hour or so later Harry had got the children to bed when he heard the click of the phone, and then he heard the tears and the murmurs of conversation as Maureen got her wish.

'If I could take back one day in my life…' Maureen said. 'I know you can never forgive me.'

Marnie closed her eyes but not in anger.

'I do, though,' Marnie said. 'I know you were just angry.'

'I'd have loved him, though, Marnie. I was so cross but I'd bought a little coat for him and I was looking at cots. I was brought up in a world where the worst thing was your daughter getting pregnant, but it wasn't the worse thing, it was losing Declan and losing you…'

'I'm here, Mum.'

'I'm proud of you, Marnie. I know I didn't act as if I was then. Have you been to the cemetery?'

'With Craig,' Marnie said.

Yes, Marnie had chosen well.

She had a son.

He had a father—that foolish mistake wasn't so foolish all these years on.

That Declan was buried in Australia had been the only thing that had kept her here at times, but now, finally, she knew the reason she was here. Finally she felt at home.

'Let me come over. I don't want you to be on your own.' Gushing in, high on maternal waves, Maureen wanted to be with her child, but when Marnie said no, this time it wasn't because she was avoiding her.

'I'm with someone, Mum.'

'Craig?'

'No.' She looked around the bedroom, a room she'd never so much as kissed Harry in, but she could feel the love.

'His name's Harry and he's got twins.'

'Twins!'

'Their names and Charlotte and Adam,' Marnie said. 'You'll get to meet them soon. Harry's a consultant where I work.'

Maureen sat silent for a moment as Marnie opened the doors to all the separate compartments of her life and finally let her mother in.

'It sounds as if the two of you are serious.'

She wasn't serious, though.

Marnie was happy.

As he crept in the room later, trying not to disturb her, Marnie watched as he undressed, and then Harry saw the glitter of her eyes in the darkness. 'You're awake!'

'Very.'

Oh, it was lovely to feel him climb into bed and lie there beside her, and Harry lay wondering what to say to her.

Or if they might...

No, not tonight, Harry told himself.

'Are you just going to lie there?' Marnie asked, and Harry found himself laughing. 'I told my mother we were serious,' Marnie warned him, 'so you'll have to marry me now.'

'Done.'

'On one condition.' They turned to face each other. 'We're keeping this house.'

'Marnie,' Harry warned, 'we'll be buried under renovations.'

'I don't care.'

'Can we talk about this another time?' Harry said, because their legs were twining around each other's.

'I like to know what's happening,' Marnie said. 'I like things organised.'

And he knew then he had her for ever.

'Yes, Marnie, we'll keep the house.' Harry smiled as he kissed her.

Marnie had found her home.

# EPILOGUE

'I SWEAR THAT she is.'

Kelly took off her shoes and stretched her feet. 'Her dress is too tight and she never takes that jacket off.'

Harry just smiled to himself and carried on watching the television.

'Her boobs are bigger,' Kelly went on. '*And* she's being nice. I've got the next four Saturdays off.'

'Marnie doesn't do nice,' Abby grumbled, because Marnie had just given her a long talking to about being consistently late, which, of course, Marnie never was.

Not once.

'She's so cold that if she is pregnant she'll lay her eggs in a river—'

'Hey!' Juan said, because Juan liked Marnie and the way she ran the place.

Harry just smiled.

Juan had an inkling but the rest of them had no clue, and that was the way Marnie had wanted it. She was determined to prove, before everyone found out, that they could work together and argue and clash at times, and Harry certainly got no favours.

At work.

Marnie was twenty weeks pregnant, and everything

was going perfectly. The children were besotted with her and called her Marmie—a mixture of Mummy and Marnie—and it was their own in-joke. Marnie had found a day-care centre near their home rather than in the hospital. It was one Evelyn could walk to if Harry or Marnie couldn't get there, but that happened rarely. Marnie took her management days at home and the occasional sick day too, and somehow they had a routine and the children were absolutely thriving

Charlotte was doing ballet; Adam was desperate to be an older brother. They had put in an offer on the house, even though it needed a demolition ball. Marnie had listed every single thing that needed repairing and read off the list to a very weary Dave, several times, until finally their offer was accepted.

Marnie came in and opened her salad and stirred in the dressing, just as she always did.

She was still slim, but even with her jacket on it was getting more obvious with each passing day and she really needed to speak to Cate about filling in for her when she went on maternity leave.

'I'm sure you've all heard the rumours,' Marnie said, and Kelly gave a triumphant eye-raise. 'And they're correct. I'm getting married next Saturday.'

'Marnie!' Juan came over and Marnie stood as he gave her a kiss to congratulate her, and so too did his wife, Cate.

'Oh!' Cate looked at the engagement ring on Marnie's finger. 'That's beautiful.'

'I know,' Marnie said. 'I'm just wearing it to show you. I'll be taking it off at the end of lunch break.'

Cate suppressed a smile. Marnie *loathed* anything

other than the simplest of jewellery, lest there be a germ beneath it.

Marnie looked down at her beautiful hand and even more beautiful ring, and it made her so happy that she couldn't help smiling.

'And, yes...' her cheeks were a bit pink as she told her colleagues what they probably already knew '...I'm expecting.'

'I'm thrilled for you, Marnie,' Juan said.

'I'm thrilled for myself,' Marnie said. 'Now, it's just a small wedding, well, as small as it can be with my massive family, but you're all very welcome to come—all very informal but there'll be a good party after.'

'I didn't know you were seeing anyone,' Abby fished.

'I don't bring my personal life to work,' Marnie said.

'Will you be changing your name?' Kelly asked.

'No.' Marnie shook her head. 'It would be too confusing.'

'Confusing?'

'Marnie Worthington,' she said. 'I think having the consultant and the manager with the same surname...'

'You mean...?' They all looked at Harry, who smiled back at them, and although they never usually showed affection at work, in this instance, he reached out and pulled his soon-to-be wife onto his knee.

'I'm very disappointed in all of you,' Harry said. 'I can't believe that you didn't work it out sooner.'

Harry watched as Abby's cheeks went purple as she remembered her little reptilian comment earlier, but he just smiled back at her.

Harry couldn't stop smiling.

He loved it that no one could quite work out Marnie, not even he at times.

But he'd spend the rest of his life trying.

'Harry?' Juan went over, his smile never wider, and, because it was Juan, he wrapped Harry and Marnie in a hug. 'This is wonderful, unexpected, amazing…'

'I know,' Harry said. 'Like Marnie.'

\* \* \* \* \*

*A sneaky peek at next month...*

## MEDICAL ROMANCE™

THE ULTIMATE IN ROMANTIC MEDICAL DRAMA

*My wish list for next month's titles...*

In stores from 7th March 2014:

❏ Waves of Temptation — Marion Lennox

& Risk of a Lifetime — Caroline Anderson

❏ To Play with Fire & The Dangers of
   Dating Dr Carvalho — Tina Beckett

❏ Uncovering Her Secrets — Amalie Berlin

& Unlocking the Doctor's Heart — Susanne Hampton

Available at WHSmith, Tesco, Asda, Eason, Amazon and Apple

*Just can't wait?*

**Visit us Online**

You can buy our books online a month before they hit the shops! **www.millsandboon.co.uk**

0214/03

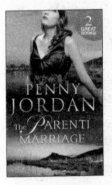

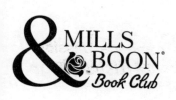

# Join the Mills & Boon Book Club

Want to read more **Medical** books?
We're offering you **2 more** absolutely **FREE!**

We'll also treat you to these fabulous extras:

- Exclusive offers and much more!

- FREE home delivery

- FREE books and gifts with our special rewards scheme

*Get your free books now!*

**visit www.millsandboon.co.uk/bookclub**
**or call Customer Relations on 020 8288 2888**

## The World of Mills & Boon®

There's a Mills & Boon® series that's perfect for you. We publish ten series and, with new titles every month, you never have to wait long for your favourite to come along.

**By Request**

*Relive the romance with the best of the best*
12 stories every month

**Cherish**™

*Experience the ultimate rush of falling in love*
12 new stories every month

**Desire**™

*Passionate and dramatic love stories*
6 new stories every month

**n o c t u r n e**™

*An exhilarating underworld of dark desires*
Up to 3 new stories every mon

M&B/WORLD4a

Discover more romance at

# www.millsandboon.co.uk

- ❤ WIN great prizes in our exclusive competitions
- ❤ BUY new titles before they hit the shops
- ❤ BROWSE new books and REVIEW your favourites
- ❤ SAVE on new books with the Mills & Boon® Bookclub™
- ❤ DISCOVER new authors

PLUS, to chat about your favourite reads, get the latest news and find special offers:

- 🔲 Find us on facebook.com/millsandboon
- 🐦 Follow us on twitter.com/millsandboonuk
- ❤ Sign up to our newsletter at millsandboon.co.uk